Praise for Lexi Mercenaries...

"I can always trust Lexi Blake's Dominants to leave me breathless...and in love. If you want sensual, exciting BDSM wrapped in an awesome love story, then look for a Lexi Blake book."
~Cherise Sinclair USA Today Bestselling author

"Lexi Blake's MASTERS AND MERCENARIES series is beautifully written and deliciously hot. She's got a real way with both action and sex. I also love the way Blake writes her gorgeous Dom heroes--they make me want to do bad, bad things. Her heroines are intelligent and gutsy ladies whose taste for submission definitely does not make them dish rags. Can't wait for the next book!"
~Angela Knight, New York Times Bestselling author

"A Dom is Forever is action packed, both in the bedroom and out. Expect agents, spies, guns, killing and lots of kink as Liam goes after the mysterious Mr. Black and finds his past and his future... The action and espionage keep this story moving along quickly while the sex and kink provides a totally different type of interest. Everything is very well balanced and flows together wonderfully."
~A Night Owl "Top Pick", Terri, Night Owl Erotica

"A Dom Is Forever is everything that is good in erotic romance. The story was fast-paced and suspenseful, the characters were flawed but made me root for them every step of the way, and the hotness factor was off the charts mostly due to a bad boy Dom with a penchant for dirty talk."
~Rho, The Romance Reviews

"A good read that kept me on my toes, guessing until the big reveal, and thinking survival skills should be a must for all men."
~Chris, Night Owl Reviews

Sweet Little Spies

Other Books by Lexi Blake

ROMANTIC SUSPENSE

Masters and Mercenaries
The Dom Who Loved Me
The Men With The Golden Cuffs
A Dom is Forever
On Her Master's Secret Service
Sanctum: A Masters and Mercenaries Novella
Love and Let Die
Unconditional: A Masters and Mercenaries Novella
Dungeon Royale
Dungeon Games: A Masters and Mercenaries Novella
A View to a Thrill
Cherished: A Masters and Mercenaries Novella
You Only Love Twice
Luscious: Masters and Mercenaries~Topped
Adored: A Masters and Mercenaries Novella
Master No
Just One Taste: Masters and Mercenaries~Topped 2
From Sanctum with Love
Devoted: A Masters and Mercenaries Novella
Dominance Never Dies
Submission is Not Enough
Master Bits and Mercenary Bites~The Secret Recipes of Topped
Perfectly Paired: Masters and Mercenaries~Topped 3
For His Eyes Only
Arranged: A Masters and Mercenaries Novella
Love Another Day
At Your Service: Masters and Mercenaries~Topped 4
Master Bits and Mercenary Bites~Girls Night
Nobody Does It Better
Close Cover
Protected: A Masters and Mercenaries Novella
Enchanted: A Masters and Mercenaries Novella
Charmed: A Masters and Mercenaries Novella
Taggart Family Values
Treasured: A Masters and Mercenaries Novella
Delighted: A Masters and Mercenaries Novella
Tempted: A Masters and Mercenaries Novella

Masters and Mercenaries: The Forgotten
Lost Hearts (Memento Mori)
Lost and Found
Lost in You
Long Lost
No Love Lost

Masters and Mercenaries: Reloaded
Submission Impossible
The Dom Identity
The Man from Sanctum
No Time to Lie
The Dom Who Came in from the Cold

Masters and Mercenaries: New Recruits
Love the Way You Spy
Live, Love, Spy
The Bodyguard and the Bombshell: A Masters and Mercenaries Novella
Sweet Little Spies
No More Spies, Coming March 18, 2025

Butterfly Bayou
Butterfly Bayou
Bayou Baby
Bayou Dreaming
Bayou Beauty
Bayou Sweetheart
Bayou Beloved

Park Avenue Promise
Start Us Up
My Royal Showmance
Built to Last, Coming May 27, 2025

Lawless
Ruthless
Satisfaction
Revenge

Courting Justice
Order of Protection
Evidence of Desire

Masters Of Ménage (by Shayla Black and Lexi Blake)
Their Virgin Captive
Their Virgin's Secret
Their Virgin Concubine
Their Virgin Princess
Their Virgin Hostage
Their Virgin Secretary
Their Virgin Mistress

The Perfect Gentlemen (by Shayla Black and Lexi Blake)
Scandal Never Sleeps
Seduction in Session
Big Easy Temptation
Smoke and Sin
At the Pleasure of the President

URBAN FANTASY

Thieves
Steal the Light
Steal the Day
Steal the Moon
Steal the Sun
Steal the Night
Ripper
Addict
Sleeper
Outcast
Stealing Summer
The Rebel Queen
The Rebel Guardian
The Rebel Witch

LEXI BLAKE WRITING AS SOPHIE OAK

Texas Sirens
Small Town Siren
Siren in the City
Siren Enslaved
Siren Beloved
Siren in Waiting

Siren in Bloom
Siren Unleashed
Siren Reborn

Texas Sirens: Legacy
The Accidental Siren

Nights in Bliss, Colorado
Three to Ride
Two to Love
One to Keep
Lost in Bliss
Found in Bliss
Pure Bliss
Chasing Bliss
Once Upon a Time in Bliss
Back in Bliss
Sirens in Bliss
Happily Ever After in Bliss
Far from Bliss
Unexpected Bliss
Wild Bliss, Coming November 12, 2024

A Faery Story
Bound
Beast
Beauty

Standalone
Away From Me
Snowed In

Sweet Little Spies

Masters and Mercenaries: New Recruits, Book 3

Lexi Blake

Sweet Little Spies
Masters and Mercenaries: New Recruits, Book 3
Lexi Blake

Published by DLZ Entertainment LLC
Copyright 2024 DLZ Entertainment LLC
Edited by Chloe Vale
ISBN: 978-1-942297-99-4

Sign up for Lexi Blake's newsletter
and be entered to win a $25 gift certificate
to the bookseller of your choice.

Join us for news, fun, and exclusive content
including free Thieves short stories.

There's a new contest every month!

Go to www.LexiBlake.net to subscribe.

Family Trees

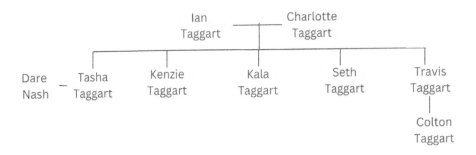

Ian Taggart — Charlotte Taggart

Dare Nash – Tasha Taggart

Kenzie Taggart

Kala Taggart

Seth Taggart

Travis Taggart

Colton Taggart

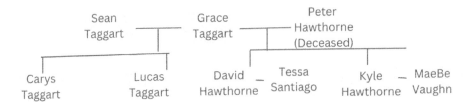

Sean Taggart — Grace Taggart

Peter Hawthorne (Deceased)

Carys Taggart

Lucas Taggart

David Hawthorne – Tessa Santiago

Kyle Hawthorne – MaeBe Vaughn

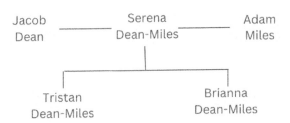

Jacob Dean ———— Serena Dean-Miles ———— Adam Miles

Tristan Dean-Miles

Brianna Dean-Miles

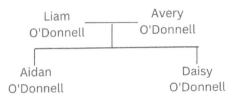

Liam O'Donnell ———— Avery O'Donnell

Aidan O'Donnell

Daisy O'Donnell

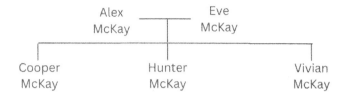

Alex McKay — Eve McKay
- Cooper McKay
- Hunter McKay
- Vivian McKay

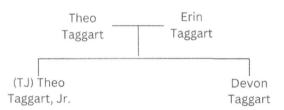

Theo Taggart — Erin Taggart
- (TJ) Theo Taggart, Jr.
- Devon Taggart

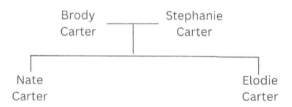

Brody Carter — Stephanie Carter
- Nate Carter
- Elodie Carter

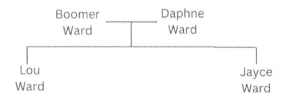

Boomer Ward — Daphne Ward
- Lou Ward
- Jayce Ward

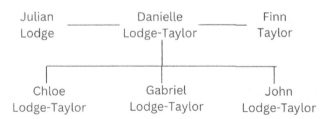

Julian Lodge — Danielle Lodge-Taylor — Finn Taylor
- Chloe Lodge-Taylor
- Gabriel Lodge-Taylor
- John Lodge-Taylor

Acknowledgments

Carys was the first Masters and Mercenaries baby and Tristan and Aidan weren't far behind, so writing their book feels like I'm closing a circle I opened long ago. *The Dom Who Loved Me* was actually written long before I started publishing. It went through a couple of versions before I finally released it into the wild in 2011. As I sit here and write these acknowledgements I can't believe it's been thirteen years. It feels both like it was yesterday when Sean took that dive into Grace's backyard pool and like an eternity I've spent with this family. Like they've somehow—despite being fictional—been with me all along. So it was with a little dread I moved into *Sweet Little Spies*. It's the only other ménage in all of Masters and Mercenaries, so it also takes me back to *The Men with the Golden Cuffs*. There was so much nostalgia for me, but I also loved seeing my older characters in the eyes of their children. We never quite believe our parents are people with full lives and histories and mistakes made. It was fun and a revelation to watch these three realize they are a link in a long, loving, a little wild chain. May the chain go on for a very long time.

Love to my whole team! I couldn't do any of this without you.

Prologue

Carys Taggart stared at the man she'd loved since they were children. Well, one of them. The other sat beside her, but he'd done nothing to deserve her death stare.

They sat on the balcony section of one of Dallas's fine dining establishments, located in an equally luxurious hotel, overlooking the city lights. It was elegant and somewhat private, and she wondered if this was where it all finally ended. At least he'd chosen a beautiful spot to end what had felt like a lifetime love affair.

"It's not forever." Tristan Dean-Miles was a gorgeous man with dark hair and green eyes. He was six foot three, and over the last few years had gone from gangly computer geek to muscular soldier.

She missed her computer nerd so damn much. The nerd wouldn't be leaving her. The hacking-obsessed young man she'd adored wouldn't be standing in front of her breaking all of his promises. She felt inexplicably weary, and it wasn't because she was in her final year of medical school. The stress of taking the USMLE was nothing compared to sitting in this restaurant watching the man she thought she'd marry let her down. Again.

"That's what you said last time." The other man she loved looked as tired as she did. Aidan O'Donnell. Six foot two, with lean muscle he honed in the gym and by running.

Her life was complicated.

"I know," Tris replied, a deep patience in his tone. "I'm sorry. I know I did, but things have gotten…complex."

She'd known they would have trouble when Tristan had announced he was going into the Army instead of grad school. They'd had plans. Plans they'd made when they were stupid kids who thought they could make a relationship like this work.

She sat there in the middle of the fancy restaurant Tristan had likely picked either as an apology for what he'd been planning to say or as a shield so she couldn't yell at him. Either way, she sat there feeling like a piece of herself had broken off, and she wouldn't get it back.

Just because Tristan's parents had made it work didn't mean they could. Tristan's unique family had made what they had feel somewhat normal. But there was a reason the world wasn't full of happy threesomes.

"Complex?" Aidan's jaw had taken on the hard line she associated with his stubbornness. It always tightened when he was working through a problem he refused to give up on. Even when the "problem" had told them again and again he didn't want to be solved. "What is that supposed to mean? Tris, we're supposed to get married in a few months. We agreed when we finished medical school, we would make this thing legal and start our family."

It was what they'd always dreamed of. At least she and Aidan. They would get through school, marry, and move in together and start their lives. They would do it without shame, and anyone who didn't like it would be ruthlessly extricated from their group.

"There is nothing I want more, but I have some things I need to do before I can settle down, and it might mean staying away from the two of you for a while."

"So you did it." She knew what he wasn't saying. This had been her fear for months now.

"Did it? Baby, all I'm doing is my job." Tris looked so reasonable. He looked like a young man from a good family in his well-tailored three-piece suit. Unlike Aidan, Tristan came from money. A lot of it.

Her family did well, too, but not like Tristan's. Aidan's was upper middle-class. He hadn't worried about college or medical school, but he'd eaten his share of ramen noodles and worked some heavy-lifting part-time jobs.

Tristan could have done anything he wanted to. Had any job in the world. He could have taken his place at his father's side and learned how to run one of the top investigative firms in the world. Miles-Dean, Weston, and Murdoch specialized in locating people who were lost or who didn't want to be found. The company did well, but it was his parents' creative endeavors that had made them wealthy beyond their wildest dreams. Between his father's software innovations and his mom's best-selling novels, there was little the Dean-Miles family couldn't afford. Tristan could be here in Dallas with them.

But something else had called to him.

"It's a job you don't need," Aidan pointed out. "Look, I understand you're enjoying the adrenaline rush of being Army intelligence, but where does it end? You said you wanted to spend the last couple of years working this out of your system. I got it. Medical school is a lot, and you thought we wouldn't have time for you."

She would have made time. Even if it had been nothing more than holding him while he slept.

"I didn't join the Army because you weren't paying enough attention to me." For the first time Tristan's calm looked slightly rattled. "I went in to see who I could be. To test myself."

"Is testing what you're doing now?" Aidan had on slacks and a jacket, but he hadn't bothered with a tie. He was the more casual of her two lovers.

Of course there hadn't been a lot of sex. Certainly not lately. She had two boyfriends, and it had been months since she'd seen some action. Tristan had been gone, and she and Aidan had been studying or working. They often fell asleep on the couch while trying to eat dinner and watching some random sitcom.

She'd told herself everything would change when Tris came home. His contract was up, and surely he'd had enough of being apart. She'd told herself Tristan would come home and the world would feel right again.

"What I'm doing now is serving my country," Tris replied resolutely. "You should understand. Your father served his. Carys's whole family did their time. I don't question your reasons for spending four years in med school. And have you thought about what happens when you pursue residencies? Are you going to turn down a great one because it's not in Dallas? Or will you ask Carys to make the sacrifice?"

She huffed. "Do you think we haven't talked this through? I'm in obstetrics. I can learn what I need to in almost any city. Aidan's showing amazing promise as a trauma surgeon. Of course I'm going to follow him if he ends up in a top program. The truth is he'll have some pull if they want him badly enough."

Aidan was the shining star of their class. She was okay with it. There wasn't any jealousy between them because she was doing exactly what she wanted to do. Specializing in high-risk pregnancies.

"So we're all supposed to follow Aidan?" Tristan got to one of their problems.

"No." This was why it couldn't work. Why her father worried so about her.

Sweetheart, Jake and Serena and Adam were set in their careers when they got married. They knew who they were and what they wanted to do. They were settled. I worry meshing two lives is hard at your age. I don't know how you'll manage three.

She'd told her dad they could do it because they loved each other. Because love was enough.

It turned out she was wrong.

"No? All right, then what are we supposed to do?" Tristan asked. "Car, you've been quiet this whole time. It scares me."

It should. She shut down when she was done with something. "I need to ask you a couple of questions before I make my decision."

A brow rose over his eyes. "There's a decision?"

"Maybe we should take this discussion home." Aidan could also be the peacekeeper. It was kind of his place in the relationship. She and Tristan could be combustible. Aidan was the calm voice of reason bringing them together.

Without Aidan, she and Tristan would explode. They would have passion but no peace.

Without Tristan, she and Aidan were floating through life, muddling by in a sea of study and workouts and routine.

They were perfect together as a threesome, but sometimes perfect wasn't enough either. "He wanted to meet us here for a reason, Aidan.

He's been gone for three months and when he gets home, he doesn't come to my place or to the place he literally shares with you and Cooper. He goes to a hotel and asks us to meet him there. He chose this place for a reason, and it's not for hot sex."

Aidan's face fell because hot sex was probably what he'd been looking for.

She knew better. This wasn't an invitation to intimacy.

It was a breakup.

"Sex is certainly not off the table, sweetheart." Tristan's bad boy made a sudden appearance, and she knew this wasn't going to go well.

So she should get it over with. "It is. You haven't touched me in months. I understand. Honestly, I don't get the whole wait-for-me thing. Be brave. Rip the bandage off. Make a clean break."

And then his scared boy was right there in his eyes. "Carys, I'm not breaking up with you. Why would you think that, baby? I know I've been distracted, but you have to admit, it's not like you're the queen of free time right now."

It was odd how cold she felt in this moment. Like an icy shroud had descended. Probably because she needed it. If she didn't have it, she might be on her knees begging him not to leave them. She wasn't sure they could make it without Tristan. They fit and without him… But no. She suspected she knew what was really behind this new delay of his.

All of her life she'd loved nothing more than she'd loved these two men. She knew beyond a shadow of a doubt if she needed Aidan to give up medicine, it would hurt, but he would do it. It was precisely why she was willing to follow him.

But Tristan had found something he loved more than them, something that fulfilled him in a way no relationship ever could. If it was anything but what she suspected, they could probably work it out.

But Tristan's secret love left no place for anything else. Not in the end.

Still, she thought she should be thorough.

"Is there another woman?" She didn't ask about a man. Tristan and Aidan loved each other, but they'd never seemed to want to get physical past sharing her.

"No." He didn't hesitate. "I've been faithful to you. I would

21

never cheat on you. Hell, I don't even look at other women."

"He wouldn't," Aidan said with a frown. "He's just being a dick."

"How is it being a dick to want to do my job?" Tristan argued.

The job was the problem. "Why didn't you come home when you could? You had leave two months ago."

A fine flush hit Tristan's face, but he otherwise didn't react. "I had some things I needed to take care of."

She bet he did. "Were you auditioning?"

Aidan frowned. "Auditioning?"

He was a brilliant man. A truly gifted surgeon who would someday save so many lives, but he missed some of the small details of life. Carys took care of them. "For the Agency."

A gasp came from Aidan. "He wouldn't."

"He did." She knew it because of all the secrecy surrounding him. Her cousins would stop talking when she walked in a room. Her uncle was an excellent liar—not a bad trait when working in espionage—but even she could see he'd been uncomfortable talking to her when she brought up the wedding. "Did you even have to audition or did the twins finally make all their dreams come true?"

Her cousins Kala and Kenzie Taggart had grown up wanting to be like their mom and dad. Their father—Carys's uncle—had been a CIA operative, and their mom an information broker. She loved her cousins, but they played dangerous games. Games that were about to kill her relationship.

Tristan sat there as though he wasn't sure what to say.

Because his life was classified now.

She felt the wall between them, the wall he'd built without even asking how they felt about it.

"Have you had a chance to look at the menu?" The waiter obviously hadn't noticed the tension.

Carys put her napkin on her plate and moved to pick up her purse. "I don't think I'm hungry anymore."

"Carys," Tristan began and his voice had gone deep and low.

He was the Dom in the relationship. The one who needed control to be fully himself. Aidan liked to drift between roles, and she was the sweet sub.

But even a sub knew when to walk away.

22

She shook her head. "You don't get to use your Dom voice on me, Tristan."

Aidan started to stand.

She shook her head. "Don't. You need to make your peace with him so we can see if we can move on. I'll be fine because I'm going to walk one block down to Top and get a drink, and you can pick me up there when you're done."

"Carys Taggart," Tristan began.

Aidan held out a hand. "Give her a minute, man, unless you want her to explode."

Tristan settled back down. "This isn't over."

Carys walked out. Because it sure felt like it was.

* * * *

"I think I'll have another Scotch on the rocks. The Macallan 20." Tristan sat back and forced himself not to run after the love of his life. She didn't understand. She couldn't possibly understand, but if Aidan was still sitting here, he had a chance.

"Just bring the bottle," Aidan said, his jaw going stubborn.

Oh, this could get nasty. Aidan was punishing him via credit card. The good news? His credit card didn't have a limit.

The waiter's focus went back to Tris, his eyes going wide. "Sir, the cost would be…"

Horrifically expensive. Yeah, he got it. Nothing mattered except placating Aidan right now. "We'll take two glasses, and have the chef make some chicken wings."

"We don't have those on the menu."

This poor guy. "And yet he will make them. Tell him I'm in the presidential suite."

"Of course." The waiter turned and walked back inside.

He should have done this in his suite. In the suite, he could have shown her this wasn't the end. In the suite, he could have gotten her underneath him, and there would be no question about how he felt.

"You're a coward."

Tristan closed his eyes and took a long breath. He'd known this would be a difficult conversation. "How? Because I assure you there's not a lot cowardly about the work I'm doing. I'm putting myself in harm's way for my country. I'm sorry I couldn't be some office worker for you."

"I'm talking about how you did this." Aidan sat back, staring at him, gesturing around at the luxurious surroundings they were in. "This conspicuous show of wealth doesn't help you."

"I wanted a special night." It was true and also a lie. He'd wanted…he wanted to go back and not open that file, not get curious, not end up in a corner.

Aidan wasn't having it. "You wanted to show her what she could have if she waits a bit longer. You know damn well I can't give her this."

"No, you give her everything else." It was an old wound between them.

Aidan shared her interests. They could talk medicine for hours and hours. Neither of them understood his need to unlock mysteries via his keyboard. They certainly wouldn't understand the forces behind the mission he was on now. Not even his uncle knew.

His parents didn't know, but then Adam Miles would have already figured the problem out and Jacob Dean would have handled the whole physical mission without batting an eye. He was the child of giants, and he felt so small.

But if he could follow through, he might prove himself wrong, might be worthy of being their kid.

Aidan sat there for a moment. "Is she right?"

Tristan didn't have to answer. His silence was enough.

"Fuck." Aidan's expression fell. "This is honestly what you want? Because I don't know how we get through this. We've put off the wedding once."

Aidan was the easy one. Tristan had known the minute he'd realized he was going to join the twins' CIA team he would need to work on Aidan because Carys wouldn't want to listen. "I need more time. That's all. Look, what Kala and Kenz are doing is something totally new. It's an experiment, and it's exciting. I know you don't understand."

Aidan held up a hand. "But I do. Man, do you think I don't get excited about getting invited to watch a craniectomy? I dropped everything including a date with Carys. She understood. But we're not talking about a five-hour surgery. If you do this, your life is classified."

"It already is. Do you think my Army intelligence job consists of me giving soldiers tests or something? I've been seeking information for the US Army while you've been in med school. The only difference is I'll be doing it for another agency."

"For *the* Agency."

Tristan glanced over to make sure the other tables couldn't hear them. There were only three on this balcony. It was as private as they could get. "Look, I know I said I would come home, but there's something I have to follow through on." He leaned in. "It's a project I started a while ago, and if my instincts are right, it's big."

"So is our wedding," Aidan countered.

"Our wedding means nothing if the world burns. And don't look at me like that. Like I'm talking in hyperboles. I've been tracking a group, one I think is behind several terrorist events across the globe." He couldn't tell Aidan too much, but he had to make him understand.

Aidan was…more than a friend. More than a brother. Sometimes he thought Aidan was half of his whole. Like they were one soul born in two bodies, and they'd managed to find the one woman who could handle them. His parents always talked about how they'd been inseparable, even as babies. Aidan's mother was his mom's best friend/personal assistant, and they'd been through everything together—even their pregnancies. It was as natural as breathing to share Carys with Aidan.

He couldn't lose them, but he also couldn't walk away. Even if he wanted to.

"There's a job, and I'm the only one who can do it," Tristan said quietly. "It's important."

"It sounds like the twins can do it. Or Cooper. You should know he's a good spy. He's been home a couple of times, and not once did he mention 'hey, I've joined a CIA team and your partner is coming with me.'" There was a bitterness to Aidan's words.

Tristan couldn't blame him. They'd been in their house for a couple of years now, and in the beginning it had been the three of them. He and Aidan and Cooper McKay had moved in together after college. Then he and Coop had gone into the military, and now they treated the house like a way station while to Aidan it was home. For now. "He'll be here in Dallas more, you know. For Coop, this is a

25

way to come home more often."

"It's a way for him to try to keep Kala from killing herself," Aidan shot back. "Coop never intended to go into the Agency. But I have to wonder now if this wasn't your end game."

"My end game is and always has been marrying our sub and living a happy life." Frustration started to well. Somehow he'd thought this would go better. "But we can't get there if this…" He took a long breath. "The man I'm tracking is an arms dealer, but the important part is he can lead me to someone much more dangerous. Aidan, you know how there are breakthroughs in medicine the public doesn't know about yet?"

"Of course," Aidan replied. "There are any number of studies and new tech coming through. They're in testing before they're released to the public."

"Weapons are the same way." A pit opened in Tris's gut. The same one he got every time he thought about this mission of his. "What if I told you there's a man out there in the world who is working on a delivery system for a bomb you can hold in the palm of your hand. A weapon capable of decimating all living things within a city the size of London and yet leave the buildings standing."

Aidan went still. "Is that what you're telling me, Tris?"

He nodded.

"Why didn't you tell her?"

He'd thought about telling her for months and come to one conclusion. "Because it won't matter to her. I'm not saying the world won't matter. I'm saying she'll be more worried about me. Does she need more to worry about while she's in the middle of her last year in medical school? Which will make her more stressed? The idea of me being a selfish ass who wants to play soldier or me being in real danger?"

"Okay. I'll talk to her. But we can make this work if you'll come home every now and then. I assure you simply spending time with her will settle a lot of her concerns." Aidan sounded so reasonable. "And there's zero reason for the wedding not to go through. You don't have to do a thing. Carys and the moms are handling it all. You show up, say I do, we go on a horny honeymoon, and then we settle down. If she's got a ring on her finger and believes we have a future together, she'll be more patient."

There were a couple of problems with Aidan's scenario. "I have to step back from you both. I don't want to, but there's a reason I've stayed away." He shouldn't be doing this, but he couldn't lose them, and he couldn't leave them completely in the dark. Besides, if his boss found out, well, his boss was his Uncle Ian, and he would likely kick his ass. "I'm going to tell you something not even my team knows. I didn't join the Agency because the twins talked me into it. I joined because it's the only way I can do what I need to do. I'm going to be working for several teams beyond the one the twins and Coop are on. The arms dealer was killed three weeks ago."

"Then what's the problem?" Aidan asked.

"I took over his operation. He worked in the shadows, and so I have to be there, too. It's the only way to find the person I need to find. The bombmaker. I find the bombmaker, I shut down his operation, and then I can come home. Until then I worry anyone close to me could be in the line of fire if it ever gets out that I'm The Jester." Bile rose in his throat. "Fuck. Now I've brought you into it, and I am a fucking coward. Aidan, I should never…"

What the hell was he doing? Carys had walked out and…

Aidan leaned toward him. "Hey, I'm sorry. You're not a coward. I didn't understand."

"I shouldn't…"

"Yeah, you should," Aidan said. "I don't know how the team works, but I can guess who else is working on it. Lou left her assistant professor job to play around in a think tank? Nah. She's working tech. I've also heard Ian and Charlotte and Tash have been mysteriously out of the office at the same time Coop is out of pocket. So if my brain functions the way it should, I can put it together, and you're the one on the outside. Kala has Cooper and Lou. Kenzie has Tash and her mom. You deserve someone to talk to. I assure you I won't say anything. Neither will Carys."

Guilt threatened to swamp Tristan. "I can't drag you into this."

"You don't have to." Aidan reached out and gripped his hand.

It was a familiar gesture and one he'd always counted on. All of his life Aidan had been there. Carys had been there.

He had to do this job. For them.

* * * *

27

Aidan walked into the bar at Top, a familiar sensation buzzing through him. He'd worked summers and weekends here, washing dishes and later as a server. Always, always watching the boss's daughter. Hell, he could remember running around the backrooms when he was a kid and begging the pastry chef for a taste of whatever he was making. There was so much of his childhood here. So many memories.

How could Tristan give all this up? Even for a little while. It wasn't something he understood, but if he was going to save the most important relationship of his life, he had to go with it.

"Hey, Aidan," a familiar voice said. "She's in the bar. Do you know why she's drinking straight gin martinis on a night when she should be celebrating Tristan's homecoming?"

Sean Taggart. Carys's father was the chef and owner of Top, but there was still an air of military authority hanging around the man decades after he left the service. He stood just outside the bar entrance, wearing slacks and a button-down that let Aidan know he wasn't in the kitchen this evening. The other thing he wore? A tight expression, a sure sign he was worried.

"Tristan needs some time." He didn't want to give his best friend up.

"Tristan is playing dangerous games," Sean said quietly. "Tell me he's not bringing you into them."

Well, at least he'd been right about one thing. He'd known damn well there was zero chance Ian Taggart hadn't talked to his brother about the CIA team he was now leading. "You could have mentioned it to me."

"I'm telling you now. I hoped he would come home and you could talk some sense into him," Sean said. "But then I saw the look on my daughter's face and realized what had happened. Did he break up with y'all?"

The fact he'd said "y'all" and not "her" showed how far they'd come. For many years, Sean had lived in what Aidan's da liked to call Delusion. According to Da, it was a nice place where one didn't have to think about one's children having sexual needs who might make a couple of mistakes along the way. Sean had been forced out of Delusion when they'd gotten engaged right here on the patio at Top.

To his credit, he'd taken a long swig of Scotch and then welcomed both Aidan and Tristan into the family.

"No. He asked for more time," Aidan replied.

"Didn't he already ask for more time and you gave it to him?" Sean asked.

"It's complicated." He wanted to talk about it. Sean would understand. Sean might be able to advise him.

But he'd promised Tristan.

"It always is. So what have you decided?" Sean studied him for a moment. "I ask because I know you're about to walk in there and convince Carys to do what you think she should do."

"Sir, is there something you would like to talk about?" It had been a rough night, but it looked like it was going to get rougher. He now knew way too much about a former arms dealer known as The Jester and far, far more than he ever wanted to know about the dark threats of the seemingly peaceful world around him. A threat that could kill everything he loved if Tris was right. And now he had to deal with his future father-in-law, who seemed to have taken exception. "Because I don't make Carys do anything. No one can. She makes her own decisions."

"Ah, but she makes them with the two of you in mind always," Sean argued. "And now I worry one of you is no longer thinking with her best interests at heart."

"Do you mean me or Tris?"

Sean sighed. "Of course I mean Tris. Aidan, I wasn't in the same position Tris is in, but I know it's damn hard for a man to give himself one hundred percent to his spouse when he's involved in the kind of job he's doing. My brother got out for that very reason. So did Ten Smith and Beck and Kim Kent. So did Kayla Summers. You find someone you love and get out. Not the other way around."

He wished Tristan had fucking come down here with him so he wasn't the one who had to face down a disappointed father figure. But no, he'd gotten a call from Lou, who needed him desperately and he'd said *sorry, I have to go*. Like always. Like Sean was telling him. The job came first. Before Aidan. Before Carys. Before anything else.

And yet he was going to defend the asshole. "It's not forever."

"How long are you going to put off the wedding? We've already done it once."

On this Aidan wouldn't be moved. Tristan was on a timer. Hell, Tristan had been the one to tell him it might be better if they went through with the wedding because it would keep up the illusion they were no longer together.

Were they together? Because he sure as fuck felt alone right now.

"We're not moving it again," Aidan replied. "At least that's what I was going to talk to Carys about. If she'll have me, I'd like to go through with the wedding. It's not like what we were planning was exactly legal."

"No, but I thought Tristan was the one who would legally marry her and then they would both take your name."

Because Carys had said she refused to be Carys Dean-Miles O'Donnell. They'd sat up late the night they'd asked her to marry them and argued about it. They'd passed a bottle of expensive champagne around as they'd lain in bed and reached a compromise.

Three kids, if possible, and their first names would be Dean, Miles, and Taggart, or a feminized version of some kind. Deana. Myla. He wasn't sure how to make Taggart pretty, but they would figure out a way if they had to. And they would all be O'Donnells.

"It doesn't matter in the end." It was a lie Aidan hoped he could convince himself was true. "I promise you I won't let anything bad happen to Carys."

"I think something bad already has happened. Getting her heart broken isn't exactly fun," Sean said with a sigh like he'd known it would end like this. "Are you sure it can work without him?"

"He's not leaving us," Aidan insisted.

"He won't mean to, but I know how this kind of job goes. How long did he say he needed?"

"Six months. Eight, tops," Aidan said, glancing into the bar. Carys sat alone, her back to him, but there was a slump to her shoulders that made him ache. "He wants to clear this one mission up and then we'll be good. The wedding is months off. Even if he needs more time, we'll be okay. If not, we'll go through with things the way we need to."

Sean chuckled, but there wasn't any humor to the sound. "Oh, if we're betting, I'll take the over." He sobered. "Are you sure you want to wait?"

Aidan wasn't sure of anything. "Not forever."

"I'm going to give you some advice, son. Postpone the wedding for a year. Honestly, I've been worried about the stress it will have on Carys even with Grace and Serena and your mom doing most of the work," Sean said.

He didn't want to wait, but it might be for the best. However, there was another problem. "The stress won't go away. If we wait a year, we'll be almost through our first year of internship. It's intense. But I get your point. If I want this to work, I might have to be patient. I don't think this is about Tristan wanting to be some big spy. I think he got involved in something, and he feels like he needs to follow through."

"He got involved with my nieces," Sean said under his breath. "I love them, but damn I worry about them. Tris will be okay. Ian's in control. But I worry about what this is going to do to Carys."

"I'll take care of her." He was going to shield her from the worst of it. He would convince her without dragging her into Tristan's suddenly dangerous world. He would hold the connection so when Tristan was done there would be something for him to come home to.

Sean put a hand on his shoulder. "I know you will. I know you love my daughter. I know Tris does, too, but sometimes it's not enough. You should talk to her. I only have so much gin."

Sean turned to go, and Aidan took a deep breath, getting ready. Tristan had his mission and now Aidan had his.

To keep them all together.

It was only six months. Then they could enjoy their engagement and wedding planning and get on with the rest of their lives.

He walked through the bar to join his future wife, sure he could handle this.

Chapter One

Two Years, Three Months, and Fifteen Days Later

Carys looked at herself in the mirror and wished her smile was brighter.

Fuck Tristan Dean-Miles. He was ruining her wedding day and the bastard wasn't even here.

"Okay, if you look like that in the pictures, your future children will worry you were forced into this marriage. You want to run, cousin?"

She glanced back and Tasha Taggart stood in the doorway looking gorgeous in her bridesmaid dress. It was a blush pink with a plunging neckline flowing to a fitted skirt. Carys stopped and sighed because it truly was lovely. Everything was beautiful.

She was letting one thing ruin the most special day of her life.

A little thing like one of her grooms wasn't here.

Still, she had to put on a brave face because Aidan *was* here. Aidan had been at her side the whole time, and he needed to know how much she loved him. She needed to believe they could make this work on their own. Without Tris.

"Devi did an amazing job," she said, forcing a smile on her face.

She wasn't this mopey girl.

Tash walked in, setting her bouquet aside. "She did indeed, but you should know Kala is complaining the skirt is too tight."

"I said no weapons." Yes, she was the bride who had to tell her bridal party they shouldn't strap on an armory, and it proved beyond a shadow of a doubt her family was filled with psychos.

Psychos she adored. Her family could be intense. Though her father had left the military and security business before she'd been born, most of her family still had feet planted firmly in that dangerous world.

She'd made peace with her cousins long ago. Her cousins hadn't forced Tristan to work with them. She'd come to the conclusion that if her cousins hadn't offered Tris a place on their team, he would have found another way. She didn't have to lose her family because one man couldn't love her the way she needed.

Tasha grinned. "Oh, you can ban weapons all you like, but I assure you there are some here, and it's not just my gang." She closed the door behind her. "Why are you in here all alone, Carys?"

"I needed a couple of minutes." Her mom was running around ensuring everything was perfect. Avery O'Donnell was dealing with the photographer.

She didn't like to think about Serena Dean-Miles being left out. She was merely another guest at this grand affair when she'd been such a big part of the planning.

I know he's going to come around, Carys. I know he loves you. I think he's in trouble and he doesn't want to bring you into it.

Serena had tears in her eyes the night of the rehearsal dinner. She'd had some wine and gotten emotional.

Carys had been shut down. Like she always was now. She was standing here in the dress of her dreams, ready to marry a man she loved, and she felt...numb.

"You could change your mind. You could walk out there and tell them you want to turn this into a fun party and wait," Tasha offered.

"Would you like to tell me why I would call off my wedding?" The words came out harsher than she meant them. Or maybe not. Maybe this was one of those times when she resented her cousins' secret world.

Tasha's face fell. "I would like to, but you know I can't. I can only tell you he loves you and he wishes things were different. We're going to figure this out. I promise. Right now I don't think it's safe for him to be around you."

"Are we talking about Tris? Because it's so not safe for him to be around," another voice said. "Carys, dude, how am I supposed to kick ass in this thing? I can't even hide a knife with how tight this is, and Devi was real rude when I suggested an adjustment." Kala Taggart. The murderiest of her cousins was in the house.

"Hey, stop. We talked about this." She was followed by her twin sister. Kenzie was Tigger to Kala's kind of evil Eeyore persona. She was bouncy bouncy bouncy bouncy, fun fun fun fun fun. Right up until she had to assassinate someone, but then Carys was sure Kenzie did it with pep to her step.

The twins were perfectly identical physically. Down to their scars. Seriously, when one got shot, the other had to find a way to fake the scar if it was visible to the public. From what Carys understood from context, the twins were known through the intelligence world as one person. They'd run an op at the club she and Aidan played at a few months back. Aunt Charlotte had sat down with the women of The Hideout and explained they were to call Kenzie Kara for the night and to not ask about why Kala was hiding in the locker room while Kenzie hung out with some dude who was probably a spy.

Carys had done what she always did these days. She'd convinced Aidan to take her to a privacy room and pushed him to spank her until she cried. She'd avoided all the spy stuff.

"You are not ruining the lines of that gorgeous dress with a small sword on your thigh." There was only one way to deal with her cousin. Boundaries. They had to be firmly in place. But simply because she had some rules didn't mean she hadn't thought of Kala. For all her rage, there was something oddly fragile about Kala Taggart. A deep vulnerability that always made Carys think about her comfort.

Kala frowned, looking at her sister and then her twin like she'd been caught doing something terrible. "I'm sorry. I was joking."

"No, you weren't." Sometimes it was fun to get Kala in an awkward position. Carys couldn't help the impish feeling rising inside. It was good to feel anything at all.

Maybe she was coming out of her broody era. Maybe she could do this.

Kala looked to her twin. "I don't know what to say because she's right. I'm not joking. I know, like, we're supposed to be all about the bride, but what if someone decides to attack the wedding? This bouquet thing doesn't even have thorns. I can probably take out a couple of eyes with my shoes, but I'm at a loss for anything else."

Yes, it was fun to tease her, but it was time to let her off the hook. After all, she'd thought of everything. "No, but I made sure the bouquet is long enough and wide enough for you to hide a knife or a small pistol in."

Kala's eyes lit up. "Seriously? Because my mom threatened me with a bunch of stuff I'm scared of if I screw this up for you."

Only one person had screwed it up, and he wasn't here to feel her wrath. She gave her cousin a smile. "Seriously. It's not like your dad's not packing. There's a reason there are no metal detectors. I would be a heinous misogynist if I didn't allow you to defend us simply because you're wearing a dress."

Kala breathed a sigh of relief. "Thank god. You're the best, Car. I'll be back. Lou's got my emergency pack in her car."

She did not want to know what Kala considered emergency supplies for a wedding. Something lethal, for sure.

Kenzie turned as her twin walked out yelling for her bestie. "She's right, you know. You are the best."

Carys held up a hand because her cousin had a very specific look on her face. The one warning Carys she was about to get all emotional and girlie. Girlie in the best way, in the way only women ever truly got with the people they loved. "Do not make me cry."

She'd cried enough. She'd cried every day for the last month, hiding out in the call room at the hospital so Aidan wouldn't see her. He was being strong. She had to be strong, too.

"Don't ruin her makeup. We can tell her how amazing she is and how grateful we are to have her in our lives when she is not wearing a pristine white dress and hasn't spent two hours on hair and makeup," Tash said with a sigh, sitting down on the luxurious couch. "But she is. Amazing. So now the question is why she didn't let us get dressed in here with her."

"Well, the room is pretty small," Carys tried.

35

Kenzie's pink hair was in an elegant updo. "It's huge and literally built for like eight women to get dressed."

Carys turned back to the mirror, taking a long breath. "Kenz, I'm barely holding on. I can't lose it today."

Kenzie moved in behind her. "And if we were in here, you would?"

"If my closest family and friends were in here, I would…" She blinked, forcing herself to stay calm. "I would think about him, and that's not fair to Aidan."

If she let herself truly feel the gravity of the day, she would melt down, and she wasn't about to do that to Aidan. She had to think about the man who actually loved her.

The man who also needed Tristan. Was she forcing Aidan into a position where he had to choose? Would he resent her for the rest of their lives? Would he wonder what could have happened if they'd waited longer? Fought a bit harder?

Why was she having these thoughts now? It was her wedding day. It was supposed to be the best day of her life and she was plagued with doubts.

Kenzie had tears in her eyes. "I love you. I could kill him for you. Well, I could let Kala do it. She wouldn't mind getting her dress dirty, but I think I look really good."

She turned to her cousin. This might be the right time to ask a few very specific questions. "Is he involved in something dangerous?"

Kenzie's gaze didn't falter. "Yes. Yes, he is, but it doesn't mean he should shut you out. My father would never shut my mom out. He wouldn't care about clearance. I've tried to talk to him."

And this was why she didn't blame her cousins. She put a hand on Kenzie's shoulder. "I know. I know you didn't bring this down on us. Tristan chose this. If he's worried he'll lead us into something dangerous, well, he forgot who my family is."

"He forgot who *his* family is," Tasha corrected. "I assure you his mother wouldn't let herself be left out of things. Even if they were dangerous." Tasha frowned. "Sorry. I meant to not mention anything about Tris. You should know we've all registered our disapproval."

Kenzie stepped back, and she was the one on the edge of wrecking her makeup. Tears pooled in her cousin's eyes. "Are you sure you want to go through with this? It might only be a couple of weeks. I understand more about the situation now. I can't talk about it, but I think we're going to fix this."

Ah, so he'd been a secretive bastard with everyone. She'd rather thought that was part of the problem. Her cousins, for all their ability to keep secrets, wouldn't leave her dangling if they had any wiggle room. The fact that Kenzie was letting some light through meant she'd only recently discovered whatever games Tristan was playing. "I don't want to put you in a bad position."

"We'll tell you what we can," Tasha promised, sitting up and offering the seat next to her.

"Everything we can." Kenzie moved over to the elegant buffet table where the owner of this gorgeous venue had set out light snacks and champagne to be shared with her bridesmaids.

Carys had asked a secondary spread be made available in the room she'd set her bridesmaids up in. Now that she thought about it, it was kind of a bridezilla move. "I'm sorry I shut you out."

"I understand, but you need to think about why you're doing it." Tasha was always the voice of reason while Kenzie popped the cork on the champagne. "This is supposed to be a joyous day. Not something you survive."

It looked like the most practical of her cousins was going to push her. "Aidan thinks this is the way to go, and I can't let him down. Of course I have mixed emotions. I know everyone thinks I should push the wedding again, but the third time's the charm. How close are you to magically fixing the problem so Tristan could potentially come home if he wanted to? Or am I asking for classified intel?"

"You know he works for other teams." Kenzie handed her a glass and poured one for herself and her sister. "Cooper and Zach do, too, but only occasionally. I think Tristan's gotten in deep."

Tasha sighed. "I don't think anyone would care if I gave you a projected date if I had one. I don't. The case is ongoing and serious. I only recently learned how serious. There's a reason for him to stay away from you."

She'd thought this over a million times. Whenever she would go to a family function and see he wasn't there, she'd asked the question. When Tristan sent her flowers or long letters where he told her how much he loved her, how much he missed her but didn't mention why he had to stay away, she'd asked this question. "Then he should have talked to me. He should have sat down and explained to Aidan and me why he chose this path and why he thinks we can't handle whatever damage he thinks he's going to take. I'm not some naïve, coddled child, Tash. I'm not some security expert, but I know how to duck, and I take it all seriously."

"He's being overly cautious," Kenzie said, sitting down, careful to not wrinkle her dress.

"I don't know about that," Tasha hedged. "I think this might be much more dangerous than he's letting on. I know Dad is concerned. But there's no question in my mind he still loves Carys."

"Just not enough to let me stand beside him." Carys took a long breath. There was something they weren't considering. "Guys, you want me to wait, but he doesn't. Tristan made it clear Aidan and I shouldn't wait for him anymore. He asked us to go through with it this time. We're here today because Tristan wants us to be."

It hurt more than she'd imagined. After she'd read his text from an unknown number months and months ago, she'd blocked him and changed her number and then blocked him again.

I love you so much, baby. I miss you. My heart isn't whole without you, and it will kill me to know you're saying I do to only Aidan. But it's not forever.

Then tell me why.

Because I have to protect you.

By staying away from me for years? You don't want a wife. You want a piece of property. I'll marry Aidan but don't text me again.

She had the messages memorized. She'd hoped they would fade in her brain after she'd deleted all of them, but nope. They were engrained there. "I know he thinks he still loves me, but it's not enough. Honestly, I think it was always going to happen this way. We were together for so long. It was inevitable at least one of them would need to see more of the world."

"He's not interested in other women," Kenzie said.

"Around you he's not." Carys took a sip of champagne. It would be better once the ceremony was over. It was what she told herself. She would get through the ceremony, say I do, and then the party would happen and she would know it was done and there was no more potential, no more chances he would change his mind. She would start her life with Aidan and it would be okay. "Of course he doesn't want to piss off his family, but honestly, this is an excellent way to get out of a relationship he doesn't want anymore."

"He's not trying to get out of the relationship." Kenzie sat back. "But I understand why you would think it's possible. He's very secretive. I know a little about what's happening, but he's holding out on all of us. He doesn't want us to talk about it with anyone, even his family."

"Which could mean it's highly classified, although our group knows how to keep quiet. Or it's a front for what he really wants. His freedom." She'd had to come to the conclusion since he wouldn't talk to her or Aidan. With the exception of those texts and the gifts he'd sent her, there had been no meetings, no phone calls. Aidan had even less.

The way he'd treated Aidan was far worse than what he'd done to her. He'd cut his best friend out of his life, and she'd been helpless to watch it.

This was what Tristan wanted, and he was going to get it. Then he would know she and Aidan would take care of each other and he could pursue his own life.

"I'm worried he thinks someone might be after him, and this is his way of throwing them off," Tasha offered.

"Then he should have told me. You guys find ways to tell us to be careful without telling us everything." She'd been around the spy stuff all of her life. It might not always have been CIA operatives, but even before her uncle and aunt had gone back in to watch over their daughters, they'd had their secrets. And not once would her uncle have left her father and mother on the outside if he could help it.

There was a knock on the door, and her mother was suddenly there. She looked gorgeous in her emerald green gown. "Hey, sweetie. It's almost time. Are you ready?"

What her mother was truly asking was—were they going through with this?

Yes. She would because she was done waiting and hoping. It was time to be with the man who'd loved her all of her life. Carys stood and smoothed out her gown. "I have to get my veil on and then it's time to get this party started."

Her mom stepped in. "Hey, I wanted you to know Serena and Adam and Jake are here. They came with Brianna, and they're sitting close to the front. I didn't want you to be surprised."

She reached for her mom's hand and gave it a squeeze. "I appreciate them coming and I'm thrilled to have them. Is Serena okay?"

Serena had been so happy the day they'd announced the engagement. She and Carys's mom and Aidan's mom, Avery O'Donnell, had been the best of friends for years, and they'd been so happy to plan their children's wedding. Not a one of them had batted an eyelash. Especially Serena, since she'd raised Tristan in her own throuple. She and Adam and Jake had been happily married for decades, and she'd seemed thrilled her son was carrying on the tradition.

She'd cried when Carys had told her she was marrying Aidan and it was okay if she didn't want to come.

"Like I said. You are amazing, cousin." Kenzie stood and placed her champagne glass on the buffet. "I'm going to go and make sure my sister doesn't decide to overstuff her bouquet, if you know what I mean."

"And I'm going to go and ensure Daisy isn't making out with her groomsman." Tasha shook her head. "Did I mention my brothers are both upset they have to escort their sisters down the aisle? I think they were planning on hitting on all the bridesmaids they weren't related to. Then they got a list of the bridesmaids."

Carys snorted at the idea of her horny cousins hitting on everyone. "If they thought I had hot friends, they do not understand the life of an intern. All my friends are family." Including the ones she didn't share any blood with. "I'm sure Lucas is right there with them."

Her youngest brother was a menace.

Grace sighed. "I love my son."

"But?" Carys grinned her mom's way as her cousins ran off to get everything ready.

"No but," her mom said with a sigh. "Just I love him. I have to remind myself sometimes. He was hitting on the wedding planner earlier. One day he's going to meet a woman who knocks him on his ass, and I pray she takes him. I really do. I wonder how Liam did it."

Carys snorted, an inelegant sound, but there was no other way to react. "Nate took one look at Daisy and fell madly in love. Well, he spent one hot night with her at the club and he hasn't looked back."

She was thrilled for Aidan's sister. Daisy had recently gotten engaged to the Dom of her dreams, and Carys couldn't wait to see what would happen at their wedding. Trouble often followed her almost sister-in-law, but she was adorable and always made the best of things.

Like Carys was going to do.

"Here. Let me help you with the veil." Her mom picked up the gossamer creation and placed it on her head with a sigh. "I can't believe you're getting married. You were a baby yesterday."

"She was a hope yesterday," a deep voice said. "She was the reason I made guacamole for nine months straight." Her father was still devastatingly handsome in his tux. Sean Taggart had been the male authority figure in her world, and she adored him. He'd managed to build a restaurant empire without ever making his children feel like they were second place. "You look gorgeous, sweetheart. You look like your mom."

Her brother stood beside him, and there was a reason all the girls loved Luke Taggart. He was following in their father's footsteps career wise. Luke was an up-and-coming figure in the culinary world. In the dating world he was mostly the stud du jour among the younger D/s groups. "You look great, sis, but couldn't you have, like, brought in some hot bridesmaids?"

Her dad shook his head and ignored her brother. "I'm serious, Carys. You look stunning, and I'm so proud of you and Aidan. This is all going to be all right because the two of you... Well, let's just say I've watched him for years, and he's loved you since he was a child. You two are going to be fine."

Nope. She wasn't going to cry. She wasn't going to think about the fact that once there had been three of them. "Thanks, Dad."

He stared for a moment as though taking it all in and then held

41

out an arm. "Ready?"

Not in any way. But she smiled and took her dad's arm. "Ready."

* * * *

Aidan O'Donnell stepped out on the balcony. The rest of the groomsmen were getting ready inside, joking and farting around, but he needed some quiet.

Just a few minutes more and he would be Carys's husband.

He loved her so much, but there was an ache in his soul because Tristan wouldn't be standing beside them.

He stared over the green fields. They'd selected a venue in the country. It was beautiful, with rolling hills, and the stars would light up the night when they danced their first dance as man and wife.

We have to figure out how to tango as a threesome. Carys likes to dance. It could get our wife all hot and bothered and ready for the honeymoon.

Aidan forced the thoughts away. He wasn't giving Tris headspace today. He was doing what the fucker wanted. He was marrying her to throw off the bad guys Tris had gotten involved with. That was all the space Tris got today.

Damn. Should he be this angry on his wedding day?

You can't tell her. Promise me. If you tell her, she'll never stay away. It won't be long. I promise.

Promises. Fucking promises.

Somehow he'd thought Tristan would show up today. He'd thought he would ride in on a white horse or something and tell him everything was okay and they could finally get on with their lives.

Years they'd spent perfecting their roles, and Tristan had blown it all up for a job.

He'd thought Tristan would tell him he was done pretending to be some arms dealer and ready to get back to real life.

All he'd gotten was a single text.

Take care of our girl.

She wasn't going to be *their* girl after today. He had to pray she never found out he'd been talking to Tristan all this time. He'd played a part in keeping Tris's secrets. If she did, she might never forgive him.

At this point he had to think it wouldn't matter because she would never come back from Tristan's distance. This was the rest of his life. Life without his best friend. Without the family he'd wanted to build.

It would be enough. It had to be.

At least he would have Carys when they eventually heard Tristan was dead. He was certain this ended in one way. He knew it in his soul.

He glanced down and saw a shadow moving through the building across the large patio where everything was set up for the party they would have after the elegant dinner. There were tables and a bar and a stage where the band would play. Seth Taggart was taking care of the music this evening, with some of his friends coming in to back him up.

They would dance under the stars and then go on their honeymoon.

His gorgeous wife was perfectly fine with her honeymoon being in Montreal where he would be attending a special symposium on cutting-edge surgical techniques.

But then neither of them had a lot of enthusiasm for a week at the beach. A luxurious week at the beach had been the plan in the beginning. Hole up on an island with a staff to take care of them and lay out in the sun and fuck their wife.

It was better this way. After all, it wasn't like he could afford to rent a villa in Barbados like Tristan had planned.

He watched the shadow move across the dining hall. Likely one of the venue's workers making sure everything was perfect since Chef Taggart was here. Boy, all the kitchen workers had freaked out when they'd realized who would be planning the menu and overseeing the dinner. Not Sean, of course, but his longtime partner Eric Vail was somewhere in the back of the reception hall braising a shit ton of meat.

He was almost certain it was a man who stopped at the doors to the kitchen and paused as though lost and then turned to walk back down the hallway.

Something about him. There was something familiar about the

way he walked.

"Hey, it looks like this train's about to get rolling, son." His father stood in the doorway. "You look good, boy. Are you feeling okay?"

His da. Liam O'Donnell had been born in Ireland, but he'd raised his family in Texas. Not that anyone could tell given his accent. His father had been known to slip back into Irish when he got emotional. Aidan hadn't bothered to learn Irish past how to curse and say I love you. It had been his sister who'd made a study of the language of their ancestors.

"I'm good. I'm ready."

His father sighed and closed the French doors behind him. "Aidan, you don't have to go through with this. I can walk down there and tell Adam and Jake to get that son of theirs here. Shotgun wedding works for me."

A smile curled up Aidan's lips because his father would do it. "I'll pass on the forced marital vows. It's better this way, and don't make me say anything else, Da. I need some delusion today."

His father moved in and put a hand on his shoulder. "All right, then. Let's go because it's almost time, and I know you don't want Carys to be worrying you won't show up. Let's get the heavy stuff over and welcome your bride into our family properly."

By properly his father meant with a whole bunch of whiskey and shenanigans. He suspected there would be a very Irish party at the end of the elegant ceremony and dinner. It was probably exactly what he needed. "Let's do it."

He followed his father back inside, gathering the groomsmen who weren't currently acting as ushers, seating guests in the gorgeous outdoor setting Grace and his mother had crafted.

Though it had been Tristan's mom's idea. She'd been the one who'd found this place. It was only twenty minutes west of Fort Worth, but it was like they were in another world. A simpler world.

"Hey, everything is ready. I saw Sean heading into the bridal suite." His mother stood in the entry hall. There were lovely covered walkways connecting the buildings in the venue. His mother was in front of the one that would lead them all to where the ceremony would take place. The bridal suite led right out onto the big balcony space where they would make their vows. The groom, however, had to make the long walk around, climbing up a set of winding stairs. "Everything is in place. Oh, Carys looks so beautiful."

His father reached for his mother's hand. "She's not the only one. Come along, my darling. Let's watch our son get married. Aidan, don't take too long, son."

His mom practically glowed as she let his father lead her away.

Aidan stood at the bottom of the stairs and heard the string quartet playing above. The afternoon sky was a perfect blue. Everything about the day was perfect with the singular exception of who was missing.

He pulled out his cell. He should have left it upstairs, but there was some hopeful part of him still praying Tris would change his mind. He pulled up the number he used to contact his best friend. It was listed as Dr. Jerry Smith in case Carys ever saw the contact come across his phone. She wouldn't question a doctor calling him, and there were so many in his department she wouldn't expect to know them all.

Keeping secrets. It was what he did these days. He kept Tristan's secrets, and it was killing him.

He typed in what was going to be his last message.

Don't call me after today. I told you what would happen if you let it go this far. I love you, man. But I have to pick her, and that means cutting off contact. Have a good life.

He hit *send* and immediately saw a set of typing indicator bubbles. So Tris had his phone.

There is no good life without you and Carys. I thought you understood. Come on, man. I love you and I love our wife. I'm trying to protect you.

It was what he always said. Aidan wasn't sure how to reply. He'd said it all a thousand times.

"I am trying to protect you," a quiet voice said.

Now he knew why the shadow he'd seen before had seemed so familiar. He turned and Tristan was dressed as a security guard with a ball cap pulled low on his head.

"I thought one of the ways you were going to protect us was staying away," Aidan said, not moving toward him.

Tristan clung to the shadows. "I had to see her. I had to watch over you both. There's a room above the ceremony space. I think it's where they store all the lighting and stuff. It's also got a small security station. I'll be up there."

So the uncles were hard at work. "Ian knows you're here."

"He is my boss," Tristan replied. "And he wants you safe, too."

"What do you think is going to happen? Beyond Carys and I getting married? I assure you my father is paranoid enough. He and Aunt Erin and Uncle Theo did a perimeter sweep before they let the bridal party in. We're not using the venue's security staff. From what I've heard, they're worried about TJ being here. I have no idea what TJ did, but I'm not letting any more spy shit disrupt my wedding."

He'd had to talk fast to convince one of his favorite people in the world to come to his wedding. He'd grown up with TJ. They were basically cousins since TJ's mom had been his father's partner for as long as he could remember. TJ was his best man. It would have been one more piece missing.

"It's not shit," Tristan said with a sigh. "And the threat to TJ is real, but I understand. It's why we're being careful. But this should do it, Aidan. This should prove to anyone watching we're no longer together. You won't be a target."

"Yes, it will prove it because it's true. We're not together and haven't been for a long time." He was angrier than he thought he was. Tristan was here and playing games again. "After today, we're done. I can't lie to her. I'll keep all your secrets but after today, there's a line in the sand."

"Aidan…"

Aidan shook his head. "If this isn't what you want, then stand beside me the way you were supposed to. If you want this to work, then walk up there and talk to her. I can't do this anymore. I can't wait. She can't wait. You chose this path. You can get off it, but this is the last exit ramp, man."

Tristan's face fell. "I can't. It's too dangerous. Aidan, it's worse than I've told you. I wanted to keep you out of it."

Aidan brought his hands up, putting some distance between them. "Then I'm out of it. Like I said, have a good life, Tristan. I'm going to go take care of my girl. You take care of yourself. You're good at that now."

"You're not being fair," Tristan said.

It probably wasn't, but it was how he felt. Angry. Antsy. Like all of this was a terrible idea and it shouldn't be this way. "Good-bye."

Aidan took a deep breath and forced himself to walk through those doors, to climb the stairs, to smile as he took his place next to TJ.

TJ Taggart gave him a big grin. "Hey, I was worried you weren't going to make it." He leaned over, and his voice dropped to a whisper. "You should know I think Tris is here."

It was good to know he was still a loyal friend. TJ worked with Tristan, so his loyalties were almost certainly conflicted. "I can confirm he is, but he's planning on staying in the shadows. I'm fine."

"He talked to you?" TJ asked.

They'd been dancing around this for weeks now. TJ had suspicions. Finally figuring out his love life seemed to have made TJ smarter. Or maybe Louisa Ward was rubbing off on him. Lou had also been in their group, growing up alongside the twins and Tash and Cooper McKay.

They'd all gone off to the Army or Navy or college far away and they'd all ended up in the same place. The CIA.

"He told me he's protecting us and getting married without him will throw off whoever is pursuing him." Aidan forced a smile on his face as he straightened the jacket of his tux. The ceremony space was intimate, with less than a hundred seats, and not all of them were full. They'd wanted to keep it fairly small, though family alone was a lot. They hadn't had a bride or groom's side since they'd all grown up together. He looked out and saw his father and mother sitting in the front row along with his sister's fiancé's family.

But right behind them in the second row was the Dean-Miles family. Adam Miles and Jacob Dean sat together with Serena in between Jake and her daughter, Brianna. Who had been a bridesmaid at one point but had dropped out when it became clear her brother wasn't coming home. Serena dabbed her eyes with a tissue while Brianna held her hand.

What the hell was he doing?

"He is trying to protect you, but I think he's going about it the wrong way," TJ whispered as the pastor of the church they'd all attended since childhood moved in behind them. "We're going to talk when you get back from your honeymoon. I promise I'm going to work this out for you and Carys."

That was TJ. "It's okay. There are things we can't fix, and this is one of them. Carys and I are going to be fine."

The music changed to Pachelbel's Canon in D, and all heads turned as the bridal party began to walk down the aisle.

Carys's niece, Diana Hawthorne, looked adorable in her pink dress. The four-year-old skipped down the aisle, joyously tossing rose petals.

Her mom, MaeBe, bit back a laugh as she walked down the aisle with Carys's brother Kyle. All of Carys's brothers were in the wedding party along with their wives, his sister, Daisy, and her fiancé, Nate, and her Taggart cousins. Tash walked down the aisle with her brother Travis, Kenzie with Carys's younger brother Lucas. Kala walked beside her brother Seth.

And then the world narrowed to one sight.

Carys stood with her father, the sun shining down on her like a fucking spotlight. Like it couldn't help but caress her with warmth, giving her a glow.

He let go of everything in that moment. Aidan allowed all of his worry to wash away because no matter what happened, she was the important part.

His love. His life. Everything revolved around the gorgeous woman who started walking down the aisle.

Her eyes caught with his, and a smile crossed her face. A real smile. A "we're in this together and it's going to be okay" smile.

It was going to be okay.

He glanced over and noticed Carys's uncle had stepped away from his chair and walked to the back of the space, standing near the railing overlooking the grounds below. Ian Taggart's body was stiff, as though he was on edge.

Something was happening. If he trusted anyone's instincts, it was Ian's.

A buzzing sound could be heard over the stringed quartet who'd started up with the wedding march.

"Is that a drone?" TJ stepped up onto the platform where the pastor stood. "Fuck."

"TJ," the pastor admonished.

Sean had stopped in the middle of the aisle, looking over to Ian. "I'm sorry. It's probably press. They'll go away. Someone shoot it down."

"Taggarts," the pastor sighed under his breath.

"I've got it," Kala announced, pulling a SIG out of the center of her bouquet.

There were suddenly a whole lot of guns.

Carys's father was a celebrity chef. Sean Taggart was known in culinary circles—and food-related television—as the Soldier Chef. It wasn't terrifically surprising celebrity media would want pictures of his daughter's wedding, although they'd been careful about keeping the logistics quiet.

"Maybe we should think about this," Aidan said.

"I've got the shot," Kala announced.

Of course she did.

Carys sighed. "Have we thought about pictures of the twins getting released to the public? I thought we were trying to pretend there was only one of them."

"Shit." Uncle Ian looked back, his cell in hand.

"I need a laptop." Adam Miles moved out of the aisle. "I can probably hack into it and figure out how to stop those pictures."

"You're getting soft in your old age," a feminine voice said. Chelsea Weston sat beside her husband, and she had her phone in hand, working on the problem. Chelsea was one of the world's best hackers. "I've already got it on my phone. Give me a second and I'll figure out who sent it. Sorry, guys."

"Diana, don't climb the trellis, sweetie," MaeBe was saying.

Carys strode to him. "I'm sorry. I should have known better. We should have been inside. I don't understand why they would want pictures. I'm not a celebrity."

"They don't," Chelsea said. "It's weird. It's not taking pictures. It's… Ian, it's sending back markers. Directions."

Aidan's father was on his feet. "Bloody hell. Everyone out. Move to the stairs as quickly as you can."

Kyle Hawthorne scooped his daughter off the trellis, while MaeBe picked up their son. Tessa Hawthorne had been sitting next to

49

Grace, and David began hustling them toward the stairs.

Then he heard a deeper thud than any drone could make.

He didn't have to be in the military to know the sound. Helicopter.

He barely had time to push Carys to the ground before the world exploded.

Chapter Two

Tristan stared at Carys. She looked so fucking gorgeous. The dress clung to her every curve. It was as timeless as Carys's beauty.

Aidan didn't look half bad either, but TJ standing in Tristan's place bugged him way more than he thought it would.

This was all for the best. It was what had to happen.

He stood in the tiny security room. This whole venue at one point in time had been a mission. They'd added on, and the gorgeous dining hall and ultra-modern kitchen were new, but this part used to be the chapel.

He might have been far too invested in the planning of a wedding he wasn't a part of.

The bell tower was the security office and part-time storage closet since he was stuck in here with what had to be five hundred Styrofoam cups stamped with *Happy Quinceañera*. It offered him a couple of monitors hooked up to the CCTV cams across the venue, but even more importantly he could see the ceremony space with his own eyes. From his vantage, he could see Carys starting to walk down the aisle with her father.

Tristan's own family was down there watching as the love of his life married another man. Well, most of them were. His sister, mother, and one of his dads were politely turned to the aisle with the rest of the guests.

His most military dad, however, had turned and looked up. Like Jacob Dean knew he was there, knew he was hiding.

It was obvious his father wasn't happy with him. None of them were.

It was precisely why he'd had to stay away. His parents would get far too curious. He would actually be surprised if his fathers hadn't already done a lot of digging. They wouldn't find anything because the Agency knew how to hide intelligence.

Still, he took a step back in case his dad could see him. He wouldn't put it past Jacob Dean to storm the castle.

Just a few more minutes and they would be safe. He didn't think anyone had figured out his true identity, but he'd come to believe it was only a matter of time, and time was what fucked him over when it came to this op. He'd already taken too much of it, and he couldn't promise anyone when this op would be over.

His cell beeped and Tristan pulled it out. This wasn't the one he'd used to text with Aidan over the last couple of years. This was the one only a few people had the number to.

"Hey, Tris. I've picked up some weird stuff on the web about The Jester." The young woman who served as his technical support when he was working outside the family team was one of the people who knew this particular number.

Tara Hahn was a cutie, but he'd always seen her as a sister. Every woman was a sister when a man had found the right one. "I'm kind of in the middle of something."

"Are you in the middle of nowhere in North Texas?" she asked.

Down below he watched as Uncle Ian stood and stepped away from the crowd. He was on his cell, too.

"What have you got?" Tristan felt his blood go cold, an icy professionalism coming over him.

His whole family was down there. What the hell was that? There was a black thing coming into view. Not a bird. A drone.

What the fuck was a drone doing out here?

Gathering intel.

"I've got movement from one of the groups we're monitoring. From what I can tell, they flew into DFW yesterday. I'm sorry I'm late with this, but they were good at covering their tracks. Honestly, if I hadn't known you were in Dallas this weekend, I might have let it go," Tara was saying. "I think I've tracked them meeting a person we consider... Well, he's basically a logistics guy for the Dark Web. He's a broker of sorts. He can get you anything you need."

A hole opened in the pit of Tristan's stomach as he heard a familiar thud.

A broker who could get a guy whatever he needed. Like guns and drones and a fucking helicopter.

Tristan dropped the phone and started down the stairs. He managed to make it to the landing as the guests were running from the upper floor.

"Move," he called, waving through the parents with kids. It was obvious even in panic mode, his family prioritized the kids. They moved quickly.

"Hey, my sister is still back there." Kyle Hawthorne had his daughter clinging to him as his wife moved past, followed by Carys's other brothers. David and Lucas were each carrying a child while David's wife, Tessa, led the older kids.

"I'll get her," Tristan promised. "You get them inside. Away from the windows."

"I'll be back," Kyle told him but called out for everyone to follow him.

The chopper closed in as he saw his mom and sister with Grace and Avery and Daisy. Daisy held her mother's hand as they navigated the stairs.

His mom's eyes widened when she saw him, and she started to move his way. He shook his head.

"Get her to safety. I'll get Carys and Aidan," he shouted, and suddenly a massive dude was at their backs, moving the women along.

Nathan Carter sent him a nod and a look that told him he would ensure everyone was safe. Nate was former Aussie Special Forces, and Tris trusted him.

Now he had to deal with the rest of his family, the ones who wouldn't be running to safety.

Where the hell was Aidan? From what he could hear, the chopper would be right on them now. Tristan rushed onto the big balcony in time to watch the helo swing in and gunfire start.

An explosion came from his left. Grenade? They were lobbing fucking grenades at his wedding? Anger and fear flared, but he shoved them down as smoke covered the balcony and the sound of gunfire exploded through the air.

He barely avoided one of those bullets as he crossed the space, trying to work his way to the altar where he saw Carys on the ground, covered by Aidan. Sean had moved in, lending his big body to protect his daughter, too.

Aidan looked up. "What the fuck is happening, Tris?"

He heard Carys gasp but he didn't have time to talk. "Stay down." He looked over and Ian and his fathers had taken up refuge behind the balcony wall. Luckily they'd stayed somewhat true to the original architecture and hadn't switch it out for wrought iron. It was a thick wall that protected them from bullets.

The hail of bullets went on for what felt like forever. He was forced to huddle behind one of the big pillars while Carys and Aidan were behind the wall. He could barely see the white of her dress because her father and Aidan protected her so completely.

But he wasn't there, and if he didn't figure this the fuck out he never would be again. Aidan had been serious. He'd meant to cut Tris out after today.

He'd agonized for years over the decisions he'd made. He thought he'd come to terms with all of them. But standing here and not being able to take his half of the burden was killing him. He couldn't do this. He couldn't be without them for the rest of his life.

The sound of the chopper hung in the air and then he risked it to get a look. Tristan moved to the side, and the chopper was starting to pull away.

"Are they leaving?" Carys asked quietly.

He glanced over to where his cousins were huddled. Kala and Kenzie looked worse for the wear, but neither was panicking. Kala caught his gaze and lifted her chin slightly.

She wasn't letting anyone leave. Neither was he. If he didn't take the shot, his cousin would.

He nodded and then the twins were moving, firing to give him some cover. The helo was starting to turn. Cooper was suddenly at Tristan's side.

"Hit the fuel tank," Cooper said, his eyes narrowing as he lifted his weapon. "They're too close right now."

Tristan knew exactly where to hit, but they had to let the fucker get further away. There was a responding set of gunfire, and Cooper ducked but Tristan stood there. He stared at the fuckers who were likely looking for him. He was the reason for all of this. A bullet flew by him, but he stood firm.

The gunfire ceased, and for a second the quiet was unsettling.

"Girls, get down now. Tristan, Cooper, take them out." Uncle Ian yelled.

He was sure Ian would have preferred to do the taking down, but he and Coop were in a better position. The helo started a sweep up, and he and Coop fired.

Two shots. It was all they needed. Two shots and then they heard the whirring of the engine right before the whole thing exploded.

Tristan felt the heat from the blast and realized Coop had taken cover. Everyone had. They'd all protected themselves, but Tris needed to see it, needed to feel the power of the blast, to know beyond a shadow of all doubt at least these fuckers wouldn't be coming after his family.

"What is wrong with you?" His dad's eyes were wide as he stalked across the space, pointing Tristan's way. "Do you have a death wish, son? They were close. You are lucky the blast didn't take you out."

"Hey, are you okay?" His papa was calmer, though he could see what it had cost Adam Miles to stand down while the rest of them took care of the situation.

"I'm fine." He took a long breath and turned to help Aidan up, but Sean Taggart was already there. He had Aidan on his feet and reached for Carys, but she was already holding her hand up for Aidan.

"Yeah, I need a cleanup crew," Big Tag was saying into his cell.

Liam O'Donnell rushed in as Aidan helped Carys to her feet.

Her dress was ruined. It was torn in several places and covered in some form of soot. Her hair had come down, and the veil was barely hanging on. She held on to Aidan as she looked back at her dad. "Is everyone okay?"

Charlotte Taggart came in from the bridal suite where it looked like she'd taken the guests in the back half of the balcony to hide. She

55

was in a designer gown but had her favorite accessory. A pistol. "We clear?"

Her husband nodded. "Yeah, but now we have to deal with the fallout. Carys, sweetheart, I'm so sorry…"

She held up a hand. "The wedding's off. We need to check on everyone, and then you need to figure out what's going on. I understand. All that matters is everyone is safe. Does anyone need medical treatment?"

She was surreally calm as she pulled the veil off her head.

"I think we moved them all out in time, sweetie," her dad said. "I need to let your mom know you're okay."

"I'll come with you. I want to check on everyone," she replied, cool as ice.

"Hey, we need to check on you first." Tris moved into Carys's space. She was in shock, and she needed to know she was safe now. Even while the helicopter burned a hundred yards away. "Come on, baby."

A crack sounded through the air, and his head snapped back before he felt the actual pain. She'd slapped him. Not in a girlie way, in a bitch-goddess, feel-my-power way.

"How dare you," Carys said. "You were hiding? You were spying on us?"

"I was watching over you." He looked to Aidan, who was pale but calm as well. "Aidan, I was just…"

His best friend shook his head. "We have to check on the others. We can talk later. I'm sure you have a debrief to attend."

"Hey, Car, I take back what I said about the dress." Kala strode up as though the wedding was still happening and nothing had gone wrong. The bridesmaids dress she wore now boasted a long slit up the side. "Once I ripped it a little, it was totally easy to move in. Did you see the way that fucker went down?"

"What I saw—and anyone who was looking—was you aren't wearing underwear." Cooper pointed a finger Kala's way. "What the hell?"

"Hello, panty lines," Kala replied.

They started to argue about whether going commando during an impromptu firefight was a good choice, but Tristan couldn't take his eyes off Carys.

Who turned and walked away, letting Aidan lead her down the stairs.

"Well, this is a hell of a thing," Aunt Charlotte said as another boom shook the air around them.

Tristan stood with his dads and watched the loves of his life walk away.

* * * *

Carys took a long drag off the martini Tasha had put in her hand. Her cousin had switched out the champagne for vodka after the horrors of the afternoon. According to Aunt Charlotte, vodka solved most problems. She was pretty sure they wouldn't solve hers, but she would take the detachment it might bring.

She was still in shock. An hour later and she was still trying to process what had happened.

"That's the last of the guests with kids." Kenzie and Kala were in the bridal suite as well. Her cousins had told her they wouldn't leave for anything.

Of course they might be playing bodyguard. They kept watching the door and tensed whenever it opened.

"I had to talk Kyle out of staying." Her mother had a grim look on her face. "He wanted to help with the cleanup, but he doesn't have clearance anymore."

Yes, she was left with the Agency crew. The wedding she'd planned for years had basically been firebombed, and the only good news of the day was no one was seriously injured. She had no idea what she would say to her coworkers at the hospital when she eventually returned to work. *Uh, didn't actually get married because someone tried to kill us all, and then we had to deal with a helicopter exploding, and oh, my ex showed up to save the day and I was fairly certain he'd been okay with dying.*

So why did she feel oddly relieved?

Shock. Yep, it was still shock. She wasn't secretly okay with the fact that she hadn't said I do. Her heart hadn't thudded in her chest when she'd realized Tristan was here. Nope. Anger was all she'd felt. The slap across his gorgeous face had been about anger. It hadn't because she couldn't figure out another way to touch him.

Because she couldn't let him hug her, couldn't allow him to kiss her.

Even though her first impulse had been to throw herself into his arms.

No one was injured. No one had died. Well, the dudes in the helicopter had absolutely died, but they had been far past her medical skills the minute Tristan had blown them out of the sky.

She'd been under her father and Aidan, but she'd managed to watch Tristan stand beside Cooper and take down the helicopter in seconds. Cooper had ducked, but Tristan had stood there and watched, his eyes hard.

He hadn't cared if he'd gotten hurt. He'd wanted the storm to sweep over him.

There had always been a darkness in Tris. Since they were kids, he was the one who could brood and lose himself in dark thoughts.

Like she could. She'd needed Aidan's light and Tristan's darkness to balance her own needs.

Her dark side was so fucking hungry.

She took another sip of martini. If there was any vermouth in there, she couldn't tell. Her cousin had a heavy hand. "He needs to be with his kids. Diana was upset."

"Well, Rand told me it was the best wedding he'd ever been to," her mom said with a shake of her head. "MaeBe had to haul him away because he wanted to go out and see the wreck."

They were huddled in the bridal suite while her uncles and Tristan handled the situation.

Actually, she was now surprised her cousins were still here. "Shouldn't you guys be meeting with... What did Uncle Ian call it? The cleaners?"

Kala's nose wrinkled. "In this family men deal with the bodies. I know I seem like I would enjoy body disposal, but it's kind of gross. I have no use for them once they're dead. Also, I just had my nails done. Personally, I think we should have gone through with it. Diana was way more upset Kyle yelled at her for climbing the trellis than she was about the chopper going boom. The kids are all right, if you know what I mean. I feel like we kind of quit."

"Hey, we couldn't go through with the ceremony. There's a whole-ass helicopter burning right outside the ceremony," Kenzie argued. "You can't expect the wedding to keep going."

"I don't see why not," Kala replied. "She wanted fireworks and they wouldn't let her have them. So we got organic fireworks."

Only Kala would call those blasts organic fireworks. She chuckled. Maybe the vodka was already doing its work if she could see some humor in the situation.

"Uhm, personally I think you did the right thing by deciding to reschedule." Louisa Ward appeared to also be a member of the men-body-disposal movement. She worked with her cousins' team, likely behind the scenes since Lou was a certifiable genius when it came to computers and math and engineering. She was also TJ's girlfriend, though she was fairly certain they would get engaged soon.

Everyone seemed to be starting their lives. Daisy was engaged to Nate. Tasha and Dare's wedding was coming up, though they might need to think about eloping after today.

"Oh, I don't think I'll try this again." Carys shook her head. "Nope. I am listening to the universe, which is telling me in no uncertain terms I should have a small wedding. Maybe at a courthouse. Or a drive-through chapel in Vegas."

If they stayed in their car, they would have a good chance of getting away if someone started shooting again. She'd never considered exit routes from her wedding. It had been a definite mistake.

Or they could live happily in sin. Sin was fun.

Sin left doors open.

"Don't say that." Her mother somehow still looked perfect, like she was ready to greet guests and look elegant while she made everyone comfortable. "You know we can try again once we get everything sorted out. Your uncle and aunt will make sure they take care of the situation."

Carys was pretty sure she looked like she'd survived the apocalypse. "I don't even understand what the situation is."

She looked around, and Kenzie and Kala were perfectly blank. Tasha took a long drink.

Lou had gone a nice shade of pink.

Lou was the weak link among the Agency set. Oh, she wouldn't give out classified intel, and Carys was sure if a bad guy was in the room, Lou would also be perfectly blank. But Lou had never truly learned how to shut it down when she was with her friends and family. Lucky for her, most of her friends and family had high levels of security clearance. "So this has to do with you? Or TJ?"

"Why would it have anything to do with TJ?" Her mother took a drink from Tasha, who was working through her anxiety via bartending.

Her mom was right to ask the question since TJ was an overly large golden retriever. Not that he wasn't deadly. He was a Taggart and was in the military, but he was sweet and helpful, and she couldn't imagine him pissing off someone so much they decided to ruin a perfectly innocent wedding.

She was pretty sure the photographer was going to need therapy. At least all the catering staff had come from her dad's restaurant and were therefore mostly ex-military who knew there was one freezer you did not walk into.

"I mean it was probably about TJ." Kala shrugged and looked at her sisters. "Don't judge me. She just had her wedding raided by assholes. She deserves some explanations."

Kala was the one she could see attracting vengeful killers. But right now she was also the most reasonable. "Yeah, what Kala said."

Kenzie sighed. "Okay. In broad terms TJ might have a fake connection with a worldwide arms dealer, and said arms dealer is apparently the only one who supposedly has the number to this person who makes bombs better than anyone else, and so the bad guys might be putting together one and one to make an unknown two."

Kenzie wasn't good with simple explanations. "I don't understand."

"Okay, let's see if I remember this language," her mother said. "Someone set up TJ to be close to an arms dealer, likely so it would either hurt TJ or your uncle and aunt. But the arms dealer has this other valuable connection, and they think TJ either knows who the bombmaker is or can get them to the arms dealer who does."

Kala's eyes went wide, and she leaned toward her sister. "I think Aunt Grace might know too much."

Her mom's eyes rolled. "Oh, child, I know far too much, but this is just me speaking spy." She shifted her gaze to Tasha. "Was it your old fiancé? The dead one?"

It was Tash's turn to be surprised. "Uh, yes. He set up a long-

60

term kind of revenge on me. He thought it would look bad if TJ was connected to this guy, and no one turned it off when he died. In this case his organizational skills kind of bit us all in the ass."

"Then why would they try to kill TJ?" Carys didn't think the twins' explanation made sense. "They need information out of him. It would feel like it would be better to kidnap him."

Kala waved her off. "They already tried to kidnap him."

"Hey," Kenzie said. "Classified."

"Aidan had to examine him after you came back from…wherever it is you went since you couldn't say." They'd both known something had gone wrong. TJ had been okay, but Aidan had told her about the cattle prod burns on his body. "It's not a hard leap to get to he got kidnapped and tortured for information. You see doctors have to put together many puzzles. Patients lie a lot. Out of shame or to hide something, and in this case out of the information being highly classified. I get it. But this happened here. It happened to me and Aidan. We have a right to know. Maybe not legally, but I have walked into enough sketchy shit to know legal isn't always the family way."

"How about we wait for the inevitable debrief," her mother advised.

"Because I don't usually get invited to debriefs." It was well known in their family that if you found yourself sitting in the conference room at McKay-Taggart, you were in serious trouble and likely to find yourself in some form of lockdown.

If they got sent to Sanctum and locked in, Aidan would miss his once in a lifetime chance to meet with surgeons who could help his career. He was the youngest invitee to the conference, and it was a huge opportunity for him. She couldn't let him lose it.

"I'll make sure you get an invite to this one," her mother promised.

It would be best to avoid getting involved further. She knew how her uncle handled these things. It could be hours, and she would have to sit there with Tris the whole time. "I think I'll pass. This seems to not be about me and Aidan, so it's likely best to stay away. It makes it way easier on you guys."

Tasha joined her sisters, all of them staring at her with suspicion. "Not what you said mere moments before. I thought you deserved to be in on everything."

Kala nodded. "She totally did."

"And then Kenz pointed out all the problems with being in on everything, and here we are," she said, hoping she sounded confident. She hadn't exactly mentioned her honeymoon plans beyond they were going to be spending some time in Canada.

Her parents might not like knowing their "honeymoon" was more like a work trip. They didn't understand the needs of a resident.

She didn't mind. She was actually looking forward to it, but her parents would say it was one more reason to put the wedding off. One more way they thought she was screwing this up.

She hadn't needed to screw anything up. Tristan fucked things up for all of them.

Lou looked at her, blinking, likely because she wasn't used to wearing contacts. She'd insisted on them, though Carys had told Lou her normal glasses looked great with the dress. "She's hiding something."

"Ooo, I love a mystery," Kenzie said with a smile and a clap of her hands.

Sometimes Kenzie's weird positivity was scarier than Kala's...well, scariness. "Not hiding anything. I simply don't want to get involved in something that isn't my business."

"Or you want to avoid Tristan since he's apparently back." Tasha frowned. "I thought he was in DC meeting with Drake and Taylor. He didn't call any of you?"

"He didn't want any of us to know he was going to be skeeving on the wedding," Kala replied with a shrug. "Which is weird because that's something you're supposed to do when you weren't invited to be an actual part of the vows and shit." She held off her sister's admonition. "I'm only being honest. The dude could literally be enjoying his honeymoon right now if he'd wanted to."

"Oh, I forgot about the honeymoon. Carys has been a little secretive about it," her mom said. "All she'll say is it's a surprise and she'll send pictures. I'll be honest. I hoped she was so quiet because Tristan was going to join them."

"No, he's not." She hadn't considered her mom might think she was keeping a secret. She wasn't really. More like trying to avoid a minor argument.

"I thought they were going to Bermuda or something. Don't they have like a whole beach house rented?" Kenzie replied.

Kala shook her head. "No. They were going to the Caribbean when Tris was joining them in newlywed bliss."

Lou gasped and put a hand to her heart as though she'd heard something horrifying. "He took back their honeymoon? Like I know why he did the rest, but taking back a beautiful honeymoon seems rude."

"Guys, he didn't take it back." If she let this go, there would be a couple of assassins pissed at Tris, and he had to work with them. And Lou could do a lot of damage on her own. "In fact, he tried to pay for the wedding. But he's not a part of it so we turned him down."

It had been the only thing to do.

She didn't want his conscience to rest in any way. She knew when he was trying to buy her off, and he could go to hell.

Wouldn't it be fun to tell him that in person? How long has it been since you had someone who would fight with you, who would go toe to toe and call you out when you're a brat?

"Then where are you going?" Tash asked.

Carys sighed. "We're going somewhere perfectly safe." It was time. They would all know in the end. "We're going to Canada."

She would have sworn a tear formed in Kenzie's eye and glistened there like she was thinking about something infinitely sad.

"Eww. Why would you go to Canada?" Kala asked. "Assholes live in Canada."

Kenzie nodded and seemed to put on a brave face. "They do."

"Hey, and super nice guys like your soon-to-be brother-in-law," Tasha pointed out because her fiancé was from the Great White North. "But it doesn't seem like the hottest location for a honeymoon. Oh, tell me you're not going to Niagara Falls. Honey, it's a tourist trap."

"We're not going to Niagara Falls." They wouldn't have time. She had maybe one day with him, and she planned to get Big Red Bus tickets and explore the city. Like interns did. Because they had no money.

"Vancouver," Lou guessed. "It's beautiful, and you know Aidan likes to hike."

She did not. Hiking and wilderness things were activities she'd been more than happy to send Aidan and Tristan off on while she took a long soak in the tub with a good book.

There had been a lot about being a threesome that worked for her.

"We're going to Montreal."

Tasha frowned. "For your honeymoon? Don't get me wrong. I love Canada. My fiancé is literally from there, but it wouldn't even make the top ten of our potential honeymoon destinations. If you wanted a city, you could have gone to New York and seen some shows. What are you going to do in Montreal?"

She growled, a frustrated sound. "We're going to a medical conference. Okay? That's what we're doing. Well, what Aidan's doing. He got an invite a while back to this prestigious conference, and it happened to fall on the week after our wedding so we're going and spending a couple of days exploring the city and then he'll work."

"You're going to a medical conference in Montreal," Kenzie said in a flat tone. Like she was working something out in her head. "One Aidan was personally invited to."

"Fuck," Kala said. "Well, cousin, you're definitely going to be in the debrief."

"What's going on? Why is it important she's going to Montreal? Though I think it's crappy you're not having a proper honeymoon, I do understand," her mom said. "Is this the foundation thing Aidan mentioned? He said it was one of the world's leading groups to study new medical technologies."

"I don't understand what the Huisman Foundation has to do with any of this," Carys admitted. The Huisman Foundation was universally acknowledged as one of the world's premiere research centers.

"Oh, you will," Kala promised.

Carys looked to her mom, who seemed every bit as confused as she was.

It looked like it was going to be an even longer day.

Chapter Three

Aidan sat in the reception hall, a glass of Scotch in his hand.

"Son, are you all right? Can I get you anything? I sent your mom home with Daisy and Nathan, but I stayed in case you need a ride." His father sat across from him. "Or you need to talk. I know you prefer to talk to your friends, but I'm here for you, too."

His father. His da. "I'm okay. I talked to Mom before she left. We'll give it a couple of weeks and then we'll figure something else out. This is a setback, but the one thing in the world I know is I want to be Carys Taggart's husband."

"Of course you do. It's what you've wanted since you were a kid. A baby, really. You would follow after her when you were in diapers. I swear you learned to walk so you could toddle beside her." His father studied him for a moment. "Tristan's back."

Didn't he know it. Apparently everyone did. "Yeah, and he brought helicopters full of armed assassins with him. Guess he was serious about being a danger to us."

His father pointed a finger his way. "I knew he thought he was protecting you. You've talked to him?"

He didn't want to lie to his da. "Yes. But Carys doesn't know we've been communicating on a regular basis. She absolutely doesn't know he's the guy I've been playing games with online for the last year or so. It was oddly the easiest way for us to talk."

Because Tristan knew how to ping a signal across the globe.

"Do you want to keep something like that from your fiancée?" his father asked.

"Tristan didn't think it was a good idea to bring her in. He thought she would freak out. And he's not wrong. Carys can be stubborn when she thinks she's right." It was one of the reasons their threesome worked. He was the go between for two very strong personalities.

He wasn't certain Tristan and Carys wouldn't self-immolate if left alone. Not that he didn't have his own situation. When he and Carys were alone they fell into patterns and routines, and found it difficult to break them. Especially since they were in the same field and could understand the pressures on each other. It sounded like perfection, but sometimes they required an outside force to remind them both there was something to life beyond studying and surgery and rounds. Tristan would have laughed if Aidan had told him they needed to go to a symposium on cutting-edge surgical techniques for their honeymoon. Tristan would have told him to stuff the conference or if it was important enough, to postpone the honeymoon. Instead, he and Carys had decided to be practical.

Tristan was the one who constantly pushed her boundaries. The one who could get her to cry.

Aidan was fairly certain Carys hadn't cried in two years.

Was it all about to fall apart? He had no idea what he would do if he lost Carys, too.

"What's going on, son?" His da stared at him with intelligent green eyes. "I know you haven't wanted to talk about it, and your mother and I have honored your privacy, but it's past time."

Aidan shook his head. "I know very little, Da. I know a few years ago Tristan got involved in a long-running operation with one of the Agency teams he works with, and it got dangerous."

"But Ian says he doesn't know anything."

The man known as Big Tag had been his father's "brother" for most of his life. Aidan wasn't about to throw him under the bus. "According to Tristan, he didn't tell Uncle Ian. This wasn't the team he's on with the twins. Because Tristan is technically Army intelligence, he's allowed to work all over the place. He works with

66

military teams and Agency teams, but he doesn't share information between them. I don't know entirely how it works, but I know everyone's frustrated with him. Unless they're all lying to me and they're in on it."

"I know the twins. They would find a way to tell you if they knew something. If they believed this would all get sorted soon, they would have found a way to..." His father frowned. "Oh, I hope this wasn't Kala's way of forcing you to postpone the wedding. Sometimes that girl likes to play god. I wouldn't be surprised if she found someone she didn't like and set them up to do this knowing damn well we'd shoot an encroaching helo down."

His cousin could be ruthless. "I don't think so, Da."

"Oh, she could do it," a deep voice said. "If my daughter thought she could help her cousins out and get rid of someone who annoyed her at the same time, she would set it up. She believes in multitasking, however, I assure you she wouldn't have put the kids in danger."

Aidan looked over and the man, the myth, the legend himself was standing there, and he wasn't alone. Tristan was beside him, looking worse for the wear. His security uniform was wrinkled, and his usually perfectly messy hair was just messy. He had a small cut on his jawline, and there were singe marks on the sleeve covering his left bicep.

He hadn't thought to check on Tristan. Damn it. He'd been so fucking angry he hadn't done his job. "Did you get hit?"

Ian huffed and slapped a hand gently upside Tristan's head. "He's fine. He got a taste of what could have happened because unlike the smarter members of my team, he forgot to duck when the bullets went flying. I've trained you poorly. Come Monday you'll be back in school. After a couple of spontaneous sniping attempts, you'll get better at ducking."

"I didn't want to let them out of my sights," Tristan corrected and frowned at Ian. "They could have gotten away."

"They could have put a bullet through you," Ian argued, though there was an oddly cheery expression on the man's face. Like he genuinely enjoyed the chaos.

It had been odd, realizing Tristan was standing over them as the gunfire seemed endless. He'd been covering Carys, but he'd gotten a look at Tris looming over them like a stalwart guardian.

It had been that moment Aidan had known things would be okay.

So why was he still so fucking mad? It rolled through him and took everything he had to keep under control. This wasn't him. He was logical and cool. This rage he felt wasn't going to fix their problems. It wouldn't help Carys. "And did you honestly think the helicopter could hide? Like where would it go?"

Tristan's eyes narrowed, and Aidan knew he'd poked the Dom inside his friend. "Well, it showed up pretty fucking fast, so I figured it could manage to leave in the same fashion. Would you like me to perform your next surgery? Since we all seem to know how to do the other person's job."

It was good to know he could still slide under Tristan's skin. It oddly made him feel seen. He probably needed therapy but for today it felt good, and he was going with it. "Somehow I think my job requires a little more skill."

"Are they going to throw down?" Ian whispered the question to Aidan's dad. "And do we think they're going to fight, or is this going in another direction?"

Tristan's eyes rolled. "We're not going to fuck."

"It might help," Ian threw out with a shrug like he didn't see the problem.

The problem was it never came up. They'd never talked about potentially exploring the boundaries of the relationship. When Carys teased them, they always shut her down. "Our kink was never each other. It's always been about the girl. For one of us. Tristan kind of comes and goes, and mostly he goes now."

"Hey, we should go and get a drink, son." His father seemed to want to play the voice of reason. Which was odd since reason was usually his mom's job. "Eric's packing up all the food, but we can probably get a plate or two and hash this all out over some whiskey."

"Yeah, lubricating these two is going to lead to good choices." Ian nodded. "I wholeheartedly agree, and I would be with you except we're heading back to Dallas. We need to talk about this in a safe room, and the only one that comes close is the conference room at MT. So I'm sorry to leave you, Aidan, but this is serious. I'm leaving two bodyguards behind, and I expect you to listen to them."

"Of course he will," his father agreed.

Because he was always the good kid, the responsible one. He was the guy who helped everyone move and listened to their troubles and gave sound advice no one ever took. His sister was a rolling ball of good-natured chaos, and he'd been tasked with protecting her at a young age. He protected everyone.

Which was probably why the image of Tristan standing there, ready to take every bullet that came their way, made him feel…safe.

It was a lie because Tristan would leave them again, and he would be all alone trying to give Carys what she needed.

"Why do I need a bodyguard?" The impulse to go along with whatever the military branch of the family said was practically ingrained in him, but he pushed it aside. The last thing he and Carys needed was to be under armed guard. They'd lost their wedding day. He wasn't about to lose their honeymoon. No matter how much it would suck as a romantic getaway. It was theirs, and the truth of the matter was he was now the dominant partner. Carys might kick his ass if she knew he even thought the word outside a kink setting, but it was true. She needed someone who made her life easier, who took care of the little things like another whole human being watching them twenty-four seven. "This wasn't about us. Congratulations, Tris. I now fully admit you've been right all this time. We're safer without you. I'll take my wife…fiancée, and we'll be out of everyone's hair for a couple of weeks."

"We don't know who this is about yet, Aidan." His father looked slightly surprised at his outburst.

Because he was never a brat prince. That had been Tristan's place, but he'd been filling in for Tristan for a while now. He might as well handle this aspect, too. "We know exactly who this is about. Tristan Dean-Miles. He's been telling me for over two years how dangerous his life is, how he can't come home because he's too busy chasing his James Bond dreams."

"Hey," Tristan began.

Aidan held up a hand, staving off the argument. "Sorry. I was wrong about the James Bond comment. You're not chasing some fictional character. You're still an eight-year-old hoping one day he can be as good as his dad."

"Aidan," his father admonished.

Ian shrugged. "It's a fairly accurate description. You learned a lot from your psych rotation."

He'd been good at it.

"Fuck you, Aidan," Tristan replied. "And you will take the bodyguards. You can take them with you or you can go into a safe house. Those are your only options. The honeymoon, like the wedding, is over before it began. So you're the big guy making the decisions. Which one is it going to be? Keep some freedom, or are you going to behave like an angry child and get both you and Carys locked away?"

His rage was starting to beat out his fear. Tristan didn't get to walk back in and start giving him orders. "You wouldn't."

Tristan's lips curled up in a sneer. "Oh, I would. I will. You want to make me the bad guy? I can play the role. I'm excellent at it. Ask anyone. And while we're at it, don't expect to go back to work."

"I have two weeks and then I need to be back. I can't exactly call in sick."

Tristan's broad shoulders shrugged like he didn't care. "Nope, but you can quit, and that's what will happen if I decide it's too dangerous for you. Make no mistake. I'm in charge here, Aidan."

"Or you can hang with a bodyguard for the next couple of weeks," his da said, his gaze going between the two of them like he was trying to figure out what was going on. "The guard will be happy to go to Canada with you. We'll handle everything. All you and Carys have to do is sit back and enjoy the trip. There's no need for fighting."

"Canada?" Tristan's expression turned an odd blank. "Why would Aidan go to Canada?"

"They're honeymooning in Montreal," his father explained. "They were thinking about going to LA, but they ended up choosing Montreal."

He hadn't exactly told his da why he was going to Montreal. "It's romantic."

Tristan frowned. "No, Paris is romantic. Bora Bora is romantic."

Did Tris want to shame him? "Montreal is what we can fucking afford. I don't know if you know this, but we're not made of money."

"Montreal isn't exactly a cheap city. I told you I would pay for everything," Tristan insisted. "You're being stubborn."

He was being practical. "Which I would let you do if you were actually a part of this marriage, but you're not. You are not a member of our family, Tristan. You gave up your place when you decided the

70

Agency was more important than our wife."

"I never said that." Tristan got into his space, his shoulders going back, and Aidan wondered if they were going to start throwing punches. It might feel good. "We had an agreement. You were going to take care of her while I figured this shit out. You know you're not the only one with a job."

"You're the only one who chose a job over our relationship. You shut the rest of us out," Aidan said. "I might not be able to talk about specific patients with you, but I can discuss my day with my partners. Your whole fucking life is classified, and look what it brought us to. You think I'm going to let you back in after today?"

Tristan's jaw tightened. "I think Carys will."

"Maybe you don't know her as well as you think you do."

"Oh, I know exactly how to get Carys to let me in." Tristan's voice went low, a sure sign whatever he said next would piss Aidan off. "Tell me something. How's the sex, A? You been giving her the really kinky stuff?"

"Hey," his da said.

He wished they weren't having this fight in front of their family. "Are you serious? Should we pull out our dicks now and let the uncles measure them? If all you have is you're better at fucking than I am, then I've already won this fight, Tris, because I'm the one who's taken care of her for two and a half years. You've been gone for two and a half years. You don't get to walk in here and nearly take a bullet and get back in bed because you're the fucking stud."

Tristan had paled. "I didn't say that."

"I get it. The two of you have some things to work through." Ian sighed, a weary sound. "But I need to know if I'm sending bodyguards or kidnappers. And I would like an itinerary for this Montreal trip. After today, I have to consider someone knows exactly who Aidan and Carys are, and now they're involved. Tris, have you thought about what it means they're going to Montreal? No one mentioned it to me. Li, you want to maybe elaborate?"

His father turned to Ian, his hands coming up. "Why would I? No one asked where they were going. I was unaware I needed to put in a request for my son to take his wife on a honeymoon. You know I'm starting to understand Aidan's position. You all expect him to behave a certain way, but you don't give him the whys, do you? Those are

71

classified."

He didn't want to cause a rift between his da and Ian. "Don't blame him. Uncle Ian's been left out, from what I can tell."

"But he can blame me," Tristan said, bitterness in his tone.

"Yeah." He wasn't letting Tris off. "Da can absolutely blame you. Everyone can. Ian didn't tell you to get involved in arms dealing."

Ian's brow rose. "Nor did Ian tell him he could announce it to the world. Aidan, you should understand that while I didn't know exactly what Tris was doing until recently, and I think he's a dumbass for getting involved in this without bringing anyone else in, I do understand why he wanted to protect you. The people who are after him are serious killers, and they proved it today. I don't know why you think an attack at your wedding has nothing to do with you, but I'm here to tell you it fucking did, and while Tristan might piss you off, he's right. Look, I can't force you to do something, but I can assure you my brother will protect his daughter."

"And I'll protect my son." His da's tone had gone stubborn and dark, his Irish thick on the tongue. "He'll go to the safe house, and he won't have a choice about it."

"Da," he started.

His father shook his head. "No. Not after today. If you're going to be ridiculous about this, I'll take over, boy. I'm not about to let my son die."

Okay, it was oddly soothing to hear his father say the words. He was always more concerned about Daisy, but something settled inside Aidan when his father declared he would be utterly unreasonable and assholish when it came to Aidan's protection. "Da, we should talk about this."

Ian stared a hole through him, and Aidan suddenly realized this wasn't his funny, sarcastic Uncle Ian. This was the Agency operative. "Why Canada?"

Tristan seemed to realize something. "Ian, it doesn't have anything to do with…you know who. I'm sure Carys thought it was pretty, and they probably found a good deal on a hotel there. Honestly, it's more a fuck you to me than anything else. They knew I would pay for the honeymoon. They probably figured I would try to show up or something."

72

It was infuriating. He heard the door behind him come open, but he was too angry to turn around and see who was there. "It has absolutely nothing to do with you, Tris. You want to know why we're going to Montreal? I got invited to a symposium, and Carys understands my career is important."

Tris had gone a pale white. "What? What fucking symposium, A? Tell me you didn't accept an invitation from Emmanuel Huisman."

"He finally gets to the point," Ian said under his breath. "Fucking right hand doesn't know what the left is doing. This—this is why I didn't want to get back in the Agency bullshit."

The last was said to someone behind him, but Aidan wasn't concerned. "This has nothing to do with the Agency, but yes, I got invited to a very exclusive meeting of some of the best cutting-edge surgeons. As a resident. It's going to make my career."

"It's not about you, Aidan," Tristan said with a sneer. "It's about me. Who the fuck do you think is after me? It's Emmanuel Huisman. You're nothing but a pawn in this game of ours, and the fact that you never bothered to tell me about it proves you have no idea how to play. You've been talking to me every week for years, but you decide to keep me out of this for petty reasons?"

A gasp came from behind him, and Aidan turned. Carys was there with her cousins and Louisa Ward. They stood in the doorway like a phalanx of beautifully dressed Valkyries. Except Carys, who looked like someone had gutted her. She'd changed into yoga pants and a tee, but she was so gorgeous his heart ached.

She knew he'd lied, had kept things from her.

Nothing would ever be the same again.

* * * *

Two hours later Tristan took his seat in the conference room. His fucking heart ached because he'd known the minute he'd realized Carys was in the room, Aidan would never forgive him for telling the truth he'd promised to hide.

But damn it, what the hell else was he supposed to do? Was he supposed to let the people he loved the most fall into the clutches of a man who wanted to burn the world down? They didn't know it, but they had become pawns in a dangerous game, one Tris had worked so fucking hard to keep them out of.

"I need to understand how Huisman knew about Aidan." Kala had changed into jeans and a tank top, showing off her toned arms.

"We don't know he does." Cooper sat beside her, making sure to get a seat that would keep him close to her. "Aidan's top of his class. The Foundation is known for finding up-and-coming doctors."

Kenzie's pink ponytail shook in the negative. "It's too much of a coincidence."

The gang was all here, with a couple of extras. The big boss had opened up the room to Sean and Grace and Liam and Avery. Tristan had protested when Ian wanted to bring in his parents. He'd told Big Tag he wasn't a fucking civilian and he didn't need mommy and daddy here with him. Or his papa.

So his parents were pissed at him, too. Everyone was. He was the bad guy, and there was nothing he could do to change it. The only thing he could do was embrace the role.

"Huisman is a world-renowned neurologist." Aidan sat next to Carys, but it was clear they hadn't hashed it out yet. She wouldn't look at him. She'd ridden over with TJ and Lou, and Aidan had come with his father, leaving Tristan to ride with Big Tag, who'd spent the hour and a half telling him what a dumbass he was. "Beyond his medical work, he runs the foundation. He's literally known for his philanthropic work."

"And he knows Aidan because of our ties to Owen Shaw and his wife, Rebecca," Liam pointed out. "Rebecca speaks highly of him. Ian, what's going on?"

"She speaks highly of him because I asked her to," Ian said, sinking into his seat at the head of the table. "They work in the same field, and Dr. Walsh-Shaw is something of a legend. There would be talk if she had a problem with Huisman. I don't need problems right now. At this point, the war has been kept to the shadows. Li, I didn't tell you because you're not involved with that part of the business. You and Alex pretty much run this place now. I didn't want to overload you."

"And it's classified." Aidan's father waved off the issue. "I don't expect to be kept up to date on Agency matters, Tag. But you might give me a heads-up to watch certain situations more closely."

Big Tag's gaze slid Tristan's way. "Well, up until a few weeks ago I didn't understand the situation. For the most part my team works directly under me, with Drake and Taylor Radcliffe acting as our Agency liaisons. The twins, Tash, and Lou don't work with anyone else. Cooper rarely takes other assignments. Zach will occasionally work with military intelligence or Special Forces teams. But this one loves to spread his talents around. How many different Agency teams are you working with, Tris?"

The man made him sound like a cheating lover. "I work where the Agency needs me to work. In this case I'm working with a small team in conjunction with military intel. It's about a project I started over two years ago. I actually worked on this before I started with the Agency, and I transitioned it over when I joined the team."

"No, you didn't because I never got the memo," Big Tag shot back.

"Neither did I." Kala looked at him like she was sizing him up.

Of course he'd fucked over her beloved cousin, and neither of the twins were known for letting things go. He glanced over to Carys, who sat between Aidan and her dad. She hadn't looked at him. Not once. What the hell was going through her head? He knew it was bad because she'd shut down utterly. He could handle a raging Carys. This closed-down woman scared the hell out of him.

"I didn't transition it to your team. I brought the case with me, though. It was supposed to be nothing more than retrieving intel. A few years ago an arms dealer named The Jester came onto the radar. He moved a lot of guns out of the Philippines in the beginning, but after making enough money, he started dealing weapons of mass destruction, as we like to call them," Tristan explained. "The Jester worked mostly on the Dark Web, and no one knew what he looked like or where he physically resided."

"Until you found him," Big Tag said.

He somehow managed to make it sound like a bad thing. "Yes, I managed to track down one of the world's most infamous arms dealers when no one else could. Well, no one except the man who killed him. Luckily I took him out before he could report back to the man who'd paid him. I killed the assassin and then sat down at the arms dealer's system and sent the group a message."

"Let me guess," Sean said, eyeing him like he was going to use one of his fillet knives soon. The Taggarts had intimidating stares down. "You walked in, ready to arrest him, found him dead, and decided the smartest thing for you to do was to take over his identity."

"Yes, I did." It was obvious this was a trial of sorts, and he was guilty. "I took over his identity on the web and managed to take over his whole business. It wasn't even hard since no one really knew what he looked like. He hid in the shadows. I unfortunately also discovered he had some dealings with government entities. I've been trying to track those down, and I think I'm close. Which brings me to the mission I was supposed to clear with Drake and Taylor this weekend."

"Oh, it's my turn to guess." Ian took a long breath. "Is it to infiltrate an upcoming medical conference?"

Tristan barely managed to not wince. "I was going to ask if we could find someone who was going and send Kara in with him. I thought maybe Dare would know someone. I don't think we should send Dare in since we still don't know how much Huisman understands about how we work."

"He knows everything," Kala assured him.

"He's met Dad and Tash," Kenzie hedged, proving she wasn't entirely in step with her twin. "He definitely knows who Dare is and his connection to our team."

"He knows I run this company," Ian said. "We're a private firm, but it can't be too hard to find out who works here. And he knows I work for the CIA. He's got the money and the resources to figure it all out. He absolutely knows Tasha is Agency. I have hopes he doesn't know about the twins. They managed to avoid him entirely while we were in Australia. The question is how did he figure out Tristan has taken over The Jester's business?"

Grace shook her head and leaned forward, a worried expression on her face. She glanced toward her daughter before posing the question to Ian. "I don't understand what's going on, but I know after today we have to think someone is coming after Carys or Aidan. They need to be in a safe house."

"Grace," Aidan began.

His mother, Avery O'Donnell, shook her head. "No. I don't care about your career, Aidan. You're going to do whatever Ian decides is best."

Aidan's eyes closed—a sure sign he was trying to get control of his emotional state. He opened them and looked at Ian. "Fine. Where is this safe house? If we're going to burn down both our careers so Tristan can get the glory, we might as well start here and now."

TJ had been sitting next to Lou at the far end of the table. He raised a hand. "Uhm, or it could be me they were trying to get."

"So there's another possible explanation," Carys said quietly.

"The best option is a safe house while they figure the situation out," her father insisted.

"For how long?" Carys turned to her father. "I know you want to protect me, but I can't trust there's some timeline that could save my career. I didn't go to school for all those years to watch it go down the drain. So the obvious thing to do is Aidan and I go to the conference and we provide cover for the team."

"Absofuckinglutely not," Tristan said, the idea turning his stomach. "It's not happening, Carys."

The whole room erupted, everyone arguing. The twins thought it wasn't a terrible idea, promising they could train Carys and Aidan. Cooper thought he could watch over them. The parents all thought it was the single worst idea anyone on the planet had ever had. Lou tried to explain all the ways tech could keep them safe.

And Ian sat, quietly watching.

The knot in Tristan's gut tightened because the truth of the matter was only one person mattered. "Ian, they can't do this."

The man he'd called uncle turned his way, his eyes slightly cold. His voice was low, meant for Tristan's ears only. "You would rather they lose their futures instead of trying to find a real way out of this situation? They won't forgive you, Tris. This might be your only way out, too."

"Then they never forgive me." He'd always known it could happen.

Ian's head shook. "I don't think they're going to let you make the decision for them. Can you address Carys's question? How long will you keep them in limbo? How much of their lives are you willing to ask them to give up?"

Why couldn't anyone understand? "I'm trying to save them."

"And they don't get to decide for themselves?" Ian asked.

"They don't understand this world."

Ian shot him a disappointed look and sat back. "Then they're

77

lucky we do." Ian held up a hand and raised his voice. "Everyone stop." He looked at Carys. "Is this what you want, niece?"

Sean's head fell back. "Damn it."

"Yes," Carys replied simply and reached out to her mother. "Mom, I need to do whatever I can to fix this. My cousins won't let me die."

"I won't let you die." Had she forgotten he was fucking here?

"You need to do this?" Grace asked, tears in her eyes.

Carys nodded. "Then I'll have my life back, and I can figure out what to do with it."

She'd always known what she wanted. Him and Aidan and a weird family and a career. A house with dogs and a cat. A life they could all enjoy.

He'd burned it down for all of them.

"Then let's sit down and figure out the op's parameters," Ian said, pushing back his chair. "I need to go call Langley and give them an update. The rest of you take a break and figure out where you're bunking down for the night. Aidan and Carys, you can stay with your parents or at Aidan's if Coop and TJ stay with you. Otherwise, I think it would be best for everyone to stay with the twins for a couple of days. When does this conference start?"

The better question was when had he lost control?

"Thursday," Aidan replied. "We were flying out tonight and staying at a nice hotel before we joined the group at the compound."

A brow rose over Ian's eyes. "This isn't being held at a convention center?"

"Like I said, it's exclusive. We're staying just outside the city. Dr. Huisman has a number of guesthouses on his property. It's more like a meeting of some of the greatest minds in the business. Though we are supposed to get a tour of the foundation," Aidan explained. "I got the feeling it's a lot of talk around a fire pit and stuff. Exchanging ideas."

Aidan could get him into Huisman's home?

There it was. There was a part of Tristan that loved the chase so much he actually excited at the thought. One percent of him. The rest was terrified, but he couldn't deny the thrill was in there, too.

If they were on this mission, they would also be working under him to some degree. No one could cut him out. No one. Not even Ian

Taggart.

"But I don't want to work with Tristan," Carys said in a firm voice, her chin stubbornly up.

"Then you won't work at all," Ian replied. "Because he's the subject matter expert here, and I'm not in charge of him when it comes to this. Make no mistake. I will take care of you. The team will watch out for you, but Tristan's pulling the strings here." Ian turned Tristan's way. "Tell me, who would you call if I tried to take you off?"

"The director. I would go straight to him." He wouldn't waste time moving up the line. The director of the Central Intelligence Agency was well aware of what he was doing.

"And there you have it." Ian stood. "Think, niece. You work this op, you'll work with him, and you'll likely have to take some orders from him. Now I've got calls to make including to Canadian intelligence." He sighed. "I said that without laughing. My world is dark now. Get something to eat and figure out your situations. Sean and Grace, Avery and Li, come down to my office so we can get the shouting done and I can tell you how I'll protect the babies with my balls."

Kala sat back, looking cool and collected. "Nah, we'll be the ones protecting them."

Tasha groaned. "That's what he meant. We're the product of his balls."

"Eww," Kenzie said, nose wrinkling.

"We'll take care of them," Cooper promised.

The parents all left, following Ian, and he was damn straight happy he didn't have to sit in on the meeting. He was sure they were going to Ian's office to conference in his folks.

Would Adam Miles ever find himself in the same place? Never. He would have figured it all out and managed to make it to his incredibly luxurious wedding like the boss hero he was, and Jacob Dean would have been right beside him. His dad and Papa didn't fight. They worked as a team, and never at cross purposes.

They were absolutely in synch with how to take care of his mom.

"And I'll head out and make sure our place is set up for you, Aidan." Cooper pushed back from the table. "You and Carys should be comfortable. TJ, you want to come help me make sure the security system is working?"

Kala snorted. "Carys isn't going home with Aidan and Tris."

"We have a lot to talk about," Aidan said almost pleadingly.

Carys's brows rose. "Do we? It seems to me like you've been doing a lot of talking. Maybe we don't have anything to talk about and my cousin is right. I'm going home with them. You and Tristan can spend all the time you like together. It's obvious I don't have a place as anything except the toy you want to protect."

"You are the woman we have both loved since we learned the word. And how are you going to avoid us when we're all working together?" He might be terrified for them, but there were some upsides to Carys's stubbornness.

The tension was so thick as Carys stared at him. He could feel it. It was anger and hate and sex and need.

She hadn't been getting everything she needed. She'd been lovingly taken care of, but Aidan couldn't top her the way he could. He didn't even want to.

Sometimes, though, she couldn't ask for what she wanted. Sometimes she used D/s to get what she wanted without saying it. She simply pushed him, and he knew she had a safe word. They'd talked about it, decided it was an odd form of communication between the three of them. She would push and push, and he would punish her until she found what she needed. Then they could breathe again. Then they could talk.

"Carys, you might think about this." TJ was the only one who wasn't watching them with wide eyes. He was completely oblivious. "The only free bed is the one in the… I think they call it an office, but it turns into a torture chamber at bedtime, and not the fun kind."

"She can have my room," Kala said, her gaze going between Tristan and Carys.

"Oh, that's nice of you," TJ replied with a smile. "Maybe it's for the best because everyone needs some space."

Tristan didn't need any space. He needed her. His cock tightened. "I think I need to talk to Carys and Aidan alone."

Kenzie frowned. "But it's getting interesting."

Tasha stood. "It's totally time to go, sis. I need to call Dare. And you need to think about who the Canadians are going to send. There's no way they let us run an op in a Canadian city without oversight."

"Fuck. Ben Parker." Kala shoved away from the table.

Ben Parker was the Canadian operative Kenzie had a thing for. Except he'd nearly gotten Lou killed, and now they were all supposed to hate his golden boy ass. He didn't have time or brain space for Parker right now. Not when his whole body was humming.

Lou threaded her fingers through TJ's as the group moved out of the conference room. "You do know Kala's going to end up in bed with us, right?"

TJ frowned as he started to walk out. "Wait, what?"

Lou pulled him along.

It was well known in their group that Kala often slipped into her best friend's bed. Usually after a sweat-inducing nightmare she wouldn't ever acknowledge. She would wake up screaming sometimes and head to a safe place. He would bet TJ didn't even know she was in bed with them since Kala was an early riser and TJ slept like the dead.

"Are you three sure you should be alone in here?" Cooper asked. "There's an undercurrent between the three of you I'm worried about. Maybe we should call my mom in."

Dr. Eve McKay, who would want them to have a therapy session. His cock said absolutely not. "Coop, you might need your mom to help you navigate the relationship with your subs, but I do not."

"Dude, I was trying to help," Cooper shot back.

"I am not your sub," Carys announced.

"I'm definitely not your fucking sub." Aidan sat back, an angry gaze in his eyes.

But they were, and he'd left them. He didn't think he'd had a choice, but he'd left them, and it was time to show them the boss was back and they could relax.

Except they were insisting on going into all the danger he'd been trying so hard to keep them out of. It looked like fate was going to throw them together all over again.

Starting here and now.

Tristan calmly stood and walked over to the door, turning the lock and hitting the button that lowered the shades.

It was time to start winning back his subs.

Chapter Four

The shades slid into place, and it suddenly hit Carys why there was a lock on a conference room door and why those shades were so technologically advanced. It got plenty dark in here. They didn't need the shades.

Also, what the hell was she doing?

She'd agreed to go on an Agency op with her fiancé and the man who should have been her other fiancé. Who the hell did that? She wasn't an operative. She wasn't the girl who looked for an adrenaline rush. Carys Taggart was the responsible one who always did the right thing, not the dangerous chick who took on the world. Nope. She left the adventure to her cousins.

She was the woman who'd never looked at a man beyond the two she'd been in love with since she was a child. Falling for two guys and keeping them both had been her life's rebellion.

Except it hadn't felt like rebellion. Loving Tris and Aidan had been natural.

So how the hell was she here?

All she knew was she'd been sitting there, and she'd known it couldn't be over. Not yet. It had to end because they'd lied to her, but she needed closure. Closure that wouldn't cost her every ounce of her dignity.

Closure? Did she fucking want closure?

She was so angry with them both, and she didn't know where to put it.

"Carys, do you want to talk?" Aidan asked.

Aidan was the sweet one. He was also the one who could get lost in his work. Tris had always been the one who remembered things. Tris was the one who poked them and reminded them they had physical needs.

"She doesn't want to talk," Tristan said, and his voice had gone dark and deep. "She needs something else."

Aidan frowned, his gorgeous face going sullen. "I hardly think she wants sex right now. She would rather yell at us."

"I'm not going to yell," she said quietly. When she went quiet, everyone knew she was serious. She didn't yell and shout when she was angry. She shut down, and she sometimes required a little discipline to get out of the corner she put herself in.

What did she want more? To punish them? To walk away and feel self-righteous? Or did she want to use them so she could cry and try to get some perspective?

If she stayed here in this head space, she wouldn't process anything that had happened today. There would be nothing but her clinging to cold logic, and despite the sense logic seemed to make, this was something she needed her heart to process.

But she couldn't ask for it. Not with words.

"Carys, are you going to make this hard on me?" Tristan stood there looking so stunning. He wore a slightly too large T-shirt he'd almost surely borrowed from TJ or Cooper, but she knew what his chest looked like.

Or did she? It had been so long.

"I'm going to make it impossible," she whispered. The impulse to go was checked by her desperate need to get him to push her until she broke. She couldn't start to heal unless she truly broke.

"Then I'll have to remind you that any disrespect is going to be punished," he returned in a softer tone. "Any sarcasm or nasty words will have to be dealt with."

"What the fuck, Tris?" Aidan asked.

But he was actually doing her a kindness, reminding her there was a map to follow if she couldn't ask for directions.

Tris gripped the back of the closest chair, using it to hide his raging hard-on. She'd seen his pants tent the moment they were alone, and he'd felt the vibe she was sending out. His dick didn't care that he'd broken her heart.

"I need to know." She didn't want to elaborate. Elaboration would mean talking, and they didn't need to talk. But she had to know.

"Know what?" Aidan was shifting his gaze between them like he wasn't quite sure what was happening.

"She wants to know if I've been with other women." Tris simply stared at her, his eyes seeming to go dark. "Absolutely none. Two and a half years. No one but my right hand and my vivid imagination."

Aidan moved in beside Tris. "Baby, he wouldn't cheat on you. I know he's been kind of a dick, but I wouldn't have trusted him at all if I thought for a moment he was cheating on us...on you."

"You had it right the first time." Tristan's gaze sharpened. "We're all involved in this relationship. Anything outside the three of us is cheating, and I never even once thought about it. I had a job to do. I wasn't looking for a different life or a way out. I've been desperately trying to find a way back in."

"Okay." Aidan took a long breath and got his "I can fix this" expression on. "We'll go into the break room and get some coffee and talk this out. Carys, I'll tell you everything you want to know."

Tristan huffed. "She doesn't want to talk. Look at her. Her shoulders are tight. Her hands keep clenching open and shut, but otherwise, she's perfectly still. Like she's afraid to move. She doesn't want to leave, but she also doesn't want us to think she wants to stay. Stop thinking like her boyfriend. Start thinking like her Dom."

This was absolutely what Tristan brought to the table. He was infinitely more physical than Aidan. Aidan would be happy making love and holding her. He didn't mind the kinky stuff, but he didn't seem to need it the way she and Tris did.

She'd had perfection. A sweet lover who thought about her all the time, and another who looked smooth and normal on the outside and inside was a fucking feral beast.

How the hell had he been gone for two and a half years? "I don't believe you."

A brow rose over Tristan's suddenly icy eyes. "You don't believe I didn't fuck someone else?"

84

It felt good to let a little venom flow. It had been building and building, and she'd had to be the sweet almost bride who delivered babies and did everything right. She'd suffered years of pitying looks, and this resentment had been inside her for so long, she forgot how good it was to give some of it up. "I know you. I know how much you need sex, Tris. I also know you're a spy and probably fuck for intel. That's what he's not saying, Aidan. Maybe he's been faithful in a purely personal way, but he's a professional."

Aidan's eyes widened like he didn't know her, but Tristan simply chuckled.

"Yeah, there you are, baby. I've been waiting for your inner alpha bitch to show up. Tell me something. Is she clawing to get out now that we're in the same room?" Tristan taunted. "You wouldn't let her take a swipe at Aidan because you don't think he can handle her. Personally, I think you're wrong. A's got some thick skin and a deep desire to give you everything you need, including taking some battle wounds."

"What are you two talking about?" Aidan looked her way, his eyes pleading. "Carys, baby, there's no need to fight."

"She wants the fight," Tristan insisted. "She needs it tonight. She needs to hit me and hard. Go on, Car. Poke at me until you wake up the predator that's always right here in my gut. I keep him tightly leashed. I know how to be a gentleman. I learned all the rules and codes my fathers trained into me. But they also taught me there's a time and a place to let it go. Is it time, Carys?"

"I've been taking care of her." Aidan's jaw tightened.

"Yes, you've given her what she needs from you," Tris acknowledged. "Now she needs something else. Tonight, she doesn't need to be a beloved girlfriend or an equal partner. Tonight, she needs to be prey. She needs us to take her down physically so she can find her way out of whatever room inside her head she's locked herself in. You believe in good guys and bad guys, A. You think not every man is a closet predator. In your world there are black hats and white hats, but she needs a little gray today."

He was wrong about one thing. "I assure you I think you're the bad guy, Tris."

He shrugged like he wasn't about to argue with her. "I'm whatever you need me to be, and I didn't fuck for intel. Never. I

85

assure you while I was putting my body on the line my dick remained perfectly and pristinely pure. I tell you that because you should understand what's about to happen. I won't be able to be sweet and caring. You need me to be the bad guy who makes you cry? I can do it, but I'll get what I need, too."

"And you need to hurt me?" Carys asked.

"No," Aidan argued.

"Stop it or leave the damn room," Tristan hissed as he turned to his partner. "Normally we would sit down and discuss a scene we were about to play out. We can't tonight because the minute we leave, the door in her head locks and she builds walls. Has she cried?"

Aidan seemed to think about the question, and then his eyes closed. "No."

"She's been through this whole shitty day without shedding a tear or having an emotion beyond icy anger," Tristan pointed out. "Are you the good guy who wants to do some very bad things to the woman who is acting all calm and composed? What are your instincts telling you about her? Don't bring yourself into it. Don't bring your fear into it. This is about her. What does she need?"

She fucking hated the way Tris could see right through her. Hated it. Craved it. Needed it so badly.

The moment Aidan's gaze went hard, she knew she was about to get the fight she wanted. "She's wound so tight she can't breathe. She's held it together because she can't fall apart in front of anyone else. She might not want to break down in front of us, but it's acceptable. She wants to tear us up, to have us hold her down and force her to feel because if she doesn't, she worries she might never feel anything again."

Tristan cocked a brow his partner's way, firmly in bad-boy mode at this point. "So do you want to clutch your pearls or help me top her?"

Aidan calmly pulled his shirt over his head, tossing it to the side. He moved from his everyday persona to the one he put on for her. He might not need the dominance the way Tris did, but he could play the role. He was actually much harder when Tris was around. In every way. "Are you scared, Carys?"

A thrill went through her, and she could feel her damn nipples tighten. "Why would I be afraid, A? Of you? Should I be afraid because your boss is back? You going to do what Tristan tells you to do?"

Tristan sighed even as he was pulling his own shirt off. "See, it's a form of therapy, too."

"You want to take a piece of me?" Aidan asked, his hands in fists on his hips. "You feel the need to tear me up, baby? Am I the reason for all the bad shit that happened today?"

"If you were working with him, then yes," she shot back, but there was something in Aidan's eyes...some rage of his own, and it was directed at her.

Tristan chuckled as he pulled the belt from his jeans. "You're always so careful with sweet Aidan. Is it because you worry you'll hurt his tender feelings, or are you afraid he can tear you up, too? I'm intrigued. I'd love to see the two of you go at it because once you unleash Aidan's beast, there won't be any shutting that cage again."

Her breath rose fast and hard, and she felt adrenaline flood her system. She'd thought she didn't chase that particular drug, but damn it was heady.

"What's your safe word, Car?" Aidan's face looked carved from granite.

"I don't need a safe word." Along with the adrenaline came a sense of unease. Like maybe this was a bad idea.

Yeah, she liked how that felt, too. Maybe because it was the first time in a long time she felt anything but anger and worry. This wasn't the same. This was the worry of a deer in the presence of two wolves who wanted to eat her alive.

"You need one if you're going to be my submissive." Aidan seemed taller than before. And closer. When had he moved around the table? She'd been watching Tris and then Aidan was right there.

"How about we don't make her think too much. How much do you want to use the word *no* tonight?" Tristan sounded so fucking calm. Like they were at the club and about to run a perfectly normal scene. Like he hadn't blown up their lives. Again.

"I like the word *no* when it comes to you, asshole." She had to force herself to breathe because they'd maneuvered to either side of her. They'd blocked off all routes to escape.

"I thought you might." Tristan blocked the door, the belt in his hand. He slapped it against his palm. "You should know this conference room is soundproofed, so feel free to say no as much as you like. Plead as much as you like. Beg me. Nothing stops unless you say the word red."

Harsh, but again, a map for her. There was always an out, but there was also a place for her to hide, to let this piece of herself hold sway. She felt hard hands on her waist as Aidan jerked her back. She fell against his chest, hands instinctively going to Tristan's shoulders for balance. She could do it because they'd trapped her. She looked up at him, eyes wide, lips parted.

"I don't want to think about why they soundproofed the conference room, do I?" It was a stupid question, but her nerves were working overtime. She was here. Where she'd wanted to be for years. Between them, and it had to be one of the last times.

Not the last time. They had the mission.

She winced inwardly because now she knew why she'd taken the mission.

Tristan's hand slid into her hair. Slowly, deliberately, he made a fist, pulling her hair tight. She sucked in air, breasts rising. He stared down at her, eyes on her mouth. "I'm sure they would say it's because of all the classified intel, but we know the truth. Tell me how hard you want it, because if you knew what I want to do to you right now, you might use your safe word."

"You stayed away for two and a half years. I bet you can't even get it up anymore." She wanted it pretty fucking hard. She was sure he would prefer to get to the good stuff, and she would want that eventually, but for now she wanted the belt in his hand, wanted for her body to feel what her soul felt. Constricted. Forced into a shape she found uncomfortable.

He brought their hips together, proving her wrong. She didn't need proof. It was all words to push him like he'd pushed her. "I assure you I can take care of you tonight, baby."

She smirked up at him, letting her inner brat flow. This wasn't her normal submissive self. She was the sub everyone looked up to, the perfect one who never stepped out of line. She didn't have to because Tris always seemed to know when she needed it rough. He'd ruined their perfection, and now he got the brat. He'd made her this way, and he would have to deal with it. "Great. I'll get three-minute Tris."

His lips peeled back in an approximation of a smile, but it was more a bearing of teeth. "I promise I'll give you more than three minutes."

She felt heat on her ear and then a hard nip from Aidan.

"You know damn well I can go all night," Aidan growled. "You are pushing my buttons. I'm every bit as emotional as you are. Do you want to do this? We don't play like this."

She turned. How fucking dare he equate them? He'd been talking to Tris all along. She'd been alone, left out of their boys club like a blow-up doll they passed between them. Like the cypher she'd always worried she was, nothing but the woman they needed because they weren't wired to want each other sexually. "We don't play at all. You pretend to be him."

"Damn it," Tris cursed.

Aidan's hand gripped her neck, and he lowered his mouth to hers. She expected the sweet, long kisses he always drugged her with. His teeth caught her lower lip, biting down hard enough to make her jerk. He'd never done *that* before. There was something deep and dark in his eyes when he tightened his hold on her, forcing her upper body to arch back and against Tris, who was behind her now. "No matter what the fuck you think I've done to you, I don't deserve that. Take your clothes off. Or do you need to run to daddy now that it's getting serious?"

Oh, he was obviously ready to play. "I can handle myself."

"Can you, baby? Because I'm the one who handles everything for you," he shot back. "And now I'm wondering if you appreciate any of it at all or if you sit around wishing I was him."

The words sparked through her. This wasn't what she'd meant at all. Aidan had been here for her. Why the fuck had he had to lie? Why had they forced her to the outside? Still, she couldn't bring herself to say the words that might soothe him. "You don't have to worry about it anymore. You and Tris can find someone new to fuck since that seems to be all you need me for."

"Clothes, Carys," Tristan ordered. "You aren't capable of anything but tearing us apart right now. You can take the clothes off or I'll rip them off for you."

Anger swelled, hot where it had been icy before, but it was impossible for her to be cold when they were so close.

Her only lovers. Since they were seventeen and they'd solemnly made love after prom. After they'd all promised to never leave.

They'd fucking lied.

She gasped as Tristan turned her forcibly toward him.

"Hold her still," Tristan ordered, and he took the sides of her shirt and ripped the T-shirt she was wearing in half, baring her torso and the lacy bra she wore. It was supposed to be something sexy for her first night as Aidan's wife.

Aidan's arms became a cage, and it made it easy for her to fight back. It felt good to get physical. To be more than a precious, fragile thing everyone loved and protected and kept to the side. So she fought even as Aidan held her tight and Tristan started to drag her clothes off. She kicked out at him, knowing she couldn't really hurt him. He was far too strong and knew how to fight. She was helpless as he efficiently got her naked, tossing her bra to the side after ripping it off. The delicate undies she'd selected for her wedding night were trashed with a single tug of his strong hands.

Tristan stared at her for a moment, his eyes on her breasts. "I forgot how gorgeous you are. I thought I remembered every detail, but I didn't."

She didn't want to hear his soft words. She jerked back, trying to force Aidan to drop her hands.

A sad look came over Tristan's face, a wistful, longing expression, and then he stepped back. "Let her go. See if she runs or if she knows when she's finished."

Asshole. Aidan let go of her hands and she pushed back, turning to put some space between them, every minute feeling a spark she'd been missing for forever. The conference room was large and gave her space to run. She moved to the back of the room where the high-tech screen hung down, framed by several lovely works of art Aunt Charlotte had curated. She was naked and standing in a room with two men she shouldn't trust. Her family was somewhere in this building, and she was about to get fucked hard. When she decided to go bad, she went all out.

Aidan growled and then charged. She spun out of the way, but he'd anticipated the move and grabbed her elbow as his momentum carried him past her. What he hadn't expected was for her to stick out a foot and trip him.

He took several stumbling steps before crashing into the wall. The screen trembled and so did the paintings, the closest one falling off its hook and hitting the carpet with a thud.

She was about to pick it up when Tris clotheslined her, hauling her up by her waist. A gasp came from her chest as he plunked her down face first on the conference room table. His big hands pinned her down.

"Take her wrists," Tris ordered in an almost guttural tone. "Carys, don't give me more trouble. I'm emotional, too. I want to give you what you need, not rip us entirely apart."

"You already did that," she hissed back, anger surging. Anger felt good. Anger felt warm and active, even though they were holding her down.

"No, I fucked up, but it doesn't have to be over. And I'll show you why." Tristan put a hand on the flat of her back.

She was caught between them, utterly helpless, and somehow being so vulnerable, being unable to move, helped her face what she hadn't been willing to before.

They'd betrayed her. They'd plotted behind her back and treated her like a child. She was a toy.

Tristan's hand came down on her ass, the sound cracking through the room like thunder, and she was happy she came from a family of perverts because she shouted out. The pain washed over her, and she felt the shock start to wake her up.

He'd dropped the belt when he'd come after her, but his hand was more than enough.

"More," she said through gritted teeth. "Give me more."

How long would it be before she found this again? Before she got to be in this place where she could face anything? Good, bad. Not indifferent. Never indifferent here. She'd used this space to handle stress, to face her fears. Now she was going to have to use it to deal with a heartache she'd never thought she would have to feel.

Over and over Tristan struck her ass and thighs, spanking her until she could feel how hot and red her skin must be.

It wasn't enough. The tears wouldn't quite come even though the pain felt like everything in the moment. She ached and hurt, and it wasn't enough to overtake the break in her heart.

He stopped.

"More," she insisted.

"You can't, baby. I'll hurt you if I give you more," Tristan said.

Aidan released her hands, stroking back her hair. "He can't safely give you more." He stared at her for a moment, and his handsome face took on a resolve. "But I can."

"A," Tristan began.

Aidan straightened up. "You have your way of taking care of her and I have mine. It's my fucking turn. Turn her over and hold her down."

What the hell was he talking about? Carys winced as Tristan flipped her over, her back against the table now, her ass at the edge. Every muscle was sore. But the peace she'd hoped she would have hadn't come. It was incomplete. The ritual wasn't finished, and she realized she might never feel peace again, not the way she had.

"Stop it. Let me up." She needed to get away from them. It wasn't going to work. She needed to be alone. Needed to start figuring out how to be alone.

"No," Aidan said, sounding more sure than she'd heard him in forever.

He pressed her ankles out, forcing her legs to open wide and keeping her off balance. Tristan was the one on the conference table now, one hand holding both her wrists, the other fisted in her hair. "You stay still."

And then she felt Aidan move, and suddenly he buried his face between her legs. She'd almost expected fingers and got lips and tongue. Her labia spread wide as he passed his tongue between the folds. Pleasure curled through her, making her scalp prickle and toes curl.

She hadn't wanted this. Hadn't thought she wanted this. She'd wanted the pain, but this… The pleasure was so sharp it made a contrast to the pain, a reminder of everything she was going to lose.

He repeated the caress, this time ending it by pushing his tongue into her, his face buried so deep in her pussy that her labia were against his cheeks, his nose nudging her clit.

She ground against him, and he thrust his tongue into her again and again, shallow penetrations. It felt so fucking good, so like normal.

All the days came rushing in. The days she'd spent with them, the sweet looks and hand holding eventually leading to kissing. First Tristan and then Aidan. She'd turned from one to the other because she'd known she was at the center, and she couldn't leave either out.

Aidan fucked her with his tongue, and the tears finally started because this was what she would lose. These intimate moments when the world got locked out and no one mattered except the three of them. Nothing mattered but this moment with them.

Even as her body tensed and the orgasm threatened to overwhelm her, so did the pain. She'd needed both—Tristan's discipline and Aidan's sweet, giving nature to fully understand what she'd lost.

She sobbed as she came, the tears rolling down her cheeks, and suddenly Tris wasn't holding her down. He was twining their fingers together, stroking her hair.

"It's okay, baby." There were tears in his green eyes, too, though he didn't shed them. "I'm going to make this right."

Aidan moved from between her legs and hauled her up, his arms wrapping around her. "Come here. Let me make this better. I love you, Carys. We're going to get through this."

"We?" The words came out shaky because she was still holding back. "Don't you mean you and Tris? You two make all the decisions. I'm just along for the ride."

Aidan paled. "It wasn't like that."

"It wasn't," Tristan agreed, starting to move in behind her. "Baby, I wasn't trying to leave you out. I was protecting you. I'm still going to protect you because I'm not about to allow you to go to Canada."

Yes, there it was. She pushed back. This was stupid. She was crying and naked, and if she let them she would fuck them both and be their doll again. "Red."

"Carys." Her name was a plea from Aidan. "Don't do this."

Tristan's hands had come off her the minute she'd said the word. Her safe word was a blunt instrument when it came to Tristan. "You need aftercare. I can't leave you like this."

"You've left me in much worse situations than having my ass red," she snarled his way.

"Let me look at you." Aidan reached for her.

"You can't touch her," Tristan insisted. "She said her safe word."

"Red," she said again. "I want you both out. If you insist on aftercare, send my cousins in."

"Then tell me about the last two and a half years. Tell me everything. I want to know what I missed and how it hurt you," Tristan insisted.

She shook her head and picked up Aidan's T-shirt. He could go down and grab one from the bodyguard unit. They always had extras. "Leave me alone. I'm sure Aidan will happily tell you everything. It's what the two of you do. Leave."

She couldn't do it. She'd thought she could, but she couldn't break down with them here.

"Car," Aidan began.

"Are you going to honor my safe word?" Carys asked. She could feel the tears on her cheeks, but she couldn't let go. Not yet.

"This isn't a fucking scene," Aidan insisted, and he took a step toward her.

Tristan had pulled his shirt over his head and put a hand on Aidan's broad shoulder. They looked so gorgeous standing there together.

They would make a lovely couple.

It was a bitter, nasty thought, but she couldn't deny it.

"She's done for the night," Tristan said. "I'll have the twins check on her. But Carys, you might be done, but we're not. We'll talk in the morning and then we'll figure out how to protect you while I finish this mission."

She stood there and watched as Tris convinced Aidan to let her have some privacy.

Nothing had changed. He would shut them out again. Well, shut her out and bring Aidan into his secret life. Hell, if it was Aidan, Tris would probably convince him to join the Agency, too.

When the door closed, she realized she didn't need to cry.

Carys screamed, the sound matching the anger in her soul.

Chapter Five

Aidan turned because he could have sworn he heard something from behind the door they'd closed. The one between him and Carys.

Fuck, he hoped they hadn't closed it forever.

"I can't leave her like this." He could still taste her on his lips. They'd been close. Close to breaking her down. She'd cried. Not in the way she'd needed to, but it had been a start.

"You walk back in there and she will use it like bricks to build her wall. I know you don't think what happened now was a scene, but I assure you it was." Tristan stared at the door, but he wasn't making a move toward it. "She's retreated to D/s because it's all she can handle right now. We need to talk about how we get through to her."

She'd screamed. He knew it. Shouldn't they break down the door to get to her?

"She needs some time and space," Tristan concluded.

"Does she? Because you've given her a hell of a lot of it and she's still screaming alone." He'd forgotten how pissed he was at Tristan. Tristan was the cause of all of this trouble. He and Carys had been fine on their own.

No, you weren't. You need him. You and Carys will break because you're not a couple. You're a threesome. It would be different if he'd died, but he's right here, and you have to find a way to make this work.

He hated being the reasonable one.

Tristan huffed. "I know you're angry. I didn't mean for her to find out we've been talking. You know I've been trying to talk to her, too. I've sent her flowers and cards and gifts. Anonymously, of course, but she's not unaware. I simply haven't made a bunch of loving social media posts lately. I kind of thought she would know."

"Well, she got the real message when you wouldn't get married the first time." He needed a damn shirt. Naturally the big bad Dom had to show off how strong he was by ripping off their girlfriend's clothes. Like she hadn't been through enough today.

And yet she'd needed the intensity. She hadn't had it for years.

"Hey, don't walk away from me," Tristan said, putting a hand on his shoulder.

Aidan spun around, his heart thudding in his chest. His emotional state was far too ragged, and he knew he needed a time-out, but those warnings were a distant alarm bell he had zero intention of listening to. Tris was his best friend in the world, his other fucking half. It hadn't been Aidan who'd broken them utterly. "I'm not the one who walked away."

"Uh, guys, maybe we should think about doing this in like a therapeutic session," a familiar voice said.

Suddenly he realized they weren't alone. He looked over, and the gang was all here. Tris's gang, naturally. They were all friends, but this was Tristan's team. Lou had a can of soda in her hand, while TJ seemed to have raided the vending machines. Cooper stood with the twins, all of them watching carefully.

"Dude, where's your shirt?" Kala asked. He knew it was Kala from the expression on her face. She'd changed into her normal uniform of all black—jeans and a tee and combat boots. It was truly helpful when they weren't working and wore whatever they liked. Kenzie wore bright colors and girlie dresses while Kala took the goth-girl route.

"Don't worry about his shirt," Tristan said, stepping beside him. "Your cousin needs... She needs aftercare."

"What?" a deep voice asked.

Aidan groaned at exactly the same time as Tristan, likely thinking the same thing.

Big Tag.

Why did they let the man out of his office?

"What did you do in my beautiful, sparkling clean and sanitary conference room that would lead to my niece needing aftercare?" Ian asked.

Aidan turned, but Tristan was already facing down the biggest authority figure in all their lives.

"Nothing that hasn't already been done in there, Uncle," Tristan said. "My sub was hurting. She needed a session, but she doesn't want aftercare from me. I'm pretty much doing exactly what you and my parents taught me. I'm taking care of the submissives in my charge. Carys requested her cousins deal with her aftercare. I'm sure she would appreciate Lou being there, too."

Ian's expression softened. "Should I get her mother?"

Kenzie stepped up. "Absolutely not. She needs her sister subs, and you know it. Dad, we can handle this part. You try to get Aidan into some clothes before his parents get worried."

Kala sent him and Tristan a look capable of freezing fire. "Yeah, maybe the Doms should think twice about causing a scene they can't control. The parents are freaked enough." She looked back to her dad. "We'll handle it. Well, Lou and Kenz will do the sub thing, and I'll make sure nothing goes wrong."

Lou grabbed a bag of chips and a candy bar from her boyfriend's stash as she followed the twins. "Send Tash in when she gets back. She's out calling Dare and keeping him updated. She wouldn't want to miss the girl time."

Aidan didn't want to miss the girl time, but he heard the lock slide into place after the door closed.

Kala would guard her cousin like the precious gift she was.

He never thought anyone would have to guard Carys from him.

"If you want to avoid your dad, you'll head down to the bodyguard floor," Ian said quietly. "They'll have clothes. And a boxing ring, if you need it. You two have to get your shit together. She needs you."

"She said she doesn't. She used her safe word," Aidan replied, wondering if he really wanted to avoid his da. His da might give him some advice. He utterly hated how he felt right now. Vulnerable and stupid, but he hated how she'd looked more. Angry. Desperate. Hollow.

97

Tristan sighed. "She used it in an emotional fashion. It had nothing to do with her being hurt."

Ian's brows rose.

"Not physically," Tristan corrected. "She's not injured. She's devastated emotionally, which is precisely why she used her safe word. She's also angry. I need you to understand I'm not letting them go to Canada. I might be persuaded to allow Aidan to go if he can prove to me he can handle himself, but Carys is going to a safe house."

"Sending her away is a mistake," Ian said with a frown. "But it's one you're going to make no matter what I say. You're the single most stubborn asshole I've ever worked with, and I've worked with Ten Smith. You should also know once this mission is complete, I'm going to ask the director to reassign you."

"It's probably for the best," Tristan said. "I'm glad you're not trying to get me fired."

Ian's stare sent a chill through Aidan. He had zero idea how Tris was still standing up to the man. "Oh, we both know I likely couldn't do it. You're also a ruthless bastard. I approve of ruthlessness. You're excellent at protecting the parts of your life that are truly important to you. But I won't watch you ruin your life a second longer, Tristan."

Tristan's shoulders lowered slightly, his hands coming unclenched and tone softening. "And if I promise to get out? To get off the other teams I'm working for?"

"If you promise to come home and deal with your family, then we'll talk." Ian turned. "And think about letting Carys be something other than a pretty prize you show off. You ruined her relationship with Aidan when you convinced him to leave her out. If you don't fix it, she'll shut you both out. Especially if you take him and not her. If you shove them both in a safe house, Aidan might have a chance. I like that outcome better than Carys being alone. So I think it's an either-or situation."

Ian strode back toward his office.

"And someone better Lysol my damn conference room," the man grumbled before walking through the door. "This generation is rude. Someone get Adam on the phone. I've got some complaints."

"I meant what I told Ian," Tristan said quietly. "I am going to leave the other teams."

Sure he would. Aidan strode down the hall leading to the stairwell. He ignored the elevators. He didn't want to be stuck in a small space with Tristan, and he was pretty sure Tristan would follow him. "I don't care. I think you should do exactly what Ian told you to do. Send me and Carys to a safe house, and I'll take care of her. But we need an end date."

"I thought you wanted to face Huisman. I thought Huisman was some hero of yours."

He had. There had been a moment when he'd thought going on this mission—all three of them—might heal the breach, but he was past the idea now. Wasn't he? "Carys means more, and after what happened, I can safely say she needs me. She needs me to focus on her and not to get involved in the very thing that broke us."

"We are not broken," Tristan said.

Aidan stopped right before he reached the door, pointing his best friend's way. "Were you in the same room I was? How the fuck can you say we're not broken? She used her safe word."

"I told you. She was emotional, and it's all she's got. She wanted to send a message, and it's been received." Tristan opened the door, allowing Aidan to go first. "I don't have to be in Canada for a couple of days. We'll take Carys to The Hideout tomorrow night. The good thing about having a completely private club is you can open it at any time. I've already got a message out to Gabriel Lodge, and he's handling the arrangements. He was having a training meeting with a new class, but he told me he'll turn it into a watch and discuss session. We didn't get a wedding, so we'll have a stress relief party."

What the hell? He blew past Tris, jogging down the stairs. "You honestly believe she's going to the club and submitting to you tomorrow?"

"I do." Tristan sounded like the confident asshole he liked to pretend to be. Or maybe it was who he was now. "I think she'll go because it's her safe place, and she won't be able to resist. She'll end up in a privacy room with both of us. I expect she'll likely use her safe word then, too. This is going to be a process."

How could he talk like this? Aidan reached the door leading into the bodyguard unit. He thought some of the sales unit was down here, too, but he needed the space of the men Big Tag called the Douche. Yeah, it was what Carys's uncle called a group of bodyguards. The group also included women, who should be more outraged by the title. "It's not a process. It's a relationship. At least it was once."

"Maybe everyone is right and we need to sit down at the Ferguson Clinic," Tris said with a long huff as he followed Aidan inside.

The clinic had been around as long as Aidan could remember. Founded by therapist Kai Ferguson, it was housed in a building next to the old folks' home…Sanctum. He probably should never make the joke out loud. There was no need to go to the clinic for throuple's therapy because they weren't a throuple anymore.

Except for a moment it had felt so right.

The stairwell door led right into the office portion of this side of the floor. A bank of cubicles were to his left, the first one belonging to Nate Carter, the newest bodyguard and Aidan's sister's boyfriend. Daisy had taken one look at the big Aussie and she'd been a goner.

He'd never felt that rush of new love. He'd simply always had it. Carys had always been there, a piece of him he'd never thought he could lose. He was happy for his sister and Nate, but he had no desire for the kind of crazy new love they had. He wanted Carys.

He wanted Tris. Or rather he wanted the Tris his best friend had always been. Sometimes he didn't recognize him now. He'd been okay with the soldier. Tris had still been recognizable in the soldier. The operative scared the shit out of him.

"Somehow I don't think a handful of therapy sessions are going to solve this," Aidan shot back.

Tristan ignored his opinion. "Nate's shirt is going to be way too big on you. Landon Vail is closer in size. Or they keep some MT shirts in the locker room."

Aidan was about to tell him he could dress himself when his cell trilled. He wanted to ignore it but what if it was Carys? What if she'd changed her mind and she needed him? He pulled it out of his pocket and glanced down at the screen.

The Huisman Foundation.

"Ignore it," Tristan ordered. "We need to talk about how to handle her going forward."

What the hell was the Huisman Foundation doing calling him on a Saturday night? When he was supposed to be dancing with his new bride. Of course it wasn't like he'd sent them an invite. No one at the institute would know he was getting married. He'd never talked to the man himself.

Had they figured out he didn't belong and they were calling to tell him it was all a mistake and then this fight was a moot point?

"Aidan." Tristan somehow made his name an order.

An order he wasn't taking. He slid his finger across the screen, expecting to talk to someone in administration, likely about the upcoming conference. "Hello."

"Dr. O'Donnell." A warm voice with the hint of an accent came over the line. "My name is Emmanuel Huisman."

The room went cold as he realized he might not have an option of a safe house anymore.

* * * *

Frustration welled in Tristan as Aidan answered his damn cell phone.

It was fucking Saturday night. Who would be calling him? His father was upstairs. His mom and sister wouldn't bother him now, and Carys wasn't talking to either of them, but apparently this was his punishment. Aidan would rather talk to some fucking telemarketer than talk to his best friend.

If Aidan thought he was about to leave because he wanted to discuss his Internet usage and how such and such company could save him a few bucks, he was underestimating him. He could stand here all night. It wasn't like he had anywhere else to go.

"Hello, Dr. Huisman."

The world seemed to slow down.

Emmanuel Huisman was calling? On what he should think was a random Saturday night? Calling a man he'd never actually met before?

Tris had his cell out in a second, sending Ian a text letting him know what was happening and to be quiet if he came down.

Aidan looked up, a shocked expression on his face.

Speaker, Tristan mouthed.

Aidan nodded, and suddenly Tristan could hear the man he was investigating.

The man he was absolutely sure wanted to burn the whole world.

"I'm sorry to call so late, but I only today became aware you're going to be a part of our symposium," Huisman was saying. "I'm afraid I've been busy lately, and I'm just getting around to acquainting myself with the residents the selection committee invited."

He sounded so reasonable. So gracious. It was a mask.

Aidan stood there like he wasn't sure what to do.

Tristan waved a hand, a gesture for him to talk, to be natural.

"Well, Dr. Huisman, I can't tell you how happy I was to be invited." Aidan sounded stilted, but they could work with it.

"Calm down," Tristan whispered as quietly as he could. He saw the white board and realized he could communicate without Huisman realizing anyone was with Aidan. He pointed to it as he found the dry erase marker.

"My team is tasked with inviting the best and brightest to come to these meetings," Huisman was saying. "I trust their judgment completely, but I like to make sure I know a little about our attendees, especially the new minds. I was impressed with your essay, but when I read the paper you wrote on using ultrasound as a potential alternative to some forms of surgery, I knew they'd truly found a gem."

"It's still surgery," Aidan corrected. "The ultrasound alternative, that is. It still requires all the precision of a blade. In some ways more."

Damn, but he was smart. All of his life Tristan had been considered the brains, but Aidan might revolutionize the way surgery was conducted. However, he wasn't great at the spy game. He wrote on the board.

Act normal.

"Yes, I can see that," Huisman replied. "I am so fascinated by your work. I wanted to call because as I said, I'm excited about your research. I can't wait to talk to you and learn more about what you're doing. You're coming out on Thursday?"

He was fishing. Shit. Huisman was fishing.

The stairwell door came open, and Ian and Cooper slipped out quietly. Cooper sat on the edge of Nate's desk, but Ian moved in close to Tris.

"That's the plan," he said, though he didn't sound sure. "To come to the symposium on Thursday. It's when it starts, right? Sorry, sir. I'm afraid I'm flustered. I didn't expect you to call."

This was precisely why Aidan needed to go to the safe house.

Ian ran a hand over his hair, a frustrated gesture.

"I think he's fishing," Tris whispered. "I think the people he sent in didn't report back, and he wants to figure out what the fuck happened."

Ian nodded gravely. "So do I. Which means Aidan can't lie."

Fuck a duck.

Ian was right. Tristan turned to the board.

You have to tell him what happened today. Be honest. He knows because he sent them in. Tell him and then explain you can no longer attend.

Ian growled, but he stood back.

"Well, I was wondering if you might want to come out a bit early," Huisman began.

Tristan shook his head. No way it was happening.

"I'm sorry, Dr. Huisman. I had a kind of rough day. I was supposed to get married today," Aidan admitted.

Ian nodded, confirming it was okay to tell him.

Because Huisman already knew. Because Huisman wanted to know if Aidan would lie to him.

"Married?" Huisman sounded surprised, but then the fucker was an excellent actor.

"Yes." Aidan wasn't, but he didn't need to act now. "We put it off a couple of times, so I wasn't willing to disappoint my fiancée again. She's a doctor, too, so she understands how important being invited to this symposium is."

This would be an excellent way to let Huisman down. And it would be all his own damn fault. The doctor wanted Aidan and Carys in his grasp. Well, it wasn't happening. If Huisman hadn't pulled this shit today, Tristan would have had to work much harder to come up with a reasonable excuse to get Aidan out of this trap.

"But you said *supposed* to get married." Huisman's voice was all sympathy now. "Did something go wrong? Forgive me if it's none of

103

my business. I know you might not understand, but we actually have a connection, you and I. I didn't realize it until I saw where you were from. You're Liam O'Donnell's son, right?"

Sure, he hadn't realized. Tristan was sure Huisman knew who they all were and what they did. And how close they were to exposing him. Which was precisely what Tris had been trying to avoid. By splitting off from Aidan and Carys publicly, he'd hoped to take them out of the line of fire.

He'd failed. Well, everyone had told him he was a dumbass.

"Yeah, he's my dad." Aidan was looking to Ian for his prompts. Not to him.

Ian nodded, letting him know to keep going. But then Ian turned to the white board and wrote.

This is your choice.

It took everything Tris had not to growl right back. It wasn't Aidan's fucking choice. It was his. He wrote again.

Tell him you have to cancel.

Aidan turned away. "Li O'Donnell is my dad. And we had some trouble. I'm still not exactly sure what happened. My family and Carys's family... They're involved in the security and intelligence worlds. I think maybe her uncle's business came back to bite us in the ass, or shoot us in the ass, so to speak. I'm sorry. I'm still a bit rattled."

Thank god. He was going to bow out. It was going to be okay. He was surprised at how hard his heart was beating.

Aidan was talking to Tristan's biggest fucking nightmare. It was everything he'd attempted to avoid, but it was going to be fine because Aidan was sane. Carys would do it just to throw him her middle finger. When Carys got mad, things could go seriously south, but Aidan was reasonable. Aidan would make the right choice.

"Of course you are," Huisman said. "Is everyone okay?"

"Well, the dudes in the helicopter aren't," Aidan replied with a long sigh. "I'll be honest my fiancée's uncle has some...rough connections. I think something went wrong and someone was looking for revenge. I won't probably ever understand it. I'm sorry I can't talk about it. I'm sure it's classified." Aidan groaned. "I shouldn't have said that."

Maybe Aidan was better at this than he thought.

Cooper had made his way over while Ian watched Aidan. He leaned in. "I looped Zach in earlier today. He said he'll be in Dallas in the morning. I'm sure he'll want an update."

Zach Reed.

On the outside they were simply teammates on the group run by Ian and Charlotte. They weren't even very good friends. Zach held himself somewhat apart, though he hung out with Cooper a lot. When he was in Dallas he was friendly with the gang at The Hideout.

No one knew Zach was his partner in tracking down The Jester and had been since the beginning.

"Good," he whispered. "We'll debrief in the morning after we've settled Aidan and Carys into the safe house."

A brow rose over Cooper's eyes. "Sure."

"It's not a problem, Dr. O'Donnell," Huisman replied. "It sounds like you had a troubling day, but you don't have to worry you've said something you shouldn't. Like I said, I have some ties to your family. I assume this has something to do with the Taggarts. Your father is an executive at McKay-Taggart, correct?"

Aidan's frown deepened. "I'm sorry, how would you know that?"

"Our families go back quite a ways," Huisman admitted. "It's why I was so surprised to see your name and called you on a Saturday evening when I should have waited until Monday morning."

Sure, that was the reason for the call. Tristan didn't bother to hide his eye roll.

"I want to assure you you've said nothing to betray your family," Huisman continued. "Mere months ago I approached Mr. Taggart about a problem I found myself in. I consider him an intelligent and wise man. Please feel free to talk to him about the symposium and contact me. I can assure your safety and comfort. If your worried, I'm more than willing to make arrangements with him."

Ian's jaw tightened, but his eyes remained on Aidan. He gave him the slightest nod.

"I don't know. I worry I won't be able to concentrate, and the last thing I want to do is drag everyone down."

He was going to praise his friend so much. Aidan was playing this perfectly.

"I scarcely think you could drag us down," Huisman reassured him. "I've read this paper of yours twice now. Dr. O'Donnell…"

"Aidan. Please. Call me Aidan."

A soft chuckle came across the line. "I do think we'll get along, Aidan. I like a man who isn't so arrogant he must go by all his titles. I, too, prefer to simply be called by name. You must call me Manny. All my friends do, and I think we could be friends, you and I."

He was the fucking devil trying to make a deal. But lucky for him, Aidan couldn't be fooled.

"Well, Manny, I'm afraid I also don't want to bring my trouble to your doorstep," Aidan replied.

"Is it *your* trouble?"

This guy wasn't taking no for an answer. Tris went back to the white board.

Tell him you have to take care of Carys. Tell him no, and be firm about it.

Aidan read the note. "No real idea. I'm afraid I get left out of the meetings. You have to understand, I'm not a part of that world. Neither is my father. We're close to the Taggarts, but we don't have ties to the intelligence stuff. Not even my fiancée, who is a Taggart. Her father's a chef, so this is not something we're used to."

"Then bring her to Montreal," Huisman offered. "You sound like you could use some time away, Aidan. I have several guesthouses around the property. I'm happy to offer you one of the bigger ones. Perhaps one large enough you could bring a bodyguard. Or a companion, so your fiancée isn't lonely. Come to my home and surround yourself with some of the best minds in our business. I include you in this. I truly believe you have extraordinary potential. Come to Montreal and think about the future."

Tristan huffed, trying to get Aidan's attention. It was past time to hang up on this motherfucker. He would find another way in. Maybe through one of the other doctors Huisman invited.

"All right," Aidan said.

Tristan gasped and started to say something, but Cooper had a big arm around his neck, his hand covering his mouth.

"Don't you dare," Cooper whispered. "His choice, Tris."

Now he knew why Ian brought Coop down. Bitterness welled. Carys and Aidan were his. Fucking his.

"But I need a couple of days. Carys and I were going to spend them in the city, but given our situation, I think we'll come in later in the week." Aidan sounded like this was all normal. Like he wasn't fucking up the whole world. Like he hadn't put their love in danger.

Tris thought seriously about breaking Coop's hold. Oh, he had an inch and some muscle on him, but Tris could fight dirty. Tris could twist out and kick the fucker in the balls, and then they would see whose choice it was.

"Well, I will look forward to it, and I'm serious about talking to Mr. Taggart if you think it would help make everyone comfortable." Huisman sounded pleased with himself.

Because they'd given him everything he wanted.

"I should get back to my fiancée," Aidan said. "But I appreciate you calling, Dr…Manny. I think this might be exactly what I need."

"I'm glad I could help. See you soon."

There was something ominous about the words, but Tristan doubted anyone else would hear it. Cooper's arm came from around his neck, and Tris fought the urge to clock him. Ian was watching him now as Aidan hung up his phone. Watching and likely hoping for a reason to try to sideline him.

It wasn't going to happen.

Aidan turned to Ian. "Do you think he bought it?"

"Bought it?" Ian asked. "I think you just made a choice."

"Yeah, I know," Aidan agreed, "but did I come across as reluctant? Because I was going for reluctant. I thought I shouldn't sound too sure after what happened today. He knew about what happened today, right? That's why you wanted me to be honest with him. Because he already knew. Because he's the one who sent them. Why would he send them?"

"Isn't that the million-dollar question," Ian mused. "Tris, you going to freak out on me?"

"Would it help?" Tris asked, bitterness welling.

"No," Ian said with a sigh. "The path is set, and you're going to have to get on board. Do you want to give him a training crash course or should I?"

"Oh, it's definitely going to be me." If anyone was going to train Aidan, it would be him.

Aidan held up a hand. "Training? Like what kind?"

At least one good thing might come out of this. They would all die, but Aidan would get an education.

Tris felt a nasty smirk cross his face. "You'll find out."

He might have been out of control tonight, but Aidan would find he was still the boss come morning.

Chapter Six

"Are you sure?" Carys was still feeling vulnerable hours later as she stood in her cousin's room. "I can sleep in the office."

Kala had changed into boxer shorts and a tank, looking lean and predatory even with magenta pink hair piled on her head. She waved off the thought. "I sleep with Lou about half the time anyway. Bad dreams and stuff. I know. It's a bad habit I haven't broken yet, and tonight I have a perfectly valid reason."

Her cousin had some secrets. She didn't worry about Kala physically. Emotionally was another story altogether. "So TJ is cool with you sleeping with them?"

"Oh, I totally wait until after they're done with the sex stuff. And then I leave before the morning sex stuff. He's got a very specific pattern," Kala admitted, and she looked around the room. "Maybe be careful in here. I can't remember where I put all the weapons. Though I did disable all the traps. I think."

"There are traps?"

Her pink-haired cousin's head tilted slightly. "Of course. Who doesn't have traps?"

"Me."

"And that is why you fail."

Her cousin was such a weirdo. "I will try not to touch your stuff.

Luckily I had packed since we were supposed to spend tonight at the Ritz-Carlton before we got on the flight to Montreal tomorrow. Maybe we should still go. Aren't we supposed to be pretending like nothing's wrong?"

The door opened and Kenzie strode in with a couple of extra pillows. She handed them to her twin. Unlike her sister, Kenzie wore super feminine satiny shorts and a camisole top. "Did you disable all the traps? The last thing Carys needs is an arrow to the head."

"What?" Carys asked.

"She's kidding." Kala frowned her sister's way, but she could have sworn her cousin had said "it's fine" under her breath.

Maybe she should sleep in the office. Or at her parents'. It had been a viable alternative, though she would have to have taken a bodyguard with her. Her mom had cried and asked her to come home, but she couldn't do it. If she'd gone home, she would have let her mom and dad coddle her and talk her out of what she needed to do.

Go to Canada. Finish this thing once and for all.

We're going in. I got a call from Huisman. Your uncle thinks he's the one who sent the helicopter. We're going to Canada on Wednesday, Aidan had said when they'd all sat down in her uncle's office since he'd told her she'd violated his precious conference room.

Her dad had tried to not listen to that particular messy conversation.

All her conversations felt messy as hell now. Especially the super-stilted ones with Tristan and Aidan.

There had been little said beyond Aidan explaining he'd talked to Huisman and now Tris couldn't keep them out. He'd said it like he was giving her a gift, like he'd done it for her.

She'd been both afraid and gratified. And oddly invigorated.

They were going to finish this. It was going to end one way or another.

"As to if you should go to the swanky hotel you were going to consummate your marriage in, the answer is no," Kala said. "Unless you want a bunch of us sleeping with you. Personally, I think you're better off here. Have you thought about what would have happened when you're getting all down and dirty with Aidan and suddenly oops, Tris is there?"

"He wouldn't have…" Except he'd been at the wedding, and he

110

was an arrogant bastard who probably thought he could sneak into her bed. Maybe it was something he and Aidan had been planning all along. She wouldn't put it past them.

"I bet he would have." Kala frowned. "After all, the dude is willing to sleep on the couch."

Kenzie's nose wrinkled. "Yeah, I should warn you about that. They kind of broke in and took over the office, so you should know they're probably going to be here in the morning. By probably I mean will be."

"Unless you want me to get rid of them." Kala's expression had brightened.

"They have their own place to go to." She'd assumed they would go to their house or to the apartment close to the hospital she and Aidan had recently moved into. There were no rooms at this particular inn. They were kind of filled to the brim at this point.

The twins' sister, Tasha, had moved out, but it hadn't been more than a few days before Tristan's sister, Brianna, had moved in. She'd lived in her parents' guesthouse for a long time and had jumped at the chance to be on her own. Kala had explained how it didn't hurt they now had someone who could easily watch after the big mutt they called Bud Two and the house when they were off galivanting around the planet.

So all four bedrooms were full, and no one apparently wanted to stay in the office.

"Cooper tried to convince them to come back to his place, but they were not listening," Kenz said. "Like not even to each other. They both argued the other one should go to Coop's or The Hideout, and then they argued about how the other one was trying to cut them out. It was a lot of boy drama. Are you sure you want two dudes? It feels like a lot of emotional turmoil."

It normally wasn't. It had worked for so many years, and then it simply hadn't. "Well, I probably don't have to worry about it now. I mean afterward. I really have to worry about it now since I'm stuck with them until we get back from Canada."

Uncle Ian had gone over the parameters of her mission.

Don't get fucking killed.

He had a way with words. Basically they were going so Tristan and Kala/Kenzie—who would be playing her best friend/companion/

111

bodyguard—could get access to Huisman's estate and hopefully find some dark lair where he kept all his secrets. They talked about him like he was some comic book villain who could murder her with a snap of his fingers. She was there to look pretty and be quiet.

She got that a lot these days. It was starting to rankle.

"Or you could, like, talk to them," Kenzie said quietly. "They're out in the living room arguing about who should take the first watch."

"There's a watch?" They must have come in after she'd showered and gotten ready for bed. Likely because they'd had to get Tristan's bags from wherever he'd left them. "Also, why did you let them in? I thought we were going to be an all-female refuge. Well, all women and TJ and Bud Two."

"Bud's kind of half dude since he lost his balls. And TJ is proof you can't trust any men. I mean he's good for carrying heavy things and stuff, but he folded when the guys showed up," Kenzie admitted. "They started whining about how they would sleep outside your window and he let them in."

"I would have told them to go for it," Kala replied. "I happen to have a great trap on the window. You can totally go out of it if you need to, but anyone coming in is getting some new scars, if you know what I mean."

Her cousin was terrifying. "They were going to sleep outside?"

"They have sleeping bags and everything," Kenzie explained, sinking to the bed with a wistful sigh. "I kind of thought it was romantic."

"It's stupid," Kala corrected. "But the fun part was Brianna yelling at her brother."

"Because he's a butthead." Brianna stood in the doorway, the frown on her face softening when she looked at Carys. "Hey. Sorry, I was on the phone when you came in and then you were in the shower. Are you doing okay?"

Her parents had blessed her with three brothers and not a single sister. Her relationship with Aidan and Tristan had given her the sisters she'd so desperately desired. Brianna Dean-Miles was precious to her, and the idea of not being in her life made Carys ache. She held open her arms. "I'm okay, sweetie. How are you?"

Brianna sniffled and walked into her arms, hugging her tight. "I was so worried about you. I'm sorry. Tristan is being an idiot, and I don't know what to do."

Carys hugged her. She remembered doing this the first time Bri got her heart broken. Bri and Daisy O'Donnell had been her baby sisters, the ones who looked up to her, who came to her for advice. Even more so than her cousins. The twins were a force of nature and had Tasha to look up to. But Bri and Daisy had been hers.

"There's nothing for you to do," Carys said, stroking Bri's gold and brown hair. "None of this is your fault."

"No, it's Tristan's," Brianna replied.

Damn. This wasn't like a normal breakup. It was like a divorce. She'd never thought about all the people who'd come to depend on the three of them being together. They were breaking up whole family systems. She hadn't even thought about how it would affect her parents. They were all so close.

All of her life she'd simply accepted she would marry these men, and this was her family.

Did she honestly know what she was doing? The first thing she had to do was love her friends and make this easy on them. She squeezed Bri and then leaned back so she could look her in the eyes. "Sweetie, it's not his fault. He was trying to do his job, and it got away from him. I don't think he meant to get so lost and hurt me, but sometimes we don't have control over outside forces. I'm going to be okay. You'll be okay, too, and even though I'm not with your brother anymore doesn't mean we can't be friends."

"We're more than friends." Brianna brushed away her tears and stepped back. "And it was his fault. I love you for trying to protect him, but I'm not a kid anymore. I know when my brother screws up. I can be mad at him and still love him. He's not only doing it to you. He's locked me and our parents out. I feel like I've lost my brother, and I can't lose you and Aidan, too."

Her heart ached for her little sis. "You won't. You can't lose me, Bri. I'm always here for you. Why don't you try talking to him? I've heard he's around."

Bri sighed. "Not tonight. I'm too tired. He should know if he doesn't talk soon, I think Dad is going to do something. I saw our parents plotting tonight. There was a meeting, wasn't there? Back at the MT building."

"Yep," Kala revealed. "And my dad wanted to call your parents in the same way he did Uncle Sean and Aunt Grace and Aidan's parents. Guess who pulled the 'I'm a professional' card?"

Brianna groaned. "Well, it's his fault now because he seems to have forgotten who our parents are. Mom is not the most patient woman, and she married two guys who would do anything for her. I'm supposed to go to their place for brunch tomorrow. I'll see if I can mitigate the damage. Good night."

Bri walked out.

"Now I kind of want to kill him myself," Kala said with a huff.

She turned to her murderiest cousin. "Somehow I think him dying would make things worse."

"Well, it wasn't like he was trying to avoid it." Kenzie's eyes had widened. "I couldn't believe he stood there while they were shooting. It's a miracle all he got was a scratch."

"Has he always been this reckless?" She realized what she'd asked and backed down. "Sorry. You can't answer."

The twins exchanged a look, and then Kenzie turned her way.

"He was known in Army intelligence for being super reliable. Like Tris was the guy who did his job and did it well. He was the dot all the I's and cross the t's guy. He was also passed over for Agency work because it was deemed he had too many close ties to really do the job."

"They were looking at him pretty much from the time he joined the military," Kala explained. "Because of who his fathers are."

Jacob Dean and Adam Miles had been Special Forces at one point, but Carys knew it was what they'd done after they left the military that likely made the Agency interested in Tristan. After years at McKay-Taggart, they'd formed their own company along with some other brilliant minds. Miles-Dean, Weston, and Murdoch was known for cutting-edge facial recognition software every intelligence agency would like to get their hands on.

"From what I understand, the Agency discussed bringing him in early, but after consideration they decided he wasn't morally gray enough," Kala explained, winking her sister's way. "We didn't have the same problem. You should know something. Kenz and I are the only ones on the team the Agency actively recruited. Everyone else was brought in as backup. Cooper McKay would never have been considered if we hadn't insisted on it. And neither would Tris."

Carys was confused. "Why? I guess I don't understand what you mean by morally gray. I get it in a romance novel hero sense, but not here. I mean everything you do, it's to protect your country."

"Of course," Kenzie said.

"Eh," came Kala's reply. "I mean, sure. But it's about how far we're willing to go. The big bosses didn't think Tris would be willing to go far enough."

"Well, he showed them, didn't he?" It hurt when she thought about it. This could have been avoided.

Or maybe he always would have changed.

"I tell you this because once he started working with my team, he signaled a willingness to work outside it as well," Kala continued. "Tristan has some very specific skills."

"He's addicted to the Dark Web." He always had been. Even as a kid she'd known how dangerous it could be.

"He's an excellent hacker," Kala corrected. "He's good at putting things together and gathering intel. Turns out he's good at tracking a signature."

"And pretending to be someone he's not," Kenzie finished, and she studied Carys for a moment. "Have you thought about the fact that he's basically been undercover for two and a half years? He didn't think it would be this long, didn't think he would have to go so deep. Sometimes when an agent is undercover for so long, they take on aspects of the character they're playing. They kind of have to in order to survive. Tris became incredibly secretive."

"And reckless," Kala added. "He wasn't as reckless in the beginning but lately... Well, I've been worried we're going to bury him. The only one he talks to is Zach."

She'd seen the handsome Army captain at The Hideout, but she'd never spent much time with him. "They don't act like the closest of friends when he's in town."

Kenzie sat back against the headboard. "I think they do it on purpose. They're both technically Army intelligence. At least that's what it says on the books. Cooper is technically military, too, but what he does is logistics and transportation."

"The point is there's a lot we don't know, but we're worried about Tris," Kala continued. "You're now a part of this, and since we'll be with you, I need to know how hard a bodyguard I'm supposed to be."

"Well, I would prefer not to die," Carys replied.

"She means do you really want us to keep Tristan away from you? Right now he's planning on going in as Aidan's bodyguard," Kenzie clarified.

"How can he do that?" Carys was confused on how all this worked. "If this doctor person knows about the wedding, how could he not know about Tris? I know when he entered the Agency they scrubbed him off socials, but there are still records of him."

The first awful indication life had changed because of Tristan's job had been waking up to all her socials being taken over. She wasn't a slave to her socials, but they had been a way to memorialize some of the nice parts of her life. She'd woken up one morning and they'd been changed. All the pictures of Tristan had been gone. All her posts about him, messages to him...simply gone.

It should have let her know how the next years of her life were going to go.

"The Agency is excellent at changing a narrative," Kenzie insisted. "In this case, we're McKay-Taggart bodyguards, and we don't have to pretend. Which makes me sad because I like the undercover aspect. I would have been Carys's friend from work. Kally the nurse. I had a backstory and everything."

"Not a nurse." Kala's reply let Carys know they'd been arguing about this for a while. "Do you know nurse things? We can dress a wound in the field but there's more to nursing. I'm glad we're going in as a bodyguard since we'll be walking into a nest of highly trained doctors. What would happen if they ask specific questions we can't answer? You and your back stories."

She wasn't about to mention most of these doctors would be arrogant assholes who thought nursing was beneath them and they wouldn't ask anyone without an MD for anything except maybe another coffee. "It's for the best. The medical world can be kind of insular. These are guys in highly specialized fields or in what we consider sexy fields like trauma surgery. They won't pay attention to you. Hell, when they find out I'm in obstetrics, they'll completely shut me out. I will be considered Dr. O'Donnell's girlfriend."

Kenzie frowned. "Well, now I kind of want to take all of them out."

Carys shrugged. "It is what it is. Maybe we can use it to our advantage."

"I'm sure we can," Kala said. "Now how hardcore should I go on Tristan's ass? Am I guarding the bedroom door?" She turned slightly, looking at the doorway. "What do you say, buddy? Do we need to have a talk? I'm not worried about your friend there, but we do have to work together."

Carys followed Kala's gaze, and there they were. Tris and Aidan stood in the doorway. Well so much for respecting her boundaries. "I asked you to stay at your place. I'm perfectly safe here."

"My place is our apartment," Aidan insisted, and she wished he didn't look so damn delicious. He'd changed into PJ pants and decided he didn't need a shirt. "I'm not leaving you, and I know Kala thinks she can intimidate me, but I'm not about to crawl away in the hopes my cousin won't take my balls."

"And she won't be able to keep me out." Tris hadn't changed yet, but he stared at her with dark eyes.

With eyes that reminded her of everything this man could do to her. Had done to her. He could make her feel in a way no one else could. He could also rip her heart out.

"Are you planning on letting Aidan and I do our jobs?" Carys asked since he'd been suspiciously quiet during the hours' long meeting discussing how this mission was going to work.

"Not at all. I plan on talking you out of it. Aidan's put us all in a terrible position," Tristan admitted. "He got overly emotional, and now we have to find a way out. I'll come up with it. I think our best way out is to replace you with an actual operative. It's not like Huisman will have studied you."

"Because I'm nothing more than a prop." It was good to know they were all on the same page.

Tristan frowned. "I didn't say that."

Kenzie stood. "I think they have some stuff to talk about, sis. You sure you don't want to bunk down with me?"

Kala followed her sister. "It's more fun to freak TJ out." She brushed past the boys and turned. "You sure you can handle them? I can toss them out. Or sic Bud on them."

"Yeah, Bud might lick me to death," Tris said under his breath.

The massive mutt her cousins had rescued wasn't exactly a guard dog. She didn't need one in this case. It was time to start dealing with the problem. "I'm good."

When the twins were gone, Tristan closed the door. "I'm sorry for putting you in this position, Carys. Aidan wouldn't listen to me, but I do have a plan. I've already contacted a woman I work with, and she's trying to find an operative who looks similar to you. I can think of a couple, but we have to make sure we can get her here soon so she has time to familiarize herself with Aidan. I wish I could do the same for Aidan, but I don't know any surgeons who also happen to be operatives."

He was such an ass. "What are the requirements to pretend to be me? Similar-sized boobs?"

"You know she's a doctor, too." It was obvious what play Aidan was making. He was pretending to be on her side.

"I know how smart she is, but you know not a one of those fuckers is going to view her as anything but your girlfriend," Tristan argued. "The type of medicine she practices, while of the utmost importance, is viewed by them as basic."

"I don't treat her like that." Aidan moved toward the bed. "She knows a lot about trauma. She's my first and best sounding board. If anything, I'm the one who's dumb about what she does."

He wasn't at all. Aidan often challenged her. When they'd been in med school they would test each other. Even as they'd found their specialties, they'd tried to keep up with each other. "He's quite proficient at obstetrics, but you're right about the rest of them. They'll see me as his girlfriend. Whoever you bring in won't need to know much."

"He's not bringing in anyone," Aidan declared. "If he tries, I'll pull out. Tris, you think I'm some moron who got caught up in the moment, but I thought it through. Carys needs this. I do, too. We're not going in a safe house. We're going to end this."

"The fact you think this is the end only tells me you have no idea what you're doing. This is an intel-gathering mission. We're not going in guns blazing," Tris argued.

"He wasn't talking about ending Huisman." She needed to be plain with Tristan. "Once we're done with this, we'll be out. You and Aidan can go your way and I'll go mine."

"Not what I meant at all." Aidan looked stubborn. "I don't care about Huisman. After we do this, Tris can decide if he wants to be with us or if he wants to run around the world playing superhero."

"We are not sure there is an *us* at all." It looked like she would have to be clear with Aidan, too. "You lied to me. You worked together behind my back, and I need some time to deal with it. The truth is today might have been a blessing."

"Getting shot at is a blessing?" Aidan asked, his eyes wide, and then his face fell. "You mean because we're not married. So you don't have to divorce me because I lied to you."

She sighed because it sounded so harsh. The day had been dreadful, and she knew in her logical mind she might feel differently in the morning. Or in a few weeks. She needed time. "I don't know. Do I have to make a decision tonight?"

"No." Aidan looked lost. "You don't have to make a decision at all, baby. I made a mistake. I honestly thought I was protecting you, but I understand how that made you feel and it's not okay. I'll do whatever you need me to do to earn your trust back. But we're going into something dangerous, and us being at odds isn't going to help. The tension between us… I'm worried it could get us killed. Get you killed."

"I'm a pretty good actress," she replied.

"You're not." Naturally Tris wanted to argue. "You're a terrible liar, and Aidan's right. He's even worse than you are, which is precisely why this is such a terrible idea."

Aidan's head shook. "I'm not arguing tonight. It's getting late, and it's been a fucking awful day. Carys, will you let me sleep with you?"

The idea of going to bed alone made her ache. He was right. It had been terrible, and the best thing in the world would be to wrap herself around him and sleep. "No."

She couldn't do it. Not yet.

He nodded as though he'd expected her answer. "Then Tris, you can take first watch. Wake me in a couple of hours."

Aidan strode out, and it took everything she had not to go after him, to shove all this anger aside and hold him. If she did, she would cry all over again and still not get what she needed. She was a ball of stress, and not the kind she was used to. Carys could be perfectly cool under pressure. She could shut it all down and concentrate on her

119

patient, but there was no patient. There was only her and Aidan and Tristan. There was only the rest of her lonely life if she couldn't figure this out.

She was fairly sure she couldn't figure this out unless she went to Canada. Unless she finally faced whatever had taken Tristan from them. "You think I'm such a terrible actress I can't pretend I still love him? I don't have to pretend. I do love him. The question is can I trust him?"

Tristan moved into her space, and she immediately felt her body heat up. "No, the question is do the two of you work without me."

She wasn't about to back down. "We've worked for two and a half years without you."

"Have you?" He loomed over her. Tristan had a good half a foot on her, and his body had gone from lanky boy to muscular man in the last couple of years.

She wished she didn't want to get her hands on him, to explore the changes in the body she'd loved so much. The afternoon had done nothing but stimulate an appetite she'd hoped she'd outgrown.

Shouldn't Aidan be enough for her? Shouldn't she be enough for him? Why couldn't she be normal and make this work like other people did? Like her parents. And almost everyone she knew. Except Tris's parents. And some of her friends' parents.

She couldn't let Tris see her weakness. "We've been fine."

"I don't think so, baby. The fact that you fell apart so quickly lets me know the truth. You are not an unforgiving woman, Car. When you think about it, you're going to understand. I tried to talk to you but you refused."

"You wanted me to be your secret," she pointed out. "It's not the same. You were sending me cards and gifts as a placeholder. You weren't trying to let me know what was going on. You didn't keep me in the loop the way you did Aidan."

"You want to know why?"

She didn't need an explanation. "I'm sure you were trying to protect the little woman."

Tris groaned. "Little woman? I wasn't afraid you would fall apart. I was terrified you would try to save me. I was scared you would ride in like the Taggart woman you are. You talk about how you're the sensible one and you're the reasonable one in your family.

120

Your family has Kala and Kenzie in it. Of fucking course you're the reasonable one. Anyone is reasonable compared to your wild-ass cousins. I don't know if you've given this any thought, but you're not exactly a shrinking violet. What happened when we got called out as a threesome in high school?"

She and Tris had gone to the same high school while Aidan had been at one across the city. It had been fairly easy for a while to keep their threesome status from their classmates. For several years, everyone thought Tris was her boyfriend and Aidan was a guy they saw occasionally because their parents were friendly. And then they'd been outed.

She hadn't ever cared. "I told the ones who called me a whore to bite my ass. They were jealous I had two hot boyfriends and was living the dream."

"And where did you say it, Car?"

"Fine. I said it over the loudspeakers because I wanted everyone to hear it," she admitted, remembering the day fondly. She'd gotten serious detention, and they wouldn't let her do morning announcements ever again, but it had been worth it. None of this meant she should be left out of a deep and important part of his life. It had been far easier when she thought she hadn't been the only one left out.

"Yeah, I'm talking to that woman right now. I was scared you would decide it was too dangerous for me and you would show up in the middle of an arms deal," he said with a shake of his head. "I talked to Aidan because I knew he would stand down. I needed him, Carys. I needed someone to ground me because I couldn't talk to my team."

The whole reason she'd initially felt somewhat comfortable with Tris going into Agency work had been his close proximity to her cousins and Cooper McKay. "Why?"

"Because my team is made up of you on steroids. All Taggart women. If I talked to Coop, it's like I'm talking to Kala, and Uncle Ian would have smacked me upside the head and caused all kinds of trouble." Tris paced the length of the small room and then back again, an anxious predator in a too-tiny cage. "I went into this particular mission because I was the only one who could do it."

"The only one?" Tristan could be a bit on the arrogant side when it came to some things. "No one else in all the world?"

He sent her a look that let her know he wished they were in a club. "I was the only one in place at the time with the skills to track down The Jester. Once I had assumed his identity, I realized how truly dangerous this mission was, and I knew I had to protect you."

"So now they know you're The Jester." She was confused. Maybe because her brain had been churning all night. She was still in shock. It wasn't the best time to absorb years' worth of mission information.

"We don't have confirmation anyone knows anything." Tris stopped, his arms crossing over his chest. "I think they were likely after TJ. You were listening when Big Tag explained what happened in Germany?" He sighed, softening slightly. "Of course you didn't. You shut down and then our scene didn't work, so you've stayed shut down. I don't suppose you'll let me spank you until you cry."

She'd thought about it. "It won't work. I need more than a simple spanking and more time than I'm willing to give you tonight."

His brows rose. "Tonight?"

"The twins told me The Hideout is open tomorrow." Beyond how pissed she was, the idea of playing with him again… Well, it all swirled around in her brain like a toxic cocktail waiting to do some real damage. "My first instinct is to tell you and Aidan to find a sub and have fun."

Tristan's jaw clenched. "We would never. There's one woman in the world for us. You know that, right? You realize if you walk away, Aidan and I break, too. You seem to think you're some sort of ancillary arm of my friendship with him. You're not. You're the base of our triangle. You leave and we fall apart. I'll make a deal with you."

She barely managed to avoid rolling her eyes because she knew exactly what he was about to say. "You'll think about letting me on the op if I play with you tomorrow night."

He chuckled, though it wasn't an amused sound. "Oh, I thought you knew me."

"I do."

"You're going to have to accept that the last few years have changed me. I've got scars you've never seen before, baby. On the outside and the inside, and I've always known there was one person in the world who could even start to heal them, and it's not Aidan. No, I wasn't going to offer you some tiny deal. I'm pretty sure this is beyond my fucking control unless I want to never be allowed to come home again." He stared down at her. "If I wasn't a selfish bastard, I would do it. I would call in a couple of favors, and you suddenly wouldn't have a choice about the safe house. No one would. Not even Uncle Ian."

"You honestly believe you can outmaneuver my uncle?" As far as she could tell, Uncle Ian and Aunt Charlotte were in control of everything concerning their team. To her they were fun relatives. Uncle Ian was goofy and had a ton of dad jokes and was way too sex positive, while Aunt Charlotte was exactly the kind of woman they all wanted to grow up to be, but she'd learned as she got older there was another side to them.

It was hard to believe Tristan could go up against them. Would dare to go up against them.

"I know I can. If I want to shut this down I can, but I'm asking you not to make me," he said quietly. "I need you to think this through. What I'm offering you is training. I'll train you so if I can't find a way out of this without losing my whole family, you'll be safer."

"The twins are going to train me." She felt the need to remind him of a few truths about her life. "Though you should remember my father put me in karate when I was six. I have a brown belt."

"And I have a black belt. I recently used it in a fight where my opponent was trying to gut me," Tristan shot back. "When was the last time you practiced?"

Years. It had been years, and he knew it. "It's been a while."

He let a moment go by before sighing. "I'll talk about work. I'll talk about what's happened and why I did what I did."

She hadn't expected the offer. "I thought it was classified."

"Well, it is, but if you're going to be a part of this, you should know."

"I thought you were going to talk me out of it."

His head tilted slightly, acknowledging the truth. "I am, but I'm not going to force it if you agree to my terms."

"That I sleep with you."

"That you play with me," Tristan corrected. "Think about it. You need a session, likely more than one. You play with me and Aidan and I answer your every question openly and honestly."

Well, the man knew how to tempt her. "It won't change things. I'll admit I don't know how long I'll be able to stay mad at Aidan, but I don't think I'll ever trust you again. I'll always be waiting for you to leave me."

"Then you don't have anything to lose. Then you can take what you want from me and walk away at the end. You can know how much it's going to hurt me if you leave. Show me everything I'm going to miss because I fucked up."

"But there's no guarantee you won't pull the whole mission?" She could see all the ways he could wriggle out of the position Aidan had put him in.

"That's the risk you take. What do you say, Carys?" It was more of a challenge than a question. "You get anything you want information-wise out of me. No holds barred."

There were a few problems with his offer. "You could lie."

"Ask me something. Something you think I would lie about."

"Have you been with someone else?" She wasn't sure she believed him. Or maybe it would make everything easier if he admitted he'd been unfaithful.

His head shook like he was disappointed in her. "I told you. No one else. Not ever. You're the only woman on earth I've ever had sex with, and Aidan's the only other human I've shared any kind of intimacy with. Try again. Ask a hard one."

"Did you miss me?" The minute the question was out of her mouth, she regretted it.

He started to take a step toward her but backed off. "Of course. I've missed you every single day."

"Would you take it back?"

He hesitated. "I don't know. Part of me says yes. Part of me....part of me is addicted to this life. Part of me can't stand the thought of not having this kind of power. I want to tell you I'll walk away and come home and work for my dad. But I don't know if I can."

Well, he'd said he would be honest. She glanced at the clock. It was so late. "Can I take the night to think about it?"

Tristan nodded and moved to the door. "Of course. If you decide it's a no and you still need a session, Cooper can run one for you. Kala wouldn't mind helping."

They would give her the pain she needed but none of the pleasure.

She knew what she was going to say but she couldn't give it to him tonight.

If this was the end, she wanted something from him. From them.

"Okay," she agreed. "I'll let you know tomorrow."

"It is tomorrow." Tristan yawned. "Can I have a pillow?"

She picked up the extra. Kala's room was oddly spartan. The most decoration she had was a wall of pictures of her and her family and friends. There was a pic of her with Bud One, along with his old collar hanging off it. A pic of her and Lou and Cooper and TJ in high school.

Her and Aidan's apartment was filled with memories. Did she want to lose them? Would she even be able to look at the pictures if they broke up?

She handed Tristan the pillow, careful not to touch him. "You staying on the couch? It might be better than the office, or so I've heard."

He opened the door and stepped just outside. There was a sleeping bag rolled up on the floor. "I've been told the only place I should sleep tonight is outside your door. Your father gave me a whole lecture on how it's the traditional sleeping place of a Taggart who fucked up."

Her father was mean, but she'd certainly heard the stories. "My mom kicked him out of their bedroom once, and he slept outside her door. He was worried about her at the time."

"And apparently your brother did the same for MaeBe." Tristan unrolled the sleeping bag. "But this is where I'm smarter than they were. I only have to take half the night because I have a partner. He might be pissed at me, but he'll do his part. Also, I came prepared. I got a bunch of complaints about how crappy it is to sleep on the floor. This baby has a new type of memory foam built in."

"Good for you," she said and couldn't keep the sour note from her tone.

"There's room for two," he offered. "Or I could stay with you."

She hadn't let Aidan stay with her. She certainly wasn't about to invite Tristan in. She slammed the door in his face.

"All right, then," he said. "I'll be out here doing the Taggart tradition proud."

Carys turned off the lights and forced herself into a lonely bed.

* * * *

Tristan came awake suddenly with the knowledge he wasn't alone. Adrenaline flooded his system as his brain came back online.

He reached for his gun, kept hidden under the pillow, and brought it up.

"Hello." Daisy O'Donnell sat cross-legged at the end of the torture device the twins called a pull-out sofa bed.

Fuck. He was at the twins' place. He wasn't out in the field. He wasn't The Jester here. He was Tristan Dean-Miles. He was himself. Whoever that was anymore.

He'd offered to stay on watch when Aidan had come to relieve him at four this morning, but Aidan had insisted, and his best friend had obviously had enough, so he'd given up his fairly comfy spot for this...punishment of a "bed."

He pulled the gun away and forced his body to an upright position, taking a long breath to banish the fear response. "Sorry."

"Oh, it's fine," Daisy said with a wave of her well-manicured hand. Aidan's sis was a few years younger and what Aidan liked to call a walking ball of chaos. She had good intentions, but things went haywire around the gorgeous brunette. Today she was dressed in shorts and a pink halter top, her hair piled in a messy bun. She'd ditched her shoes at some point, or at least he thought she had. Daisy might have taken to the barefoot life. "It's totally not the first time I've had a gun in my face, so don't worry about it. I do not take it personally."

He was actually surprised she'd managed to sneak up on him. He was a light sleeper. Since the episode in Taiwan, he was definitely concerned with people attacking him while he slept. It was the very incident he'd mentioned to Carys the night before where his black belt had come in handy. "What are you doing here? Aidan's sleeping..."

"In front of Carys's door," she said with a wistful grin. "It's romantic."

"Well, he's taking his turn." He felt the need to point out Aidan wasn't the only one watching out for Carys. "I took the earlier shift."

She shrugged, the action making the massive gold hoops in her ears shake. "Well, I'm sure that was easier. It would be better if he was in bed with her, but I can understand why she's upset. I have recently had to deal with men not treating me like the grown-up, capable woman I am. And I'm here because I thought we should talk. We haven't talked in a while, have we, Tristan?"

He wasn't sure they'd ever really talked. She was his best friend's kid sister. Daisy was close to Carys and to her brother, but it had been years since he'd been in a space with the younger O'Donnell. The truth was Daisy kind of scared him. "No, we haven't. I'm not sure what we would talk about."

Were there cameras on him? Was this some kind of prank?

He felt...weird. Like someone was watching him. He glanced around the small room the twins and Lou used as an office. Brianna, too, now. His sister was living here, and she didn't want to talk to him at all. She'd laughed in his face when he'd suggested he could sleep in her room on her large-enough-for-the-two-of-them, comfortable bed. It wasn't like they'd never gotten shoved into a small space together. They were brother and sister. How many times had she gotten scared and spent the night in his room? They'd survived a childhood together, but would she do her brother's back a solid? Nope.

Something was definitely wrong but he couldn't put his finger on it. Every instinct he had was tingling, but it might be the cloud of craziness that followed Daisy around.

"You can't think of anything? Not a single thing?"

He sighed. Daisy could be relentless. "You want to talk about Aidan?"

She nodded like she was thrilled a toddler had figured out how to solve a problem. "Very good, Tris. Yes, I thought it would be good to talk about my brother. We should throw some Carys talk in, too. Lucas and I had a long discussion after the whole helicopter thing. I think I convinced him not to poison you."

Carys's brother used to be one of his best friends. "Poison?"

"Well, he knows you can probably take him in a fight, so he's using his talents," Daisy said like they were discussing something normal and ordinary and not his death by food. "Like I said, I think I talked him out of it, but like me, Lucas takes his sister's happiness seriously. Now Kyle and David are another story. You would think David would be the reasonable one, but he's studied a lot of history."

"Kyle and David want to murder me, too?" Carys had a lot of brothers.

"Yes, but there's some torture involved before your death. Like I said, David knows a lot about medieval torture techniques." Daisy nodded, and her spine straightened as though she was ready to get serious. "I don't know if it's occurred to you, but you've been unfair to my brother and Carys."

He had so much to fix. It made him kind of want to run. "So I've been told."

"Oh, good. Then you're aware of the problem."

"Dais, of course I'm aware." He needed to handle Daisy with some delicacy. Could he still handle people with delicacy? He'd spent so much freaking time pretending to be someone else, he forgot the charming man he used to be. Could still be. He hoped. "I know how much I've screwed things up with Aidan and Carys. I can only tell you I'm trying to make it better."

"Are you?" Daisy asked, staring at him as though this was a session and she was his judgmental therapist.

He could probably use some therapy. "Yes, but there are things I need to do to ensure their safety before I can even think about being in their lives the way I want to be."

"Things like leaving them for two and a half years? Except you truly only left Carys because you talked to Aidan behind her back."

He winced. Well, it was good to know everyone had heard the story. He should have expected it. This was one of the reasons he'd kept to himself. "It wasn't like that."

Daisy pinned him with her stare. "It feels like it was. I would bet Carys feels like it was."

He knew how Carys felt, but she wasn't thinking about the situation logically. He had a few days to work on her before he had to make the ultimate decision on how he was going to handle the Huisman situation. He'd already sent a text to Tara about finding someone who could take Carys's place. His tech had promised to do the job. "I know she does, but she shouldn't. I thought you were here to talk about your brother."

He glanced around the office again, trying to decide what was making all of his instincts fire off. He was getting paranoid. This was a safe house. His cousins had made sure of it. He was actually a little afraid of walking around too much. He'd thought about making a survey of the place but had found a trip wire outside, and he hadn't wanted to figure out what it was attached to.

"I am, but Carys is such a part of him. It's like their souls are combined." She said it with a sigh as though they were goals as a couple.

They weren't a couple.

"Uhm, you know I'm a part of that. They're my soul mates, too. I've been there since the beginning." Then why the fuck had he let this vast chasm open? They were his soul mates, and he'd been empty without them. He'd become more and more the asshole he played out online.

"I mean, you were, but then you weren't," Daisy said, waving a hand like all those years meant nothing.

It was annoying. And yet hadn't there been times when he'd seriously thought about ending things so they never had to know everything he'd done? He had blood on his hands, and they saved lives. "This is precisely why I kept talking to Aidan. I never meant to leave them forever. I'm involved in something dangerous."

"I'm always involved in something dangerous. I can walk down the street and somehow I end up breaking up a criminal ring," Daisy said with a smile. "See, this is why I thought I should consider law enforcement as a profession. But then I don't look great in those costumes they wear. It's why I didn't go into the military. Army green is not my color. Now if they'd opted for emerald..."

The thought of Daisy with a military-grade weapon was disconcerting. "I think it's better you're going back to school."

From what he'd been told his sister's best friend was going to get her master's in psychology, with an emphasis in childhood development. She'd spent a couple of years trying to find a job that fit her unique personality. And one that didn't blow up, get raided, or went under shortly after she was hired.

Her brief stay at McKay-Taggart had begun with a street chase and ended with her distracting a couple of kidnappers. At least the building was still standing. He wished Nate Carter all the luck in the world. He was going to need it.

"Me, too. It's going to be fun. But my point is couples don't break up because things get dangerous. Or rather the good ones don't. I've had many a dude break up with me because he couldn't handle the heat. Or the explosions. But Nate is totally solid. I mean he pretty much told me I was his right after a cartel trying to kill me shot him instead. It was how I knew he was the one." She had a dreamy look on her face.

"I'm happy for you." Had someone moved the chair? He was almost certain it had been sitting in front of the closet since the bed pulled out across the space where it would sit at the desk.

Daisy must have moved it. But then wouldn't the sound have woken him?

He'd been dreaming about someone stalking him. That's what it must be. His brain had been stuck on someone following him and him leading the bad guys right back to Aidan and Carys, and now he couldn't stop thinking about it.

It was the only explanation he had for the instinct tugging at the back of his head. The one that told him something was wrong.

Daisy nodded. "Me, too. And I want the same for my brother. So you're going to fix this, Tris. You're going to do whatever it takes to make this up to my brother and Carys and get back to normal."

He wasn't sure what normal was anymore, but finding it again was definitely a goal of his. "Yes, it's why I'm here."

Daisy's gaze narrowed suspiciously. "I thought you were here so you could sneak into their marital bed."

Well, that sounded bad. "I came to make sure they were safe."

"So you weren't going to show up on their wedding night?"

"No." It was mostly the truth. He'd kind of thought maybe he could talk to them after they were married and had proven to the world they were done with Tristan Dean-Miles and he was done with them. He'd only taken out the room at the Ritz because it was conveniently located near the airport. If they happened to want to sneak him in... Fuck. "Yeah. Okay, yes, I tricked myself into thinking I was only doing it to protect them, but I probably would have tried to talk to them. I tried to talk to Aidan before the ceremony."

"And he told you to fuck off."

Not exactly, but close. "It doesn't matter now."

"It does because you should learn from your mistakes," Daisy informed him primly. "It feels like you're making another one. Da gave us a debrief on what's happening, and you are screwing all this up again."

It was good to know Uncle Li was serious about sharing classified intel. It was precisely why he didn't think any of the parents should be involved.

His parents. They'd sent text after text and called him at least twenty times. He was going to have to deal with them. Brianna would have told them he was here. It would shock him if one or all of them didn't show up at some point to try to talk to him.

The idea of talking to his parents made his gut churn. What the fuck would he tell them? His dads were heroes. His mom was beloved in her profession. How did he tell them he'd made a mess?

How fast could he get to The Hideout? They might not look for him there.

"Tris, are you even listening to me?"

Tris shoved the covers off. He wore a T-shirt and pajama pants, thank the universe since apparently he didn't get any privacy. "I am, Daisy. I promise I'm thinking about Aidan and Carys. I'm going to do right by them."

"I don't think our versions of *right by* are going to line up," Daisy mused and then sighed. "Oh, well. I was going to blackmail you into doing the right thing, but I suppose I'll simply do the right thing by my friend." She eased off the mattress, straightening her shirt. "It's been a real predicament for me. Do I use what I know to help my brother or fess up to help my friend? Thanks for helping me figure it out."

Tristan put his weapon into its lockbox in case Daisy decided to go commando on him. "That sounds like a threat."

Her dark hair shook. "No, not a threat at all. The opposite. I was going to blackmail you, but I can see it probably won't work. Nate said you were too thick. I don't think he was saying anything about your body though. He wouldn't body shame anyone. He speaks Australian. I think *thick* means you're not very smart."

Sure, because that was better. "Awesome. Tell Nate hi for me."

She smiled brightly. "Okay. I will. Good luck."

She was obnoxious. "Daisy, what were you going to blackmail me with? You could at least tell me."

She'd stopped at the door. "Oh, I was going to offer you a choice. Fix things with my brother in the next couple of weeks or I'll tell your mother that you went to all the Doms at The Hideout and threatened to kill them if they played with your sister. I wouldn't tell Bri because it could hurt her feelings. I know they hurt mine when I found out you and Aidan had done it to me. I was starting to think maybe I wasn't pretty or something. But I will totally tell your mom."

Holy shit. Sometimes when he was in real danger it felt like the world slowed down. This was one of those times. "Aidan told you?"

It wasn't easy being the big brother. Especially in a kink-friendly world. If he'd been born to a normal family, no one would be like *hey, take your sister to the sex club you founded with your friends.* He didn't live in that world. He lived in the one where if he didn't give his sister a membership, she would go and find her own and then probably get in a shit ton of trouble. What was he supposed to do? Let those assholes use his sister?

They were mostly his friends and had been super vetted by him and Lou, but damn it, there was also Lucas and Seth to deal with. They were walking, talking red flags when it came to women.

Maybe he could have talked to Bri instead, but then he would have had to talk about sex with his sister, and it was far easier to threaten the fuck out of every Dom at the club.

"He didn't have to," Daisy said with a shrug. "I figured it out. You know I could have been a detective. When I confronted him he admitted you helped him and you did the same with Bri. Also, he said TJ told you his sister was a grown-ass woman who got to make her own decisions, so good on TJ. I don't have to go to Aunt Erin. But I think Aunt Serena will be interested in this…intel."

His mom would be pissed. His dads would likely understand, but they would be way more afraid of his mom than they would be of standing up for Tris's right to protect his sister from a bunch of men he regularly hung out with.

When he thought about it, he was kind of an asshole. Would she see it as interfering or the act of a loving brother?

Yeah, she was going to kick his ass, though nothing like what his mom would do. His mom would write him into a book and kill him off and never, ever let him forget he was part of the patriarchy. It would be awful.

"I could also tell the twins," Daisy mused.

The twins… He didn't want to think about what Kala and Kenz would do if they decided a fellow woman was being infantilized. He'd faced down some of the world's most dangerous spies, and nothing had quite scared him like Daisy O'Donnell. "I'll get them back. I'll do it. I'll make sure they're safe, and in a few weeks I'll ensure they let me back in. I'll take care of them, Dais."

Her eyes narrowed as she looked him over. "I don't know if I believe you."

"If I don't, then you can always tell her later," he offered. All he knew was he didn't want his mom to find out. She would kill him. He suddenly felt like a kid again.

And all he wanted was his family.

He couldn't have them right now. He had to get through this, had to fix it so he didn't stand in front of his parents like a naughty boy. When he was the hero, he could have them again. He would be worthy again.

He'd thought he could give all of this up in order to protect the people he loved, but he was facing the actual truth of it now and he couldn't…he couldn't.

He couldn't lose them.

"I could wait," Daisy allowed.

"If it helps, I think I see how it might have been wrong to do it," he replied. "Now I'm worried I might have interfered in a bad way."

Daisy's eyes widened. "You think?"

"Well, I thought I was protecting her."

Daisy pointed his way. "Yeah, that's the problem."

"Protecting her is a problem?"

A bright smile crossed Daisy's face. "I'm glad we understand each other now. So any way I could convince you to join your sister? She's going over to your parents' place for brunch."

His mom's Sunday brunches were legendary. She often invited all her friends over, but even when it was just the five of them, she made it special. He missed those Sunday mornings. He missed being home.

Everyone else got to go home for long stretches of time. It was part of their cover.

He'd had his head down for so long he'd forgotten how much he missed home.

But not the reason he hadn't been able to go there. "No. I can't go back yet. I have to handle this situation and then maybe I can go home."

Daisy's nose wrinkled. "Oh, well, I guess it's going to be the hard way then. Uncle Jake, he said no. You should do that stuff you said you would do."

What the fuck? He turned as the closet door came open, and his freaking father was standing there. His father, whose nickname in the Green Berets had been Ghost, so he knew his dad still had it. He'd ignored his instincts, and now it came back to bite him in the ass.

And his father owned a tranquilizer rifle, which was totally in his hands.

"The hard way it is, son," Jacob Dean announced.

"Dad..." Tris began. He could reason with his dad. This was ridiculous.

Then his dad shot him. Right in the chest. The dart stuck out of his right pec, and he hadn't held back on the dosage. The world immediately started to go fuzzy.

"Should have come home," his dad said as he caught him right before the world went dark.

Chapter Seven

Aidan yawned as the door came open and Carys looked down at him, a frown on her gorgeous face. Damn, but she was pretty. Even when she was mad at him. "Morning. How did you sleep?"

She ignored his question. "You actually slept on the floor?"

He sat up, stretching. "It's tradition."

Sean Taggart had been explicit the night before. When he'd heard Carys wanted to stay at the twins' place without them, he'd explained in no uncertain terms how this was a bad idea.

"So I've been told. Somehow I think whatever my dad did it was like a minor thing," she said with a shake of her head. "Like he annoyed her. He certainly didn't lie to her. My dad would never lie to my mother."

A deep chuckle came from the end of the hall. "Oh, you infants think you cornered the market on angst and drama, do you?"

Adam Miles. Tristan's obvious bio dad stood at the end of the hallway dressed as casually as the man ever did in slacks and a button-down. He would occasionally wear sweats and a T if he was playing basketball or working out, but Adam was always stylish. Rather like his son. Adam was an older version of Tristan, though he doubted the father had ever been as relentlessly stubborn as the son.

Carys's brows rose. "Hey, Adam. Are you here to talk to Tris? He's in the office."

"I'm aware," Adam replied. "I'm afraid I'm not the only one who wanted to talk to my son. As my conversation with him is going to take a while, I allowed the other interested party to have her say."

He was about to ask who he meant when he heard something going on down the opposite end of the hall.

"Dude, how the hell did you get in?" Lou's door had opened, but it was Kala who popped her head out. Then her whole body. "My security system didn't go off. Did Bri give you the code? My alarm still should have gone off. I get notifications whenever someone enters or leaves the house. I also have perimeter alarms."

Adam's handsome face lit with the most arrogant smirk—one he'd often seen on Tris's face. "I overrode your system. As to why I'm here, I'm picking up Tristan and Brianna for brunch. Now let's talk about why Carys's dad slept outside her mom's room. I was there, you know. I should also probably protect their privacy, but that's not a big thing with us."

"Uh, no," Kala said, staring at Adam. "I want to know what you did to my system. Lou? What's happened to the security system? TJ, put that thing away. Eww."

"I can't help it. It's morning. Damn, Kala, go back to your own room," a deep voice said.

Lou made an appearance. She was in an oversized T-shirt and fluffy socks. She pushed her glasses up her nose and looked down the hall. "Hey, Uncle Adam."

Adam was frowning. "Is there something I should know? Like I'm all for a threesome, obviously but, uhm, TJ's your cousin, Kala."

Carys snorted, and her lips had curled up. Aidan decided he should probably not be the only one lying on the floor for this discussion. He forced himself up, folding the sleeping bag. Also, he would like the story about why Carys's sainted father had to sleep on the floor. It might help him out. Carys fully believed her parents were perfect.

Aidan's father was Liam O'Donnell. A great man, but not one to pretend to be perfect. He would call it his Irishness. His father had been open about the trouble he'd had at the beginning of his relationship with Aidan's mom. And how his mom was a wonderful woman who put up with all his crap.

He'd always known his parents weren't perfect.

Kala's nose wrinkled. "Ewww. I'm not like their third. Eww. I had to give up my room for Carys because your son is an idiot, and she's rightly decided to not sleep with any men ever again. And I built the system myself. It is unhackable. Aidan, where is your shirt?"

"Uh, totally didn't say I wasn't sleeping with men again," Carys said, obviously a little confused.

"And yet I hacked it with my phone. Your security system, that is," Adam said and looked Aidan's way. "How can he show off his cut chest if he's wearing a shirt? Good move, son. If Carys is still interested in men, you gotta use all your assets."

Carys sighed and tied the belt on her robe. "This is weird now. I'm getting some coffee."

Adam looked down the hallway Kala's way. "I also got into your car's system. You'll find your radio now defaults to the Love Channel."

Kala huffed. "This is not over."

She disappeared into Lou's room.

"I would like to know how you did it," Lou began. "I told her she was playing fast and loose with some of those protocols, but she can be stubborn. And I like the Love Channel. It's soothing in the morning. If you could hack her AC, I would be so grateful. She likes it really cold."

"Lou," Kala yelled.

Lou gave them a wave and followed her bestie.

TJ rushed out, shaking his head and tugging a T-shirt over his broad shoulders. "Good one, Uncle Adam. Although the secret is she listens to a lot of ballads. Like she pretends to be all about the death metal, but I saw some girlie songstresses on her playlist. I really preferred it when I didn't realize most nights she sneaks in and sleeps with us. We need to get our own place."

"Oh, cool," Carys said, joining her cousin. "I'm looking for a room."

Aidan groaned. "No, you are not."

"I might be," she said over her shoulder. She moved down the hallway and stopped when she got to Adam. "Is everyone okay after yesterday? I know Serena wasn't hurt, but I've been worried about her."

Adam's face lost its arrogance, and he was the "uncle" who'd always welcomed them. "She's worried beyond words, sweetie. How are you? I wanted to be there, you know. At the meeting."

Carys sighed. "I do, but Tris is insisting he can handle it. I'm not great since I was supposed to be married today, and I spent last night with two guys taking turns sleeping on the floor outside my borrowed room. Not how I thought they would be taking turns."

"Carys," Aidan said, shocked.

Her shoulder shrugged. "Like he doesn't know."

"If they're taking turns, they're doing it wrong," Adam said, his calm tone not giving away even a hint of embarrassment. "I'll talk to them."

The last thing he needed was a sex lecture on how a ménage worked. It would likely be incredibly detailed and way over the top. There could be an embarrassing PowerPoint presentation in his future. "We know how a ménage works."

"Do you?" Carys asked. "Because I haven't seen evidence recently."

Adam chuckled. "Oh, she's moving on from tears to sass. That's probably a good sign."

"Or I'm simply moving on," Carys replied. "Only time will tell. I'd like the story, if you don't mind telling it. Somehow I can't imagine my dad doing something to deserve sleeping on the ground."

"Does Tris know you're here?" Aidan asked, following them through the living room. The house was quiet, though it was midmorning. They'd had a late night. He was surprised Cooper was sitting in the kitchen, a mug of coffee in his hand.

"He'll know soon enough," Adam said. "Morning, Coop."

"I heard what was happening from Bri. Well, from Hunter, who heard it from Devi, who heard it from Bri. Thought I would come over and see if I could mitigate the damage," Cooper offered. "Is she freaking out?"

There was zero question in Aidan's mind who Coop was talking about. His friend was always concerned with Kala Taggart.

Adam snorted. "She thinks she's untouchable when it comes to security. She's been touched, so yeah, she's pissed. I already called her aunt, and she's upping our security for a while. Daisy thinks she's the one who deleted my high-tech virtual assistant. I figured out it was Kala. This was a bit of revenge. I know how to handle a Taggart."

Aidan rather thought what Adam knew was how to have never-ending prank wars with a Taggart.

Cooper grinned. "In her defense, the AI was nosy. And she did not hold back on the relationship advice, which I believe was her downfall with Kala."

Adam sighed. "I thought it was probably something like that. I was training Tess in human relationships. I will admit she was extremely confident in her advice for an artificial intelligence who's never actually been in a relationship."

"With anyone except you," Aidan pointed out with a chuckle. "Aunt Serena hated her. I wouldn't be surprised if she cheered Kala on."

"Hence the light revenge," Adam admitted. "Sometimes we get obsessed with projects we should let go of, with jobs that cause more problems than they do good."

Cooper stood and grabbed a bag from the bar. "To the highly paranoid, I assure you this revenge isn't small. She'll be freaking out about the system for weeks. You know when you think about it, your revenge was actually against me and Lou. Thanks so much, Uncle Adam. Luckily they had chocolate croissants at Daphne's Delights this morning. You guys are on your own."

He stalked off down the hall.

"Mom was happy when Daisy deleted Tess." Brianna walked into the kitchen. She was dressed for brunch in a pretty sundress and strappy sandals. She went on her toes and kissed her father's cheek. "And I think it was Daisy. Dad's systems are complex. Only some crazy chaotic crap could have led to her being deleted so completely. Kala's good, but not that good. Lou might be able to, but she would never delete so much work. Ever."

"Or it was Aunt Chelsea," Carys pointed out. "If anyone knows how to take advantage of a situation, it's my aunt. I know she sent Daisy a cookie bouquet."

Aidan pointed her way as he pulled down two mugs and started pouring coffee. "I'm going with the Chelsea scenario. Daisy knows nothing about programming."

His sister had gotten into some crazy situations, but she certainly wouldn't destroy someone's work. Well, she wouldn't mean to. He found the creamer in the fridge.

He'd missed this. On the weekends they used to come here or the gang would come to the rambling house he'd shared with Coop and Tris, and they would all somehow put together a big breakfast on Saturday mornings and talk about what had gone down at the club. Carys's brother Lucas would show up wearing the clothes he'd worn the night before, and he would actually cook something. They would all just be. He and Tris would crowd Carys while they watched movies and the twins argued and Lou set up games for them to play.

Then residency had started and the world had been a blur and he and Carys had barely managed to see each other, much less their friends who were like family.

"Well, if it was Chelsea, I don't want to know." Adam had gone into business with Carys's aunt a long time before. "I prefer to believe it was Kala, and Coop's right. She'll love having a reason to upgrade all the security here. Maybe this time she'll even get an actual guard dog. Hey, you large cuddle bug. When was the last time you ate an intruder?"

Bud 2 ambled in, his tail wagging like this was the best day of his life. Every day was the best for Bud. He set his head on Carys's lap, and she started to pet him.

If he was a big hairy, lovable dog, maybe Carys would pet him, too. He poured some Italian sweet cream into her coffee, making sure it was the right color. A lush mocha brown. He liked his black but Carys needed some sweet, and she wouldn't want breakfast for another hour or so. She never ate right after she woke up. He hoped there were some eggs and toast. He could work with eggs and toast, especially if Tris was heading to his parents' place. Tris ate like a horse. Aidan moved to the table and placed the mug in front of Carys.

"You didn't…" Carys sighed and put her hand on his. "Thank you."

"Of course." When he sat down next to her, she didn't move away. It was how they started most mornings these days.

Wake up, shower, make coffee, go over notes, go to work, rinse, and repeat.

"So your parents never told you how they met?" Adam asked.

Carys took a sip and then sat the mug down. "Of course they did.

Dad was investigating Mom's boss, and he saved her from him.'"

It was a way easier story than his parents'. "My dad was also investigating Mom's boss, but he kind of got close to her so he could get intel. When he finally told her, Mom had some problems with it."

Adam grinned. "I remember it well. Your mom was pissed. She walked right out of the privacy room at the club we were at wearing very little, according to Ian."

"I do not need to know that part," Aidan insisted. He knew they'd met in London during an op. In his logical brain he knew it likely meant they'd spent some time at the BDSM club called The Garden, but his "they're my parents" brain skimmed over some pieces of knowledge.

"Well, your dad was honest with you. Sean is not telling Carys the whole story." Adam sat back.

Bri grabbed a coffee. "Have you never read Mom's book about it? *The Spy Who Left Me.* There's a movie and everything."

Carys frowned. "Of course I have, but Aunt Serena added drama. I know it's loosely based on what happened, but it is fiction. She had to add some stuff in. It's not like my dad lied to my mom and slept with her so he could get…"

Carys stopped, her brain seemingly working through some not-great scenarios. She stared at Adam.

They might need some whiskey. "Do you want me to make it Irish for you?"

"But in the movie the character who was like you…also liked my mom," Carys said carefully to Adam.

It could be so rough to realize your parents had these whole lives before they were moms and dads. Lives where they did dumb shit and made bad choices. Like how his dad had slept with half of Dallas before he married Mom. His parents talked a lot, and the older generations' relationships had been messy.

Kind of like they'd been young once, too, and somehow survived it.

Adam sighed with a shit-eating grin on his face. "Oh, your mom was hot. I can discuss your mom's hotness because Serena agrees with me. Grace Hawthorne was a goddess on the club floor. Yeah, I totally tried to hit that. Almost wrecked my friendship with your dad over her."

He got up and went for the whiskey.

"But it's fiction. Aunt Serena writes fiction," Carys insisted. "Like there's this scene in a pool... I mean the pool scene didn't happen in real life. It couldn't have. My mom wouldn't... She wouldn't swim without her bathing suit."

Like Carys didn't? It was kind of hypocritical, but he wasn't about to point it out to her. He'd already slept on the floor one night. He had hopes the club might work out for him tonight.

He gave her a nice splash of the good stuff. He would buy the twins another bottle. He could use a little, too. "Drink up, baby."

"Are you talking about the whole *all characters in this story are fictional and bear no resemblance to real life and events* legal thing in front of every book?" Adam seemed to be having a great time. "It's meaningless. Sure, Serena adds some stuff for drama, but sometimes she doesn't need to. Your parents gave her the good shit."

"We're drinking this early?" Kenzie bounced into the room, dressed for a workout. "Hey, Uncle Adam. Did you really bust through sis's security system? Because she's already paranoid enough as it is. She's talking lasers now. Only the idea that the possum who beds down in the garden sometimes might get cut in half is stopping her." She looked at Carys, her eyes widening. "Oh, no. What did Tristan do now?"

He reached out and put her hands around the mug. "Wasn't Tristan. She just found out Aunt Serena pretty accurately depicted her parents' love story in a romance novel."

"And a movie," Brianna said with a grin. "I always knew. I totally skip *The Doms with the Golden Whips* when I read Mom's backlist."

"Oh, I've read my mom and dad's book. I love the part where Dad's the biggest asshole and then Mom tells him she's spent five years plugging her own asshole to keep herself ready for him. I mean at first I kind of wanted to vomit, but then I thought it was beautiful, you know," Kenzie said. "I'm pretty sure it happened because Dad talks about it. My childhood was weird. Is she freaked out because her dad offered her mom up to you and Uncle Jake when he thought she was in league with the bad guys?"

"What?" Carys sounded a bit desperate.

He poured some more.

"Oh, I thought she read it." Kenzie gave her a tremulous smile. "Hey, we've all had this moment when we find out our parents are like total freaks. I'm serious about my mom and the butt plug. It bothered me at first, but then I decided I want to find a man who makes me want to plug my own asshole for five years just so I can be ready to have filthy sex with him." She sniffled. "I thought I met him. Then he turned out to be a jerk who tried to kill Lou. I hate him."

"Your father will be relieved to hear it," Adam said, glancing down at his phone. He stood and slid it back into his pocket. "I heard he was Canadian. You must be trying to rebel, Kenz. You have to know your sister took the only spot for a foreign national. You'll have to find an American guy now. Bri, Dad's got the package. It's time to go."

Bri swallowed the rest of her coffee in one go. "Awesome."

"Hey, brother." Daisy strode in. "Good to see you're up." She frowned when she took in Carys. "What did you do to her?"

Aidan put an arm around his sister, shaking his head. "She recently found out her parents are human."

Daisy nodded, sympathy in her gaze. "Oh, when I found out about my dad... His ho phase is still legendary, apparently."

"I don't think we should call it that," Aidan said with a shake of his head, then his jaw dropped because Adam wasn't the only Dean-Miles dad here. Jacob Dean stood in the living room, and Tristan was splayed across his big shoulder.

"Hey, come on," Jake huffed. "He's heavy."

Brianna gasped. "Dad. You said you were going to talk to him."

Daisy shook her head. "He was not reasonable. And you know I don't think he was getting good sleep when we snuck in his room. A nap could help him out. TJ swears by tranqs."

TJ looked up from where he was sitting in the living room, looking at his phone. He gave them all a thumbs-up. "It's really restful."

Cooper walked back in, frowning. "Now we've got a fight club scheduled. Thanks a lot, Uncle Adam. Chocolate croissants did not work. I mean she totally took them but then kicked me out because I've got balls. At least that's how she explained the problem. I was going to eat one of those. Dude, is Tristan dead?"

Jake readjusted his son. "Nah. Just sleeping until I can get him back home."

Aidan was so happy his father had a bad back. "I know it might not be my place, but he was my partner for a long time, and I should tell you he's going to see this as an attack on his bodily autonomy. And his pride. Also, can we talk about how dangerous it can be to shoot up our loved ones with drugs when we have no idea how they're going to react?"

"Fuck his pride," Carys said, obviously forgetting her whole Hippocratic Oath thing. "You go, Uncles. And I think fight club sounds perfect. I haven't hit anything in a long time." Her fists clenched. "Yeah, some sparring might be exactly what I need."

He didn't like the sound of that. Especially since he knew who she would be sparring with. "Maybe you should start slow, baby."

Cooper shook his head. "Nope. We don't fuck with female fight club unless we want to get taken down by female fight club. You need to understand if you get involved you might be perfectly fine around Kala. Because they will take your balls."

Adam gave them all a salute. "I wish you well. We'll have Tristan back this afternoon. Dais, you want to join us? We've got eggs Benedict."

"Thanks, but I want to watch fight club," Daisy admitted. "It's always super fun."

The Dean-Miles clan strode off with their son/victim… He wasn't sure what he thought of Tris's kidnapping. The best friend part of him knew it could go poorly. The other best friend part of him said fuck it, Tris deserved it.

Carys downed her coffee/whiskey in one go and had a look in her eyes she got when she was going to do something dumb. Usually because she was too stressed to be reasonable. Like the time she gave a debate speech in front of the whole school about how coaches shouldn't teach history because they neither understood it nor understood that young women didn't want to be sexualized in class.

Though it had gotten the asshole fired.

The thing was when his baby had enough, she kind of exploded, and he might be dealing with two and a half years' worth of suppressed rage.

Thank god he was well versed in trauma. He thought he might face a lot of it today.

"I'm going to take a shower. Tell Kala I'm ready whenever she is."

"Oh, not a good idea." Kenzie had been watching the whole scene from her place at the bar, sipping her coffee while the show played out. "Maybe you should start with like Lou. Or Dais. She's been taking self-defense."

"I just got my nails done," his sister said. "I'm strictly audience today. The only pounding I intend to take is from Nate tonight. I'm excited about the play party. I thought we were going to skip the whole weekend because of the wedding thing."

"I did not need to hear that, Dais." There was a lot of info he didn't need to know floating around today.

"No, I can handle Kala," Carys said, stretching one arm over her chest and then the other. "Do we have any protein bars? I'll eat it after I shower. I can handle this. I can."

She walked off.

Aidan started after her.

Cooper put a hand on his shoulder. "She needs some time. This is woman's work, man. We should make breakfast and pray they don't take it out on us."

"I could eat," TJ said.

Aidan sighed. It was going to be a long day.

* * * *

Tristan came awake in a crazy, groggy state, the world hazy around him.

What was wrong with his arms? He couldn't move them. His whole body felt...tight.

What the hell had happened? Had he been kidnapped? Was this it? Someone had finally found him, and he would be tortured until he had to admit he didn't know who the bombmaker was and they killed him because he was fucking useless. He hadn't been able to solve the problem, and it cost him everything.

"He's waking up," a familiar voice said. "You were right. I thought he would be out longer."

"Yeah, I know Big Tag. Aidan thinks Tris has never taken a tranq dart before. Big Tag thinks shooting his employees with tranqs is training," another voice said. Just as familiar.

Was he dreaming? He groaned as he felt a feminine hand on his face. Somehow he knew it was feminine. But not Carys. Carys might never fucking touch him again.

"Sweetie?" Was his mom here? "Are you all right? You should know I was against the whole use of the tranquilizer. I thought they could just, like, tie you up or something. Your dad's good at that, as you're about to find out. Don't struggle too much."

"Mom?" He managed to get his eyes open.

Was he home?

Why was the rest of his body not working? He managed to focus. His mom was kneeling beside him, concern in her eyes. "Are you feeling okay?"

He seemed to be in the dining room in the house he'd grown up in. His parents had a beautiful home in North Dallas in a wealthy neighborhood where the lots were big enough for a pool and a guesthouse his sister had been living in up until recently. Every inch of this house was coated in memories.

It was probably why he hadn't been home in years. Everything would remind him of what he'd lost.

"Could someone tell me what's happening?" Tristan asked. "The last thing I remember I was having the weirdest conversation with Daisy. Also, am I shrink-wrapped to a chair?"

It's what it felt like. He legit couldn't move his arms or legs. He was pretty sure his feet moved, though, and he could turn his neck. It was how he knew his dads were sitting across from him, both enjoying what looked to be an excellent brunch.

"It's more like plastic wrap." His sister was here, too. Good. He wanted an audience for this humiliation. "The last time I went camping with the dads they were trying out the whole plastic wrap as a hammock thing. They shouldn't be allowed on TikTok. It gives them ideas."

"Not where I got this one," his papa said with a wink his mom's way.

Adam Miles. Papa. The one who hadn't shot him with a tranquilizer dart but had almost certainly been involved in the planning. Because his papa and his dad were always in step. They didn't miscommunicate or get awkward around each other. They always took care of his mom.

They were everything he wanted him and Aidan to be. Aidan measured up. Aidan did everything he'd promised. Tristan had been the one to fail.

"Okay, Carys already had to face some terrible truths about her parents. I think it's enough revelations for the day," his sister said and gave him a brilliant smile. "I think they're talking about Mom's sudden interest in mummification play."

"It was for research, but I found it oddly soothing." His mom eased into the chair beside him. "It's good to know there are boundaries to be pushed after all these years."

"You're still the most open-minded woman I know," his dad said with a wink as he picked up a piece of bacon. "And as usual your crazy research came in handy because I think Tris would be able to bust out of some zip ties. Probably even handcuffs. Big Tag would make sure."

"You know what Big Tag wasn't prepared for?" Papa asked.

"Some nutjob wrapping my unconscious body in what has to be forty-two pounds of plastic wrap?" Tris asked.

His dad nodded, obviously proud of himself. "Exactly."

He should have known they would pull something like this. Though he'd expected them to show up at the house he shared with Coop. He looked to his sister. "You tell them where I was?"

"No," Brianna said with a frown. "But if I had, I wouldn't feel bad about it. You know you do have a tracker thingee."

"Uh, that's classified." What the hell was happening? "Did my boss let you track me?"

Papa sat back, gesturing around. "Has everyone forgotten who the hell I am? I don't need Big Tag to give me a damn invite."

"You hacked the Agency?"

"Like it's hard." Papa sighed. "I was hacking military and government bases long before you were a thought, child. Look, Tris, we've been patient with you."

"Adam," his mom began. "Remember what we talked about."

"Your mother thinks we should handle you with delicacy," Dad explained. "She's worried we'll harm your tender feelings. Personally, I think you're way tougher than she's giving you credit for. After all, you've had absolutely no thought for her feelings for a couple of years."

"Do you have any idea how many times you've made your mother cry?" Papa leaned forward.

Tristan's gut twisted. "I didn't mean to. I've been working. I'm sorry if my job doesn't come with normal hours. It's not like I haven't checked in."

"You've sent emails and called occasionally," Dad pointed out.

His mom was sniffling, using her napkin to dab at her eyes.

It was everything he'd tried to avoid, and in the moment he cursed Big Tag for not being paranoid enough to foresee a time when one of his operatives would find themselves wrapped in plastic. It was quite well done. He couldn't get any traction. His fingers were against his thighs, and he couldn't use them to start making a dent in the wrappings.

Soothing his ass.

How many women was he going to make cry? His mom. Probably his sister. Definitely his Carys.

"I did what I could do. I'm mostly in Europe or Virginia."

"Only because you want to be." Papa took a sip of his coffee.

Coffee smelled good. Not that he could drink some.

How did Carys take her coffee now? She used to love some sweet cream in it. Had she become a hardcore addict like Aidan was? Had long nights at the hospital changed her habits?

"I don't." He was going to be as honest with his parents as he could be. The truth was it was time. "You can let me out. I won't leave."

"Sure you won't." Dad passed Papa the French toast.

It looked tasty. His papa was actually an excellent cook. "I won't. And I'm kind of hungry."

"Are you?" Papa asked. "You know what I've been hungry for?"

Papa was also the one who would draw this out with sarcasm. Dad would be satisfied he'd gotten Tris here, but Papa would want a pound of flesh. "I'm sure it's information about what the hell your son thinks he's doing."

"I really would like to know, son," Papa agreed.

"You don't know what it's like to be on the outside," Brianna said quietly.

What was his sister thinking? "Oh, I don't? I assure you I've been on the outside of the most important relationship of my life for years."

Brianna's eyes narrowed. "Oh, won't anyone think about how hard this has been on Tristan? Poor Tris. They shut him out. Except they didn't. They begged you to come home. Like we begged you. You should know I'm the one who voted against this plan because I think it's futile. You don't have any interest in your family. You've moved on."

What the hell was he doing? He was getting defensive when he was the one who'd offended. "That's not true."

"You've missed every event in the last few years," Bri accused. "Travis had a kid. You weren't even around to make fun of him or to welcome Colton into the family. Papa had surgery and you weren't here."

"What?"

Papa waved a hand. "It was my gallbladder. I don't even notice it's gone. It wasn't a big deal."

"It felt like a big deal," his mother said.

His papa had surgery and he hadn't even known? Why hadn't anyone told him? "No one said anything."

"I didn't tell anyone because it was a minor surgery, and I'm fine now. I was back in the office a couple of days later."

What he wasn't saying was why he'd kept it quiet. He wouldn't have done it out of vanity. Or because he didn't want anyone to make a fuss. Papa quite liked a fuss. "You knew Big Tag would force me to come home."

"I knew he would try, and at the time I didn't want the answer to the question of how hard you would fight him," Papa replied. "I didn't want to know if you would care or not. I'm afraid I've been avoiding some truths, too, and that's on me."

What had his family been through?

He'd gotten so lost. He'd thought what he was doing was important, and then it was dangerous. He'd thought he was sparing them pain, but he'd caused them more.

"I would have come home, Papa." Was he speaking the truth? "I don't know. It would have depended, but you should know I care. I love you. I'm just... I can't talk about it because it's classified, but it's a complicated case."

"Yes," Dad said. "Dealing with international arms dealers is complex. It's even rougher when you're trying to pose as one to connect some very nasty dots. Do you have any idea where to look for the bombmaker? You didn't find any intel on his system when you tracked him down?"

Tris felt his jaw drop and knew exactly where to look. "Papa, you can't hack into the fucking Agency that way. Do you know what they could do to you?"

There was the sound of the doorbell chiming. Dad glanced at his phone and put his napkin on the table. "There he is."

"What do you think they're going to do to me?" Papa asked as Dad walked down the hallway.

"Tris, you can't expect us to sit back and let you ruin your life," his mom said, tears in her eyes. "You are going to lose them. I know somewhere in your head you're justifying this behavior by saying you're protecting them, but it won't matter in the end."

"I was trying to protect all of you." What the hell had they done? "Do you think they can't ruin Mom's career if they want to?"

"Why would they want to?" Bri asked. "We have a lot of friends in the intelligence world. You're pretending we're on our own. You know the twins have made it plain if we need something, we should come to them. They protect all of us and they don't have to shove us away."

His sister understood nothing. "They aren't in the position I'm in."

"The position you put yourself in," Papa corrected.

"We don't know that, Adam," his mother said. She had a cup of coffee in front of her but her plate was empty. And not because she'd finished. "You promised you would go easy on him. We don't know what he's been through."

"I promised I would do whatever it took to get our son back," his father replied, and there was a coldness in his tone.

Brianna's jaw had tightened, and Tristan realized this was an argument they'd had more than once. Way more than once.

He was tearing his family apart. Somehow he'd thought they would simply accept that this was his work. Like the work his fathers had done. They'd been Special Forces. But it wasn't the same. His fathers had taken leave, and after they'd left the military, even when they'd done intelligence work, they hadn't iced his mom out. Adam Miles and Jacob Dean had been incredibly present fathers.

How could he ever have a family himself if this was how he handled his work?

"I don't think this is the way," his mom said tightly.

He had to fix this. "I don't know, Mom. I think wrapping me up is a pretty good wake-up call. If I promise I'm not going anywhere, could I get my arms out? I'm really hungry, and it's been forever since I had some of Papa's cinnamon rolls."

His mom looked his way with a watery smile. "Of course."

Papa didn't seem as sure.

"Papa, I promise you I'm not going to leave until you're comfortable. I do not want to cause this tension," he said. "Bri, I'll answer all the questions I can. I don't want you to think the twins will protect you more than I will."

"I never thought you wouldn't protect us. I thought you might be willing to sacrifice yourself to do it," Bri replied. "I know it sounds noble, but there are things we can't ever give up. Mom and the dads, they don't get to stop being your parents because you became a CIA operative. I don't get to stop being your sister. I don't think Carys gets to stop loving you. She can try, but I think it would be as if she stopped being who she is. Same for Aidan."

"You're in over your head, son. There is nothing weak about leaning on your family. I would understand it if you thought we weren't strong enough," Papa began.

"It's not that." He'd never wanted to admit this, but in the face of the damage his lies had done, the truth was the only way out. "I didn't want you to know how bad it had gotten. It was my pride."

His mother's tears flowed freely now. She put her hands on his cheeks. "There is no place for pride in a family. Not the way you mean it. You say the word *pride*, but it's actually ego. I'm begging you to let your love for us win this war that's going on inside you. And when it comes to Carys and Aidan, baby, if you had gone to Carys and asked if she would rather be protected or trusted and loved and a part of you, I know what she would have said. There are worse things than death, and one of them is thinking our love is worthless."

Fuck. He felt the tears slip from his eyes. No one could get to him like his mom. She was weird and quirky and comfortable with herself

151

so everyone around her was comfortable too. She was brave and kind and had never once let him down. Oh, she had a big career, and sometimes that had meant she missed a baseball game here and there, but she'd been the strong base on which his life was built. "It's not, Mom. It's absolutely the opposite."

She leaned forward and kissed his forehead. "Neither is Carys's. Baby, you will regret it the rest of your life if you don't fix this. I know it feels like you have the weight of the whole world on your shoulders. It feels like the damn fate of it all is on you, but it's not. It doesn't have to be. You have a team, and you have a family. You have a partner, and you have a woman who would be your wife right this second if you allowed her to be. Think about it. You denied her the right to be beside you while you're in the toughest fight of your life."

He'd done so much damage. "How do I fix it?"

His mother was a romance novelist. If anyone would have a game plan, it would be her.

"I'm afraid this conversation is going to have to wait, kid." Papa stood. "Zach, thanks for coming."

Tristan looked up, and Captain Zach Reed stood in the dining room beside his dad. He had a duffel slung over his shoulder and a ball cap on his head.

"I was unaware I had a choice, sir," Zach said, and then his lips curled up as he took in Tris. "Now that is something we didn't prepare for. How's the whole saran wrap thing working out for you, buddy?"

"It was a real oversight," he admitted. The fact Zach was here meant one thing. "So they've brought my papa in?"

The Agency had been trying to find a way to bring Adam Miles in for a long time. He'd said no to money, to power, to information.

It turned out Tristan was his Achilles' heel.

"I was supposed to get here tonight. Had the flight scheduled and everything. But this morning the head of our department told me to get my ass here ASAP and deal with our new consultant." Zach dropped his duffel on the floor out of the way and pulled up a chair. "I'm glad I did since apparently they have some torture techniques the Agency doesn't prep us for. You know there's a kink called mummification. You're real close to that right now. Oooo, bacon. I had to fly commercial, so I have not eaten. This looks delicious."

His mom slid back into her chair. "Please, eat up. Do you want a moment with Tristan? Brianna and I can take our plates out on the patio."

Brianna sighed, like she'd known she would get left out.

His sweet, creative sister. She'd been his partner in crime when they were kids.

"It's up to you, Tris. Your dads are cleared for pretty much everything," Zach said, reaching for the bacon. "But we both know our primary team doesn't work the way the others do. Big Tag is taking over, if you let him."

The instinct to say no was still right there, but his instincts kind of sucked. He'd thought he had to change to become The Jester. Had to go cold and be alone.

What if what he'd always needed was his team? What if it didn't matter if he fucked up because it wouldn't change the way the people who loved him felt?

He looked over at Zach. Zach didn't ever talk about his family beyond the aunt who'd raised him. As far as Tris could tell, Zach was alone. The military had become his family, and Zach was a rules guy.

Yet he was sitting there telling Tris if he wanted to bring his mom and sister into the classified briefing, he was cool with it.

Because somewhere along the way the military had been superseded by the Agency team, the experiment Zach had been tasked to oversee and take apart if he could.

He'd never tried. He'd pretty much loved them all from the beginning. He was one of them now. Zach was letting him know it was time to stop being a secretive operative. It was time to be a team player. A family member.

"Mom, you're going to want to take notes." He was sure his whole fucked-up mission would show up in one of her novels, complete with explosions and anal play. Because that was how she rolled.

A slow smile crossed his mom's face. "Really?"

He felt something lift, something heavy that had been sitting firmly on his chest. He could breathe again. Well, he would be able to if someone would cut him out of all this wrap. "Yeah, really. You know you want to. And Bri. But you have to be open and take notes, too, and Mom isn't going to ask you what you're writing. You know she's not ready."

His mom's eyes narrowed as she looked at his sister. "Maybe if she spent some time wrapped up, she would think about listening to her mother's excellent advice. You know I do have some experience as an author."

His sister stood. "I'll get us some paper and pens. We should definitely take notes for later fiction writing that will absolutely happen. Please don't mummify me."

His sister ran off, but she would be back.

"Jake, would you please let Tristan out?" His mom reached for the muffins, calm in her movement. As though she had some faith again.

He hoped he wasn't bringing them all into serious danger, but he had to trust his fathers would protect his mom and sister.

He had to protect Carys and Aidan, but he'd realized something profound. While he'd protected their lives, he'd done a number on their souls. He would have a long talk with his mom. And maybe Bri. Tonight he would start winning them back.

Right now, he would work with this part of his team. The best part. His family.

His dad used scissors to gently cut the wrap, loosening it enough that Tris could wriggle, and then he was free.

"Someone pass me the bacon before Zach eats all of it," he said, stretching.

He was suddenly hungry again.

Chapter Eight

Carys took a deep breath and tried to find the calm place she'd been taught to go to before a fight.

Though they hadn't been called fights. Matches. Kumite. It was one of the three main parts of karate, along with kata and kihon. It was sparring with and learning from another student.

She'd enjoyed her time in karate. She'd started her training with Kenzie and Kala, though they'd quickly blown past her.

"How much do you remember?" Kenzie was dressed in shorts and a tank top, showing off toned arms. Her cousins were incredibly fit. Deadly.

"Enough to know I should pay attention to my flight instinct," she admitted. It might be for the best all the way around.

Kenzie grinned. "She's not going to hurt you. Now if Uncle Adam was here…"

She'd seen Adam and Jake carry Tristan out, and for a second she'd felt a worry. Then she'd let it go. Surely he'd been through worse than being kidnapped by his family. Not that he would ever talk to her about it.

Her cousins knew far more about the man she'd loved than she would ever be allowed to know.

"I think Adam is about to discover how stubborn his kid is." She couldn't imagine whatever Adam and Jake were planning would go well. Tristan would get pissed and get his pride on and then he would find a way out, and he would have blocked off someone else who could have helped him.

He seemed determined to be alone, and she was tired of fighting him. She couldn't help but think about all the times she'd pleaded for him to come home, to talk to her, to be with them. She'd told him how lonely Aidan was without him.

Except Aidan hadn't been alone at all.

"I don't know," Kenzie said, sitting on the bench.

The Hideout had a room deep inside the club the regulars all called the fight club room. It was one of the larger spaces, with a padded floor and bleacher seats on either side. Cooper had obtained the seats from a local high school in the middle of renovations. Her uncle had looked at them and sworn they would rot away from all the adolescent angst, but it had been mold that had caused problems. Lucky for them Gabriel Lodge was incredibly interested in carpentry and had replaced the bad rows promptly.

"I think he might be coming around." Her cheeriest cousin was also overly optimistic.

Carys stretched one arm over her chest, opening up her shoulders. "Last night he promised he would answer any questions I had."

Kenzie's eye sparked with enthusiasm. "See."

"And he also told me he's going to replace me on the op with someone from the Agency."

Her nose wrinkled. "With who? It can't be Kara. We're going in as the bodyguard. Also, we have to dye our hair and go by something else because there's the slightest chance the doctor will remember us from Australia. We didn't have direct contact with him, but he could have seen us at the conference. And contacts. I hate the colored contacts."

"Uhm, isn't it going to cause trouble if he remembers you?"

Kenzie waved the worry off. "He won't because of the hair color and the eyes. Also, we know how to dress to minimize the girls, if you know what I mean."

"It's the three biggies for women operatives." Tasha sat down beside Kenzie, handing her a water bottle. "Hair, eyes, and boobs. It's what most men see and remember, though I worry Huisman pays more attention to detail than the normal man."

156

"Is this coming from Ben Parker?" Kenzie asked as though the question meant not a thing to her.

Which meant it was important. "Okay, who is Ben Parker?"

"Is he the Canadian dude who was here a few weeks ago?" Daisy sat on the bench closest to them, Devi Taggart at her side.

Devi looked preoccupied with her phone but she answered. "I think his name *was* Ben Parker. He was totally into Kenz. You remember it was the night Kala was so pissed because she couldn't play, and Uncle Ian was here in the conference room and then he walked through the dungeon with a blindfold on like he would die if he saw something."

Daisy grinned. "Cooper put a couple of spanking benches in his way, and Auntie Charlotte let him fall over one. It was funny."

"Yes, I remember the night, but I didn't catch his name," Carys said.

"He was only into me because of my boobs," Kenzie said with a frown. "Or maybe everyone is right and he's been playing me all along. All I know is I can't forgive him for the shit he pulled with Lou."

"What happened to Lou?" She seemed to have missed a lot in the last few weeks. She'd had no idea her cousin had a crush on some foreign operative. A rival, it seemed.

Things were happening so fast. Tasha had come home from Australia with a fiancé. Lou and TJ had finally gotten their shit together. Kenz had a crush. Daisy had a boyfriend.

She was the only one going backward.

"Nothing," Tasha replied. "Ben used a situation Lou was in to confirm Huisman is at the very least involved in some shady dealings. You should understand Huisman is dangerous. I know Dad gave you a briefing, but I suspect you weren't listening. I told him to hold off, but my dad powers through."

"Ben set up the situation. The situation didn't exist until Ben made it happen," Kenzie corrected. "Lou could have been killed. But I do think he's right about Huisman. You need to be careful around him, and Aidan definitely needs to be careful."

"I got the whole Huisman bad thing," she admitted. "I'm not sure Aidan believes it, but then it's not like we've talked. Though I'll be honest, I didn't get a lot out of the briefing. I was thinking about

Tristan. It was the first time I'd seen him in forever."

"Oh, hey, Car. I did not know Aidan was talking to him," Daisy said. "I swear on my feminine soul I would have told you."

There was never any doubt. Daisy was her girl. "I know, sweetie. It's okay."

"It's not okay because he's sitting over there and you're here," Daisy pointed out. "You two have barely talked. And did he really sleep on the ground?"

"Not like the ground ground," Kenzie corrected. "The inside ground. Aidan protected his love in the true Taggart male fashion."

Like her dad had protected her mom after she'd found out the whole basis of their relationship was a lie and her dad had climbed into her bed as part of an op. And into her pool. And on her boss's desk.

She wished she hadn't read the book. There should have been a trigger warning. *Read this book and you'll never look at your parents the same way again.*

It was disturbing, but when she thought past the sex stuff—if it had really happened—then her parents had gotten through some traumatic stuff. Stuff Carys would have said was a deal breaker.

Could she get through it? She wasn't even sure Tris truly wanted to get through it. She glanced over to where Aidan was sitting with Cooper. They'd shown up a couple of minutes before with her brother in tow. Lucas sat beside them, a frown on his face as he watched her.

He was going to be trouble. Her younger brother was a walking red flag. She loved him but he slept his way through whatever space he happened to occupy. Sometimes she thought her brother's out-of-control libido was the only reason her dad had pretty much just accepted the whole "my daughter's in a threesome" thing with a shrug and a sigh and yes, some whiskey. It was what her family did.

She was a bit worried her brother—who had half a foot and seventy pounds of muscle on her—was going to take it upon himself to try to deal with Tris.

And while Lucas was excellent in the kitchen, a true star on the rise in the culinary world, Tris was a trained killer who was on the irritable side right now.

Would he even show up for play night tonight? Or would his parents' interference send him right back to the airport, shutting them all out again?

"I wish you two were talking," Daisy was saying. "It's weird. Like something stable in my world isn't stable anymore. You should think about this, Car. You've never had to date."

"Dating sucks," Devi agreed.

"It's true," Kenzie said. "The dating world is filled with land mines, cousin. You never know if the beautiful man who seems so into you is only trying to get into your pants for intel."

"I don't think I have to worry about someone working me for information. I don't know anything," Carys admitted.

Kenzie shrugged. "Neither did your mom and yet…"

Tasha sent her sister a frown. "Hey, she's sensitive about the whole her parents had sex thing. Uncle Sean and Aunt Grace are way more circumspect than our parents."

Everyone was more circumspect than Ian and Charlotte Taggart. Everyone in the world.

"Oh, I understand," Daisy said with a shake of her head. "I recently learned my father was the player of choice when it came to Hooter's waitresses back in the day. Though I don't think he kept it to Hooter's. I think it was all the chicken wing places. He really liked chicken wings."

"Girl, do not bring that fight to us," Tasha said, gesturing to her sister. "Our dad was apparently Mr. Dom and did every sub at Sanctum while Mom was dead."

Kenzie nodded. "Yeah, but he was sad she was dead. He was looking for comfort. Uncle Li was just looking for chicken wings."

"Well, my parents are practically perfect." Devi sighed. "Dad died, but Mom didn't like rip through a bunch of dicks. Probably because Dad left her all kinds of knocked up. You know when you think about it, we have a real trend of dying and coming back."

Actually, they had a real trend of epic love stories. When she thought about it, all their parents had something serious to get through. She was sitting here thinking she was the only person in the world who ever felt this way, but she knew it wasn't true. She was a freaking doctor, and she listened to her patients. They all had stories. They all had heartaches.

Maybe it was time to start listening to her elders. How had they gotten through it?

Aunt Erin had lost Uncle Theo to a crazy woman who'd kidnapped him and wiped his memory. They were happy today.

Aunt Charlotte had faked her own death, and Uncle Ian had been under suspicion he'd killed her for years. They were happy today.

Apparently her dad had been a massive asshole, and her mom had found it in her heart to forgive him.

And they were happy today.

"You know Dare didn't know who I was when I slept with him," Tasha said quietly. "I lied to him because we were in the middle of an op. I knew I was in love with him and I lied. I let my team bug his room and download his laptop. I almost lost him. In some ways, I think I would have if I hadn't gotten shot and he had to face a world without me. We're together today because of his generous heart."

Kenzie sniffled.

"Nate didn't know who I was," Daisy said. "I stole a night of passion from my big Aussie bastard and he forgave me."

She knew this story well, and Daisy was embellishing. "You were after his dick, sweetie. Not his secrets. It's not the same. You didn't cause Nate a shit ton of heartache. Just a little confusion."

Daisy sniffed. "Well, that makes me sound like a novella. You know like when Aunt Serena needs a break from the big books. You don't think she'd make me a novella, do you?"

Carys snorted. "Never. It was epic."

Now she wondered if hers was epic. It had simply always been there. Aidan and Tristan had always been there, and until Tris decided to run off to the military, they hadn't had a ton of drama. She hadn't cared when some jealous girls called her a whore. Her parents had accepted them with relative ease.

Was she wilting in the face of the first real trouble they'd ever had?

Tristan had told her what he wanted, and she'd shut down. She'd gotten her feelings hurt and let him go.

"Hey, are we doing this or are you going to admit you remember nothing and promise you'll duck behind me when shit goes down?" Kala had on shorts and a sports bra, her magenta-colored hair up in a high ponytail. "Because shit is absolutely going to go down."

"Hey, Kala, you could go easier on her," Kenzie complained.

Cooper stood up. "Maybe we should talk about this first."

She rather thought she knew what her cousin was doing. Kala was poking at all her sore spots to point out her weaknesses. To show her how hard this was going to be.

Because she was soft.

She was a Taggart, too. Oh, if things had gone the way they were supposed to she would be Carys O'Donnell, and maybe the name didn't change things, but maybe it would have.

She was still Carys Taggart, and it was time to prove it.

Carys got into Kala's space. "The good news, cousin, is I can put you back together after I take you apart."

Cooper winced. "I don't think that's how this is going to go."

"Baby, why don't you spar with Lou?" Aidan had joined Cooper.

Kala's lips curled into a snarl she still managed to make look cover-model worthy. "Really? You think you can take me, doc? You've been in your ivory tower for too long. It's fucked with your reasoning skills."

"Yeah, well the Agency is the only reason you're not covered in tattoos and traveling the world in a built-out school bus," Carys shot back.

Kenzie laughed out loud, but everyone else went still as though waiting for carnage.

Lou gave her a weak smile. "I mean, she is right about the tats. You complain about it all the time. It's also the reason she's not pierced all over."

"Except in the good places," Cooper said with an entirely masculine smile. It made Carys wonder what was really going on between those two.

Kala's eyes narrowed. "Thanks, Coop. As for my sweet, naïve cousin, let's go." She frowned suddenly. "And I wouldn't build out a freaking school bus. Ewww. I would be fully tatted up in a tiny house in the middle of the forest with a small goat army. Thank you."

And then her cousin punched her. Right in the gut.

The air whooshed out of Carys's lungs, pain flaring as she tried to get enough oxygen.

"Hey." Aidan stepped in front of her. "That wasn't fucking fair."

"There's no fair where we're going," Kala replied simply. Aidan had a couple of inches on her and a lot of muscle, but her cousin wasn't afraid of him.

Because she knew damn well she could handle herself. Despite what her cousin had said, her reasoning skills were top-notch, and she knew admiring her most psychotic relative for her cool under pressure probably wasn't the healthiest thing. Kala had a lot of issues. Being sure of herself in a fight wasn't one of them.

"Hey, let's get into the locker room and let Aidan look you over." Her brother reached for her hand.

"Maybe it would be for the best," Kenzie said with a wince.

"Yeah, Carys, let the men take care of you," Kala taunted.

She'd been letting everyone take care of her for the last two and a half years. Poor Carys. Her man left her. Aidan had to take care of her all alone. The sympathy was nauseating when she thought about it.

She'd just taken it.

She wasn't taking it anymore.

They weren't playing fair? She sniffled and held a hand out to her cousin. "I get it now. Forgive me."

Kala frowned as though deeply disappointed in her. "Sure. It's okay." She reached out to shake her hand. "Like I said, I'll watch out for you."

Carys found her cousin's radial nerve and pressed her thumb down, causing Kala to gasp. She took the moment to kick her right between the legs, probably hitting whatever piercing she had in there.

The whole room went still.

"That's right, baby. You give her hell," a deep voice said.

She looked over and Tristan was standing in the doorway with Zach Reed in tow.

Kala had fallen onto the mat, and every man there took a step back.

All of them except Aidan, who was still trying to protect her. "She's going to get hurt."

"Sometimes we need to get hurt to remind us how resilient we can be," Tristan said. "I'm putting fifty on my baby. She's mean, and she knows pressure points."

She'd forgotten how much Tris loved it when she was an arrogant brat. Aidan loved her sweet side, but Tristan craved the bad girl. She hadn't been a bad girl in far too long.

Kala's legs came up, and she was suddenly on her feet again. "Nice move. It won't work again, but you're right to use my preconceived notions against me. Do it with every fucking man you meet. They will underestimate you, and then you can take them down."

Cooper moved back. "You're insane, Tris. I'll take your bet. Kala, don't kill her. Deep down you love her."

Kala looked his way. "Why the hell else would I be doing this?"

"Because you love to fight," Cooper replied.

Kala shrugged. "Truth. But I do love her, and this is absolutely for her own good. Show me what you got, cos."

Carys felt a surge of energy go through her, felt Tris watching her and Aidan's worry.

And then let it all go as Kala threw her next punch and the fight was on.

* * * *

"You could have died." Aidan put an ice pack on his previously sane girlfriend's wrist. What the hell was she thinking?

"She wasn't going to die." Tris sat across from her in the lounge where everyone had retreated for drinks and snacks after watching two women try to kill each other. "Carys, you handled yourself well out there, but you should know…"

"She took it easy on me," Carys said with a sigh and a wince as she sat back.

"Easy?" Aidan couldn't believe what he was hearing. It had been brutal. They'd gone at it for more than thirty minutes. Carys had gotten flipped and punched and held down with an elbow in her back. "There was nothing easy about what I just saw."

And there had been nothing he could do about it because every time he tried to stop it, Tris put a hand on his shoulder and made him sit back down.

She needs this, he'd said.

Needed to get punched? Needed to get put on her belly like she was some kind of wrestler?

Carys sighed. "She totally pulled her punches."

"She did, and I'm glad you saw that." Zach Reed handed her a glass. Amber liquid with one large ice cube.

Bourbon. She took it with her free hand. "She was never going to truly hurt me. She wants me to understand what happens if I get into a real fight."

Zach was six foot four and corded with lean muscle. He sat down across from Carys. "And what do you do if you get into a real fight?"

Zach had come into town to help Tris. Because they'd been working together for a long time now. Had Zach taken his place?

Fuck. He might be jealous of Zach.

"Get out of it as fast as possible and hide so Kala doesn't have to worry about me," Carys said and then knocked back the bourbon.

"Excellent." Zach gave her an approving nod. "Then you're halfway there. You have some good moves. Now the question is how prepared is Aidan?"

"I'll take care of Aidan." Tristan sat in his chair, his own bourbon in hand.

"No one needs to take care of me." Was he now considered the softest one? "I know self-defense and all the same pressure points Carys does. I'm not exactly helpless. Also, I thought we were probably going to a safe house."

"Told you I can't send you because you promised Huisman you would be his pet resident," Tris replied. "And it was recently pointed out to me that I don't get to walk away for two and a half years and come back in and start barking orders. Carys, you want to do this?"

There was a part of Aidan praying she would tell him no and he was on his fucking own.

There was a bigger part praying she didn't give up this chance. If she walked, he wasn't sure they ever came together again. If they were together, they had a shot. If she said no, it would be too easy to let time go by, to come up with excuse after excuse why to put off trying again.

"I want to go," Carys said, handing the glass Aidan's way. "I need another."

Something eased inside him. He would get his shot. He would get a chance to decide if they could work in this new world they found themselves in, the one where Tris was different but still so familiar.

And that meant starting to act like the man he wanted to be. He took the glass. She hadn't listened to a thing he'd said all day. "Not if you're going to play, you don't. You're right, baby. You're tough. From what I can tell nothing's broken and you won't even bruise. So are we playing or should I get you another drink?"

Tristan's lips curled up in a decadent smile. "You sound ready to play, partner. I think she wants it. I think her inner brat is begging for it. The fight with Kala was nothing but a warm-up."

Carys sighed, and her eyes closed as she sat back. "It won't mean anything. Not anything beyond I need a session and it would take forever to train a new top."

"Sure, tell yourself that, baby," Tris shot back.

Her eyes opened. "Just because I play with you tonight only means we're sexually compatible, and I'm lazy when it comes to finding what I need. It doesn't mean we're together."

"It's exactly what it means if we're running this op," Tris said. "You're with me through this op or this op doesn't happen."

"What?" Zach looked at Tris like this was completely new information to him.

Tristan sat back, his eyes still on Carys even though he was talking to Zach. "I've decided they're more important than taking down Huisman. If she won't let me close to her, I can't protect her. Same with Aidan."

"You can't be serious." The captain sat up straight, leaning over. "You know what's at stake. You've always known. We have reason to believe someone got files out of the Tandy Medical Group the night the Canadians raided. Huisman knew what was there. I think it was him. He has the formula for the weaponized anthrax. If he finds the right delivery system…"

"Anthrax?" Aidan took a seat beside Carys. "No one mentioned bioweapons."

Carys's eyes had opened, and she was suddenly way more interested. "Yes, this is new information. What is Tandy Medical? Is it a pharmaceutical company?"

Zach stood and looked out over the lounge, waving at someone. It was mere seconds before Tasha walked up, her hand in her fiancé's. Dare Nash had come in during the middle of the sparring match, sitting beside Tasha and wincing with the rest of them as the cousins had seemingly tried to take each other out.

He was being overly dramatic. When he looked at Carys he could see she wasn't truly injured.

And she'd been kind of hot as she'd taken on a woman most men

165

in the group would be wary of sparring with.

"Hey, Zach. We didn't think you would join us until we head to Canada," Tasha said.

Dare held out a hand, shaking Zach's. "Good to see you again."

Zach offered them the cozy love seat, switching to a padded table for himself. He looked way too big, but it held. "You should know we've got a contractor on this op."

Tasha sat back. "Does his name rhyme with Shadam Giles?"

"Yep." Tristan snorted slightly but he smiled, a genuine smile and not the fuck-the-world expression he'd seen on his best friend's face so often in the last few years. "My father called in some favors. He's pretty much done with me…how did he put it…fucking up my whole world, and he's sick of waiting to bury me. Uncle Ian's right. Papa is overly dramatic. Anyway, he's coming in, and we should expect the olds to be super feisty. You know how they like to go at each other."

"What does Adam joining the team have to do with bioweapons?" Aidan asked. Having Adam on the team meant someone might have half a chance of reining in Tris's reckless streak.

He wasn't sure what had happened with Tris's parents, but Tris seemed more like Tris than he had in years.

Tasha's brows rose in obvious surprise. "Wow. We're doing the whole talk about classified intel around Zach now? I thought we usually left him out of those fun chats so he has plausible deniability."

Zach shrugged. "I'm going with the Taggart flow. If we're bringing in civilians, they deserve to know what's at stake and in plain terms. Telling them Huisman is probably a supervillain isn't going to cut it, and if they have doubts, it could cost them their lives. So I thought Dare would take this one. They asked about Tandy."

Dare sighed, a weary sound. "Tandy Medical was part of my father's company. The Nash Investment Group used to fund medical research, and we owned stakes in a bunch of research companies. They did cutting-edge stuff."

"Like the Huisman Foundation," Aidan pointed out.

"Yes, though Huisman is bigger than we ever were, and I would say we were pretty big," Dare replied. "Tandy Medical was doing research into emerging viruses and bacteria. Funguses sound funny, but they pose a real threat to humanity as we move through climate change. Tandy was supposed to research ways to combat those threats."

One of the worst things a surgeon had to worry about was infection. A surgeon could do miraculous work, and it could all fall apart because of a tiny bit of bacteria. Staphylococcus, streptococcus, pseudomonas were simply the most common. There were always new threats to deal with.

They didn't have to go looking for them or figure out a way to make one do its deadly work better.

Of course he could come up with a couple of reasons… "So they were planning on selling the research?"

"I'm sure my father would have at some point," Dare agreed. "He's in prison right now awaiting trial. He wasn't a good man. Money was my father's god, and he didn't care how he got it."

"This is one of the things we learned while we were in Sydney. Tandy was potentially developing a stronger version of anthrax," Tasha explained. "A stronger version, one that could be dropped on a large population for maximum effect."

"Why would anyone want to make anthrax more deadly?" Carys asked. "I don't mean to sound naïve, but I'm expected to believe a world-famous doctor, who's known for his philanthropy, is behind a plot to murder hundreds of people?"

"Oh, if my intel is correct, we're talking thousands. Maybe hundreds of thousands," Tris said quietly. "Murder, though, isn't the principal motive. What we believe is happening is disruption. We believe Huisman is the head of a connected network of groups called Disrupt."

"I've heard of them, but they're not some terrorist group." Aidan was confused. "Disrupt America is about dismantling systems that no longer work in the modern age. They press for things like health care reform."

"Our hospital recently got a grant from DA to buy high-tech crash carts built specifically for maternity patients." Carys leaned forward. "I wrote the proposal myself. Texas has one of the First World's worst maternity outcomes. Disrupt is trying to help us change that."

"The surface organization does excellent work," Tris explained. "But we believe there's a smaller, more elite group within the group."

"Like a star chamber or an illuminati society," Zach continued. "They use all the resources the public face has to push their own agenda. Which is chaos. We have reason to believe the inner membership has targeted a couple of large cities in Southeast Asia as test runs. Especially looking to disrupt trade routes."

"Canadian intelligence took out the Tandy Group and found the research Huisman told us would be there." Tris sat back. "But I looked into their systems, and I found a hack roughly two hours before the raid. They pulled down most of the research files, including the anthrax project. It took me a while, but I managed to trace the hack back to Montreal, where the Huisman Foundation now resides."

"And the arms dealer who kidnapped TJ verified it was Huisman he was working with," Tasha agreed.

Aidan had been the one to check TJ out after he'd come home from his adventures with a German cattle prod. He'd been physically all right, but it proved how dangerous the job was.

Tristan sighed and took a sip of the water he'd selected over beer. "So that's what we're working with. Oddly, no one is listening to the criminal over the doctor. Not that we've pushed it. For now we're in this odd place with Huisman. He knows we're a CIA team investigating things that happen around him. How much more he knows is a mystery."

"It's one of the things we think you can help us figure out." Zach set his glass on the table next to Tristan.

Tasha threaded her fingers through her fiancé's. "If we're right and Huisman is the one behind the attempt on your life, then we have to worry he'll try it again."

Zach's head shook. "We can't be sure Aidan and Carys were the target. I would say it's unlikely. If I were to bet on it, the attack was about TJ. There's a faction of the illegal arms world that believes TJ is connected to The Jester."

"Or someone's finally figured out I took over the role, and this is about me," Tristan concluded. "Either way, we're going in knowing this is a dangerous situation. I don't think Huisman is going to try anything while we're in Montreal. We're too close to his home base, and if the man values anything in the world, it's the Huisman Foundation. He won't allow any scandal to taint it."

"Or he's good at pretending and he doesn't care about anything and we're walking into a trap." She sighed and sat up, pulling the ice pack off her wrist. "Either way, I need a session. I get the feeling the rest of the week is going to be a whole lot of my cousins trying to kill me so they can save me. Not really looking forward to it."

How did he go from worried everyone he loved was going to die to horny as hell in the space of a couple of seconds? "You should go and get dressed."

She stood and frowned down at him. "So you can talk to Tris behind my back?"

"Yes." They needed to game-plan. "We always talk about play sessions." He should be honest with her. "Even when he's not here. You should know most of the time we did some hardcore kink play it was because he talked me into it."

A brow rose over Carys's eyes. "You talked to him about our sex life?"

Since he'd first known what sex was. "It's always been our sex life. The three of us. It's hard to break habits."

"It's not a habit. It's who we are," Tris argued.

Zach stood up. "And this is turning into a therapy session. I think I'll play as long as I'm here. You three get your shit together."

"I'll see you in the locker room," Tasha said as she and Dare joined Zach. "We can talk more if you want."

Carys waited until they were gone. The lounge was starting to empty out as everyone began getting ready for the evening. She turned to Tristan. "What do you mean I'm with you until the op is over? You genuinely expect me to sleep with you while we're working? I understand I have to keep up appearances with Aidan, but you're supposed to be his bodyguard."

"And I assure you I know how to sneak into your bed, baby. I've slipped through Sean Taggart's excellent security system more times than I can count. It wasn't Aidan who hacked the system and shut off the sensors to your bedroom window and looped the cameras." Tris crossed one leg over the other, looking like a decadent brat prince. "If getting into your silky panties is the reward, I can make anything happen."

Sometimes he had to translate for Tristan. "I think what he's trying to say is, it's inevitable so let's not play games. You honestly think you're going to be in a high-pressure situation and not end up in bed with us? Tell me you're not already rationalizing how this evening's going to go."

"I don't know what you're talking about." Carys's expression had gone blank.

He could speak Carys, too. "You don't? Let's see if I get this right. That beautiful brain of yours is arguing with your wounded heart. And I understand, baby. I truly do. We hurt you, but your logical mind is wondering if it's worth it to lose everything. You're wondering if you can forgive me. Maybe Tris can be the sacrifice you make so no one thinks you're a doormat. No one thinks that, but this is where your pride comes in."

Tristan sighed. "I got a lecture on pride already today. I was told in no uncertain circumstances that pride has no place in a relationship. You know when you think about it, she's a little like me."

Carys's eyes flared.

"Don't help me out," Aidan complained. "Like I said, your head is at war with your heart. Your heart reminds you how much you have invested in this relationship and prays there might still be a way to save it all. The problem is you've spent years and years being taught to shut down your emotional side so you can do your job."

"So you think I'll choose you and sacrifice him. Then why let him in our bed?" Carys asked as though the question didn't matter.

He'd thought about this for freaking years. "Because we don't work without him, and you know it. There's a reason we didn't follow through with the first wedding. There's a reason we've waited for him. He was an asshole, but he's our asshole, and without him we're floating through. Hell, the only reason we were getting married this time around was his insistence."

"You didn't want to marry me?" Carys asked, her voice tremulous.

"Of course I did and I do, but baby, we need him. I worry if we're alone, we drift apart. Like we've been doing for a while now," Aidan said. "I love you, but you need more than me. You need him, too. And that's what he's trying to show you. He's not trying to steal some sex before it's all over. He's desperately attempting to prove to you we can still work."

"I don't think we can. I don't think us sleeping and playing together for a couple of days is going to fix our problems," she argued.

"But you'll do it because while your brain and heart are at war, your pussy is going to sneak in and take what it wants." This was what he hadn't done in forever. He hadn't challenged her. They'd fallen into ruts, neglecting their bodily needs while they both tried to pretend they didn't miss Tristan. He'd hidden his worry from her and she'd done the same, both afraid to upset the other. "Your pussy hasn't had what it really needs in a long time. Two men worshipping you, pushing all your boundaries. Showing you that while your cousins are badasses, they're not the ones who are so fucking incredible they require two men to satisfy them. Tell me you're not thinking you can sleep with Tris and walk away and get some revenge."

"Of course she is," Tris said, his eyes steady on her.

"What if I decide I don't need either one of you?" Carys asked.

"Then you lose nothing." It wouldn't happen. They could prove it to her. He was still pissed at Tristan, but he was self-aware enough to know he didn't want to break with him.

"And if he leaves again?" Carys sounded more vulnerable now.

This was the heart of the matter.

Tristan was quiet.

Aidan moved into her space. "Then I will figure it out. I'll figure out how to be enough for you."

Carys's hand came up. "It's not…"

He shook his head, hand coming up to keep hers against his cheek. "No apologies. This is who we are, but we have to figure it out. I want to give it one more try, but if he fucks up again, I'm not willing to give up on us. I'll find a way."

Carys's eyes closed briefly but when she opened them again her expression softened and she went on her toes to press her lips against his. "I needed to hear that. Thank you. And you know my pussy is going to win this war, so I should go and get dressed. I don't know how this is going to work, but I will give you this time. Even if it means I have to give it to him, too."

"I'll take it," Tristan agreed. "Feel free to punish me as much as you like in the vanilla world, but understand on the dungeon floor, you're my sub and I'll deal with you as I see fit, brat."

Carys kissed Aidan again and walked away, moving toward the

stairs leading to the locker rooms.

"I was hoping getting her ass kicked would put her in a better mood," Tristan said with a long sigh. "I suppose I have a lot of work to do, but at least she's not forcing the issue for now."

"She'll want to know what your plans are at some point." Aidan took the seat across from Tristan. "I know I'll want them. If you're planning on going back to working for months at a time with no word, we should think about ending it here and now."

"And if I decide I'll only work with Uncle Ian's team? Would you be satisfied with that outcome? The twins are never gone for more than a week or two. I could resign my military post and take a job with my fathers as cover," Tristan offered.

"I thought you were trying to avoid working at MDWM."

"Maybe it wouldn't be so bad. Someone's going to have to run it someday, and it's not going to be my sister," Tris admitted. "I don't know. I only know I have to find a way to fix this thing with her. With you. I hurt you, too."

"Are you sure? You've made new friends." Aidan had been thinking about this for days. "You know it would be more normal for you to drift away. Not many people are lifelong friends. Things change. Circumstances change. You have more in common with Zach now than you do me."

Tristan seemed to consider what to say next. "We're not friends, Aidan. We're not lovers, either, but I think it's closer to that than some bro friendship where we watch sports and bitch about our girlfriends. That's never been what we have. We don't like to talk about it, but we love each other, too. We're probably never going to get physical, but we're still more than friends. Not really brothers. Something more, and we always have been. Zach is a friend. That's all. I'm not looking to replace you. There is no replacement for you. If you leave, that spot you fill inside me will be empty forever."

Aidan stared for a moment, shocked. "I thought we didn't talk about this."

Tristan shrugged. "You get shot at as much as I've been lately, your masculine ego suddenly doesn't seem so fragile. I don't care if people think we're fucking each other. Honestly, if we were wired that way, I would in a heartbeat. If Carys thinks it would be sexy, I say we go for it."

It had always been the only real awkwardness between them. They didn't talk sex unless it was about Carys. They pretended there wasn't a spark between them. It never had to go anywhere. It could be something they contained. Or something they decided to explore. "I don't care what anyone thinks either."

A brow rose over Tristan's eyes. "And yet when I call you my sub…"

Aidan pointed his partner's way. "You've never called me that before, asshole. It was a shock. I'm sorry I fought back a little when you walked back in after years and tried to take control. It's a dick move."

"But you *are* my sub," Tristan insisted. "And you know it deep down. We fell into our positions naturally when we were kids, and they hold up to this day whether we publicly acknowledge them or not. Which is precisely why it was such a dick move to leave you both on your own. I haven't said this plainly enough, A. I'm sorry. I thought I was protecting you but what I was doing was marginalizing you. I was treating you and Carys like possessions I wanted to protect, not like partners I trust and love and need."

It was a lot of emotional growth from where he'd been the night before. "What did your dad do to you?"

Tristan's lips curled up in genuine amusement. "Trapped me in plastic wrap. It was a whole thing. Not earth friendly when you think about it though. But, more importantly, my family made it clear I hurt them more by pulling away than I would have bringing them into my problems. It's the same for the two most important people in my life. I am sorry."

The words were a balm to his wounds. "All right. I meant what I said though. If you fuck up again, I have to pick her."

Tristan stood and reached out a hand. "I know. And I won't. I promise. We get through this and I'm out. I'll hand it all over to someone else and I'll come home."

It was everything Aidan wanted. He reached for Tris's hand and pulled him in for a hug. "We have to work on her. She's got a wall up."

Tris wrapped his arms around him. "The good news is I know how to take a wall down."

Aidan hoped he did.

Chapter Nine

Carys stepped out of the locker room, expecting Aidan to be standing there. He seemed to always know when she was ready. Or perhaps he simply changed quickly and waited for her so she never walked around the dungeon alone.

They'd spent no time in this club as a threesome. Aidan had been her only Master here. The Hideout had started in the house Tristan's parents had bought for him after college. It had housed Cooper and Aidan as well. They'd taken the large garage to make a play space for them.

Of course her first club had been Julian Lodge's fabulous, luxurious place. The three of them had gone through training there. It was beautiful, but she'd always preferred The Hideout.

Because it was theirs. Because she'd helped install the lockers in the locker rooms and had helped design the lounge. The founding members hadn't simply put precious cash up. They had sweat equity in this place. It wasn't perfect, but it reflected where they were in their lives.

"Are you sure you know what you're doing?" a deep voice asked.

Of course it was also weird because her brother was here. A lot. Lucas was deeply invested in the lifestyle. Carys used it for stress relief and as a way to connect with her men, but sometimes she thought D/s was the only thing Lucas took seriously besides his career. Sex for Lucas was casual, but dominance was a serious thing.

She was glad she'd chosen a fairly modest corset and miniskirt. Modest for the club. Her brother wore a set of black leathers that proved there was one other thing Lucas Taggart was invested in. Working out. "Do I know what I'm doing when it comes to taking down a possibly evil doctor? Or do I know what I'm doing playing with Tristan and Aidan tonight?"

She kind of thought the answer was the same to both questions. A big old resounding no.

"The twins will take care of you." Lucas looked like a younger version of their father. While she'd gotten their mom's red hair, Lucas's was a sandy blond and was always the tiniest bit overgrown. "Uncle Ian's going to be there. I'm not worried about it. They swear your part is minor, and Kala will be with you all the time."

"Yeah, she's promised we'll have so much fun." She still had some aches and pains from her cousin's version of fun.

Lucas frowned, getting to his point. "But I want to know why you're giving Tristan a second chance. He's broken your heart over and over again. You should know I'm going to talk to David and Kyle about this."

Their older brothers. David and Kyle were from their mom's first marriage, but the half-brother status meant nothing. They were a family, and she knew how they would react. David would say she's an adult and they should support her choices. Kyle would get pissed off and go all "protect the women," and then his kickass wife would kick his ass and get him on the "Carys is an adult" bandwagon. So realistically she was only dealing with the youngest of her brothers. "I don't know I am. Giving him a second chance. I told Tristan plainly this doesn't mean anything."

"You're going to fuck him. I would say it means something."

She felt her brows rise. "I'm surprised you would say sex has meaning at all. Did it have meaning when you took home those two friends of Devi's who were visiting? How about the night after those two when you went home with the new server? Does Dad know how many decent servers he's lost because you can't keep your dick in your pants?"

Her brother flushed. "It's diff…"

She pointed his way. "You better think before you finish that sentence. You want to tell me it's different because I'm a woman? Is it different for all the women you go through? Or are they different from me? Do you have, maybe, a name you like to call them to differentiate from the women like me?"

A whistle came from her left and there was Tristan, leaning against the wall looking fucking delicious in his leathers. He was six foot three inches of gloriously decadent male, and there was something primal about him. Tris tended to dress well in his daily life, to look like he could be walking a runway in Milan, every inch the modern, stylish man. But in leathers, he was stripped down to the predator he hid under expensive shirts and tailored trousers.

Her brain and her heart were definitely quieter than her pussy in this moment. Aidan was right. Her lust had taken over, and she wasn't thinking about anything but how good it would feel to be with them tonight.

"You do not want to poke that particular beast, Lucas," Tristan said, winking her way. "I would definitely not finish the sentence."

Her brother frowned, obviously not as impressed with Tris's smoldering sensuality as she was. "I'm trying to take care of my sister. She hasn't exactly dated a lot. She doesn't have the same experience. And you know I'm always open and honest about what I'm looking for. I never lead anyone on. Any woman I spend time with knows I'm not looking for anything long term. You lied to my sister."

Tristan straightened up, getting serious. "I did. I thought I was doing the right thing at the time, but I have to face the fact that I hurt her. I'll do whatever it takes to get her back. Even if it means leaving my job."

News to her. News she wasn't sure she believed. After all, the source had proven himself unreliable. "You're never leaving the Agency."

"I'm leaving the military," Tris said, going sincere. "I'll only be working for Uncle Ian's team, so my schedule will look a lot like the twins' does. I'll spend a good deal of time here in Dallas. If it's not enough, then I will quit everything and I'll work for my father."

Lucas studied him for a moment. "You're going to take care of her? Because she hasn't been the same since you left. Aidan loves her, but he can't top her the way you do. She needs a strong top or she buries herself in work. Aidan needs one, too. They've always needed you to balance them, and you fucking left them alone."

"Lucas," she began, surprised her brother had seen those truths about her. She'd thought she kept those hidden.

Tristan held up a hand. "No, he's right, and it's nothing I haven't already been faced with today. I got a lecture from my fathers earlier today. They said the same thing. I went into the military to prove something. To myself. To my dads. Probably to Carys and Aidan, too. They've always been so focused, and I was left out. I needed to prove I could do something that wasn't handed to me. Everyone expected me to take my place at Papa's company and someday take over. I needed a career that was mine. I did it, and now it's time to come home and appreciate everything I have. Had."

Lucas seemed to consider his words. "I can understand. I have to prove myself every time someone new comes in. They all think I got where I am because I'm the boss's son. I'm going to open my own place."

Again, news to her. She wondered if their dad knew Lucas had plans. But she had to admit, Tristan was handling her brother with grace. Lucas's shoulders had come down, and there was an unmistakable air of relief around him. Like he was damn happy the Dom was back in the house, and he didn't have to watch her fumble more.

She wasn't fucking fumbling. Was she?

"Let me know if you're looking for investors," Tris said. "I think you'll find a lot of us would be thrilled to back you. But do it because you want to prove to yourself you can. You're the only opinion who matters here. You've got nothing to prove to your father or anyone else. We know how good you are, but sometimes we have to test ourselves."

Lucas held out a hand and suddenly didn't look like he wanted to pound on Tris. "Thanks so much, man. I appreciate it."

Tristan shook her brother's hand and put his free hand on Lucas's shoulder. "And I will take care of my subs. I'm back, and I'm not going to let anything come between us again. I promise you."

Lucas shook his hand and nodded. "Okay. Thank you, Tris." He stepped back and suddenly looked younger, like Tristan's vows had let some worry slide off him and he was a carefree young buck again. "You guys have fun in the privacy rooms. I'm going to go meet up with Seth. Apparently we've got a new group of trainees coming in for a tour. It's good to get a look at the newbies."

Her brother was gross.

"We're on the main stage tonight," Tristan announced.

It was an evening for wild revelations. "What?"

She had a million questions, but Tris had cleverly managed to make it so the answers she wanted about him promising all that crap to her brother were secondary to where they would be playing this evening.

"Oh, really? Are you sure you want that, man?" Lucas put a hand to his perfectly toned gut and looked slightly green. "She's never wanted to play publicly before. I don't know how I feel about it."

She was the one who would be having a talk with their big brothers. It was obvious Kyle and David needed to teach Lucas a thing or two. "Your feelings are not required, brother."

Tristan shrugged. "You can feel like hiding in the locker room because your sister is probably getting naked tonight. I told you I would take care of them, and there's a streak of exhibitionist in her. She's certainly played publicly. You weren't a member back then, and I've heard since they moved The Hideout to this space, she and Aidan prefer privacy rooms. But I'm back, and we're ready to get our freak on. We're ready to dive back into this world, so we might need to make a schedule because I won't be sparing your tender eyes."

"Like how freaky?" Lucas asked.

"You should hole up somewhere, Luke."

That was the moment she realized somehow Aidan had come up behind her. He wore an identical set of leathers as Tristan but looked entirely different. They were hot for different reasons. Tris was the smooth player who hid his predator. Aidan was her sexy smarty pants who sometimes got lost in his work. He wasn't now. He stared at her like he could eat her up.

Her brother winced. "Yeah, maybe I'll stay in the lounge this evening. If I sit in the back, I won't be able to see the dungeon floor. Sister, when you get back, we have to talk because if you're going to get your freak on regularly, we need a schedule."

"We'll see about that," Carys said with way more confidence than she felt because her men were making her the slightest bit nervous.

And it did something for her.

Her brother gave her a wave and walked away, passing Tristan to get to the main part of the club.

"It's good to know you're going to coordinate schedules with my brother. Good luck with that," Carys said.

His hand came up to brush her hair back. His voice went low. "Remember where we are. You might not think I deserve your respect, but as long as we're in here, I'll have it. Otherwise we should set up couple's therapy for three. I've heard it's all the rage."

Sitting around and talking about her problems seemed awful. Besides, they hadn't had any problems before Tristan left, so she wasn't sure why she needed therapy. A couple of good orgasms and a sore ass seemed like a better bet. "Yes, Sir. I will certainly respect you as my Dom in this space."

"In every space when we're in the field, too," Tris insisted. "From the moment we get on the plane until you're home safe and sound, you're mine and you'll obey me. Not your uncle. I make the decisions when it comes to you and Aidan. Am I making myself clear?"

She wanted to spit bile back his way, but there was a piece of her that was so relieved he was taking control.

How would he dominate her? This was a different Tristan. He'd been bossy, pushing her to try new things. What changes had time wrought in this man she'd loved?

Aidan tried, but the sex always ended up being fairly vanilla. She didn't think he was satisfied, either. Somewhere deep down, Aidan kind of wanted a top, too. Though he would never let her top him. It was lucky she'd never had the urge.

Had they never truly settled comfortably into their places when it came to sex? Had Tris needed this time apart to figure out who he was, to learn he was better with them? Could she truly blame him for not understanding what he was doing?

Tristan's hand tangled in her hair, and he tugged just enough so she felt it. "I asked you a question, Carys. You've already started earning punishments."

179

He was so close. She could feel the heat of his breath against her cheek. This was not the boy who'd tried to mirror their teachers at The Club. This man was dangerous and knew what he wanted. He wasn't pretending to be a Dom. He'd come into his own somehow while he'd been gone.

What did he want from her? Her compliance. Her submission.

She hoped he wanted her body.

"Yes, Sir. I heard you and agree to your terms, though you'll have to talk to my cousins. I'm sure my uncle will happily hand me off, but my cousins could be troublesome." Some of her tension fled because he was making it so easy for her to find her submissive space.

Aidan moved in behind her, and she could feel his hips against hers, one hand coming out to flatten against her stomach. "I'll handle your cousins."

There was a streak of unexpected confidence coming from Aidan.

The door behind them came open, and her Taggart cousins were walking out.

Kenzie grinned her way. "Oh, that's so sweet."

Kala rolled her eyes. "They should keep it to the actual dungeon floor. This is a hallway, dude. It's for walking."

"Sure, because you never do weird things in hallways," Tasha said.

"I respect the space," Kala proclaimed.

Devi stood behind them, wearing a corset and boy shorts, showing off her gentle curves, her red hair in curls trailing down her back. Devi was willowy and graceful and looked the slightest bit nervous. Her gaze went to the left, toward the men's locker room.

Aidan didn't seem to understand they weren't alone. His hand moved over her belly and started in a downward motion.

"Taggarts, I have explained to my subs that I'll be in charge of them in the field," Tristan announced. "I feel the need to make it clear to you as well."

"That's so romantic." Kenzie put a hand to her heart.

Kala simply shrugged. "You can totally get Aidan killed. Like go for it, buddy. But if you think I'll let you hurt my cousin, you haven't met me. Would you like to meet me, Tristan?"

"So says the woman who punched her in the gut not three hours ago." Aidan stared at Kala with a frown. His hand came back up, wrapping around her waist and pulling her closer to him as though she needed protection.

"She'll back off," Tristan said confidently. "Or she'll meet me."

A low groan came from behind them, and Cooper was there with Zach and Dare. "She's wound up enough as it is. Could we notch down the testosterone, please?"

Kenzie leaned over, whispering in a way everyone could hear. "He's talking to you, sis."

Kala snarled her sister's way.

Cooper moved in, putting a hand on Kala's back. "Come on. I've got a scene set up for you along with an imported pain slut. Julian sent this guy over because he claims no one can give him what he needs."

"Sounds like a challenge." Kala's lips curled up, and for a bare second she seemed to lean back into Cooper's hand. Then she straightened up and got her Domme face on. "Are you watching or helping tonight, Master C?"

"Oh, I think you'll need help with him, Mistress," Cooper said, his voice low. "Let's go make sure the space is up to your standards."

Kala's head turned, and her expression softened. "I have no doubt."

Then she strode off, Cooper following behind her.

"I wouldn't hate a session," Kenzie said. "I think I'll go see if any of The Club guys are here. Gabe won't try to get into my thong."

"I thought you wanted someone in your thong," Tasha snarked as she joined her fiancé.

"I think I'm choosing sanity for a while," Kenzie declared. "And by sanity I mean celibacy. How about it, Zach? You know you've wanted to slap my ass for a long time. I mean that in an I'm-annoying way, not a you-think-I'm-hot way."

Tristan snorted and whispered in her ear. "Watch the big bad soldier run away."

Captain Reed didn't run, but he did wince. "Too much like my sister. Nope."

Kenzie pouted and turned. "Your loss."

She flounced off, leaving Devi staring at the captain.

Zach looked her over. "How about you? You're Devi, right? You need a scene partner?"

Something close to a squeak came out of Devi's mouth, and she turned and disappeared back into the locker room.

Carys was surprised because she'd kind of thought she'd heard something about Devi having a crush on the handsome captain. Of course she'd also heard there was one Taggart sister he didn't view as a familial relation. The rumor was Zach had declared his love for Tasha, though he hadn't fought her when she'd fallen for Dare. Maybe Devi was in self-preservation mode.

Zach sighed. "I guess that's a no. Do I smell bad or something? All right. Looks like I'm watching tonight. You three have fun and know you're going to have to deal with Kala in the field. She's serious."

"About letting me die, apparently," Aidan said with the cutest frown. "I kind of thought we were friends."

"Focus," Tristan commanded. "Or do you need some correction, too?"

She felt Aidan's arm tighten. "Are we going there now?"

"Only if you want it," Tristan promised.

What the hell was going on between them?

How did she feel about it? It wasn't like she'd ever told them she kind of had a fantasy where they also played together.

She'd thought they were settled before Tris left, thought they knew everything about their relationship. What if they'd been in a rut and she hadn't even realized it?

Again, a thrill of excitement went through her, and she couldn't help the brat attack that came next. "Aidan couldn't handle a real spanking, Sir."

She gasped when she felt Aidan's teeth sink into her earlobe, nipping her in a way that sent her heart rate soaring.

"I won't let you push me, brat," Aidan vowed, "But I also won't let preconceived notions hold the three of us back. However, tonight is all about you. And we're not going easy on you like we did the other day."

"Easy?" It wasn't like they'd held back in the conference room. Except maybe they had. Maybe they all had. She'd pushed and pushed and not found the place she'd needed so badly.

"You didn't really want me," Tristan said, his hand on the nape of her neck. They were surrounding her, letting her know there was nowhere to run. "You wanted to cry and wanted an orgasm, but you didn't want to connect. I'm going to change your mind tonight. I was in a place where I wasn't willing to push you hard because I didn't want to lose you. I'll lose you if I'm not what you need. I'll be what you need tonight."

"We'll be what you need tonight," Aidan vowed.

Carys took a long breath and let go of her tension. If they were willing to try, she was, too. "Then lead on, Sirs. Your sub is ready to play."

* * * *

Tristan was deeply aware of the eyes on him as he stepped onto the main stage. There was a group of unfamiliar faces standing at the front, the regulars giving way to the new trainees. Gabriel Lodge ran the training class and shared the main job of actually running the club with the founding members.

"If you don't mind talking a bit about what you're doing, I know the trainees would appreciate it. It's their first night in the club," Gabriel had told him before he'd led Carys on stage.

Aidan had gone ahead, testing the equipment for the tenth time. Aidan would always be thorough.

"Find your place while we get things ready, love," he said to his sub.

His fucking gorgeous sub. Just being here with her sent him into top space. Knowing everything was in the open now did something for him, too. He was in charge. Aidan could top Carys, but he topped them both. They were his.

It sent a savage sense of satisfaction through him.

Carys moved to the center of the stage, lowering herself gracefully to her knees, her legs spread and head down, palms up on her thighs.

He could eat her up, but first he was going to give her a reason to go wild. Carys was restrained, disciplined, emotionally reasonable. She needed to let go and scream, needed a safe place to vent her rage.

Then he would remind her there was a safe place to put her passion, too.

He moved to the center of the stage where he'd assembled the metal frame structure he intended to use to torment his sub this

183

evening. Aidan had moved to her side, but he didn't sink to his knees.

He might never feel the need, and that was fine with Tristan. They weren't going to be restrained by the relationships they'd seen before. His fathers topped his mom, and neither would ever give up the dominant position, so they shared it. There were other threesomes, though, where there was a clear top and the other man in the threesome was a sub.

They would find their own way. Aidan could float between roles or choose to simply be a Dom and Tristan would make space for him.

"Welcome to the trainees," Tristan said. "I'm Master Tristan, and this is Master Aidan and our lovely submissive, Carys. Tonight we're going to show you how to properly frustrate the hell out of your sub. By the way, Carys, we're on stage and we're now in high protocol."

Her head came up, eyes going big. "High protocol?"

Aidan snorted. "She's going to be fun tonight."

She was going to behave precisely as he'd planned she would. "Yes, love, high protocol, and that's the only warning I'm going to give you. You're going to follow our commands or there will be punishments. Of course if this seems too much for you, there's always a way out. My sub can say her safe word and then someone else will run a scene for you tonight."

Carys's head dropped back down.

Tristan leaned over and kissed the nape of her neck then straightened. "So now she's made her choice, and we can move forward. She has to make the choice every moment we're playing. Any time she chooses, we stop, but I'm sure Gabe will go over consent with you. So let's move on to the part where I make her crazy. There will be times when a simple spanking is all your sub needs, but other times you need a framework to build the tension, to make the fantasy a bit more real. My sub has some rightful anger toward me. She isn't willing to take tenderness from me, so we're going another way."

"Should you explain our form of high protocol, Master Tristan?" Aidan seemed far more comfortable than Tris had thought he would.

"Carys will end every sentence she speaks to us with the word *Sir* or *Master*. Normally I would choose what I wish to be called, but like I said, her anger is understandable, so allowances will be made." Tristan moved around the stage, the better to look at her from every angle. "She will obey quickly and without complaint. She will keep her eyes on the ground unless Master A or I say otherwise. Any infraction will be punished. How does that make you feel, love?"

"Like you're an asshole," Carys said. "Sir."

Oh, she wanted it bad. "Excellent. I didn't think I had to mention it but all communication will be respectful on the part of the sub, so that's a hard ten. I'm keeping the count low because she's going to rack it up over the next half an hour or so."

His whole body hummed in anticipation. He'd trained for this, spent years planning how he would handle her if he ever got his hands on her again. She would never know exactly how much time he'd spent thinking about this, planning it out and practicing so it could be perfect.

He'd spent at least an hour getting Aidan ready. He nodded Aidan's way, and his partner moved in behind their sub.

"Allow Master Aidan to help you up, love," Tristan commanded.

Tristan watched as Aidan caressed Carys's arms and shoulders, big hands moving over her before he helped her stand. He guided her to cross her arms loosely on her stomach before gathering her hair with gentle hands.

Tris felt his cock twitch when Aidan wrapped Carys's hair around his fist and jerked her head back.

His free hand spanned both her forearms, gripping tight and pinning them against her body.

They made an impressive, imposing picture. Aidan, tall and broad, looming over their sub's shoulder, his control of her body sure and resolute. Carys was soft and relaxed despite the tension on her hair, her arched neck. The light hit them, casting dramatic shadows.

Every eye was on them, and they were fucking his.

Aidan turned Carys's head just enough so he could kiss her, his mouth mastering hers.

Tristan vowed she would kiss him before the night was over. Last night she'd avoided kissing him, but he would get his mouth on hers tonight. He would start working his way back into her life.

"Arms up, Carys." It was time to move this along. From what he could tell, Carys and Aidan had been fairly vanilla while he'd been gone. If he didn't stop them, they might simply go at it, and what fun would that be?

Pretty fun, but not the point of the evening. It would be pleasure without pain and not what she needed. He was sure she would take the pleasure, but it was the pain that would connect them.

Carys's hands came up even as Aidan still held her. Aidan ran his nose along her neck and Carys held still, giving both Masters what they wanted.

Tristan pulled out the restraints he would use on her this evening, holding them up so everyone could see them. He opened the first cuff. "The sub will know she's restrained but these won't weigh her down. This is our choice of restraints. Of course there are many others, and you and your play partners will need to make those choices on your own."

He looked at Carys, who was still held by Aidan. "These have an easy button on the side so I can get you out quickly if I need to."

"I'm not afraid, Sir," she replied, biting her bottom lip when Aidan's hand slipped over her breast. "Of anything except you being a bastard and withholding sex."

He winced.

"Sir," she said with the slightest smile.

No. He didn't have to worry about her saying her safe word. The brat had found something today. There was a confidence in Carys he hadn't seen in a long time. Sparring with Kala and getting ready for this mission had freed something inside her. It was time to chisel away at those walls of hers. "Aidan."

Aidan's hand slipped under the bodice of her corset and her eyes widened, a gasp coming out of her mouth as he gave her nipple a tweak.

"That's another ten," Tristan promised. "This is not going to end well for you."

He gave her his sternest voice, the one he'd practiced when he'd kept up his training at the club in DC known as The Court. He'd gone with Zach and their bosses, Drake and Taylor Radcliffe. He'd never touched a sub in a sexual way, but he'd practiced in the hopes of one day being right here.

He nodded Aidan's way and Aidan backed off slightly, taking her hand and leading her to the freestanding metal frame. Carys watched as Tristan attached the cuffs that would hold her in place. When he was satisfied the apparatus was safe and secure, he allowed Aidan to lead Carys in, getting her into position.

"It's important to check on the safety of any equipment you use on your sub, which is why you should carefully plan out any scene requiring toys." Tristan took her right wrist and brought it to the place where straps waited to be attached to the cuffs on her wrists. He connected the restraint. He did the same with her left wrist, slipping his index and middle fingers under the cuff to ensure they weren't too tight.

"You should understand why your sub enjoys certain types of play." He spoke the words but he was staring at Carys. He hadn't forced her out of her clothes yet, and it was easy to see she was perfectly comfortable with all the lights on her. She couldn't see out into the crowd, but she would know they were there. "Tell them how you're feeling, Carys."

"Vulnerable but also safe, Sir," Carys said, lightly pulling against the cuffs as though testing them. She was in heels, which made it easy for her to comfortably stand. "This is a safe place to play out some fantasies that could be considered kinky, to feel things I wouldn't want to feel if I wasn't in a contained, loving space."

"That's how you feel emotionally," Aidan said, getting to his point before Tristan could. "How do you feel physically? What does being restrained by men who care about you do to your pussy?"

"It gets me wet, Sir. It makes me wonder what you and Master Tristan are planning to do to me. And when you talk about planning, everything inside me tightens because I know you're taking my needs seriously. I know you've sat with him and talked about how you'll fuck me, how you'll take turns using me like a toy you pass back and forth. Your favorite toy. I enjoy pretending in this setting, though I will admit it annoys me in the real world."

She wanted to play that way? "Another ten, brat. I assure you this is the real world. It's very real for you and me and Master Aidan. Pull at those restraints all you like. We're going to begin our scene now."

"I thought we already had," Carys said, again with a bratty smile on her gorgeous face. She was in a confident space now, but he would show her he could handle her. "Sir."

"And another ten. You're making this fun for me, baby." He gave her his own arrogant smirk before turning back to the audience. "For the rest of the time I will not be your tutor. Watch and learn, trainees.

This is how you get under a sub's skin and make her scream for you."
He looked to Aidan. "And why are we making her scream?"

"Because she needs it," Aidan replied.

Because she needed it. And he was going to give it to her. Then they could get what they needed—her.

Chapter Ten

Carys let her head fall back, hair brushing her bare shoulders, as Tristan pulled things out of his kit and whispered something to Aidan. She'd meant what she'd said. The idea of those two plotting to torture her made her feel wanted and loved. Maybe the thing that had hurt most was the idea Tristan hadn't given her a thought while he was gone. Though he claimed it wasn't true, it was hard to believe mere words. What they were doing now was starting to shake her walls.

Tonight wasn't the time to think about walls. It was the time to stop thinking and let herself feel.

The spectators were vague shapes beyond the lights. She couldn't tell how many people were watching them. She was still properly clothed, and it gave her some cover. Would they get her out of her clothes? Would they demand she strip down for them?

Not while she was cuffed, of course, but Tris seemed to allude to a long scene. In the past they would play some truly fun games. Would she still find them fun?

How long had it been since Tristan set her up for the kind of spanking that made her ache and also opened her up?

Her men prowled across the stage toward her. Prowled was the right word. Tristan was leaning slightly forward as he walked, while Aidan moved and not around to her other side. He was behind her, and she had no idea what he was doing, what he was planning to do. A thrill of alarm worked its way down her spine.

She knew they would never hurt her—well, they would hurt her plenty, but only in the ways she craved. She wasn't sure she could trust them with her heart, but she absolutely trusted them with her body. Though even as she stood there bound and helpless, she was a little afraid.

And that fear made her nipples tight and pussy throb. It was a heady feeling, a feeling that shoved out all the others and left her blissfully in the moment where she didn't have to decide anything at all. All she needed to do was comply with her Masters' commands and accept their punishment and their pleasure.

Tristan stopped in front of her, and she could feel his focus, his attention. He was no longer paying attention to the crowd. He was so much more commanding than he'd been before, and it was addicting.

"You look gorgeous tonight, love," Tristan said, his voice dipping low as though he meant to keep the words private between the three of them, as though telling her, even with an audience, there was no one in the world except the three of them.

"Fucking sexy as hell." Aidan's hand slipped under her skirt and cupped her ass. "I want to show you off tonight. I want everyone in this club to know how stunning our submissive is."

Tristan's lips quirked up. "Everyone who isn't hiding in the lounge."

She frowned. "Do not take me out of my sexy moment, Tris."

Aidan's teeth sank into her ear. It seemed to be his go-to move tonight, and it had her going up on her toes at the thrill of pain. "Bad sub. I'll move down your neck next. I like leaving a mark, baby."

Tristan loomed over her. "Another ten."

Then he lowered his mouth to hers, the kiss unexpectedly tender rather than fiery and demanding the way she thought it would be. His tongue touched hers, then ran along the inside of her lower lip.

When he broke the kiss she was soft and ready. She'd known them all of her life, but in the moment everything felt fresh, like they could have both the comfort of a long-term relationship and the thrill of something new. Like they could reinvent themselves however they wanted. She could be the calm and collected doctor during work and their wild sub here. They could have the loving partnership they'd formed, and also this crazy, reckless passion.

If she could only trust they wouldn't lie to her again.

His lips clung to hers as he pulled back, a tender moment, as if he couldn't bear to be parted from her.

Then his hand was around her neck, the movement snake-quick and so unexpected she jumped, letting out a short scream of surprise.

"Thank me for kissing you," Tristan demanded.

Carys leaned into his hand, increasing the pressure of his fingers around her throat. Showing him he wouldn't hurt her. She wanted his dominance, enjoyed the sensation of his hands sinking into her skin. "Thank you, Sir."

He smirked, then pushed his thumb against the bottom of her jaw, forcing her to tip her head back. He bent, nipping the skin on her neck and sucking.

A hickie? It had been a long time since she'd had one of those. Not since high school when they'd fumbled around, learning what they liked, what made her hot. They'd teased that if one of them put a mark on her, the other needed equal time, space on her skin.

Tristan was taking his the way Aidan had.

She might end up covered in reminders of the night, and unlike high school, she didn't think she would hide them now. She would enjoy them.

Tristan released her neck and stepped back and to the side so his body was no longer blocking the audience's view of her.

"We're going to play a game now. It's not a thing I would do if we hadn't played like this many times before. Our beautiful submissive is damn-near perfect, so we have to get creative when we want her to earn her punishments. By nature she wouldn't ever earn a single one." His expression changed, turning dark and dominant. The top was in the house. "On your knees, sub."

Carys blinked at him, looked first left, then right, at the cuffs and straps, and back to him, arching a brow. They had played these kinds of games before. Usually when she needed to really unleash tension. Tris would come up with wicked games, giving her orders she couldn't possibly obey. It was something he did when she couldn't ask for what she needed.

Did she trust him enough to play like this with him?

Tristan crossed his arms over his big, muscled chest, staring at her like he could force her to do his will. Against all the rules of science.

Aidan slapped her ass. "He gave you an order, sub."

There was still a chance he wasn't playing a game. The apparatus was a large, upright rectangle made out of heavy galvanized piping that screwed together. It was about nine feet tall and six feet wide and looked like a demented doorway, or the frame for a photo backdrop.

It was clear either Gabe or Cooper had been to Home Depot again.

It could have breakaway pins. During play of this kind, sometimes they would use breakaway pins. All the sub would have to do was apply enough pressure and the restraints attached over her head would come out of place and she would be free.

Carys turned her head up, trying to examine the latch and connectors that bound her cuffs to the straps looped over the frame, but between the lights and the angle, she couldn't see the metal tube-like piece that would separate when the correct amount of force was applied.

This could be a part of Tristan's plan. He might want her to demonstrate how the breakaway pins worked and get her on her knees at the same time. It would put her in a good position to suck his cock. Would he order her to suck him while Aidan spanked her ass? As plans went, she didn't hate it.

"Yes, Sir," she said, and started to kneel, expecting the pins to move as she put more weight on the cuffs.

Her knees never made it to the stage. Carys's shoulders and wrists protested as the restraints pulled taut. She grunted in a combination of discomfort and surprise as her body weight hung on her wrists, her knees a good twenty centimeters from the stage.

"Problem, sub?"

She awkwardly got her feet under her, shaking out her arms. "No, Sir. I just need a moment."

Bracing her feet, she twisted her wrists, gripping the hardware of the cuff, and yanked. Hard. She wasn't weak. She'd proven it earlier. While she didn't work out as intensely as her cousins did, she was strong.

Carys yanked on the cuffs, listening for that cracking sound of the breakaway pin snapping.

Nothing happened except her wrists hurt.

She shifted to the side, bringing her wrist as close to her face as she could.

No breakaway pin.

Aidan chuckled behind her. "Did you think we put breakaway pins in? You're not a newbie, baby. You don't need them."

"I do if I'm supposed to get to my knees," she argued back and then winced. "Sir."

Tristan arched a brow. "I didn't tell you there were breakaways."

He was on her in the next breath. His hands gripped her hips, jerking her forward. Carys inhaled sharply.

"I gave you an order, sub. I expect to be obeyed."

"I literally can't." She waved her arms, making the metal hardware and chains clank. "Sir, do you think I don't know what you're doing?"

"I think you need to feel everything tonight. This used to help you push through when you were locked down. It reminded you there are things you can't control. I was good at getting you through all the stress and tension. This was one of the ways we played, but, baby, I also know this is how I treated you in real life. I put you in a position where you couldn't win. I need you to know I understand the difference. This is the place to play the hardass Dom, when it's your pleasure and relaxation on the line. Not when it's your heart."

Tears pierced her eyes. It was a perverse way to apologize, but this was a connection she hadn't felt in so long. If they could get back this piece of themselves, could they have it all?

"If you can't trust me, I understand," he whispered. "We can try this another way. But I need you to know I'm never going to stop trying."

She'd always found this type of play frustrating and oddly freeing. It was a game, one where the goal was sexual satisfaction. And often emotional release. "I think we should give the newbies a good show."

Tristan leaned in, brushing his mouth over hers. "Thank you, love. Don't hesitate to use your safe word if it gets too much. This is play, and it's for you. If it doesn't work, we try something new." He leaned back, his eyes going hard. "That's twice now you haven't called me Sir."

And they were doing high protocol.

Carys knew her eyes went wide before she dropped her gaze. Shit. She'd walked right into that.

Did she need this excuse? Had they decided to put her in a corner in order to give her what she needed? He promised to make her scream. She'd thought it would be in pleasure, but what if what she needed was to release the poison in her system?

His words had already done some of the work. He knew what he'd done. He took accountability. It made it easier to sink into this role they wanted her to play.

They were going to push her and push her until she broke. The realist in her knew she needed to break.

"I'm sorry, Sir," she said, instinctively trying to go to her knees. If she could have, she would have dropped all the way down.

But she couldn't. Because sometimes she couldn't do things even when she wanted to. It was the odd lesson to this experience. She wasn't at fault. She'd done nothing wrong. The "punishment" was nothing more than a way to get her where she needed to go.

"Are you? You don't look sorry." Tristan started to circle her, ducking under the straps holding her arms.

Aidan followed him, switching positions so now she was facing him. "Actually, we're not looking at very much of you. Strip."

Yes, this might be exactly what she needed. They would force her into impossible situations so she "earned" an amount of punishment absolutely sure to make her cry, to make her break. Carys looked down at herself. She had on her favorite corset and the skirt she used when she was looking for a more modest night. Getting out of a corset was easier than getting into it, but it required hands. She couldn't simply shimmy out of it.

It was easier with Aidan in front of her. She could deal with Aidan. She wasn't so sure about Tris. "Sir, would you help me?"

Aidan stepped back, considering the request. "Help you how?"

Asshole. And where the hell was Tris? Her heart rate ticked up as she realized he could surprise her from behind. What was that bastard planning? "I need help with my corset, Sir. I want to comply with your orders, but I can't use my hands because you locked me in."

Tristan pressed against her back. The feel of his hard dick compressed by the leathers was familiar but no less exciting because of the familiarity.

"Do you want me to show everyone your tits?" Tristan whispered the question against her ear.

His arms came around her from behind, and she leaned back into him.

"If that would please you, Sir."

His lips touched her shoulder, and she felt the smile.

"You're too well trained to make fun mistakes," he murmured against her skin.

"I was trained well, and Aidan's taken care of me," she breathed back, turning to kiss his temple. Somehow here and now the words weren't an accusation but rather a way to honor Aidan.

"I can see he has," Tristan whispered. "And that's why we have to get creative with reasons to punish you."

Aidan smiled, an entirely predatory expression. "Very creative. I had a whole lot of last night to think about ways to torture you."

"You don't need an excuse to spank me."

"You're right, I don't. But if you don't disobey, then I don't have a reason to call you my bad girl." Tris straightened, and she knew the intimate byplay was over.

"Do you want me to show everyone your tits, sub?" Tristan used a stage voice, letting the audience hear him.

Did she want him to? He'd said she had an exhibitionist streak they'd never fully indulged. Did she want everyone to see her body? Or was it more about having her Masters be so proud to show her off? Was it actually putting their relationship on display because they were proud of it, because it brought them pleasure, brought the people around them pleasure? "If putting me on display would please you, Sir. Does it also please you, Master Aidan?"

Aidan's eyes were already on her breasts. "You know it will. I've always wanted to show you off, wanted to parade you around this club and show the world I have a beautiful sub."

His hands gripped the bottom of the corset, squeezing the edges together until the hook and eye closures came undone and the bottom few inches were unfastened.

"You want us to share our property with other people?" Tristan asked in a dangerous voice.

Every possessive word caressed over her skin. She needed to

believe him, needed to know she was his because it was the only way he could be hers again.

"I want to please—" She couldn't get the rest of the words out as he gripped the top of the corset, thumbs slipping under the fabric, sliding back and forth over her nipples.

Pleasure sizzled through her from that simple touch. Her moan became a gasp when two quick movements unfastened her corset, and it fell to the stage around her heels.

He pulled at the skirt, dragging it down her hips and off her, leaving her in only a silky white thong.

The lights warmed her now bare breasts, and when Tristan's fingers danced over the underside of them she strained forward, wanting more of his touch. Wanting to tempt Aidan to join them. She could see the bulge of his aroused cock tenting his leathers.

Tristan cupped her bare breasts, lifting them. Displaying them for the people in the audience. His thumbs flicked her nipples, quick casual motions.

"I don't like all these strangers looking at what's mine," Tristan said.

There was a faint "bullshit" from someone in the unseen audience. It elicited a snort from Carys because while whoever said it was an asshole, he was also right.

She moaned as Aidan reached out and twisted her nipple, bringing her back into the moment.

"Pay attention, sub," Aidan commanded. "He said he didn't like all these strangers looking at you. Are you his?"

Was she? She felt like his. In this club, she was definitely theirs. "Yes. I'm his."

"You are his, too, aren't you?" Tristan asked, his body big and warm at her back.

Always had been, always would be. No matter what happened. Even if she walked away in the end.

"Yes, Sir."

"Who decides if you get pleasure…" Tristan circled her areolas with his thumbs, then gently gripped her nipples. It was a barely there touch, but she was so aroused it felt like she'd been shocked with a live wire when he applied faint pressure.

"…or pain?" He pinched her nipples. Hard.

Carys cried out, arching her back as he pulled on her nipples, distending them from her body, and then twisted viciously.

He released her nipples abruptly, her breasts bouncing. She moaned softly, pressing back against him.

Tristan's hand gripped her hair, hard, her scalp lighting up with pain. "Answer me."

"You do, Sir. You and Master Aidan decide."

He grunted in satisfaction and released her hair.

"Cover up, sub."

Carys didn't hesitate this time. "Master Aidan, would you put my corset back on me, please?"

He walked around to face her. "No."

"Sir, I can't cover up unless you help me because I can't use my hands." Carys raised her brows and once more jiggled the restraints. Her nipples felt hot and tender, and she knew her pussy was almost embarrassingly wet. The eyes she could feel on her only added to both sensations.

She realized her mistake. "Please, could you help me, Master Tristan?"

Tristan moved to stand beside Aidan. His lips curled up as his eyes took in every inch of her body.

"No," he said, echoing his partner.

She stared right back at them, loving how they looked standing there torturing her together. Those men had been her everything for so long. Wasn't it worth the risk if they could find their way back? If Tris was really ready now?

Aidan leaned in, looking her straight in the eyes. "Sub, where are you supposed to be looking?"

She'd been looking at them as she sorted through her tangled emotions, examining each of his familiar features.

But they were in high protocol.

Carys dropped her gaze to Aidan's boots. "I'm sorry, Sir."

"You should be. You've already earned punishments," Aidan said. "All you're doing is adding to the total."

Her body thrummed in pleasure at the promise of impact play.

The folded flap of leather at the tip of a riding crop caressed her lips. Carys gasped in surprise because she hadn't noticed he'd grabbed it from his kit.

"Last chance to show us that you can be a good girl," Tristan said.

She could only see their boots, four of them standing together. Despite her gaze being on the floor, the image of them together formed in her mind, Tristan and Aidan—her men—standing together, working together to punish her. To please her.

The words were all part of the act. She was their good girl and they her loving tops. They might have thought frustration would be the way to break through, but she suddenly didn't feel the need to scream. She only wanted to be with them. In every wicked way possible.

Aidan flicked the crop against her nipples, then pressed the tip hard against the underside of one breast, lifting it. "Spread your pussy open and show us how wet you are."

She did her best to follow the order without her hands. Carys spread her legs as wide as she could, lowering herself until her arms were pulled tight, and she would have lost her balance if she hadn't had the restraints to pull against.

She felt her labia part, knew her pussy was open and vulnerable.

But not visible.

Because while he'd taken her skirt, he'd known what he was doing when he'd left her in the thong.

She still had one thing on, and while it didn't cover much, it covered what her Masters wanted to see.

The crop flicked against the inside of her left thigh. A quick strike, the pain bright and sharp, fading fast.

"I'm sorry, Sirs. I want to be obedient."

"But you aren't." Tristan's words were soft. "You're always such a perfect submissive. My dream sub. But tonight you are pushing me."

She was pushing him exactly where they all wanted to go. "This isn't fair, Sir."

The crop cracked against the inside of her other thigh. Carys flinched, the delicate skin feeling hot and thin.

Aidan rolled his shoulders, tipping his head first one way and then the other. She knew that look and did her best to brace herself.

He brought the crop up in an underhand strike. The sound of leather on flesh was loud as it snapped against her inner thighs. Again and again he struck her. Not their normal pace of impact play, but the sweet pain made her lick her lips. Aidan would spank her when she asked for it, but this was something different. This felt like a real Master. She expected it from Tristan, but Aidan was a revelation.

"Sir, do you want me to count?"

"Count?" Aidan asked.

"Count each strike of my punishment?"

Tristan chuckled, a deep sound that rolled over her like a drug. "Punishment?"

The crop cracked against her pussy. Pain and pleasure blossomed in her, and Carys screamed, as much in shock as pain. Aidan struck her right above her clit, and as the stinging heat faded, a pulsing throb started up, making her clit feel swollen and needy.

"This wasn't punishment." He dropped the crop to the stage and cupped her sex in his big, hard hand. "That was me enjoying what's mine."

Aidan's other hand fisted in her hair, forcing her head back so he could devour her mouth even as he pulled up on her pussy, making it throb harder.

He bit her bottom lip. "Now it's time for your punishment."

* * * *

Aidan had never felt so fucking in control before. The love of his life was wet and ready for whatever he gave her.

And he had to acknowledge the only reason this worked was because Tristan was here.

Tristan was right. They weren't merely friends. They were something more, and acknowledging that, allowing it to be whatever it was going to be, made a massive difference. It took away any slight awkwardness they'd had before, when Aidan wasn't sure of his place. Now he settled in.

Carys was oddly calm. He could tell from the set of her shoulders and the serene look in her eyes. Tris had been right about this, too. When they'd decided on this form of play, Aidan had worried. Tris had explained it was his way to show her he wouldn't ever do this to her again. That he would put her needs, her peace, first.

Outside of the dungeon. Inside the dungeon, they would sometimes push her limits, though they didn't seem to have truly done so tonight.

And he had to admit, it was fucking fun. He knew one thing. She wasn't thinking about anything but him and Tristan. The rest of the world had floated away.

She'd "disobeyed," and now they got to punish her.

His whole body felt alive in a way it never had before. He'd shoved down all his anxiety because he needed to stay calm in the face of an attack. But now this felt like a fucking reward. He'd done what he needed to do, proven he could stay in control, and now he got to truly top her.

He rubbed her pussy and she tensed, adjusting her position. The fabric of her itty-bitty thong was soaked, and she felt warm and soft against his hand. She'd feel warmer and softer against his dick.

Aidan lifted up, her plump pussy grinding against his fingers. Standing with her legs spread wide wasn't a sustainable position. She was strong, but it would be too easy for her leg muscles to tire. If she dropped any further, she might hurt her legs or arms as she pulled on the restraints, or both.

Being a good Dom, he'd help her stand up straight. He pulled up, hard, his hand digging into her. Carys gasped, scrambling to bring her feet together and stand up to alleviate the pressure.

His fingers slipped between her outer labia, the warm, slick flesh cradling him. Her thighs, pressed together, kept his hand in place.

She ground down on him, hips shifting as she tried to rub her clit against his hand.

"Spread," he commanded. "Enough so I have easy access to this pussy."

She adjusted until her feet were a little more than shoulder width apart. He dropped his hand away from her sex.

Then gave her pussy a friendly spank.

Tristan had been behind her the whole time, and now he chuckled. "I think she's definitely ready to move on."

Carys groaned, her head tipping back against Tristan's shoulder, her knees tilting to the side, spreading her thighs wider and forcing her hips forward.

When her pussy was spanked, she didn't clamp her legs together. She spread them, offering her sweet flesh up for more. There was his sweet sub, and he realized what they'd been missing. Sex was good between them, but this was more. This was a connection they'd been missing.

Aidan reached between her legs once more, but now his fingers were gentle. He molded the wet fabric of her thong against her pussy, making sure it clung to every fold and contour.

Tristan moved in, his hand sliding against Aidan's as he traced Carys's clit with gentle fingers. His fingers slid along Tris's, reminding him in a visceral way that he wasn't alone.

He'd been so alone.

She arched her back, pulling against the restraints.

"Does that feel good?" Tristan asked.

"Yes, Sir," came the breathy reply.

Then it was time to shake her up. "And this?"

Aidan carefully scraped her clit with his nail.

Carys let out a shocked sound that was almost a scream.

He did it again.

Carys came. He felt the warm rush of her arousal against his fingers. He hadn't dreamed she was that close. He doubted she knew she was so close because if she had, she would have warned him.

Tristan stepped back, frowning.

Aidan moved to join him, forming a solid front. "Did you come, sub?"

"Just a little one, Sir."

Tristan snorted. "And little orgasms don't count?"

"That sounds fair to me, Sir." Carys's cheeks and chest were flushed, her hips moving restlessly. That really had been a minor orgasm because she didn't look satiated and satisfied. She looked like she was already on the edge again. Right where they wanted her.

"Did she just, uh, orgasm from being punished?" The question came from the audience.

Aidan couldn't tell who had said it, but he bet it was one of the newbies because he heard Gabe start in on a low-voiced lecture about how to behave during a scene.

Aidan simply snorted. They'd come to learn. They were about to. "That wasn't her punishment."

Carys's eyes widened but she didn't look totally surprised.

Aidan picked up the crop he'd dropped earlier, watching his sub as her eyes tracked the movement of his hand.

He whipped the crop through the air, quick enough that it made a soft whistling sound. Carys took deep breaths, her posture softening.

Her shoulders dropped down and back, her fingers lovingly curled rather than gripping the strap above her cuffs.

He looked to Tristan, who was still standing there watching. Tris gave him a nod, telling him they were ready for the next part of their well laid-out plan. Aidan carefully flicked her nipples with the tip of the crop.

"You're going to crop her breasts?" someone in the audience asked. Except it wasn't merely a question. It was an accusation.

Aidan bit back a chuckle because Gabe was going to lose his shit on this new group. Someone was getting kicked out. Aidan simply snorted and thought about telling the newbie that if he pulled some macho, protective bullshit and tried to "save" Carys, it wasn't Aidan or Tris he'd have to worry about. Carys would kick his ass herself.

"As a punishment? Nope. This is for fun." He added a smack to the underside of each breast. The sound of leather on flesh echoed.

Aidan looked at his sub, and despite how deep in subspace she was, she met his gaze. Her eyes flicked to the audience and then back to him.

Tristan reached out and gently forced her chin up so she could look at him. "What do you think your punishment is going to be, love?"

She was almost naked in front of a crowd, had orgasmed right here in what was essentially public, but if she was bothered by it, he couldn't tell. She was strong and proud, and her lips curled up ever so slightly as she replied. "Spanking, Sir. It's going to be a spanking."

"And you're ready?" Aidan asked, already knowing her answer.

"Yes, Sirs. I'm ready."

Aidan's cock twitched in his leathers, and he realized he was ready, too. Ready to start this brand new, utterly fascinating part of their lives.

Chapter Eleven

A spanking. They were going to give her a proper spanking, not just a casual swat to her ass as Aidan passed her in the kitchen. Even the one last night didn't count because their hearts hadn't been in it. They'd been doing it for her, getting nothing from it themselves.

This would be for all of them.

Aidan tucked his crop back into his kit before folding his arms. He looked stern and imposing, his biceps, deltoids, and pecs all bulging.

She wanted to bite him. Bite those muscles. He'd bite her back. He seemed to have found out he enjoyed leaving his mark on her. Tristan always had.

The surprise orgasm had taken the edge off, but only for a while. She needed her Masters' hands on her. Needed both of them to hurt her and pleasure her and love her.

Tristan stood beside Aidan, his eyes roaming up and down her body. "Why are you being punished?"

Carys knew what he wanted. She cleared her throat, speaking up so the crowd could hear her. Gabe seemed to have gotten control of whatever asshole needed to learn a thing or two before he came back into a club. "Because I was a bad girl, Sir."

Her toppiest Dom smirked. "Yes, you were, but let's hear some

203

specifics."

Aidan sighed. "Be very specific. How can you learn if you don't understand what you did wrong?"

He was getting into his role. In a way he never had before. She'd often worried she and Tris were far more invested in the lifestyle than Aidan was, but he seemed to have found his groove tonight.

It made her start to think this could work. It made her question if her anger was truly worth breaking them over.

"I forgot to address you properly," she began.

Aidan nodded. "Ten."

Ah, so this was how they were going to play it.

"What else?" Tristan asked.

She thought about the evening. How had she "fucked up" next. "I looked up without permission."

"True. Five." Tristan paused for a long, dramatic moment. "Anything else?"

Carys exhaled, anticipation and fear punching against one another in her gut. They were serious, and she had the sudden, delicious worry she might not be able to handle them. "I didn't obey your orders, Sirs."

Aidan nodded. "Be specific. How many orders?"

They weren't giving her a damn inch. "I'm not exactly sure, Sir."

Tristan shrugged. "If you don't give me a number, I'm going to say twenty and use that to calculate."

Carys licked her lips as her brain worked furiously. They'd ordered her to kneel at least twice. Did it count as one order, repeated, or two? They'd also told her to strip, and she'd obeyed in the end, but only because they'd helped her. Then Tristan told her to cover up, and given she was still naked with her thong stuffed into her pussy in a weird, sexy wedgie, she hadn't obeyed. Finally, he'd told her to spread her pussy so he could look at her. She'd tried, but again failed.

She could say three. Knees, cover up, pussy on display.

It was risky, because what if he counted each time he'd told her to kneel as one order? He'd given the command at least twice. And what if he was counting the strip command, since technically she hadn't done it? He'd been the one to remove her corset.

"Ten, Sir," she said softly.

Tristan stilled. "Ten? You sure?"

She tried to project some kind of confidence. "Yes, Sir. I rounded up, but I'm sure."

He studied her. "Fifty."

In addition to the fifteen she was already getting or total?

"There's one more," Aidan said, warning in his tone.

How could she possibly forget? She was still shaking a bit on the inside from how she could feel both of their hands on her pussy, their fingers tangling together as they rubbed her clit. She hadn't been able to hold back. "Yes, Sir. I came without permission."

"Yes, you did." Tristan gripped her chin, forcing her head up. "Did you know how close you were?"

"No. I didn't realize I was so…" *Hungry. Needy. Ready.* She wasn't sure which word to use because they were all correct.

There was a look in her Dom's eyes. Almost like pain.

"It's been too long since I gave you what you need." The years he'd been away were there, stamped on his handsome face.

She was already softening toward him. She'd been here with Aidan, their physical presence a connection to who they'd been. He'd been utterly alone. "What we both need."

Tris moved in, kissing her cheek and then her mouth. "I need you so much. So much I can't stand it, brat."

With that he adjusted the restraints quickly, loosening the straps that bound her to the frame. She could suddenly stand easily and her arms weren't taut above her head. But he also didn't take her down, indicating he wasn't going to put her over a lap. He wanted to give her more freedom of movement but he wasn't letting her free.

Tris turned back to the audience. "One more tip. Don't be afraid to be tender and affectionate. Only assholes think a good Dom is strict all the time."

He let a long moment pass. Another form of torture.

"Time for your punishment." Tristan's voice was back to cool and stern, but his hand was hot as he stroked her back and ass.

"First we get rid of these." Aidan grabbed her thong and yanked it down.

She gasped as the wet fabric was jerked away from her pussy. Her clit throbbed and she moaned.

Aidan crouched down, helping her step out of her underwear. He grabbed her ass with one big hand and used the hold to steady himself as he stood, but not before he'd taken a deep inhale, breathing in the scent of her arousal. Once he was upright, he petted her butt with a feather-light touch that made her sure her ass was in for it.

"If you're spanking your sub for punishment, it's your job to make sure you keep it simple, so all they have to focus on is the punishment," Tristan explained.

It was clear Tris was in teaching mode, but Carys lost her train of thought as Aidan casually cupped and fondled her breasts with one hand.

"Ordering your sub to remain still or hold a stress position for their punishment can be useful, but they'll have to concentrate on more than their submission and the sensations from the spanking," Tristan said in an academic tone. If she hadn't had tenderness with him the moment before, she might have thought he was detached. "And you check their ass for heat levels. Most importantly, you fucking ask. Communication. It works wonders."

Carys wanted to smile, but Aidan was pinching and rolling her nipples with pressure that was too light. She wanted it harder. It was building again, the minor orgasm they'd given her all used up. She needed more.

"You have two options for this setup." Tris gestured to the frame. "Either you also bring a chair or a bench of some kind, and you put your sub over your knee. Or, you can keep her standing, arms restrained. But you need to hold her in place. Give her something to push against so she can concentrate on the spanking. If you're boring, you could restrain her again on the frame. I have another idea for holding my sub in place while my partner spanks her."

Tristan's hand slid between her legs. Carys spread her feet, welcoming the feel of his hot, hard hand. She wasn't sure what he was planning, but she was going with it.

He palmed her pussy, almost massaging it.

"You earned sixty-five spanks," her Dom said.

Carys didn't bother to hide her wince. This was going to hurt.

The wince became a smile. The hurt would lead her somewhere magical.

"Thank you, Sirs."

Aidan brushed back her hair. "You think I'm going to go easy on you since it's been a while?"

It had been so long, and never like this. "No, Sir. At least, I hope not."

His hand rested on the small of her back, right above her ass.

"You're going to count them. Loud enough so everyone can hear." Aidan's lips brushed her hair. "Loud enough to make sure everyone in the club looks over here and watches us spank your sweet ass."

Carys's mouth went dry with arousal, and it took everything she had to stay still and patient, her body sandwiched between the two of them.

"What I'm about to do helps if you have a partner, though I assure you all I could do it on my own if I had to. Part of being in the kind of relationship I'm in with my subs is understanding that every now and then, one of us won't be around. We have to lean on each other. So she's never alone." There was a deep tone to his voice that gave away the emotion he was feeling. Tristan had obviously felt their distance, too. Felt the miles and minutes and hours and days. He straightened up. "I'm going to use my sub's pussy to keep her still."

A thrill of…fear…arousal…plain WTF…went through Carys.

"Since you can't see, I'll tell you. I'm going to put two fingers deep in my sub's very nice pussy." Tristan matched action to words, his index and middle fingers first parting her labia. His hand slid down, fingertips finding her entrance.

He thrust two fingers up into her. Hard and deep. Filling her and possessing her.

This position put the heel of his hand right against her clit. His index and pinkie fingers rested along the outside of her labia.

Tristan curled his fingers inside her, hitting her G-spot, and Carys moaned, leaning against him. He pressed in again, forcing her ass back and up slightly. It felt like heaven.

"Louder," her Dom demanded. He ground his palm against her clit, his fingers curling inside her in a tiny *come here* finger curl.

Carys let out a high, stuttering moan of pleasure.

"Now I control her lower body." Tristan brought Carys two baby steps forward. This was why he'd adjusted the overhead hold. Now she could bend over a bit. He used her pussy as a handle to move her around until she was right where he wanted her—bent over, ass out, pussy throbbing with need.

"Now if she jumps and tries to move away from the spanking, my control of her pussy and the restraints will keep her in place," Tristan explained. "Master Aidan, our submissive is ready."

She was so ready.

Aidan's right hand swirled over her butt cheeks in a looping figure eight pattern.

She knew what was coming, knew what it meant when his hand lifted away from her skin. Yet the first spank took her by surprise.

Pain. Hard and real and hitting her like a shock to her system.

Carys gasped in both shock as a bright spot blossomed on her left ass cheek. The surface sting was there and gone, but a faint heat remained.

Tristan's fingers stroked gently, a stunning contrast to the pain. "Don't forget your count, love."

"One, Sir."

The second blow was just as hard, but on the other cheek.

This wasn't a slap and tickle. Wasn't the lackluster spankings vanilla people liked to play around with. This was pain and domination. This was being helpless and yet so safe.

By the fifteenth spank her entire ass felt warm, from the top of her cheeks all the way to her thighs. Most of the blows had gone to the sensitive spot where ass met thigh, and she was already feeling tender.

"Spread your legs," Aidan commanded.

Carys obeyed.

Slap. The top of her left cheek.

"Sixteen, Master."

Another smack.

"Seventeen, Master."

"Louder." Aidan punctuated the command with a blow that spanned both thighs, sending Tristan's fingers even deeper into her.

Carys let out a loud, long moan of pain and pleasure.

Aidan didn't stop.

Her skin felt hot and tender, almost like it was sunburned. Now the surface sting, which had faded quickly at the start of the spanking, lingered. It was a sharper sensation than the deep heat slowly building.

By thirty she was twitching, jerking with each blow. But

Tristan's hand cupped and controlled her pussy, keeping her right where he wanted her.

At forty, she started to cry. Not tears of pain.

Tears of release.

She was in a place she'd never been before, all her boundaries blown away in the face of the way these men worshipped her. She'd never felt as connected to them as she did tonight, and she believed them. They hadn't meant to marginalize her. She hadn't communicated. She'd let her fear and insecurity rule her.

Carys dropped her head, watching teardrops hit the matte black stage under her feet. Every single one felt like an offering, a way to honor the last years but to also let them go.

"You good, love?" Tristan asked softly.

She was beyond good. She was lighter than she'd been before, and yet more herself than she'd been in years. "Yes, Sir."

He curled his fingers inside her, and pleasure threaded through the pain. "You're done counting. All you need to do is submit to your punishment."

"Yes, Sir."

She'd thought maybe he'd make the final twenty-five either fast, light, or both.

Instead, the next spank was the hardest one so far. Carys screamed, pushing up onto her toes.

"Back in your position," Tristan barked.

If he'd been soft or gentle she might have wavered, but those words were an order from her Master. An order she not only wanted, but needed to obey.

She complied, and he rewarded her by rubbing her clit with the heel of his hand.

"Tell him how he's making you feel," Tristan whispered. "He's doing so well, but he worries."

Aidan. Her beautiful boy, her loving man. "It's perfect, Master Aidan. It's everything I need. I can already... It's easier to breathe now."

"For me, too, baby." She could hear the relief in Aidan's tone. "But don't think I'm done."

Tristan kept up the clit stimulation with one hand as Aidan rained hard, sharp spanks over her burning ass. The pain and pleasure were no longer two sides of the same coin. There wasn't much separation between them.

There was only sensation. Sensation and release.

Carys was alternately screaming and moaning, and even she wasn't sure if the sounds were more pain or pleasure.

"Two more, and I'm not going to go easy on you baby."

Carys sniffled, the tears that streamed from her eyes also making her nose water. "I don't want easy."

"No," Aidan agreed, one finger slipping between her ass cheeks to gently stroke her there.

She pushed back, seeking the double penetration. It had been too, too long since she'd had them both, her body connecting all three of them. She'd almost stopped dreaming about it. Almost.

Instead, he spanked her left cheek, the sound cracking through the club. He'd hit her right where she felt the most tender, the most heat.

Carys yelled out, and waves of sensation rolled from her prickling scalp down to her toes and back.

Then he spanked her right ass cheek. She didn't have air to scream, but her body arched, a movement so intense Tristan's fingers almost slipped out of her sopping wet pussy.

"Punishment over," Tristan declared. "Do you want our cocks?"

More than anything. She'd worried this would be the moment she hesitated, but there wasn't even a glimmer of a thought of turning them down. "Yes, Sir. Please, please."

Aidan groaned behind her, and she felt him rub his cock against her sensitive ass. "Where do you want it?"

"Anywhere," she moaned. "Everywhere."

"Right answer." Tristan stroked her once more and then eased his fingers out of her pussy. He held them up to her lips. "Taste."

She licked his fingers, tasting her own arousal. He shoved his thumb in, forcing her to take more. It was a sure imitation of what he wanted from her.

Every cell in her body felt electric as he removed the restraints, tossing them to the side. Her hands were free, and she knew what she wanted to do with them.

"Knees, Carys," Tristan ordered. "Then take out my cock. Aidan, I think our poor sub's pussy needs something to fill it."

"I think I can handle it," Aidan said with a deep chuckle.

Oh, how she wanted to turn her head and watch as Aidan untied his leathers, see his big, gorgeous cock that would split her pussy wide while she sucked on Tristan. But she couldn't handle another spanking, and they were damn serious about her obedience this evening. So she lowered herself to the padded floor and worked the ties of Tristan's leathers. She glanced up and caught sight of the hungry look on his face.

He smoothed back her hair, mouthing the words she'd longed to hear for two and a half years.

I love you.

They were a balm to her soul. She could do this. She could find a way to forgive him, to trust he wouldn't leave them again.

She took his big cock in her hands, and her Master's eyes closed in obvious pleasure.

She leaned in and licked his cockhead as she felt Aidan moving behind her. His hand flattened against the small of her back.

"Hands and knees, baby," Aidan ordered.

Tristan dropped to his knees, spreading them wide in a masculine approximation of how she greeted him.

Surrender. He was telling her it didn't merely go one way.

She leaned over to bring her mouth to his cock. The movement sent her ass in the air, and Aidan lost no time. His hands found her hips as she licked Tristan's cock and brought him into her mouth. She groaned as she felt Aidan's cock slide across her pussy before starting to thrust inside.

Pure sensation. They'd primed her body with perfection, the pain amplifying every second of pleasure.

Tristan's hands cupped her head, taking control of her movements and showing off the fact that he and Aidan hadn't lost their perfect rhythm. They fell into their roles with ease, as though nothing had ever gone wrong between them.

Carys let Tristan use her mouth, allowing him to move in and out, finding his rhythm and synch with Aidan, whose cock stroked over and over inside her, pushing her to the brink again.

Heat pierced through her, and then Tristan gave her hair a sharp tug.

"You take care of me first. You take everything I give you.

Swallow me down like the good sub I know you are." He growled the words, and she could feel he was close. He sounded savage and hungry, and only she could satisfy him.

She rode the wave that rolled from Aidan through her and to Tris, leaving the rational, sensible Carys behind so she could revel in being their sub. She rolled her tongue around Tristan's cock until she felt the first spurt of salty essence. Tristan groaned and held her hard as he stroked in again and again. She drank him down, feeling more powerful than she'd felt ever in her life.

Tris was right. She was totally an exhibitionist, and she could quickly get addicted to this. They would be playing on the dungeon floor a lot if she had any say in it.

And she did. Even as she sucked Tristan dry and felt Aidan deep in her pussy, she knew she was the one who had the power. All of this, all the pain and pleasure was for her.

"Give it to her," Tristan commanded. "Make our good girl come like she's never fucking come before."

Aidan seemed to know he'd been let off the leash, and he suddenly went wild. He thrust inside her while Tristan stroked her hair and kissed the top of her head.

Tenderness and savagery. It was a heady combination, sending her screaming over the edge. This was no minor orgasm. This was a wildfire lit in her veins, burning away what had come before and leaving her feeling new and young.

She felt Aidan come inside her, warming her. She fell forward, but Tristan was there to catch her, Aidan's weight pressing them all together.

A pulse of pure bliss went through her.

"You okay, baby?" He didn't sound like a Dom now. He was her boyfriend, the man she'd loved since she was a child. Tristan was all tenderness now.

"I am perfect," she replied with a smile. "But I will definitely require some aftercare."

* * * *

Tristan stood in the lounge, looking out over the dungeon floor, feeling better than he had in…years. It had been years since his soul

212

felt so settled. Since he wasn't thinking about who he was hurting and who was looking to hurt him.

He'd spent hours taking care of Carys with Aidan. Hours where they'd ensured her skin was okay, that she was relaxed and happy. Hours healing his relationship with the man who held a part of his soul. Topping Carys together and then caring for her had worked miracles when it came to Aidan.

He'd answered every question they'd had. Told them about why he'd done the things he'd done. What it had felt like to realize he had all this responsibility on him and no one to talk to. It had been a hard conversation made so much easier because they were all naked and in bed together.

Now they were napping in a privacy room, but he was too wound up.

The club, however, was starting to wind down. The main stage was dark, and there were only two of the smaller scene spaces being used. He'd been told Gabriel Lodge had given the baby Doms a long lecture before sending them to the locker room for the night. Daisy and Kenz had apparently spent time talking to the subs, discussing the scenes they'd watched.

Tris took a long swig of the beer he'd snagged from the bar and looked out over the dungeon floor with a sense of deep satisfaction. The club wasn't perfect. It was definitely a downgrade from The Court, the DC club he visited from time to time, but it felt like he belonged here.

He wished he'd been one of the people to work on the space. It didn't matter. He'd been gone and now he was back, and he would do the work it took to be a real member again.

Damn, but he felt good. He felt right. Like something had magically fallen into place. Like he was back where he belonged, and he was never leaving again.

"What is that thing on your face, brother?"

He turned and Zach moved in beside him, a beer in his hand. They were the only two in the lounge, the sub who worked the bar having long since gone home. The Hideout was big enough to have a bar but small enough it wasn't always manned. It was cool. Most of them knew how to grab their own beers.

"Thing on my face?" Tris asked. The lights were still set at play level, giving the whole place a club atmosphere, and he was reminded there was still some fun going on downstairs since he could hear the snap of a whip and then a masculine groan. "Are Kala and Coop still at it?"

Zach snorted and leaned against the railing, looking out over the dungeon. "They are hardcore, and so fucked up it hurts to watch them. Is the problem with them that they're both tops? Also, I was talking about the smile on your face. I don't think I've seen you smile before. It looks weird on you, man."

He playfully gave his friend the finger. "Fuck you, but also, I am happy tonight. And the problem with Coop and Kala started a long time ago. They never discuss it but one day they were doing this sort of dating thing, going on doubles with me and Carys and A, and the next she didn't talk to him for a year. They got back to being something like friends before the end of high school, and then rarely saw each other until Drake and Taylor brought the twins in and they built the team."

Zach nodded as though he'd had something confirmed for him. "Kala says her dad forced her to take Coop on the team. I've never believed that."

"Because it's a lie she tells herself." He didn't want to think about Kala and Cooper tonight. He wasn't sure they were salvageable, and he didn't blame Kala for all of their problems. She'd been so in love with him as a kid she would have forgiven him almost anything. So whatever had happened, it had been bad. He studied Zach. "You know you have a weird expression on your face, too. Almost like you had a nice night. Did I see you with Devi?"

He could have sworn when he'd looked out in the audience, he'd seen Devi standing in front of Zach, one of his hands almost possessively resting on her shoulder.

Zach's lips kicked up. "Well, you know I'm not a man to kiss and tell, but I did get the chance to spend some time with her. After she got brave enough to come looking for me. Turns out she's kind of got a crush on me."

Zach seemed pleased with himself, but there were problems with the scenario. "She's TJ's sister, you know."

Though he'd been given a hearty lecture from his own sister about staying out of her romantic choices. He would. He would totally stay out of them until the moment she picked an asshole who hurt her, and then he would kill the son of a bitch. See. He was allowing her to make her own choices.

He wasn't sure how TJ would feel about his sister hanging around big, dangerous-looking Zach.

"I am well aware, and I wouldn't have played with her at all if I wasn't interested in seeing where it goes," Zach said. "I've always thought she was cute. Now I know she's beautiful and funny and kind of awesome. Did you know she's a fashion designer? Erin and Theo Taggart's daughter designs fancy dresses."

"She definitely gets it from Theo," Tris snarked. Aunt Erin was not known for her fashion sense. Her ability to take out the bad guys in numerous violent ways was another story. "But seriously, I don't know she's someone you should play around with. You might think because her mom's super tough, she is, too."

Zach turned his way, his expression going serious. "I didn't say I was playing."

But Tris knew something Zach hadn't mentioned. "We all know how you feel about Tasha."

"And she's marrying someone else. Look, I admit I had a hell of a torch for that woman, and I have the scars to prove it. But I am capable of moving on, and I'm not pining. I never expected she would care for me the way I wanted her to. I'm happy she's found someone she loves." Zach paused as though he wasn't entirely sure he wanted to continue. Then he sighed and took another swig of beer. "I think it's all the coupling up going on around me. I might be like hormonal or something, but I've kind of started to think I want a real relationship with a woman I could come to love. And I think I might have found her tonight."

Tris actually felt his jaw drop. Zach was kind of the player of the group. He was the one they sent in when they needed a guy to flirt with a target. Cooper was incapable of charming anyone who wasn't Kala Taggart, though it was kind of wasted on her. And Tris himself wouldn't because he was taken even when he pretended he wasn't. "Big Tag's going to be so upset. Unless you plan on keeping work and home separate things."

Zach snorted. "Nah. If this thing works between us, I'll have to close down my honey pot days." He chuckled. "I kind of never thought I would settle down. And it's like super early between us, so don't take this as a promise or anything, but I will be able to tell TJ I'm serious about giving it a shot. We have a date planned. We're going to go to dinner and maybe a movie. That's good, right? It's a normal person date?"

He said the words like he'd had to consider them for more than a hot minute. "Dude, when was the last time you dated?"

Zach seemed to think for a moment. "I went out with Leah Johnson all my senior year of college, but mostly we fucked in the back room of the GameStop we both worked at. She was the assistant manager, so I was kind of screwing my superior. Mostly we fucked and tried out new games after hours. She was excellent at first-person shooters. I tried to convince her to go into the Army. But we went to the Chili's for lunch most days. That's a date, right?"

He and Zach had talked a lot over the years. He probably knew Zach better than anyone on the team. But they hadn't talked much about prior relationships. Now he wondered if it was because Zach hadn't had any. "Nope. Eating skillet queso during your lunch break after getting it on in the break room doesn't qualify as a date. Are you telling me you didn't date in high school? College?"

Zach groaned and moved from the landing to one of the comfy couches. "See, this is why I only talk about sports and manly shit. Big Tag is right. All the other stuff is bullshit."

"Well, I'm sure that attitude is going to serve you well with the artistic sub you seem to want to experiment with." Tris joined him. He knew he should go back to the privacy room where his subs were sleeping, but he was fascinated with a side of Zach he'd never thought he would see. What had Devi done to the man? Zach seemed like all Dom all the time, and not the one who was looking for a particular sub. It had kind of made sense when he'd found out Zach thought he was in love with Tasha. He kept his encounters to the surface, always explaining what he was willing to give and what he wasn't willing to give. Always, always, always with a contract. Actually, now that he thought about it… "Whoa, did you talk to her or did you…because you don't like carry around a contract. Tell me you don't have a blank contract for the subs you sleep with."

Zach's head fell back, and he groaned. "I wish I could, man. But no, I did not have Devi Taggart sign a contract."

Tris breathed a sigh of relief. So this was still at the talking stage. "Good, because again, I think you should be careful with her. You're gone a lot, and I think she probably needs more stability."

A brow rose over Zach's eyes. "More than Carys and Aidan need? Because what happened on stage tonight looked pretty fucking serious."

Well, he had to tell him sometime. "It was serious. I'm out. I'm going to let Big Tag get me out of my contract, and I'll only work for our team from now on. After this op, I'm handing the whole Jester mission to you and Tara, and I know you'll find someone who can do a magnificent job. Hell, Taylor Radcliffe might want to take it herself. She's good at this kind of an op. She can't physically be The Jester, but she can handle anything online. You can do all the physical stuff."

"Uh, I was going to talk to my CO about maybe moving my base of operations from DC to Dallas and focusing as much as I possibly can on our team," Zach admitted.

Again, he was floored. "That must have been a hell of a talk if you're willing to give up The Court."

Tris went every now and then when he felt like he needed to keep his skills up or when there was a social event requiring his attention. Zach was there all the time.

"I prefer this place. I know The Court is luxurious and stuff, but I'm… I think I'm more me here. Or I'm becoming the me I want to be. Yep, I'm just going to do it. We never tell Big Tag this conversation happened. Am I clear?"

Oh, he was so deeply curious. Zach seemed like a rock. He wasn't exactly forthcoming when it came to personal stuff. They'd been working together for years. Zach was the one who took care of the subs Tris topped at The Court since he would never touch one in a sexual fashion.

Huh, had he been trying to replace Aidan? Like he always needed a partner…

He shoved the self-reflection aside because finding out what made Zach tick seemed way more interesting. "As crystal."

Zach sat back. "Okay, and if I get too…I don't know…personal, tell me, but I might need some advice because I don't date and I don't want to scare this girl off. I can be intense, though she handled me fine tonight. So I didn't date in high school because I didn't have time. My dad ran off when I was young, though not before he knocked my mom up twice. She was actually super smart. She was like a STEM girl before it was a thing."

"You have a sibling?" It was news to him.

"I do, but we didn't grow up together," Zach said, taking a quick sip of his beer. "By the time she was pregnant the second time, she'd gotten into trouble. She ran into the kinds of problems a single mom can, including owing money to people who don't send you to a collection agency, if you know what I mean."

Well, he'd heard Zach had some unsavory connections. "I do indeed. So she what? Sold the kid?"

"I believe gave up for adoption is the term we typically use, though I always wondered. She was in prison for cooking designer drugs when she gave birth. I was only a year old at the time, so I often wonder why she didn't give me up, too. It was a closed adoption, and even after she eventually got out, she wouldn't talk about it. I only know the kid exists because of my aunt."

"The one who worked with Big Tag?" He'd heard the story about Zach's heroic aunt who did some work with the big boss when he was in the Green Berets. The aunt had been thrilled when she'd found out her nephew would be working under the man she'd so admired.

Zach nodded. "The one who gave up her military career so I didn't go into foster care. Needless to say, we lived in a small town and we struggled. So when other guys were partying, I worked two jobs so we could keep the trailer we lived in."

It appeared there was a reason Zach rarely talked about his family. "How long was your mom in jail?"

"She did seven years, and then she got out and got involved in some other bad shit. She lived with my aunt and I for a few years, and then one day when I was fourteen, the cops came looking for her and I haven't seen her again," Zach explained. "My aunt told me she didn't want me to come visit, and I honored her choice. Even when she was around she wasn't, you know. She was always hustling, doing whatever she could to make money. Illegally, of course. It's not like she got a job that used her degree in a good way. I wonder what she could have been if she hadn't met my father. It was my dad who got her into trouble. He worked for some bad people, and she fell in with them. According to my aunt, he enjoyed the idea of corrupting some

218

egghead scientist. So she's probably cooking meth somewhere or dead. I don't know. Anyway, I didn't date because I worked. I managed to scrape together enough to get through college and then went into the Army. I liked the Army, but it's also not particularly conducive to a relationship."

And he had some unresolved conflict with his mother that would lead to distrust and abandonment issues when it came to women.

Tris had helped test Aidan and Carys when they were undergrads. He'd really gotten something out of the psych classes they'd taken. "What changed?"

Zach seemed to think about it for a moment. "The team. Being around Ian and Charlotte. Making some friends I can actually count on. I started this whole journey… Well, let's just say my plans upended and the things I wanted back then aren't what I want now. Now I want to work with my team and come to the club with a sub who I take care of for more than an orgasm. One who sees me as more than a Dom. I want what the people in this crazy group want. You know I was sent in by the higher-ups to find anything I could to discredit this experiment."

Their team worked differently than other Agency teams. Tris could understand why some people would worry about them. Change was scary. "I think we all suspected. But we got to you."

Zach shrugged. "You could say that. My bosses aren't happy with me, but there's not a lot they can do. I'm not giving them anything they could use to dismantle the team. We have to be careful, though. We've been vigilant about protecting the twins, but if it gets out…"

"They'll both be in danger," Tris concluded.

"We'll all be in danger." Zach turned solemn. "Have you thought about the fact that the attack might not have been about TJ?"

Only every minute since it had happened. "You think someone knows I took over The Jester's identity? I've been very careful. When we needed a physical presence, I sent someone else. Always someone different, and we never gave them the full information. If it's gotten out, then we have a leak."

It was absolutely his worst fear.

"I'm worried about it," Zach agreed. "No one knew where you were. TJ's kept a low profile."

"But it's not hard to guess TJ was probably going to be at his cousin's wedding," Tristan pointed out. "The bigger problem is why they would attack the way they did. TJ can't talk if he's dead."

"It could be a message. I want you and TJ to be on the lookout for any odd communication that could be read as a threat." Zach shifted, his gaze going over to the stairs leading up from the dungeon floor. "Hey."

The biggest smile came over Zach's face, lighting him up.

Devi strode into the lounge wearing street clothes. A plain white top over jeans she rolled up at the feet for a casual look, her red hair flowing around her shoulders. She was quite lovely when he thought about it. She'd always been a little sister to him.

And she had absolutely no time for anyone except Zach. "Hello, Sir."

Zach looked weird. Giddy. Like he was the one with a crush. He stood and immediately got into her space, his hands going to her hips while he loomed over her. "You want to get some waffles?"

She was grinning as she tilted her head up. "Sounds wonderful."

Then Zach leaned down and kissed her. Not a friendly kiss. More like a "I'm going to inhale you like I've never breathed before" kiss. It went on for a while. He wondered if they were going to go at it right here. Finally, the captain came up for air.

Zach smoothed back her hair, looking at her like he'd never seen a woman before. "I'll meet you downstairs. I've got to grab my bag."

She nodded and walked away. She probably hadn't even noticed Tris was there.

"I thought you were talking to her. You two played, and maybe something more," Tris said, trying not to make it an accusation. "You told me you didn't sleep with her."

Zach's head shook as he tossed the beer into the trash. "No. I said we didn't sign a contract. And that should tell you something. I don't lose my head often. I'm going to have some waffles and probably stay up way too late, but hey, I can sleep when I'm dead. See you soon, brother."

Zach practically jogged down the stairs.

"Who the hell was that? Because the Zach I know doesn't smile like that." Aidan walked into the lounge from the entrance leading back to the privacy rooms on this floor.

Carys was behind him, wrapped in a robe and looking soft and sexy and sleepy. "I thought I saw him with Devi."

Why was Aidan letting her walk? He was going to have a talk with his partner. Tristan strode to Carys and had her in his arms in a heartbeat. "I think we'll be seeing more of them together. Zach's got a crush. Now I think we should get you home and into bed, and I am not sleeping on the floor tonight. We're going to give TJ a break and let Kala back into her bedroom."

Carys's head drifted to his shoulder, her whole body relaxed in his arms. "You better have coffee at your place."

He hadn't actually been to his place in a long time, but Cooper drank coffee. "I promise."

Aidan yawned and stretched. "It'll be good to sleep in a bed. That couch thing at the twins' is torture. I like a big bed."

Tristan's was a California king. Built for all three of them. "And I like to please my subs."

Aidan groaned, but he didn't argue.

They were making progress.

Now all they had to do was survive Huisman and he could get back to his real life. To his life with them.

Chapter Twelve

Aidan carried two cups of coffee into the small airport lounge, trying to tamp down the unease growing in his gut.

This was happening. They were getting on the plane to fly into Montreal, and by this time tomorrow, he would be meeting the possibly evil Dr. Huisman. They would fly in and then split up, with he and Carys going to the summit with Kala and Tristan, and the rest setting up in a place close to Huisman's.

He'd spent days learning how to use the communications systems and listening to lectures on how to protect himself and Carys. It involved proving he could defend them both, and he would be smart enough to know flight was preferable to fight in this case.

The number of lectures he'd gotten from the uncles on how he could be killed shocked him. So, so many ways he could die. And he was a doctor. He'd thought he'd known a lot. The uncles had proved him wrong.

But the nights had been another story...

The nights had given him hope they could get back on track, back to the lives they'd promised themselves when they were kids.

They'd spent hours in bed, hours where they'd found their rhythm again.

"Do you have everything? You have the Glock? You remember

how to use the Glock?"

Aidan fought back a groan. His da loved him. He was worried about him. It wasn't annoying. It was good his father cared.

And cared. And worried. And peppered him with questions like he was taking the SATs again.

"Da, I have the Glock. It's the one you taught me on. I know how to use it but if it gets bad, I assure you I will cover Carys with my own body and when we get a chance, we'll run and hide somewhere. Shouldn't you be at work?" He'd said good-bye to them already this morning. He'd hugged his mom and sister and shaken hands with Nate, who'd promised to take care of Daisy. He'd given his father a long hug and said he'd see him soon.

He hadn't meant this soon.

It was like he was fourteen and going away on a school trip and his father was telling him to make good choices.

"I suppose. I wanted to go over it one last time," his father admitted. "Big Tag assures me there should be no reason for you to sacrifice your life. It's a simple op, and all you have to do is be yourself. You're the cover. You're the reason Tristan will have access. You and Carys just smile and have fun at the conference. Though I don't see how it's fun."

"Because you have no real interest in talking with the finest minds in the medical field," Aidan shot back, looking around the now pretty crowded lounge. They were set to leave in twenty minutes, and Cooper was already in the hanger doing his preflight check.

The rest of the team was hanging out in the lounge. Kala was half asleep on one of the chairs, while her twin was on the phone with someone talking animatedly about the events of the last few days. The romantic ones, of course. Kenzie Taggart would have felt right at home in a Regency ballroom, gossiping behind her fan. Lou was reading on her tablet, with TJ lying on the bench with his head in her lap. Tristan was talking to his father and Big Tag, while Carys was sipping on coffee and talking to her father.

"Is Sean coming with us?" If Sean came, would his father insist on coming, too?

His da frowned. "No. He made a case, of course. Big Tag said they already had too many cooks in the kitchen. Also, he doesn't have Adam's connections, so he can't get clearance. The bastards. The man's daughter is going into danger."

Which likely meant Da had tried and gotten the same treatment. "I thought she was going to a conference."

"You know what I mean." His da sighed. "At least you and Tris seemed to have figured things out. Are you solid with him again? I've talked to Big Tag about what Tristan's been working on, and while I don't think he was right to do what he did, I can understand the impulse. He got in over his head, and he was afraid."

"I know."

His da studied him for a moment. "But what you did was worse. You understand that now, right?"

"I shouldn't have kept it from Carys. I should have insisted he bring her in so she wasn't alone." He'd definitely thought about this for the last couple of days. When he wasn't in bed with them. Playing with them. Being with them.

"Has anyone talked about what Carys did wrong?" His father glanced over to where Carys stood, looking so pretty it hurt. The private airport lounge had skylights, and the morning light bathed her, making the gold and brown highlights in her auburn hair striking.

"She didn't do anything wrong. She was innocent in all of it." If there was one thing he was sure of, it was that Carys didn't deserve anything from the torture of the last few years.

His father frowned. "Now see, I'm worried again. Until you all understand what went wrong, what each of you contributed to the problem, I don't know you can solve it. Something will come up and the wedge will be there again because the problem can't be solved by simply getting back into bed together. Tristan knows damn well what he did, and I hope he doesn't falter under the weight of it. Like I said, he got in over his head, and there's nothing shameful about it. His mistake wasn't trying, it was refusing to ask for help. It was cutting you two out. You should never have followed his orders, son. I understand he's…"

Aidan felt a flush go through him because he knew what his father had been about to say. Had everyone known but him? Was he going to avoid saying it? This was another thing he'd thought about endlessly over the last few days. Was he ashamed of who he was? He'd been more present because Tris was back and insisting they spend real time together. Not the turn on the TV, eat some take out and read a medical journal and call it quality time. And what did they call it in their world? "Just because he's my Dom doesn't mean he's always correct, and when he's not I have to push back and do what's right for all of us."

"Exactly," his da said.

"Does it bother you?"

"Like I said, I wish you'd been honest with Carys," his da began.

"I didn't mean what happened with Carys. I was talking about my relationship with Tris," Aidan said, opening a door he'd thought he would keep locked forever. "Does it bother you and Mom?"

"Why would it bother me? Son, if I could get over the whole weird threesome thing, I can handle anything." He sighed. "Sorry. Somewhere your mother is slapping me on the back and telling me to use my grown-up words. So I'm going to. Aidan, there's nothing you can do in this world that would make me turn from you. Not a damn thing. I could be disappointed in you for harming others, but it's not in you, so it's easy to say. You needing Tris in the way you do, there's nothing to be bothered about. I'm actually quite proud because you never really questioned it. I think your mother and I did well. You didn't sit around worried something was wrong with you."

"I'll be honest, I don't think I even recognized it until he was gone and I tried to be the top," Aidan admitted. "I tried to give Carys what she needed, but what we both needed was him."

"I have no doubt in my mind if Tris was gone forever, you would find your way." His father put a hand on Aidan's shoulder and stared him in the eyes. "You would adapt, but you don't have to because I believe him when he says he's coming home. But it is up to you to figure out everything that went wrong so you can look for the signs and not let it happen again."

Aidan sighed. "Or you could tell me, Da."

His da patted his cheek. "Oh, with things like this, revelation is half the prize. Now you be safe, my boy. Are you sure you have everything?"

"Li, leave the kid alone," Big Tag said. "Aren't you supposed to be running the company while I'm gone?"

"Alex is doing fine," his da groused back. He turned to Tag. "Don't you dare get me boy killed. I spent too much on his education. He's my retirement plan."

His father had done well for them all. He'd invested wisely and wouldn't need to sponge off his kids. His father was actually everything he wanted to be. "Da, thanks for coming down to see me off."

His father smiled and pulled him in for a manly hug. "Of course. I love you, son."

"I love you, too."

"I promise I'll take care of him." Carys had joined them, grinning at his father. "He thinks he'll be the one saving me, but I've been told on this team the men are usually the ones who need saving."

Aidan stepped back. "You need to stop listening to your cousins. I assure you if things go wrong, I'll expect you to hide behind me."

"I expect you to hide, too." Sean Taggart put an arm around his daughter and leaned over to brush a kiss over her forehead. "You find a place to hide and wait for your cousins."

"Or she'll go to a conference and get childbirth mansplained by a hundred obnoxious men who think they know more about it than the obstetrical resident." Big Tag shook his head his brother's way. "And don't think you're sneaking on this plane. I've already got to deal with Adam. I checked his bags to make sure he didn't stuff Jake into one of them. You know this is an Agency team not a family reunion."

Carys frowned. "Actually, that sounds worse than potentially getting shot at."

"No one's getting shot at." Tristan moved to the other side of Carys. "This is a simple op. You're going to be surrounded by people and you'll have eyes on you. My father and I are going to use the access I'll have because I'm your bodyguard to try to get into Huisman's personal systems. He has to have them, and I would bet anything it's at his house. We get in, get what we need, and you enjoy the conference. Well, Aidan will. Carys will be treated like his arm candy."

Carys wrinkled her nose and playfully elbowed Tris. "Again with the more fun getting shot at."

The door to the lounge opened, and Zach strode in. He wasn't alone. He had an arm around Devi Taggart's shoulders, and those two were in step. Like there was nothing awkward about it. Like they'd been together for years.

He hadn't known they were together at all.

Big Tag's brows rose. "Dude, did you not get the not-a-family-reunion memo? You brought my niece to an Agency meeting? You know she's not supposed to know who you work for."

Zach's arm didn't move from its deeply possessive position. "Everyone knows, and every day with this team is a freaking family reunion. Devi gave me a ride."

Carys cleared her throat. Likely because they were thinking the same thing. She sure had given him a ride. Probably more than one.

Kala had woken when her twin poked her as Zach walked in the room. She and Kenz were both staring at the new couple like they couldn't quite believe what they were seeing. Tasha had walked in from the hanger and her jaw had dropped, but Charlotte was grinning like she'd known it all along.

Only Tris didn't look shocked. He looked grim. Like he was worried.

"I just wanted to say hi, and y'all go and get whatever bad guys need to be gotten." Devi looked a lot like her mom but without Erin Taggart's solemnity. When Devi smiled there was no darkness behind it.

Big Tag sighed and shook his head. "We're leaving now. Zach, we're going to have a talk."

"I expected we would, sir." Zach said the words with respect and a hint of trepidation, but then he kissed Devi like a starving man.

Kenzie was on her phone, texting like mad. Lou had put down her tablet and watched with wide eyes.

TJ was asleep. It fit perfectly with his personal brand. His sister was getting happily mauled by an Army captain, and he was curled up on his girlfriend's lap catching some zzzs.

Devi pulled back. "Hey, don't forget you were going to warn them about the Tara person."

Zach winced. "Yeah, uhm, we're going to have to be careful with the twins because Tara's already in Montreal. I'm sorry, Tris. I just found out about it. Did she call you?"

Carys's head swiveled, looking to Tris. "Tara?"

"She works as my technical assistant when I'm dealing with The Jester missions." Tris moved into her space. If it bothered him her father was standing there, he didn't show it. This was a more confident Tristan. He cupped Carys's face. "There's no reason for any

227

jealousy. She's nothing but a woman I work with."

"Oh, I wasn't warning anyone because I was worried she would upset Carys." Zach had Devi in a half hug like she was his teddy bear or something and he didn't want to give her up. "I've worked with them both for years. Nothing there but work. However, she doesn't have clearance to know about the twins, so we need to be careful and make sure she's not waiting at the airport to give us a briefing. She said she's already met with CSIS, and they're going to have an operative liaising while we're in Canada."

"It better not be Ben." Kenzie stood and sighed. "Someone tell me when I have to hide. I hope she's not there because I'll have to hide in the stupid plane and get an Uber. A Canadian Uber."

Kala stood. "Hey, if you get an Uber, you can stop at Tim Horton's. Dad won't let us. There's an upside."

"It's only because they didn't have lemon donuts the last time, and now Dad won't forgive an entire country," Kenzie groused. "But you're right. I'll totally grab some donuts. And maybe stop and get some crêpes. You know, now I see the advantages."

Tasha stared after her sisters. "Now she's going to try to sight-see, and I'll be the one who has to point out all the CCTV cameras and that other intelligence agencies also know how to use logic and technology. Mom, maybe I should stay and make sure Uncle Alex and Uncle Li don't burn down the company."

"I won't burn anything down. You know I've been running this company for a long time while your parents gallivant around the world," his da pointed out.

"She's trying to stay with Dare," Charlotte explained, following her daughters. "He can't go with us this time because he's actually working and not using his job as a cover. It's refreshing. Come along. TJ, wake up. Your sister's being manhandled."

"Am not," Devi protested. "I mean not in a way I'm not happy about."

TJ yawned and sat up. "Is it time to go? Hey, sis. What are you doing here?"

Yeah, he was going to let TJ figure it out for himself. He already had to watch his own sister get lovingly mauled by a large piece of Australia on a regular basis. When he'd tried to "protect" her... Well, he'd been the one who'd needed protection.

"Come on," Tris said, reaching for Carys's hand. "I'll tell you everything about Tara and we'll go over the op one more time. By this time next week, we'll be home and I'll be out of this."

Aidan said good-bye to his father and followed them out of the lounge. One more week and they'd be free.

"Dude, you know she's my sister, right? What is happening?" TJ asked. "I'm very confused. Dude takes one little nap…"

"Take care of her," Sean shouted out, standing next to Liam.

"Always." He and Tris managed to say the word at the exact same time.

It was good to be back in synch.

* * * *

One more week and she would have a decision to make.

Carys looked around what her uncle had called their safe house. It was a big house outside of Montreal proper. She, Aidan, Tristan, and Kala would go and stay at a hotel downtown tonight, but the rest of the team would be staying and monitoring the situation from here.

"Mr. Miles, I can't tell you how excited I am to get to meet you." Tara Hahn was roughly thirty, with dark hair cut in a chic bob. She was pretty in an intellectual fashion. A little like people had described Carys herself over the years. The Agency employee had been waiting when they'd entered the safe house, and she'd immediately pulled Tristan and Zach away for a brief meeting before introducing herself to Uncle Ian and Aunt Charlotte.

The whole flight she'd had one of them at her side and one across from her. They'd traded seats about halfway through, Tristan complaining because he hadn't gotten to molest her the way Aidan had. It had been sweet, and he'd proceeded to make his uncle grumble about chastity and why none of the youth have it. She'd gotten off the plane and held both their hands as they'd sat in the back of one of the big SUVs that had picked them up.

And the minute Tristan disappeared with Tara and Zach, all of her suspicions came back, shaking the peace of the last few days.

"It's nice to meet you, too." Adam had on his smoothest smile, the one he used for what Carys liked to call his groupies. He was famous in the tech world for his innovative software designs. Adam had spent the whole flight either talking in low tones with Ian and Charlotte or staring at his laptop. He was serious about fixing this situation. "I understand you work tech for my son. I kind of thought my son worked tech himself. When he explained what his place on the team would be, he told his family it would be behind a computer."

Tristan sent his father a look that was half pleading and half annoyed. "Papa, you promised."

A hand came up, waving him off. "I'm adjusting."

"Tris is too good to be a simple tech," Tara announced. "He's the best agent I work with. I've been trying to convince him to leave military intelligence and concentrate all of his talents on his Agency work. He's brilliant in the field."

So while Tristan might see her as nothing more than a coworker, it was obvious Tara had a crush.

"I certainly wouldn't say brilliant," Tris countered. "Otherwise, we wouldn't be in the situation we're in today. Do you have anything new on the men who tried to kill my girlfriend and partner? By the way, this is Carys Taggart and Aidan O'Donnell. It was their wedding."

Tara frowned. "They were getting married, but she's your girlfriend?"

So he hadn't talked about her? It was a huge surprise. Tristan was the one who never worried about what "society" thought of him or his relationships.

Zach threw his big body on the couch with a grin. "I want to see how he explains this."

TJ had apparently had his talk with Zach and they were cool because TJ sank down beside Zach and offered him half a PB and J. "Me, too. Continue."

"You know they've been explaining since they were freaking kids." Cooper joined them. "They should be good at it by now."

Tristan ignored their audience. "I've been in a relationship with Carys and Aidan for a long time. It's a lot like my parents' marriage. I've told you I have two fathers and a mom."

Tara seemed flustered at the idea. "Well, you mentioned your parents had a third. I understand the implications of the term. I thought it was like a fun thing your mom did to spice up her marriage. I certainly didn't think you would call your mom's lover dad. I mean it's obvious who your dad is."

"His dad is Jacob Dean," Adam said, going cold. Carys barely stifled a whistle because she'd never seen Tristan's papa be anything but smooth and polite. Tristan's dad was intimidating for sure, but his papa was the sweet one. Now Adam reminded her he'd once been a commando, too. "He refers to me as Papa. It was too confusing when he and his sister were kids. Jake and I rock-paper-scissored for Dad. I think he cheated. I knew the minute it happened Big Tag would give me shit about it."

"Because it makes you sound like the dad in a Disney film set in medieval France." Big Tag proved his hearing hadn't gone since he was yelling it from the kitchen. "Are you going to break into song, Papa?"

Adam's eyes rolled. "See. I knew *that* would happen."

"I'm only saying, it's clear you're Tristan's biological father. He looks exactly like you," Tara attempted.

"I have two fathers." Tristan proved he could go as cold as his papa. "Biology means nothing in my family. Now, I don't require your approval, but I do need you to understand I'll ask for you to be removed from this op if you can't respect my partners. I haven't mentioned them to you because I was trying to protect them."

There was no way to miss the hurt in Tara's eyes. "From me? It has to be me since you obviously told Zach."

"I'm trying to protect them from anyone who might figure out I've been acting as The Jester for the last few years," Tristan corrected. "Zach works on this team with me, and they absolutely understand my relationship situation, so it's not the same. If I didn't work with him on both teams, I never would have told him. I've been careful with who I talked to about Carys and Aidan because I was trying to keep a target off them."

"I know you were worried about your sister and mom." Tara looked Carys's way and gave her a once-over. "I didn't realize you had a girlfriend. Or a...uhm, boyfriend?"

Cooper snorted. "See, this is why I avoid the threesome. There are so many questions."

"I'm his partner. No further explanation needed." Aidan moved closer, sliding his arm around her waist. "Now I would love an answer to Tris's question. Do we know anything else?"

"Spoilsport," Zach said.

Tristan frowned his way. "You know you're trying to get into this family. There will be payback."

Zach's grin kicked up. "I'm looking forward to it."

Lou and Kala walked in, carrying a tray of sandwiches and some water bottles. They placed them on the dining table.

"Did we get all the weird explanations of why Tristan's going to be sleeping with the bait tonight out of the way?" Kala asked. "Someone better have gotten a suite because I am not sleeping in the same room where double penetration is happening."

"She's serious," Lou said, lowering herself onto TJ's lap. "It's why we left without the chips. Uncle Ian and Aunt Charlotte are going at it in the kitchen. Do not go in there. He was inspired by the sight of a wooden spoon. We're going to have to replace it."

Kala gagged as she sat on the side of the couch nearest to Cooper. "They are so gross."

"Hush. You know it's lovely our parents still love each other." Tash entered the great room from outside where she'd been pacing and talking on her cell. "I think I finally got the package where it needs to be."

From what Carys had heard, the package was Kenz, and they would be smuggling her into the safe house where she would be confined to the attic room when Tara and the CSIS agent would be around. There had been a ton of moaning about it. Tara knew the team was run by Ian Taggart and his wife and that the members all had close ties. But the CSIS dude didn't know their familial connections, and neither of them knew Kenzie and Kala were the mysterious Ms. Magenta. Well, they knew one of them was. Not two of them were… It was confusing, but Carys knew her main job around the intelligence people was to keep her mouth shut.

It gave her too much time to think.

Although if Kenzie were the one portraying "Kara," she wouldn't complain about the possibility of double penetration. She would say it was romantic, and it was.

There was nothing better than being between the two men she loved most in the world.

If she could trust it.

"Excellent," Tristan said and took a seat close to her. He reached out a hand and tugged on hers until she was brought down on his lap.

"Uh, shouldn't we…" Carys wasn't sure they should fly their freak flag around his tech.

"Hush." His arm wound around her waist, pulling her in close. His voice went low and deep. "We're in the field. You promised to obey me in the field."

"You did," Aidan pointed out with a smirk. He took the chair next to them.

"You both did," Tristan said firmly. "And you know damn well I wasn't merely talking about when the bullets went flying. We're in my world, and I'm going to be in control when it comes to the two of you."

She wished the words didn't do something for her. She took a long breath and relaxed against him, letting her head fall to his shoulder.

Tara cleared her throat and then took a seat across from them. Carys glanced over and Cooper had a hand over Kala's thigh as she perched next to him. Tasha settled in beside Adam, and Tara was the only one uncomfortable with the situation.

She sat primly, crossing her ankles like she'd been to an excellent prep school for ladies. "Well, we did manage to find the broker who got the mercenary group their helicopter. He's angry about losing the chopper, by the way. He's threatening a lawsuit. I don't think he understands how the legal system works since he's probably never going to see the light of day again."

"It's good to know the illegal arms sector has its share of Karens. Or is it Kevins, since he's a dude?" Aidan asked. "What do we call a male Karen? Because it's pretty sexist to insinuate only women are obnoxious, angry pricks. Which they don't have. Is that sexist? Like reverse sexist?"

"Aidan, you're in a logic loop," Tristan said with a hint of a smile. "Let's not worry about the feelings of the dude who helped the dudes who tried to kill us all."

How long had it been since she'd heard Aidan go into one of his logic loops? He could get lost in one for hours. But he hadn't for years because Tris was always the one to bring him out. It could be anything from misogynistic language and its many forms to politics to whether Superman could beat Thor. Sometimes Tristan would join in on the latter, and she would usually find a quiet place to read while they argued it out.

Damn, but she'd missed how perfectly they'd worked together. Where one of them wasn't interested, the other two had someone to talk to.

She had to find a way to shove these suspicions aside. It might be time she really needed.

"So we know it was a mercenary group?" Zach asked.

Tara's eyes went wide as though what Zach had said kind of floored her. "I sent you a report."

Zach flushed slightly. "I...uhm...I've been preoccupied."

"With my sister," TJ said with a shrug. "But hey, he knows if he fucks up, I'll kill him."

"I'm not going to fuck up," Zach insisted. "Look, dude, I'm screwing up my career. I think that should show you how serious I am. And don't give me all the it's-too-soon shit. Relationships in this group go one of two ways. Either something happens and the couple gets fucked up for years before they finally get their shit together."

"See my parents," Tasha said with a grin. "And Cooper's. Oh, and TJ's. But they're all great now."

"Or they take one look at each other and they're like 'let's skip all the heartache and drama and just do it.'" Zach sat back, looking pleased with himself. "I'm in the second half."

Tasha nodded. "Me too. Though there was some heartache and drama. See, Daisy *is* kind of a novella. Nate didn't even give her a hard time."

Carys brought her head up. "Don't you ever tell her that."

Tristan groaned and drew her back down. "How about we leave the relationship stuff out of this? Tara isn't used to us. Give the girl a chance to catch up. What did we get off the mercenaries?"

Tara huffed. "Did anyone read my report?"

"I certainly did," Adam replied, and then his eyes rolled as he heard a smack from the kitchen. "Ignore them. It's all right. Lou and TJ will get them back at some point. Now, I read the report, and from what I understand, our broker gave up the mercenaries, but he wasn't sure who they were working for."

"He says he didn't have a name, and I'm pretty sure he was telling the truth," Tara replied, looking down at the tablet in her lap.

"The mercenaries were a fairly new group. As far as we can tell they'd only run a couple of jobs together, though the leader is pretty well known for working in Southeast Asia. He's worked for arms dealers in the Philippines, and I believe his group also facilitates the importing of ghost guns into the States."

"Well, then they're assholes of the highest kind," Aidan said. "I spend most of my weekends stitching up bullet wounds."

She knew the toll it took on him. He'd lost his first patient to a GSW. Working the ER in the heart of the city could be soul crushing. She sat up slightly because she was getting drowsy and there was still a lot to do. "Is there any connection to Huisman?"

"Not that I've been able to find," Tara replied. "He was paid in crypto, and the mercenaries were as well. It's damn-near impossible to trace."

"Yes, but communications aren't as hard," Adam said, sitting back. "I managed to find the leader of the merc group's Dark Web page."

"You did? I've been trying to find it for days," Tara admitted.

"Papa is excellent at his job," Tris said. "Though I probably would have found it if I hadn't been distracted."

"Sure you would, son." Adam sighed but moved on. "Oddly enough, the leader of the merc group's cell phone was one of the few things we found in the wreckage. It must have fallen out before the explosion, or I'm going to buy stock in the company who makes the case it was in. Nevertheless, I managed to crack it, and while he was careful, my team pulled enough data that I was able to figure out real names and therefore able to track down his laptop. It was sitting in a hotel room in Fort Worth. We're going through all of it right now, but the important thing we've found is evidence our mercenary was recently paid from an account associated with Disrupt Asia."

"The group Huisman's foundation works with." Carys frowned. "Damn it. I hope we get the grant before you shut the whole foundation down. We need those carts."

Tristan kissed her nose. "I'll make sure you get them, baby." He sat back and looked at his father. "So we can connect it to Disrupt Asia, but I'm sure we'll find while Huisman works with Disrupt North America, he doesn't have ties to Asia."

"He's careful," Zach replied. "My question is why. Why come

after the wedding? If he was looking for The Jester, what would the point be? It's too chaotic. Why not hire an assassin? Or someone to kidnap The Jester? I can't see how what happened at the wedding helped him. If he's looking for information about the bombmaker, killing a bunch of Taggarts is going to do nothing but piss them all off."

"Or it could be about me." TJ rubbed his cheek against Lou's. "We know the intel put out about me being close to The Jester was false, but we also know not everyone is going to believe it wasn't me."

Lou sat up straighter. "But in a way it's true. We just didn't know until later. You are close to The Jester. He's sitting right there."

There was a chiming through the house, and Tara stood. "Maybe we should continue this in a moment. I think our CSIS contact is here. Should we stop all the… What do you call it? D/s stuff around the Canadian operative and try to look like we're professionals? Is this what you and Zach do at that place... What's it called?"

"The Court." Zach sighed and sat up. "And, yes, we should go into professional mode."

Tara nodded. "Thank you. I'll go let him in. Or her. They didn't give me a name. They were kind of rude. I was surprised because they've always been so nice."

Tara went to answer the door.

Zach went into military mode, his shoulders flattening out and back ramrod straight. "Carys and Aidan, feel free to be the couple you are, but the rest of us are operatives working together on a team, and we're giving this guy nothing. Though whoever it is has almost certainly gotten a report on us. Ben Parker would make sure of it."

He was talking about the one who Kenzie was mad at.

The Court.

What the hell was The Court?

Is this what you and Zach do at that place… What's it called?

A cold wash of revelation swept through her. The Court. It could only be one thing.

A club. Tristan had been going to a club for the last two years?

She sat up and stiffly allowed Aidan to help her to her feet. Everyone around her was standing and decoupling. Kala went to the door separating the great room from the kitchen. She knocked loudly.

"Hey, perverts. We have incoming from Canada's finest, and it's probably that asshole."

Tristan stood behind her. "Hey, are you okay?"

He'd played at a club. He'd topped subs.

Aunt Charlotte came out first, smoothing her hair back and giving her daughter a smile. "CSIS is here? Sorry, we were working out dinner plans."

"Sure you were," Tasha replied and gestured to the stairs. "You need to go make sure everything's okay up there."

Charlotte nodded and jogged up the stairs toward the attic where Kenzie was staying.

Uncle Ian came out, the French doors opening to accommodate his big form. "And it can't be him because I told CSIS I wouldn't work with him."

"And they always do what Mr. Lemon tells them to, don't they?" Tara was followed by a tall man with movie-star good looks, who quickly assessed the room. His gaze settled on Kala. "Maggie."

"Fucking Ben Parker." Kala's eyes narrowed.

The team started to argue, but all Carys could think about was the fact that he'd lied to her. Again.

A familiar numbness settled over her.

"Carys, I asked you a question," Tristan said, though his tone was gentle. "Are you all right?"

She forced her lips to curve up. She wouldn't say anything here, so she had to convince him everything was fine. It was easy since she was an excellent actress. "Great. I'll go see if the conference room needs anything. I take it we're starting the meeting over again?"

Tristan stared at her for a moment. Aidan did, too. "Yes. We should be able to go to the hotel in a couple of hours. We'll talk there."

"Of course." She took a deep breath and walked away.

At least she had some time to figure out if she even wanted this battle. Or if it was time to walk away.

Chapter Thirteen

Tris watched as Carys left the room. She'd given him the smile she gave people she hated but tolerated for the sake of keeping the peace. He knew all her smiles, and the one on her face right now was the worst-case scenario when it came to him. Aidan moved in close, watching her, too. His voice went low.

"Dude, she is pissed. What is she pissed... Fuck." Aidan's face fell.

"Yeah, I hadn't mentioned I was going to a club. I honestly didn't think about it because it wasn't like I was having sex. You can't tell her you knew I was going to The Court," Tristan said under his breath.

"I told your boss I wanted to work with someone else," Ian was saying and he wasn't keeping his voice down.

"My boss is more concerned with what's best for our country." Ben Parker looked over the room with cold eyes. "You're not in charge of CSIS. If you don't want our help, you should feel free to leave. I assure you we can have a team in place quickly. Hey, Lou. How are you doing?"

"Hey, Ben," Lou replied with a smile, though her boyfriend had taken a place in front of her like she needed to be protected.

"I can't lie to her." Aidan had paled, ignoring what was going on around them. "I promised I wouldn't ever again."

He'd hoped Carys had missed Tara's mention of The Court. She was a smart woman who could put two and two together quickly. He was absolutely certain it was what had put a blank expression on her face.

She'd gone cold on him again. She hadn't demanded they talk.

She wasn't going to fight him, wasn't going to ask for explanations. She was going to do what she'd done the first time. Walk away.

"Lou is traumatized," Kala said.

"Not really," Lou countered.

Tristan barely heard the argument going on around him. His gut ached with the implications of what had happened. "I'll talk to Carys, but if she knows you knew, she'll feel alone again and she'll shut you out, too."

"Tristan, are you with us?" Ian stood staring at him, his best dumbass-is-doing-what look on his face.

Uncle Ian had perfected the look, though his dad was also giving him a good approximation.

He forced a blank expression on his face. He had to deal with this. He should be happy Carys was handling the situation this way, but he wished she was telling them all the meeting would have to wait. He would greatly prefer she upend the whole op than write him off so quickly. "Of course. Let's move to the dining room. I believe we've already set it up. Mr. Parker, did Tara send a copy of her report to you?"

They needed CSIS on this or they could get booted right back to the States. And despite what Ben had said, no team they put together would have as much access as this one.

"Do you honestly think I'm happy about working with the woman who recently took the only parachute and jumped out of a plane filled with foreign agents who were going to kill me?" Parker argued.

Ian's eyes went wide.

Shit. If Ian didn't know something, Kala was absolutely at the heart of it, and she was about to get in serious trouble. He'd known the team had worked—and he used the word loosely—with the Canadian several times in the last few months, but he hadn't heard about Kala trying to kill the dude.

Kala shrugged. "You survived, buddy."

"No thanks to you," Parker shot back.

Kala's eyes rolled. "Yes, thanks to me. You're the jackass who jumped without a parachute. I'm the one who caught you at twenty K and held onto you until we landed safely."

"And then you dosed me with a sedative and left me in the middle of a rice paddy in Mongolia." Parker loomed over her like they were about to go at it.

He was yelling at the wrong Kara. Or he was yelling at the right one and putting out sexual tension to the wrong one. Or the whole situation was way more fucked than he'd known. Maybe Parker was a masochist, and then he would do better with Kala, who was never in ten million years going to give him any more affection than a kick in the balls.

He would take a kick in the balls if it meant Carys talked to him.

"I had what I needed. I had the hard drive. I wasn't about to fight you for it," Kala said. "Besides, you looked like you needed a nap."

Parker loomed over her. "There are snakes in rice paddies."

"There certainly was one when you were there," Kala replied.

"Kara." Lou shook her head her best friend's way and proved how well Ian trained them all. Lou wouldn't screw up and call Kala by her name. "We should move on."

Kala looked around and seemed to read the room a little. She shook her now strawberry-blonde hair. Charlotte had disappeared. She usually would be in on all of the shenanigans.

But the twins had dyed their hair to something close to their natural color, which meant they looked even more like their mom. So Charlotte would deny Parker the ability to see them side by side.

Which meant Ian would be even more cranky than usual.

"Does he know?" Parker wasn't following Lou's excellent advice. He gestured Cooper's way. "Does your boyfriend know how you danced with me in Croatia? How you almost kissed me?"

Cooper's hand came up. "Told you. Not her boyfriend."

"Parker, leave it alone right this fucking second or we'll pull the op altogether and you can find your own way into Huisman's," Big Tag said on a low growl. "There was a reason I didn't want you here."

"I'm the expert on Huisman." Parker seemed to gather himself.

He took a deep breath and banished whatever he'd been feeling before. "No one knows him like I do, so you're not getting anyone else. However, if Maggie can play nice for once, so can I. I've decided you've got multiple personalities. Could we please speak to the reasonable one?"

The reasonable one was in the attic, probably losing her shit because she wasn't down here to fight him on her own. Kenzie had been so angry with him after what he'd done to Lou, but Tris didn't think it would last. There was too much chemistry between them. Kenzie had been the one in Croatia, and she'd come back from the event they'd attended like she was Eliza Doolittle in *My Fair Lady*.

He was pretty sure Kala had been the one to leave him on the plane. He'd been damn lucky she'd caught his ass.

"Sure thing, sweet cheeks," Kala said. "Let's get down to business."

"I should probably leave the whole relationship stuff out of my report." Tara watched as they walked into the dining room. "I'm not even sure how to document what just happened. Is it always like this?"

"Pretty much, and I think the big guy would appreciate you not mentioning it in your report," Zach agreed.

"They do not like each other." Tara shook her head. "I'm surprised. I've always found Kara to be friendly and easy to work with. I'm surprised to see her be so aggressive."

Because she'd only ever met Kenzie. When they needed someone to walk into Langley and charm the brass, it was Kenzie. Kala got her dour ass benched those days.

"Why does he call her Maggie?" Aidan asked, staring at the group as they walked away. "I thought her name was Kara."

Aidan was already doing well. He'd put the question in a way that wouldn't spark interest from anyone listening in. He would need to keep some distance between his subs and Parker, though. It would be hard for them. They hadn't spent years pretending the way he had. "When he first met her, she called herself Ms. Magenta. He named her Maggie despite the fact he knew we called her Kara. He said it wasn't her real name, so it didn't matter what he called her."

"He wanted a name only he called her. It's topping 101. Make a connection no one else has. He's got it bad," Aidan said quietly. "I feel for the fucker."

"Yeah, well, feel for me because I have to figure out how to explain why I joined Zach at The Court." Tris wanted to walk in there and carry her out and force her to talk to him.

"You went because your bosses were at The Court. It's practically a social event in DC for certain members of the Agency."

It was good to know Aidan was supporting him, but there was one problem. "You know socializing wasn't the only reason I went."

"You were lonely, and you needed to keep one thing from your previous life." Aidan put a hand on his shoulder. "It's going to be okay. She's going to rail and roar, but we can handle it."

Tris was worried she wouldn't roar at all. He followed Aidan in and noticed Carys had left a seat. For Aidan. Well, they were the couple for this mission. Still, he knew why she'd done it. To show her anger.

He could handle her anger. But her indifference scared the hell out of him.

"Go," Tris whispered. "Show her all the affection she needs to get through this. Then we're in for a hell of a night."

He didn't want to sleep outside the door. He happened to know the room they were in was the honeymoon suite and it had a big-ass bed, and he'd prepared for a fun night. They'd spent days reintroducing Carys's pretty asshole to a plug, and tonight was supposed to be the night when she got reacquainted with his cock up her backside.

Tristan took a place beside Ian, the one usually reserved for Charlotte, and Tara moved in beside him. He kind of wanted to put distance between them because he saw the moment Carys's eyes narrowed.

Now she probably thought he'd been sleeping with Tara. He wanted to get offended, but he'd put his own damn self in this position by leaving her alone for two and a half years.

"Parker, you know most of the team, but you haven't met Aidan O'Donnell and Carys Taggart. They're friends of TJ and Lou, who recently had their wedding wrecked via helicopter attack," Ian explained.

"Seriously?" Parker huffed. "That's some soap-opera level shit."

"Yeah, well, we're not getting those deposits back," Carys

grumbled.

"Uh, sorry about the wedding. So if TJ was the target then someone still thinks TJ is working with The Jester," Parker said.

"Duh." Kala's eyes rolled.

Ian growled, a low sound that had his daughter sighing and sitting back as though telling her dad she would be a good girl. Or at least a quiet one.

Now he knew how much Tara had left out. He glanced to Ian.

Ian's head tipped slightly.

It was good he'd learned to speak Big Tag over the years. Ian was leaving the decision to him. He'd been given clearance to bring CSIS fully up to speed if he thought it was necessary. He'd been alone with only Zach and Tara for the longest time. "I'm The Jester. Or at least I have been for several years."

Parker sat back, his poker face on. "This is new information. Did you kill the original Jester? What have you found out about him? If I'm allowed to know."

He was a prickly dude, but then he'd had his world tangled up by twins, so Tris was giving him a pass. "I didn't kill him, though I did kill his assassin. I was lucky Zach came after me because it was a close thing. Zach walking in startled the fucker long enough for me to get a shot in."

"I didn't realize Zach was there," Ian said quietly.

"It's in the official report, sir." Zach had his tablet out. "I'll send it to you. We both wrote up one. Tara and I were in town with Tris. She caught the assassin on CCTV as he was going back into The Jester's building."

"He had an Interpol red notice on him. It wasn't hard to ID the man," Tara admitted. "I sent Zach in because I thought Tris might need backup. He hadn't gotten the comms back up at the time, so I couldn't warn him. There was a jammer in place, and the assassin had knocked out the CCTVs on the actual building. Luckily I managed to slide into the ones on the underground entrance a block away."

"All right," Parker said. "So the assassin kills The Jester and then what? Went out for lunch?"

"I believe he probably heard something that scared him off," Tris explained. "Our theory is he left and when he realized no one had called the cops, he came back to get what he'd really come for. The laptop. It was in a safe. It took me a couple of hours to crack it, and then I got to work on the system itself. I had access to certain things like his basic communication system, but his financial and business records took longer."

"So you clean up the scene, leave the assassin's body behind as a fuck you to whoever hired him, and take over The Jester's online persona," Parker surmised. "Or was it more? Have you been selling arms?"

"I had to keep up the cover if I was going to find the bombmaker. Over the years I've been in contact with the man but only through encrypted messages," he replied, not wanting to look Carys's way. Would she understand why he'd done what he'd done? "I also used the position I was in to tip off the authorities if I felt the public was at high risk. The truth is most of the weapons I've sold were to cartels or syndicates, and they tend to use them mostly on each other. I'm not proud of what I did, but it was the only way to find him."

"Except you haven't found him." Parker pointed out his failure.

"I think we've come close." He prayed they had. "I had set up a buy for his new version of a dirty bomb. He claims he can do three times the damage with half the nuclear material. I was also supposed to see a test of his new detonation system. According to what we were told it could be used for biological weapons dispersion. But he never showed. And he hasn't been heard from in six months. Hence the desperation to figure out who's close to someone who can give any information about the bombmaker."

TJ raised a hand. "Not me. I know nothing, and it's how I like it. Though I do wish everyone knew so they didn't try to blow up my friend's wedding. We didn't even get cake. Lou's mom made this gorgeous cake and no one got a slice. Well, I bet Boomer did. Baby, did your dad eat the whole cake?"

"My brother helped him," Lou admitted. "But not the point. I have some questions since, unlike some of us, I have gone over the whole report."

Big Tag's lips curled up. "You know I've had a lot to do. This scenario is exactly why I have a Lou. I can count on you to study everything."

"I did as well," Tasha said. "Lou and I talked about it on the plane. Beyond questioning the entire idea that Huisman would send a helicopter to disrupt a wedding of two people he doesn't know, I have to wonder what he gets out of it."

Tris had been thinking about it, too. He had a theory. "If he is in touch with the bombmaker, then he might want to get rid of anyone who knows who he is. If he gave the bombmaker enough money, he might want the man to exclusively work for his group, and taking out anyone who possibly knows his identity would protect his asset."

"Manny was looking for the bombmaker a few weeks ago when he worked with the Germans to kidnap TJ," Parker pointed out.

"And he couldn't have figured it out in those weeks?" Kala asked, her tone respectful but with a hint of challenge. "According to you Huisman is a genius when it comes to an evil plan."

Parker nodded. "It's possible. And since we firmly believe he managed to get the formula for the new anthrax from Dare's father's company, he'll be looking for a delivery system. So I can accept that if he believed TJ was The Jester or close to him and knew the bombmaker's identity, it could be to his advantage to take him out."

"But it wasn't the best method." Carys sat up, obviously forcing herself to speak when she probably wanted to blend into the wall and forget she was here. "I don't understand. There were plenty of places to put a sniper."

Ian's head shook. "I assure you I checked them all. I ran the security since several members of my team were in attendance, and I would have found any sniper."

Carys's shoulders shrugged. "Okay, then why the wedding? Why not learn his habits and do it quietly? If I was going to kill TJ, I would figure out a way to poison the hot dog he gets almost every day from the shady food truck outside the building where Lou works."

Lou turned to her boyfriend. "You said you were cutting out processed meats. We made a deal."

TJ went a nice shade of red. "They're good. I don't know what they do to make it taste so good. But fine, Carys is right. It probably would be easier to take me out when I'm not in a crowd."

"But that's not what Manny would find fun about it." Parker's eyes seemed to go dark as he spoke. "I've known him since he was a child, and there's nothing Manny loves more than chaos. He thinks it's the ultimate shield. It's where we'll be able to trip him up. He can't resist poking a wound, and there's nothing he loves more than getting revenge on his perceived enemies. I've done some research, and I believe the real target wasn't TJ at all. I believe it was Carys."

"What?" Tris's gut turned. "Why the hell would he want to hurt Carys?"

"Because her last name is Taggart."

The whole room seemed to go still. Ben Parker wasn't supposed to know he was sitting in a room full of Taggarts. Ian had never told the Canadian operative his real name, and no one else would have. He had a cover in place should anyone go looking for him. So did Charlotte, the twins, and Tasha. Tris himself had worked with Lou to make sure they were solid, and his papa had checked their work.

But they couldn't do the same for Carys.

And the trouble was while Ben Parker didn't know Ian Taggart's real identity, there was someone who did.

Emmanuel Huisman. The doctor had shown up at their Agency safe house in the middle of the Australian op that brought him into their sphere. He'd explained himself and been incredibly helpful.

How much more did he know? If he knew about Ian, did he know about the twins? Ian had told them Huisman had figured out Tasha was his daughter.

Of course at the time he'd had a perfectly reasonable explanation for knowing what only the Agency should know.

"You're going to have to explain," Aidan said, his voice tight. He threaded his fingers through Carys's, offering her support.

"I believe Mr. Parker is referring to the incident leading up to Huisman's father's death," Ian said bluntly. "I've already considered the scenario. Mr. Parker, why don't you give me your assessment."

"Manny's father was killed by a CIA operative," Parker explained as though this was something he'd thought about for a long time. "You have to understand Manny was a kid at the time and he was on the upstairs landing when his father was murdered. He watched it all."

"I've talked to him about the incident." Big Tag's hands steepled in front of him, a gesture he used when considering a situation. "In Australia when he figured out where my safe house was."

Tasha nodded. "We asked him about it. He knows his father was in the wrong. His father had kidnapped Dr. Rebecca Walsh and a man who worked with the McKay-Taggart firm. Neither killed Huisman's father. It was a rogue CIA operative the elder Dr. Huisman had been working with."

"And Manny never lies," Parker argued.

"I don't see it. Why take your anger out on a family that wasn't really involved?" Kala asked. "It's been over twenty years. And why not go after the company? From her dossier, Carys Taggart isn't even related to the asshole who runs McKay-Taggart. The Taggart one. I've heard McKay is lovely. The point being she's that dude's niece, not his daughter, and her father is a freaking chef. They have nothing to do with any of what happened way back when."

"Nicely said," Adam offered.

Big Tag sighed. "She does have a point."

"And I'm telling you Manny lied," Parker insisted.

"It doesn't make sense," TJ replied.

"Does chaos ever make sense?" Carys asked. "Mr. Parker said this doctor loves chaos. Watching his father die at a young age was traumatizing. Sometimes our brains make odd connections. Trauma can do funny things to a person. Especially a child. Sometimes revenge doesn't make sense. Especially if you're dealing with a sociopath. Throw in some narcissism, and it's kind of a recipe for fucked-up motivations. The brain can make connections that wouldn't look rational to the outside person."

"I've read his book," Aidan added. "He wrote about how his father saw Dr. Walsh as a rival. As the woman who took his job from him. It was precisely why Huisman's father got involved with the CIA operative. He was jealous of her."

"And now he works with her from time to time," his papa pointed out.

"If he's as screwed up as Mr. Parker says, it could all be a front," Carys continued. "Or a way to get what he wants. He was a child. I'm sure he believed a lot of what his father said around him. Even though he seems to know what to say, there could be a deep-seated hatred he's hiding for all the people involved in taking his father from him. He could come after me simply for my name, and before everyone says then I should go to a safe house, shouldn't we figure it out?"

Cooper leaned forward. "I still think it was TJ if Huisman was behind the helo attack. It makes the most sense, and don't they have a saying in your profession, Ms. Taggart?"

"Yes. When you hear hoofbeats, think horses not zebras," she replied. "And it's good advice for the most part."

"But sometimes we do get zebras," Aidan added. "And if you stubbornly refuse to see it for what it is, you can lose the patient."

"I was going to argue against bringing in civilians Manny might have something against, but now I think they might be ready to do this." Parker sat back, obviously impressed. "You're sending them in with bodyguards? I can't imagine Manny invited them for any other reason than their close ties to that firm."

"I'm going in with them," Kala said. "So is Tris, and we won't let them out of our sights. The helo attack made it so he couldn't refuse the very reasonable request."

"He didn't like the idea of me not coming." Aidan sighed. "Guess it wasn't my brilliant paper after all."

Carys squeezed his hand. "It is brilliant, and you're going to use this time to meet doctors who can actually help you."

"Or Huisman will ruin me as a way to get to you and your family," Aidan posited.

"I won't let anything happen to you," Big Tag said. "But we should consider what could happen."

He'd thought about it constantly. "There are eighty people attending this thing. I'm not going to let Aidan be alone with the man, and Kara will do the same with Carys. He cares about the foundation, right?"

Parker sighed and nodded. "From what I can tell. It's mostly about the access it affords him, but I've seen some odd things happening in his financials lately. He's moved quite a bit of money around. Even in the last few days."

"He's a businessman, too." His father was studying Ben Parker like he was a puzzle he needed to figure out. "I know a forensic accountant if you would like to consult with her. She has Agency clearance."

Aunt Phoebe. She was excellent at what she did. And he was sure Aunt Chelsea was consulting, too, in some way. It was why he felt like they could solve the case this time. Because his whole family was behind him now.

"I'll talk to my boss about sending her what we have," Parker allowed and then turned to Tristan's father. "Mr. Miles, do you honestly believe you can hack into Manny's systems? I've been trying for years. My tech is excellent, but we can't get past his security."

"Your tech might be excellent, but Mr. Miles is beyond anything you've worked with before," Big Tag said, closing the cover of his tablet, signaling he was going to shut this particular part of the meeting down. "We'll get in. We're going to figure out exactly what this fucker is doing, and then we'll know how to bring him down. Canada, why don't we take this into the office and let my team get some rest? They have long days ahead, and Aidan and Carys and their guards need to get into the city. They're supposed to spend the first night at a luxury hotel to keep up appearances. Mr. Miles can join us, and perhaps we can conference your colleague in. I know of Mrs. Murdoch. She's a wily one. I wouldn't underestimate her."

Parker stood. "Excellent. I know my boss would love an update, too." He turned toward Ian. "I do appreciate you taking this seriously now, sir. Despite the problems I have with certain members of your team, I do know how effective they can be."

"Like I could effectively put my foot up your ass," Kala said under her breath.

Ian's eyes narrowed on his daughter. "*Ya razberus s toboy pozhe.*"

"*Ya v etom ne somnevayus,*" Kala growled back. "Come on. Let's get out of here. Lou, is my pack ready to go?"

Lou would have stuffed both their bags full of anything they could need. From granola bars to glasses that relayed information back to base, Lou would make sure they were kitted up.

She probably wouldn't have anything in those bags for handling a pissed off sub. He would be on his own for this battle.

Tris took a long breath and prepared for the fight of his life.

* * * *

Aidan closed the door behind the bellman and waited for the fireworks to start.

The honeymoon suite was large and luxurious, and none of it seemed to touch Carys.

He had to find a way to make her understand.

"So is anyone going to address the whole Tris has been playing behind everyone's back thing?"

Unfortunately, they had an audience.

After the near-silent drive, Tris had handled the check-in while Kala had walked around looking for things that might kill them all. She was such a fucking delight.

Carys had sat there, her jaw tight. She'd held his hand and told him she wouldn't talk about it until they were in the room.

Well, they were in the room now.

"Did you think no one caught Tara saying you and Zach are horndogs who cheat not only on your girlfriends and your Aidans, but also on your home club?" Kala continued.

"There was no fucking cheating involved," Tristan replied, his jaw tight. "And we should shut up until we…" He gestured around the room.

Aidan had no idea what it meant, but Kala seemed to. She sat back on the lush couch and propped her combat boots on the antique coffee table. "Already ran a check. No bugs. No cameras. I don't think anyone cares about who's fucking who. Or is it whom? I don't care. I do care about you playing around on my cousin."

"I didn't cheat, Mistress Kala," Tristan said, standing in front of Carys's cousin. "You should understand better than anyone D/s doesn't always involve sex. I shouldn't have to continue to say it, but I have had one and only one lover my entire life. Now will you go down to the bar or something while I talk to my subs?"

There was a bit of sympathy on Kala's face when she shook her head. The set of glasses she'd put on seemed slightly too big for her and they moved with her head. He'd been surprised by the glasses. Kala had never worn them before, so they must be some kind of disguise. She'd toned down her usual gothness and changed into white denims and a flouncy top. It made her look more like her twin.

She did kind of blend now.

"No can do. I'm supposed to guard you and be ready to call in the troops if everything goes to hell, and my father would say I can't do my job from a barstool. He would be wrong. Maybe he can't, but he's old and doesn't have my skills." She winced as though something hurt all of the sudden. "Look, Tris, my dad is already mega pissed about the whole leaving Parker behind to die thing. I can't leave this room. You can go in the bedroom. There's a door. I probably won't be able to hear."

"I'm not going in a bedroom with him," Carys said quietly.

"Carys, will you please let me explain?" Tris returned. "I'm not going to attack you."

Her chin tilted up stubbornly. "I would rather my cousin was here. She's my bodyguard, after all."

"Your cousin is currently wearing glasses that connect her to base. So it's not merely your cousin. It's Kala and probably Lou," Tristan explained. "They're smart glasses. Lou modified them in a very espionage-friendly way."

It was cool. Aidan would like to examine those. He could think of several ways to use them. "So if, say, someone was in the field and wearing the glasses, another more experienced doctor could see what his hands were doing and walk him through the procedure?"

Kala nodded. "Absolutely. But dude, read the room. This is not the time to forward your career. And it's not just Lou. She made a couple more sets of glasses, so we're kind of on a four-way call."

"So Lou and all my cousins," Carys said. "Yes, I don't mind if they listen in."

Kala winced. "I mean not Tash because Dad stole Tash's, and from what I can tell he got away from her and he's barricaded himself in a bathroom. He's dedicated to the drama."

Tristan held up his middle finger right to Kala's glasses. "Fuck you, Uncle."

"That just makes him stronger," Kala advised. "Since no one wants to talk, I will. So how did you end up at The Court, Tristan?"

"I don't care," Carys said. "He lied to me. Again."

"I didn't lie. It didn't come up," Tristan tried. "We've had more important things to discuss."

"I think we should do this Kala's way." Yeah, Aidan was surprised the words had come out of his mouth, but it kind of made sense. Kala wanted to set up Tris's reasons so maybe they were easier to understand and Carys could forgive him. Them. Because he couldn't lie to her again. No way. "We're going to be straightforward and to the point. Carys, I knew he was going and I didn't have a problem with it. I understood why and what it meant to him."

Carys stood, moving away from him. "Well, of course, you did. I mean why didn't you take a little vacay and join him?"

251

"Because I got what I needed from The Hideout," Aidan replied. "But I think what Tris got from The Court was different. He went with Zach, but he spent a lot of time with people who are influential at the Agency there. He told me Drake and Taylor Radcliffe are members."

"Drake is who got me and Zach in," Tris admitted. "I never touched a sub in a sexual fashion, but I did use the place for stress relief. I…I grew up around it. It's a part of me. Sometimes I felt like it was the only place I could breathe."

"You could have breathed at home," Carys shot back. "But this isn't your home anymore. DC is. When we're done here, you should go back."

"You and Aidan are my fucking home," Tristan replied. "And Aidan's right. We did a lot of business in the lounge there. It's a safe place to talk. Sometimes it's not even safe to talk in the office."

"Think of it like golf for a businessman," Aidan attempted.

Kala snorted. "Yeah, he actually said that."

"Golf?" If Carys had lasers in her eyes, he would have been cut in half. "Spanking a woman is like fucking golf?"

Tris gave him a what-the-hell look. "Are you trying to help me or bury me, man?"

"How much business gets done at Sanctum?" Aidan pointed out. "How many things do we decide sitting around in the lounge at The Hideout?"

"Dad says good point. He takes back his previous dumbass comment," Kala supplied helpfully.

Aidan ignored her. "My point is a club like The Court is as much a social club as anything else. Do you remember the week I was in New York for training on robotic surgery? You had a patient with preeclampsia and you almost lost her and the baby and you needed stress relief. You didn't go drinking with your friends. You didn't have anyone to sleep with, so you went to The Hideout and Gabriel Lodge took care of you."

"It's not the same, and you knew about it," Carys said with pure stubbornness. "You know what? I think I'm going to bed. This is the last straw."

And it hit him. What his father had said.

Has anyone talked about what Carys did wrong?

His father had told him they would face this again and again until they all acknowledged what had gone wrong.

Carys wasn't being Carys. Carys wasn't willing to fight.

But suddenly Aidan was.

Carys started to walk to the bedroom, but Aidan got to the door before she could, putting a hand on it so she couldn't open it. "You're really going down without a fight?"

Her eyes went startled and then stubborn. "What is there to fight about? He lied. You lied. I'm done."

"Years, Carys. Fucking years I've loved you. Did you realize this is our first real hurdle?"

"Of course it's not," she argued.

He was right about this. "Yes, it is because we're still dealing with Tristan making the decision to pursue his own career. I'm going to ask you what if it had been the other way around. What if I had wanted to go into the military with him? Would you have given up your dreams to follow us?"

Her chin came up. "Don't be ridiculous. Of course I wouldn't have given up college to follow you around the world. That's not what we asked him to do."

"No, we asked him to stay when we could give him very little attention. We asked him to take a job he didn't want at the time, to not explore who he is and what he wants," Aidan said.

"I didn't ask him not to go into the military. I knew it was something he needed. It was the Agency I had a problem with," Carys replied.

"And yet not once did you fight with him. You accepted everything with a sigh like you kind of expected it to blow up all along. You fight for everything, Carys. You don't stand down. You literally kicked your cousin in her pussy because she pissed you off, but when Tris told us to get married, we let him push us into it when we weren't ready. There's a time to be a sub and a time to tell our Dom he's full of shit."

"Oh, yeah, you should know Dad's stealing that one. He's writing a book of helpful advice called *Ianspirations*," Kala said.

He was done with Kala. He pulled his cell and hit the number for Adam Miles. "Hey, Ian's being an ass and listening in on an important conversation and it would irritate the fuck out of him if you turned off their superspy glasses."

He knew how to get Tris's dad to do what he wanted.

Kala sat up straight. "Hey, he can't do that. Can he do that?"

Carys looked over where Tristan stood, staring at the both of them. He had a grave look on his face.

"I didn't... I wasn't being submissive," Carys argued.

"Then you don't feel the same way I do," Tristan said. "Because I feel like I've been fighting for us for years."

Carys's brows rose. "Fighting? Was it fighting for us when the Agency hacked into my socials and took down any reference to you? Did you give Aidan a heads-up at least?"

"I did not because I didn't know they were doing it. I expected to have some time, though I can see why they did it," Tris said calmly. "I thought I had another week or so, but they moved quickly after I took over The Jester project. I can imagine how it felt. It had to feel like someone took important time from you. I do have a copy. If I can get out of this, I promise I'll restore it all."

She stared at him stubbornly. "Can you restore the last two and a half years, Tristan?"

"What would he have done, Car? Did you want him here getting your coffee while you studied for a procedure?" Aidan knew he was poking a sore spot, but he was suddenly sure his father was right and if he lost this fight, he would lose the war. "He fucked up, but he didn't mean to. Tris, did you go into the military with the idea it was a way to get out of a relationship you didn't want?"

Tris huffed. "Of course I didn't."

"I think the relationship he wants is with you, Aidan," Carys said, a hard look in her eyes.

"Oh, yeah. We're getting to the good stuff," Kala said and then frowned and took the glasses off. "Damn. Adam's excellent. Guess I should take notes."

Tristan looked his way and mouthed thanks. Then he turned to Carys. "I've tried so hard to maintain some kind of tie to you. I honestly believed if you thought I was in real danger you would ride in like a fucking Valkyrie to try to save me. I knew Aidan wouldn't because Aidan would understand his job was protecting and sheltering you. I'll be honest. If I had to do it all over again, I would have talked to you because I now know I was fooling myself."

Carys's index finger came out. "Don't you fucking dare put this on me. So it's my fault because I didn't what? Get on a plane and try to force you to come home? Because I asked. I asked and asked, and then one day I stopped fucking asking because I knew the answer. Don't rewrite history."

"All right, I won't. I was at fault," Tris conceded. "But please, Carys, please yell at me. Punch me. Fight with me. Fight for us. Don't walk away like I mean nothing. You might not understand why I did what I did, but do you truly believe I did it to hurt you?"

"I think you didn't think about me at all," Carys replied, her tone going hollow.

Tristan started to move toward her but stopped. "There isn't a day in my life I didn't think about you. Not a day I can remember anyway. Every day I've lived had you and Aidan in it."

Carys's arms crossed over her chest. "Were you or were you not willing to give us up? You said you would be honest with me."

"In my darker moments, yes," Tris admitted. "When I facilitated the sale of a hundred fully automatic assault rifles to a separatist in a small African country and two weeks later the whole place broke out in a bloody civil war, I thought I didn't fucking deserve you. When I looked at the blood on my hands after I killed a man in São Paulo because he'd taken a picture of me and meant to out me as The Jester, I thought there was no way I could ever touch you with those hands again. So yes, Carys, there were times I thought it would be best for both of you if I died."

What he was saying made sense to Aidan. "It's why you stood there completely open to the helicopter on our wedding day. Everyone else hid, but you didn't care."

"I knew if I died making sure the two of you were safe, I would never have to admit how far I'd fallen." Tris seemed to falter but kept on. "How much of my soul I'd given away. I know it sounds stupid, but I thought I could fix things. I thought I could be a hero like my dads."

"Your dads got kicked out of the Army because they slept with the wrong person," Kala pointed out quietly. She stood up and slid her cell into her pocket. "Our parents are human. Don't ever tell him I said this but my father is the greatest man I know, and he's fucked up things on monumental levels. Don't put them on pedestals, Tris.

Don't put anyone on a pedestal because it hurts so fucking much when they inevitably fall off. And I thank my dad for telling me all the ways he screwed up because he made it okay for me to screw up. Somehow I don't think any of your parents told you they could only love you if you were perfect, if you never made a mistake. That's what's wrong with all three of you motherfuckers. You had it easy. Now it's hard. You either love each other and you're willing to risk it all again, or you're over and then guys, get ready to know what it means to be fucking alone because what you had was epic. You're never going to find it again. But hey, I know a dude at a shelter. Dogs and cats are great companions, and when they fuck up, well, it can get messy but not as messy as this. Since you ruined our viewing pleasure, I think I will head down to the bar. It's too hard to watch you disintegrate."

"I knew they hadn't meant to leave the Army when they did," Tris said quietly. "They didn't hide it from me. I still think they're heroes."

"I didn't know about how rough it was when my parents met, but I still think they're the best love story I know." Carys sniffled. "I don't know what to do. I'm angry and I'm not sure how to not be angry anymore."

"You don't have to," Aidan assured her. "You can be as angry as you want. You can kick us out of bed. You can call us names. What you can't do is keep walking away when we're so desperate to have you stay. Unless it's truly over, and then you should put us out of our misery."

Carys turned as the outer door shut and locked and they were alone. "I don't know what I want. Not true. I do, but we don't have a time machine. We can't go back and stop Tris from leaving us."

"No, and I can't promise I won't make another mistake in the future, though I can promise I won't leave you again. I'll leave the job if I think it's too dangerous. I promise to put you first," Tris vowed.

Tris was pushing her too hard. Aidan got into her space. "You don't have to decide anything tonight. I know what you're thinking. You have to make a decision whether we get married and start a family, but we don't."

Tris nodded, seeming to figure out what Aidan was saying. "You don't have to decide at all. All you have to decide tonight is whether or not we're welcome in your bed. We planned a future. I screwed it up. It's not your responsibility to get us back on track. This isn't an either-or ultimatum. There's no ultimatum at all. I know what Aidan said, but if you feel the need to string me along, I'll take it. I'll do whatever you need me to."

"And if what I need is you to go away?" Carys asked.

Tristan took a long breath. "Do you need me to go?"

"I don't know. I just don't, and I can't give you a timeline," she admitted.

The air had changed. It was still charged, but there was a distinctly sexual aspect to what was between them now. "You don't need to give us a schedule. And I won't let anyone push us about the wedding. We're on our own timeline. I can move back into the house with Coop if you need space."

A suspicious shine hit Carys's eyes. "I don't want to decide that either."

Tris moved to her side, allowing Aidan the other so they could surround her. "All you need to think about is tonight. What do you want me to order for us? Do you want to watch a movie?"

"What if I want you to kiss me and make me forget everything?"

That he could do.

Chapter Fourteen

Tristan felt his whole body go hard when she asked them to make her forget everything.

Time. It was the only real way to prove to Carys he was with them forever now. He had to stay close, had to be with her.

Pleasure wouldn't prove anything to her, but it definitely couldn't hurt.

He watched as Aidan took her mouth in a slow, devouring kiss.

"Do you have any idea how much I love to watch the two of you?" Tristan asked. It occurred to him he should give her every option. "If you want, I can just watch. If you're too angry with me, I can be patient."

It would be awful, but he couldn't force the situation. He'd put too much on both of them.

Did his screw up truly mean he wasn't salvageable? Kala's words were running through his head. Even earlier he'd been wondering if he deserved them, if his sins hadn't caused an unfixable breach.

"I love you, Carys. I love Aidan, too. I want another chance, but I'll understand," he said.

She sighed even as Aidan was working his lips down her neck. "Stop, Tris. Be my Dom tonight. We'll figure the rest out later. All I know is what I need tonight, and it's the two of you."

The words sent a surge of hope through his heart. It sent a surge of arousal through his cock.

If she was giving him tonight, he was going to take it, make it so good she gave him tomorrow, too. And the next day, and the next. They would string together the days and nights until it wasn't a thought in her head there wouldn't be another.

Even as Aidan started working on the shirt she wore, Tris leaned over and took her mouth, melding them together. She softened for him, and he allowed his tongue to surge inside, rubbing and playing against hers. He sank his fingers into the silk of her hair and tugged her head back, letting his tongue plunge deeper. Her blouse was tugged free.

He let his hand roam down, cupping her breast through her bra. It wasn't enough.

He stepped back. She'd asked him to be her Dom tonight. It might be one of the last times he played the most important role in his life. He put a hand to the back of Aidan's neck, the touch settling something inside him.

Aidan straightened up, reacting on instinct and obeying the silent command. "Yes?"

"I want her naked."

Aidan's lips curled up in a decadent smile. "Yes, Sir."

Carys groaned. "That shouldn't be so sexy."

But it was. "In the bedroom. I can't be certain your cousin won't get those glasses fixed and come back."

Aidan took her hand and led her through. Tristan followed, closing the French doors behind him and making sure they locked.

Aidan stopped in the middle of the luxurious room in front of the four-poster bed where they would lay her out like a feast for two men.

Tristan stopped and watched as Aidan moved behind her, unhooking her bra and tossing it to the side. His hands came around her waist, moving up until he cupped her breasts, fingers toying with the nipples as he made eye contact with Tris over her shoulder.

His partner. His best friend. Aidan was part of his forever, and he didn't care if everyone knew it. "Take off her pants. I want to see her pussy. I want to watch you make her wet and needy before she sucks our cocks."

A glaze of desire coated her glorious emerald eyes, and he saw her breath hitch. Damn, but she needed this. He hoped they'd gotten through to her, but if logic didn't work, maybe submission would.

Aidan went on his knees, dragging the slacks off her. She'd chucked her espadrilles the minute they'd walked in the room, so the slacks came off with ease, and then she was standing in silky undies. Undies with a wet spot already.

"Spread your legs, Carys," Tristan ordered. "Aidan, I think you should explore a little. See if our pretty sub is ready for what we want to do to her."

Carys's bottom lip disappeared behind her teeth. "What do you want to do to me, Sir?"

She wanted some dirty talk? He could give it to her. "I want what I've been missing all these years. I want to fuck your ass while Aidan takes your sweet pussy. I want to feel his cock slide against mine while we're both inside you. I want to imprint myself on you so you never forget you belong to the two of us."

"And you belong to me," Carys said, fire in her eyes.

"Fuck, yes, I belong to you, and I forgot what that meant for a while. I forgot it meant we face everything together, and if I feel left out or like I need to prove something, I talk to you." He wasn't going into a heavy relationship discussion, but he could tell her how he felt. "I want connection with the two people I love more than anyone in the world. Now spread your legs and let Aidan test your pussy."

She slid her legs apart, her eyes on him as Aidan shifted until he was in front of her. He pulled his shirt over his head, tossing it over on top of her clothes, and then did what came naturally. He leaned in and rubbed his nose over that damp patch of silk, breathing her in.

Carys gasped and seemed to struggle to stay standing as Aidan rubbed her sensitive flesh through her panties.

"Play with your nipples." He meant what he'd said before. He loved to watch them together. It got him hot, and his cock was pressing against the fly of his slacks. Bossing them around during sex did it for him, too.

Carys's hands came up, running over her breasts while Aidan started to slide her undies down her legs. Her manicured fingers played, rolling her nipples between them.

His clothes were suddenly far too tight. He unbuttoned his shirt and pulled the belt from his pants. Her eyes flared at the sight.

Did she want some discipline while Aidan tongued her? Tristan doubled the belt over and slapped it against his hand, letting the sound echo through the room.

Carys groaned, and he knew she was begging for it.

"This isn't about punishment," Tris began, closing the distance between them. He stared at her gorgeous backside for a moment, reaching out to touch her silky skin. "This is for fun, baby. Aidan, you hold her."

She would be caught between the pleasure of Aidan's mouth and the satisfying sting of Tristan's belt. Aidan's arms wound around her legs, catching and holding her in a cage of muscle, never letting up on the slow strokes of his tongue.

Tris pulled back the belt and then let it crack over her ass, the sound sending a thrill through him, satisfying a place deep inside him. The sadist who lived inside, who was tempered always by the man who loved. He only needed these two people, and only needed to give them the pain they needed to enhance their pleasure.

"Fuck," Aidan said. "Do it again. I swear she's already close."

He struck again and again, the belt leaving light marks that would be gone by morning, but it was enough. When he saw her spine start to bow, he realized this might be over long before he wanted. "Stop."

Carys groaned, but she didn't complain. Aidan let her go and rose to his feet, stepping back, her arousal still glistening on his lips.

"Get out of those pants," Tristan ordered while he stepped in front of Carys. He stared at her for a moment, taking in the loveliness of her flushed face, how her auburn hair tumbled over her shoulders and made a contrast to her skin. He cupped her chin, drawing it up. "You are so fucking gorgeous. I dream about you at night, and don't give me back my words because I dream about fucking you and I'm pretty sure you dream about pushing me off a high building and watching me fall."

An impish gleam hit her eyes. "Never, Sir. I dream about you falling off a boat into the open mouth of a whale."

If she was joking, they were moving along nicely. Or...she wasn't joking and he should stay away from the water for a while. "At least it wasn't a shark."

Aidan leaned in. "The shark would kill you too fast. The whale would start to digest you as you suffocated."

Definitely staying away from the water. "Good to know." But

that gleam in her eyes calmed something inside him. She was an incorrigible brat at times, and he loved it. "On your knees."

She sank to the floor gracefully, her legs spreading and body flowing into her submissive posture with ease. Her head was down. "I am ready to do Sir's will. Shall I help you out of your slacks?"

She could go as slow as possible, a sweet torture of her own. He couldn't do it tonight. All he could think about was getting inside her. This was merely an appetizer. "I can handle it. Take care of Aidan for now."

Aidan moved in front of her, one hand on her hair and the other eagerly getting his cock ready.

Carys's lips were turned up, and it was obvious she was in her powerful place. She found it in submitting. He found it in dominating. Aidan…well, he rather thought Aidan simply found it by being with them.

"Take me inside, baby," Aidan said and hissed slightly when her tongue licked along his cockhead.

Tris toed out of his shoes and quickly divested himself of his slacks. He watched for a moment as Carys worked Aidan's cock, rolling over him with her tongue before sucking him deep.

Tris moved to where they'd set the luggage and pulled out his kit. He grabbed the lube, ignoring the other toys. They would use them all eventually, but this wasn't play tonight. This was connection. This was everything.

He grabbed one other item. It was the item that reminded him he wasn't safe yet.

When he walked back in, he set the lube and condoms down on the bedside table.

Aidan was thrusting his cock into Carys's lush mouth. Tris joined them. The time for watching was through. "Take me."

Carys obediently moved over, licking his cockhead and sending sparks of pure pleasure through him. When Aidan tried to move away, Tris reached out to grab his arm.

"I didn't tell you to go anywhere." He might never spank Aidan the way he did Carys because Aidan didn't need it, but he did need a reminder that Tris was his top, too.

"I thought you wanted…" Aidan began.

Tris moved his hand from Aidan's arm up to his neck, squeezing lightly. It was easy to see the touch had an effect because his cock twitched. "You don't think about what I want. You listen to what I tell you to do. I want her to service us both at the same time. And yes, it means we'll touch, and I don't care. Or I do. I want this between the three of us."

"I know I want it," Carys said, licking her lips. "I want to touch you both at the same time. I want to play with your cocks. They're my favorite toys. I want to suck on one of you and then the other, or you could stand close together and I could lick you both at the same time."

"Fuck," Aidan groaned as he relaxed beside Tris, allowing their hips to touch. "I love it when you talk dirty, baby."

"And I haven't in a long time." She looked up at Tris, her lips pouty and full, gaze filled with need. "May I, Master?"

It was the first time she'd called him Master in years. Oh, she'd given him the honorific Master Tristan in the club. She would do that for any Dom, but a simple Master meant he was her Master. He prayed she understood how hopelessly in love with her he was even after all these years. In love with both of them, really. His life didn't work without these two people. "Yes, love. You may."

Her hands came up, taking both cocks in her palms and giving them each a stroke.

Aidan's hand went around Tris, finding a place at the small of his back. He was obviously trying to balance himself, but the intimacy sent a warmth through Tris.

And then a spark of wild pleasure as Carys touched their cocks together and ran her tongue from one head to the other.

A curse came from his lips, and he stroked her hair as she played with their cocks. They'd never gone this far before. They'd been oddly careful, he and Aidan. They'd made sure to give each other space, so they rarely touched when they were making love to Carys.

He knew it worked for some of the threesomes he was familiar with, but he rather thought they were going to get over their personal male space stage. Being this close felt good, like they were all together and nothing could break them apart again.

She rubbed their cocks together with obvious delight, and he wondered how long his sub had wanted to play like this. Carys had the sweetest smile on her face as she sucked Aidan deep and then moved to Tris. Her eyes came up, watching him watch her.

He was never letting them go again. He would do whatever it took.

Starting tonight.

* * * *

Carys had left behind everything except this moment and these men. She was on her knees with them standing together looking so deliciously sexy and…together. They looked like they were together, on the same page again at last. This was her safe place, and she'd forgotten how much she'd missed it. She'd pretended she didn't because she hadn't wanted to truly feel the pain of losing what she'd always had.

This. She'd always had this place where she belonged.

Could she ever trust it again? The doubt crept up, but she shoved it away. She would think about their situation later. Much later.

Now she leaned forward and licked the pearly drop off Aidan's cock, enjoying the salty taste of him. And the groan her action elicited. Tristan's hand rubbed against her head, but he wasn't taking over. He was allowing her the freedom to play like she'd never played before. She stroked their cocks, bringing them together and trying— and failing—to get both in her mouth.

She played for a long time, licking and stroking and sucking them deep. She loved exploring the differences between them. One was longer and one thicker. She loved to trace the vein on Aidan's cock with her tongue and find the supersensitive place on the underside of Tristan's cockhead, the one that made him moan.

Before she was ready, a hand wound in her hair and Tris was gently forcing her to look up.

His gorgeous face stared down at her, and it was easy to see the man was close. And also that he didn't want to be. She knew what he wanted, hadn't missed him pulling out the lube.

"I want you on the bed, love. Lie back and spread your legs for me." Tristan's words came out on a low growl.

Aidan reached down to help her rise to her feet. Her whole body was alive and needy, blood pulsing through her as Aidan laid his muscular body out on the bed, his back to the headboard. He helped her maneuver on, lying her back to his front. She could feel the length of his cock against the small of her back, nudging against her ass.

They'd been forcing a plug in her ass for days, but it couldn't take the place of warm flesh, of knowing both of her men were deep inside her. Aidan's arms went around her even as he tangled their legs together, pressing her ankles apart so her pussy was on full display for their Master.

Tristan climbed on the bed with the grace of a hungry tiger, his eyes on his feast. He stared at her pussy.

"He's going to make a meal of you, baby," Aidan whispered. "He's going to fuck you with his tongue and suck on your clit until you come, and then we're going to prove why we should never be apart again."

His fingers found her nipples as Tristan lowered himself down between her legs, breathing in her scent. He rubbed his nose over her pussy.

Carys writhed against Aidan as Tris settled in and started devouring her. The world went fuzzy, encasing her in a bubble of pleasure and intimacy and love. She loved these two men. She couldn't remember a time when she hadn't. They were her everything. There was nothing she'd learned in this world that they hadn't been at her side for.

Tristan speared her with his tongue, delving deep as Aidan tweaked her nipples. Pleasure and pain, the contrast heightening every sensation. Aidan whispered to her, telling her how much they loved her, how much they wanted her. He punctuated the sweet words with nips to her ears that had her moaning.

When Tristan used his thumb on her clitoris, rotating and pressing down as his tongue went deep, she couldn't hold back a second longer. The orgasm swept over her in a crazy wave.

"I forgot how good you taste," Tristan said, giving her pussy one last kiss before he got to his knees, staring down at both of them. "You manage to hold it together, A?"

"Barely." Aidan breathed against her ear. "She wiggled all over my cock. It was torture."

Tristan chuckled. "Well, let's torture you some more, partner." Tris's hand reached out. "Come on, baby. Time for you to go for a ride."

It was insane, but she felt another spark of arousal. The orgasm had been good, but it was nothing compared to being between them. It had been so long, the years becoming one deep ocean of longing. She allowed Tristan to help her turn over, to get into position so she straddled Aidan.

He grinned up at her, his gorgeous face alight with joy. It was an expression she hadn't seen there in so long. Aidan was back where he was happiest. She stroked a hand along his cheek, her thumb tracing the strong line of his jaw. His hands came out to cup her hips, his own moving as he got his cock aligned.

A low huff came from him as he started to thrust up, joining them.

It felt so good. She was slick and ready for him. She couldn't help but roll her hips, trying to take him deeper.

Aidan hissed, and his hands tightened on her. "You know we're not ready for that. Don't send me over the edge or we'll have to start all over again."

It honestly didn't sound like such a terrible idea. "Promises, promises."

A loud smack filled the air and then she was gasping, leaning toward Aidan as a sharp pain sizzled along her backside.

"Do not try me, brat," Tristan said. "You stay still until we're ready. Starting over doesn't mean fun things for you, love. It means torture, and hours of it."

She managed to not repeat her previous words—because none of this sounded bad. But she could tell when her Dom was close to being overwhelmed. He was overly stimulated, and she couldn't blame him. She was only calm because she'd already had an orgasm.

And she wasn't all that calm.

Her body tensed when she felt Aidan's hands part the cheeks of her ass and then the sensation of lube against her. She whimpered as Tristan began to work it into her asshole, his big finger circling her and then opening her up. It was different from the plug. It was so much more intimate.

"Relax, Carys," Tristan commanded.

"Relax, baby." Aidan's words were softer, punctuated with his hands stroking up her sides. "Let him in. I want to feel him against me, both of us taking what belongs to us. You taking what belongs to you."

Them. They belonged to her if she could be brave enough to reach out and take them.

One of Tristan's hands was warm on the small of her back as he worked the lubricant in, his big finger fucking her ass like his cock soon would. Tristan in her ass and Aidan in her pussy, the barest hint of flesh separating them. The thought made her shiver and still because she suddenly didn't want to start over again. She wanted what they were promising her.

When she heard the sound of a condom opening she glanced back at Tristan.

He'd been wearing one all week, unlike Aidan. She was on birth control, and neither of them had ever had another lover. After she'd gone on birth control, they hadn't bothered with condoms because they'd trusted each other. But Tris hadn't even made her ask. He'd put one on the first time he'd gotten her properly in bed and had worn one every time since.

Because she hadn't believed him.

"Did you cheat, Tris?"

"No," came his choked reply.

"Then you don't need it." She laid her head against Aidan's chest, listening to the strong beat of his heart.

"Are you sure?" Tristan asked.

She wasn't sure about anything, but she had to start trying. "Yes."

"You won't regret it, baby. I love you. I love you so fucking much," Tristan said and then she felt the head of his cock pressing against her.

She had to force herself to breathe as she flattened out her back and gave Tris the leverage he needed to work his way in. Pressure and pleasure warred as he entered her in sure, shallow thrusts, gaining ground each time. All the while Aidan held her, kissing her forehead and whispering all manner of sweet and dirty things to her.

She groaned as Tristan pressed fully in, seating himself, his hands on her hips.

"You feel so fucking good," Tris groaned. "Come here."

She tilted up, turning her head so he could lean over and mesh their mouths together.

"Thank you, Carys," he whispered. "I promise I won't let you

267

down again."

She didn't have a chance to answer because he took her breath away with a powerful thrust forward, pulling her off Aidan's cock before he pressed his hips up and surged inside her.

Carys gave over, being drawn back and forth between them. The feeling was so familiar and safe, she couldn't deny them. She told them she loved them over and over while the feeling built inside her. It rolled over her skin and connected the three of them in a way they hadn't been even in the last few days. This was what they needed. Being together. With nothing at all between them.

Her body flushed with pleasure as they pushed her over the edge, and then she felt Tris's hands tighten on her hips before he filled her ass. Aidan followed, giving her everything he had.

They fell together, a pile of satisfaction.

She felt Tristan's lips on her shoulder, Aidan's on her cheek.

She was warm and safe and loved.

For now.

Chapter Fifteen

Carys allowed Aidan to lead her into the lush bar at the back of the hotel. This wasn't the lobby bar. The hotel boasted a small, Paris-in-the-twenties themed speakeasy-style bar. Naturally when her cousin went for a drink, she'd passed by the elegant bar in front for this obvious den of iniquity. Kala sat at the bar, looking perfectly at home in the low light.

She wasn't alone, but the two people with her did look a bit out of place.

Tasha was in yoga pants and a sweatshirt, like she'd tossed something on before coming here. Same for Zach, who was in gym pants and a T-shirt.

"What are they doing here?" Aidan asked.

"Probably trying to figure out how to fix the glasses." She winced. "I supposed Uncle Ian's going to be upset we cut off communications so we could have sex."

"We cut off communications so we could have a fight not everyone would express an opinion about," Aidan corrected. "We ignored our cell phones because we were having sex. And honestly, I'm leaving this whole part to Tris, who is likely getting yelled at right now. Tash coming out was unnecessary. Are you sure you don't want me to stay with you?"

When she'd walked out of the shower, she'd known she couldn't simply slip back into bed. She was antsy, despite the orgasms. Or maybe because of them. The intimacy, really. Being with them reminded her of everything she'd ever wanted out of life. But she had questions, questions she wasn't sure Tris could answer. Or rather she wasn't sure she would believe him. Kala was a different story. Her cousin would be brutally honest with her.

"Hey." Tash turned and walked over. "I need to talk to Tris. And apparently Kala didn't mention that you can't not answer your damn cell phones. This is not a vacation. I apologize for using the glasses the way my sisters and dad did, but Adam can't simply cut off communications when Tristan wants him to."

Aidan held a hand up. "That was me. And I heard about the cells. We'll be more careful about it. I'll take you up to Tris. Carys wanted to talk to Kala."

"A drink would be nice, too," she admitted. "Tris insisted someone walk me down, and then he figured out he had forty messages on his cell, so Aidan it was. He said I would be okay as long as I was with Ka…Kara."

Zach frowned, crossing his muscular arms over his chest. He looked like he'd been impersonating her Uncle Ian and had gotten good at it. "Whatever Adam did screwed up the connection between here and the safe house. I have to take them back to Lou."

"I've got them in my bag. Let's go upstairs and talk to Tris, then we can get back to base," Tash said and glared her sister's way. "Don't let her out of your sight again."

Kala gave her a salute that managed to drip sarcasm and then tipped back her glass. "Come on, Carys. You want a drink. Pierre and I were starting a lovely friendship when Tash came in. She's got the righteous indignation thing down. Told you I'd get in trouble if I let your threesome love be a private thing."

Carys slid onto the barstool beside her. The bartender was on a landline at the back of the bar, but he quickly hung up and started filling an order.

Aidan gave her a wave before walking off with Tash and Zach.

"So I take it things went real south." Kala pushed her empty glass slightly away and sighed. "I was kind of hoping that fight would end in some nasty, soul-fulfilling sex. Guess I was wrong. The world sucks."

"Of course it ended in sex." Carys kept her voice low, though there were only a few men sitting in the back of the bar at this late hour. "And it was…everything. But it's still right there between us. I need to understand why he did what he did, and I think you might be able to tell me."

The bartender moved their way. He was an older man with thinning gray hair and dark eyes. He smiled as he slid a cocktail napkin in front of Carys. "*Tu as un ami?*"

Kala didn't hesitate to reply. "*C'est plutôt une famille. Je pense que nous allons faire une autre tournée. Elle aura ce que j'ai.*"

Pierre nodded. "*Certainement. Donnez-moi un instant. J'ai besoin d'une autre bouteille.*"

Sometimes she forgot how smart her cousins were. It was easy to chalk them up to simply being weapons the Agency pointed and shot, easy to put them against Lou and not see their brilliant minds. Kala had spoken Russian earlier, and now she'd apparently been conversing in French with the bartender. "I took four years of Spanish, and I can barely order a beer."

Kala sat back as Pierre disappeared behind the bar. "Well, I just ordered another round of vodka tonics. Don't worry. Though it hurts my soul, I asked him to go easy on the vodka since I'm working. And all he has is French vodka. What the hell kind of place is this?"

"A very French place." She didn't mention to her vodka-loving cousin that she deeply preferred grape-based vodka to potato. It would potentially start a war. "And thanks. I love a vodka tonic."

"I know." Kala turned in her seat. "I might need twenty of them since I have to explain this to you again. He thought he was protecting you. He was dumb about it, but that's kind of how guys go."

Carys shook her head. "It's not about the Agency stuff. It's about The Court. With Tris gone, going to the club was more of a social thing for me and Aidan. We went and talked to our friends and spent time in privacy rooms. I didn't feel some deep need to find another Dom."

Kala shook her head. "But you did need him. You needed his dominance."

"I didn't think about it at the time. Maybe I was too upset to really think about what was missing. I don't know. I want to understand why he needed to top someone else."

Kala's eyes closed, and when she opened them there was

sympathy on her face. "I can only tell you why I have to. Believe me there are days I wish I wasn't wired like this."

She'd come down because she'd thought Kala might be able to explain this in academic terms. She'd never thought her cousin would open up this way. She was almost afraid to ask questions because it might scare her off, but she had one she couldn't ignore. "Because Cooper's a top, too?"

"There are many reasons, but I suppose that's one of them." Kala's eyes were dark in the low light. She'd put in colored contacts before they'd left for the hotel, and it made her look even more grim than usual. "I'm not sure I got to choose."

"What does that mean?"

She seemed to think about whether she wanted to continue. Pierre came back carrying an elegant bottle. He used a corkscrew to cut through the wrapper and then came the pop from uncorking, proving the vodka not only wasn't Russian but was high-end stuff.

"It means I had something happen to me," Kala said quietly. "It happened when I was dumb enough to get kidnapped so your brother would walk into his stalker's trap. I don't talk about it so you're not getting the story, and if you say anything…"

"I wouldn't. Ever. I would never tell your secrets, cousin, but I worry if you don't ever talk, they'll take you down." She'd been aware Kyle had been in trouble once years before. They'd all gone into lockdown, and Kala hadn't been there. But she'd been assured her cousin came through it all fine. "You don't have to tell me anything. I'm sorry I asked."

Kala was oddly fragile at times. Now Carys had an idea why, and it broke her heart.

"Don't be." Kala seemed to shake it off. She smiled Pierre's way when he slid the drink in front of her and then Carys. "*Merci, mon ami.*"

Pierre inclined his head and then moved back down the bar, picking up his cell phone.

"Test it first." Kala slid a thin test strip into Carys's drink. It came back clean. "Every time someone hands you a drink, you test it. Unless you pour it yourself and you opened the bottle, you test."

Carys nodded. Kala tested her own drink and seemed satisfied with the results.

"I will." They were going into Huisman's world tomorrow.

Kala slipped the test strips back into her bag and held up her glass. "*Za tva-jó zda-ró-vye.*"

She knew this one since she'd spent many days with her Aunt Charlotte. She clinked glasses with her cousin. "To your health."

Kala took a long drink and set it back down. "All right. You want to know if there's anything sexual about Tris playing at The Court. Probably."

Carys took an even longer drink because that wasn't the answer she'd been looking for.

"But not the way your jealous mind is thinking," her cousin continued. "Tris has had a connection to you and Aidan all of his life. He was pretty much the Dom right from the beginning. In the way most Doms in our lives are Doms. He didn't make all the decisions, but when it was something important, he took control. Did he initiate sex the first time?"

"He planned it all out. He made it special," she admitted. "I think Aidan would have just done it and been happy, but Tris plotted and turned it into something magical. Then he found all the weaknesses in my dad's security system and started visiting me after hours."

They'd all been insatiable. It had been damn lucky her parent's bedroom was on the first floor and opposite hers. She'd had to bribe the hell out of her younger brother and then cover for him when his horny ass discovered sex.

"Hey, didn't we all. I used to spend Saturday nights at Coop's." She stopped and chuckled. "I would have totally gotten away with it too if it hadn't been for those meddling kidnappers."

Her cousin used humor to cover her pain. Carys had always known it, but now she wondered how deep the pain went. "Does Coop know?"

Kala's head shook. "I stopped talking to that asshole the night it all went down. We eventually became friends again, but none of this matters. What does matter is how Tris is wired. A lot of his identity is tied up in being a Dom. He was raised around the lifestyle. It makes sense to him."

"But his partners weren't there."

"It doesn't matter," Kala countered. "Being in the club, even topping subs, made him feel closer to you. Because it made him feel more like the him he was when he was with you. I can't be certain this is exactly the way he feels, but I would bet it's close. When I put on my fet wear, I tap into a part of me I like. A part of me that's not afraid of anything. A part of me that's still capable of maybe one day forming a connection with someone. Or repairing a connection with someone. A part of me that still trusts."

Her heart ached for her cousin. Would it ache for herself if she couldn't figure this out? "It feels like cheating."

"But to him it felt like reaching out across space and touching some part of you." Kala's voice went wistful. "When he was disciplining a submissive, he was fulfilling the role he always had in your life. He was using it as a touchstone. Not something that showed him all the possibilities he could have, but rather it showed him what he loved. Like a memory. Sometimes those can fuel us when everything else seems lost."

Tears pierced her eyes. Had Tristan been trying to keep a door open when she'd thought he'd locked it? The idea made her want to melt and yet… "It doesn't make it right. He shut me out. He could have had the real thing."

Kala knocked back the rest of her drink. "He did. I understand that, too. He did some shitty things to get this job done. He says it was to protect you, but some of it was about protecting him. How would his sainted doctor girlfriend feel when she saw how much blood was on his hands? Carys, it's probably time for you to call it. You know there's a point of no return in any attempted resuscitation. Not much you can do if the doc working on the patient shrugs and walks away." Kala looked down at her watch. "Time of death. 11:10 p.m."

Tears gone. She was back to anger. Maybe it had been a stupid idea to think Kala could take this seriously. "What is that supposed to mean? And don't tell me I didn't fight. I'm sick of hearing that. I asked him to come home. He said no."

"Preach, sister." Kala slapped at the bar. "He said no. Leave his ass. He's not worth it. He said no. He's stubborn. He doesn't deserve you and you can totally do better. While you're at it, Aidan's a prick, too. I mean he hid shit. You need one-hundred-percent honesty or the relationship is over. Don't worry about it. Mom will set you up with some accountant dude who will never, ever put his relationship on hold to try to save the world." She chuckled. "Not that Tris did a great job. He kind of sucked at it."

"You are such a bitch." Carys stared at her cousin.

Kala seemed to sober and fiddled with her glass, rattling the ice around. "So I've heard. Look, Car, you've come to the wrong person if you want me to give you advice. You either love him and can forgive him, or you love him and you'll feel his loss for the rest of your fucking life. Personally, I went for door number two, and I spend my nights drinking and I only feel like the me I could have been when I'm in the club and he's at my side. I'm in a box. You want to climb in with me or do you want to realize it's not worth tossing out years of love and devotion because he faltered? It's not bad, you know. The box. We have vodka and cookies and the deep sense of satisfaction that you never dragged him down with you. I can scoot over and you can sit here with me. You can let me drag you down instead. Always knew I would."

Her cousin's words were rumbling inside her, but she shoved aside the way they made her feel—antsy and angry with a big spoonful of doubt—because something was wrong. Kala wasn't sitting up straight anymore. There was a hazy look to her normally predatory stare. "How much have you had to drink?"

Kala shook her head. "That was my third, but like I said there's not much vodka in it. It's mostly tonic. Fuck. It's drugged. Car...run."

"Miss Taggart," a deep voice said. Carys started to slide off the barstool but found herself dragged off by a tall man dressed in all black. He loomed over her, staring down with a nasty smirk on his scarred face. "I'm afraid my boss would like a word. Not with you, of course. You're nothing but a pretty pawn. My boss wants to have a word with a man who we hope cares enough about you to not want you hurt."

Another man moved around them, easily hefting Kala's unconscious body over his shoulder.

Panic threatened to overtake Carys. Was Kala dead? What the hell was happening? Calm. She needed calm. What was she supposed to do? Kala had gone over all of it, and it fled her damn brain now. Tris was here. Zach and Tash were here. They probably already saw something on the CCTVs.

They were supposed to be safe here.

She tried to kick back, but he was an unmoving mountain behind her.

"She didn't drink as much as the other," Pierre said in heavily accented English, holding up a hypodermic needle. "You'll need this."

"Help," Carys shouted out. There were other people in the bar. Or had it been these men? Had this whole thing been a setup? Except they couldn't have known she would be down in the bar. Her brain was moving a thousand miles a minute, trying to process what the hell was happening. They'd done everything right, down to testing the damn drinks.

A hand snaked around her throat. "Won't help you. No one will help you here. Now the boss is ready to start a fire. Let's see if you get burned."

Something sharp sank into her arm, and the world immediately went hazy.

And clear all at the same time. She loved them. She was going to die and all she wanted was one more moment with them. The past? Didn't matter. The lies? She could forgive them.

All that mattered was loving them.

It was her last thought as the world went dark.

* * * *

Aidan didn't want to leave Carys behind, but he couldn't think of a reason not to. Kala was with her. He stepped onto the elevator, following Tasha and Zach. He hit the button for their floor and caught sight of the camera in the corner. "Is someone watching us? Like from our team?"

Tash stared straight forward. "Of course. Lou took over the CCTV cameras before you checked in. I'm more worried about tomorrow. I don't think Huisman will have cameras all over his property. I wish we could have gotten someone on the catering staff."

"We talked this through." Zach's tone was calm as though they'd already been over this a couple of times. "There are going to be sixty doctors walking around the compound at any given time. Aidan's going to stick to the public places. He'll be fine. The last thing Huisman wants is a scandal at his premiere event."

"Unless Ben Parker is right and Huisman's insane," Tash said under her breath.

"What does your instinct say, Tash? You've met the man." Tris hadn't, but Ian and Tash had talked to him.

Tasha's head shook. "My instincts tell me he's kind and intelligent. But there's something deeper that tells me I'm seeing what he wants me to see. After what happened with TJ, I think we have to consider what Ben has to say. I know Kenz is pissed at him, but I think he was desperate. I've thought a lot about it. What would you do if you knew there was a bomb waiting to go off but no one would listen to you? Ben might have been playing Cassandra for years now. He didn't mean to hurt Lou, but he felt he had no other choice."

Cassandra. He knew that one. He was never going to admit he only knew the story because of the Taylor Swift song. He hadn't paid a lot of attention to Greek mythology, though he could see where Parker might sympathize with a woman who foresaw the fall of a whole civilization and no one would listen to her.

The doors to the elevator opened, and Aidan led the way. He kind of wanted those glasses now. He wanted to be able to watch over her. Despite what everyone told him, there was an anxious place in the pit of his gut. He took his key card out and led them into the suite.

Thirty minutes before he'd felt safe and secure. Tash and Zach showing up reminded him how fast things could change.

How had Tristan lived like this for so long?

"Yes, I do understand," Tris was saying. "Uncle, you don't have to tell me how stupid I am. I know. I'll take a look at the glasses from this end." He sighed. "I won't know what could have happened until I look at them. If it's not a software issue, then I need to actually have them in my hands to check them."

So Tris was having a fun night, too.

He would be so fucking happy when they were done with this and they could be together without the threat of a mission over their heads. When he didn't have to walk his fiancée around because she shouldn't be without an escort.

"They're here." Tris nodded to Tash and Zach. "Yes, I will work on getting my head out of my ass. Aidan can certainly help. It's why I picked him."

Aidan snorted. Sometimes the only way to deal with an angry Uncle Ian was to concede everything.

Tris hung up and slid his cell in his pocket. "Tash, sorry. I have been properly yelled at, and I'm apparently looking forward to some serious torture, including being keelhauled. Your father promises he'll buy a bigger boat just for the occasion."

Tash snorted and sank down to the sofa. "Dad thinks he needs a new boat. He's looking for an excuse Mom will buy."

"But it was stupid to leave your phone where you wouldn't hear it ring." Zach stayed standing, arms crossed over his chest. "I get it, man. You're dealing with some personal stuff, but we're also in the middle of a mission. I know it seems easy…"

"Nothing's ever easy," Tris interrupted. "I know it. All right. I'm sorry. It won't happen again. And please tell Big Tag not to be too hard on Kala. We needed the privacy. We were fine. She was still in the hotel. Now she's with Carys, doing her job. So what do you have for me?"

Aidan was interested, too. When Tristan took a seat on the couch across from Tasha, he sat down beside him. "Did Phoebe find something? I heard Parker giving Adam permission to send what his agency had on Huisman's recent financials."

Tasha's head shook. "Nothing yet. It's late, though, so I would bet we won't hear from Phoebe until tomorrow. No, I wanted you to be aware of something weird we found. We managed to get the schedule for the symposium."

"Weird?" Aidan asked. "It should be a series of meetings. A couple of speakers. Meals. I know he schedules what he calls 'free thinking' time, which is basically where everyone sits around and exchanges ideas."

"The schedule isn't the problem." Zach paced behind Tasha. "Included with the schedule is a list of the attendees. When did you say you got the invitation, Aidan?"

"Two months ago. I received the invitation to apply for the symposium six weeks before that," he replied. "So my initial contact with the foundation was roughly three and a half months ago."

Tasha looked back at Zach. "So before Australia."

Before they'd met Huisman himself. "That's good, right? If Huisman hadn't even met you, then it does feel like the timing backs up the idea this was all a coincidence."

Tris had gone tense beside him. "Unless all of this was a plan and

278

we're playing catch-up."

"We can't know," Aidan said.

"Aidan's name is not on the list." Zach frowned, a grim expression. "There are sixty-two registered attendees, but no Dr. Aidan O'Donnell. Did you have to send in anything like a bio?"

"Of course." It kind of hurt, but he could come up with a couple of reasons he would be left off. "I sent in everything they asked for, including a bio and professional photo. I would bet it's because I'm the only resident in the group. Everyone else is either a fellow or an attending. I can see where he wouldn't give a resident the same page space. I'm literally years behind most of these guys. Or it could be a mistake. I can't imagine another reason they would leave me off."

"Plausible deniability," Tasha replied.

Tristan took a long breath. "You think he wants to be able to pretend Aidan wasn't there at all?"

"I don't know," Tasha admitted. "If that's his plan, then this is more dangerous than we previously thought, and it's time to get Aidan and Carys to a safe house. I'm worried Huisman will make his move the minute they enter the compound. Ben has done a lot of research concerning the house. He's got serious security, and if they're Huisman's personal army, we could be outnumbered."

Tris sat back, seeming to think for a moment. "Uncle Ian didn't say anything about ending the op. Is he leaving this in my hands?"

"I believe he is, though you should understand he knows what he wants you to do," Zach replied. "I think this is one of those Big Tag moves where he says he's leaving it up to you—as long as you make the right call."

Tris huffed out a laugh. "Good to know I'm going to make him happy. We're out. We'll pack up and return to base and we'll be back in Dallas by tomorrow afternoon. I think I'll take my subs somewhere tropical for a couple of weeks until we figure out what's going on. My father can do the work he needs to do from Dallas. I know he wanted a chance at one of us getting hands on Huisman's system, but he'll find a way."

A deep sense of relief swept through Aidan. Tris was dropping the whole op. He was coming with them. He could leave all of this behind if Tris was with them. "I'll go and get Carys."

Aidan stood, ready to get the train rolling. He'd been so excited about the prospects of attending this event, and now he never wanted to hear the name Huisman again. Even if they were wrong and it was all a coincidence and Huisman was the caring man he presented himself to be, Aidan wanted out. Something was happening and it would hurt people. He wanted to make sure it wasn't his people.

He needed to make sure it wasn't Carys and Tris.

"Take Zach with you," Tristan ordered. "I can handle the packing."

"I'll go with him. I need to talk to my sister," Tasha offered, standing up and straightening her shirt. "She's going to be pissed the op's not on."

Zach held his hands out as if telling them all he wasn't about to argue. "Definitely sounds like a Taggart family problem. I'll help Tris get packed up, and we'll meet you downstairs. Why don't you get them in the car and pick us up in fifteen minutes?"

"Sounds like a plan," Tasha agreed. "Aidan, come with me."

Tris stopped him before he could get to the door, putting a hand on his neck and getting into his space. "You do whatever Tash tells you to do. I know she's a woman and your instincts will be to protect her, but she's deadly. She knows what she's doing, and she'll keep you safe."

Aidan chuckled. "We're walking down to the bar. I think we'll be okay, but I promise. I definitely promise I'll hide behind Kala if it comes to it."

"I'm serious," Tris said. "Something's not right. I can feel it in my gut. Leaving you off that list was a choice. He's playing games with us, and I don't know the rules. Maybe we should leave everything behind."

He seemed to have forgotten who their fiancée was. "You want Carys to leave her makeup and shoes behind?"

"I can buy her more," Tris insisted.

"You told me the key to everything was staying calm." His Dom was on the edge. It was up to him to bring him back. "It's going to be okay. All you have to do is shove her skin care and makeup in a bag. You can leave my stuff. I don't care. But do not leave her e-reader. She'll be pissed."

Tristan took a long breath. "Okay. You're right. Go. We'll be right behind you."

He hugged Tris, holding on for a moment. "We'll be okay. All of us."

Tristan nodded and stepped back. "Take care of our girl. I'm sure she'll love sleeping on the couch instead of in this big, gorgeous suite."

Tasha shook her head. "Sorry, guys. I already called the couch. I think y'all will be bedding down in the van, maybe. But not all is lost. I'm sure Dad will have us on a plane before dawn. Fun times."

He followed Tasha out, retracing their steps to the elevators.

"I'm glad he's being reasonable," Tasha said as the doors closed and they started down toward the lobby. "I was afraid Dad was going to have to come and drag him away. He's changed in the last couple of days."

"He hasn't changed. He remembered who he is and where he belongs," Aidan explained. He knew Carys was still wary, but he wasn't anymore. He knew Tris, and when he said he was coming home this time, he meant it. He'd bent, and that meant they hadn't broken. Carys would see it.

A couple of weeks in paradise wouldn't hurt.

Tasha reached into her pocket and pulled out her cell as the doors opened, and they walked out into the elegant lobby. Naturally Kala had picked the tiny bar in the back rather than the big one closest to the doors.

"Hey, Lou. We're probably forty minutes out," Tasha said as they walked along the marbled floors. It was getting late and the lobby was quiet, with only a few employees milling around. "Wait. What are you talking about?"

Aidan stopped.

Tasha's brows had come together as she listened to Lou.

Aidan felt the moment his body started pumping adrenaline. Something was going wrong. They'd miscalculated some small thing, and the world was about to get upended.

"Lou says the CCTV cams went out five minutes ago," Tasha said, the cell still to her ear. She gasped and then swallowed at something Lou had told her. "Yes. I'll get us out of here right fucking now. Tell them we'll be coming in hot."

She hung up and slid her free hand around her waist, feeling for something there. Aidan had seen her keep a holster for her gun in the small of her back. Was she making sure the safety was off in case she needed to use it quickly? "Aidan, I need you to stay calm. Lou said Phoebe just called. She didn't take the night off. She did a deep dive on Huisman's recent financial transactions. It wasn't easy because the foundation is linked to a corporation which has a bunch of arms."

"I don't need a lesson in finance. Tell me what's happened."

"Phoebe found a transaction for three million dollars. It went through two days ago, shortly after we made the reservations for here. To the manager of this hotel," she explained. "His name is Pierre Allard. She sent a picture, and I'm almost certain he was behind the bar Kala was at."

The one he'd recently left Carys at.

Aidan took off running, but he already knew it was too late.

Chapter Sixteen

Tris watched the door close and sighed. It was over. The job. Probably his career. He might not lose his job, but he would be exactly what everyone thought he was—a keyboard jockey who supported the real operatives. A guy who'd failed at his first real mission. He hadn't caught the bad guy. He'd tried his hardest, given it everything he had, and still come up short like he'd always feared he would. His father was coming in to clean up his mess, and he would go home and be a dutiful son and watch after his subs and do his diminished job to the best of his ability. He would be nothing more than a son, brother, friend...husband.

It didn't sound so bad.

"I know this sucks for you, but I, for one, am not upset about heading home," Zach said. "This trip's timing was shitty for me."

He wasn't the only one who was planning some life changes, but he still had some questions. Zach was planning to shift his focus to the Agency. "You already talked to Coop?"

Zach nodded. "Yeah. We had breakfast yesterday morning, and he offered up a room. Getting a place in Dallas will be so much more convenient than constantly having to fly out for briefings. I thought Cooper might want someone to help with rent and utilities and stuff.

I've lived alone most of my adult life, so I'm looking forward to having someone to talk to every now and then. But there was something I was thinking about. Don't your parents own the place? You don't think they'll sell it now that you're definitely not living there anymore?"

"Somehow I think my parents will continue to be perfectly reasonable landlords." His mom wasn't about to chuck out her son's friends. She would consider keeping the house up her contribution to the team. "And sure you want to suddenly move in order to be closer to the team? There's not another reason?"

"Yeah, like I said, I'm kind of sick of being alone."

"So you're doing this to have a roommate?" Tris stared at the big guy, willing him to get to the real point.

"Fine. I want to see where it's going with Devi. The last week has literally been the best of my life. We went to Top the other night and Cooper and Kala were there. It was the nicest time. It was...like being around family," Zach said in an almost wistful way.

It was hard to remember some people weren't constantly surrounded by family and friends who'd known them all their damn lives. It could be annoying, but then he realized how alone Zach must feel. "I'm glad it's going well. Devi is great. And I bet Coop will be happy to have someone who doesn't immediately fall in love and move. I think Nate lasted like a week and a half before he was living with Daisy. Take your time with Devi. I think Cooper needs some stability."

"I can do that," Zach promised. "Devi's got a lot going on. I want to add to her life not give her more to do. I need some time to figure out how we can fit into each other's lives."

"Let's get going." Tristan looked around the room. "The last thing we need is Tash honking at the door."

"You okay?" Zach asked, studying him. "I know what this mission has meant to you and what you gave up for it. You seem to be handling this like a champ, but you have to know this means Big Tag's going to take over everything. Well, if the higher-ups let him."

What he'd given up was precious time with Carys and Aidan. He didn't want to lose more. "I think the fact they allowed him to take over this op means they're coming around. You were sent in to discredit the team. It's been a couple of years and you haven't managed it."

"I was sent in to report back with an unbiased eye," Zach corrected. "I'm going to admit something I wouldn't to most other people. I wasn't ever unbiased. I wanted on the team."

"Because it sounded like a beautiful train wreck?" Tris got to work. Despite what Aidan had said, Tris didn't mean to leave their stuff behind either. Though he wouldn't call for a bellman. They'd checked for bugs, but the absence of them in the room didn't mean there weren't still eyes on them. Especially once they hit the elevator. He intended to walk out before anyone could think to stop him. He grabbed his laptop and shoved it in his bag.

Zach grinned and picked up Carys's laptop bag, moving it to the table at the front of the outer room. "It is most of the time. What I loved about the idea of the team was the family aspect. It felt more military to me than Agency. I liked the idea the team would care about each other, would know each other. So often a Mr. or Ms. Black would roll in, order my Special Forces teams to do their will, and then never see a one of us again. Big Tag gives a damn about everyone he works with, and he's passed his philosophy on to his team. I wanted to be part of that."

"I can see why it would be appealing." Tristan mentally counted their baggage and the likelihood he and Zach could handle it. Luckily, he packed light. The good news was they hadn't gotten around to unpacking more than toiletries since they wouldn't be staying more than the night. It was easy to shove the dirty clothes in the outer pockets of the luggage and then roll it to the living room where Zach moved it into place. "Tell me something. Did you know about the whole taking the last parachute and leaving Parker behind to die thing?"

Zach chuckled. "I did. I kind of watched it happen, though from a distance. In Kala's defense, she didn't believe they would kill Parker. He's being kind of dramatic when he says that."

Tristan scoffed at the idea. "She did not care."

"Okay, she didn't, but what else was she supposed to do?" Zach asked, proving he would back his teammates even when they were a little psycho. "She did catch him, and she did make sure he made it safely to the ground. It was a hell of a thing."

"Why didn't it make your report?" Tris was always careful to go over mission reports even when he wasn't involved in the op.

Zach stopped, and Tris could have sworn there was the faintest flush to the big guy's face. "I don't know."

"Yeah, you do." He knew exactly what had happened, but he wanted to hear Zach say it.

Zach shrugged. "Fine. Because you don't tell on your sister. I'm not a snitch. You know what they say."

Except there was one problem with what Zach had said. "You were literally hired to snitch. Also, you should be happy you didn't because snitching on that particular sister wouldn't lead to stitches."

"Nope. It leads to a body bag, and what can I say, man? I drank the Kool-Aid and I want more," Zach admitted. "I came on board because some of the directors worried the team would be unstable. Don't ever tell our Langley handlers, but those directors wanted Big Tag and Charlie in. It's the only reason Drake and Taylor were allowed to form the team. They knew if they had the twins, they had their parents. Some of them thought if we could get shit on the team, they would have leverage over the whole Taggart clan."

Tris stopped in his tracks, feeling his eyes widen. "Ian would eat them all if he knew."

"Which is why we're not going to tell him, brother," Zach said. "It would cause problems. I handled it for him. They're no longer talking about shutting it down at Langley. Instead, they're giving the team more important assignments, and that's why I think this one is going to fall to Big Tag. Honestly, bringing your dad in is the nail in the coffin to the people who want to shut this team down. If we have Adam Miles, no one's going to argue with us."

His father was being used as a chess piece, but he had to trust his dad could handle it. Between his father, Big Tag, and Charlotte, they would likely upend the whole game and change all the rules. If there was anything he'd learned from all of this it was to trust the people he loved. "Well, then one good thing came out of all the mess I made."

He went into the bathroom and grabbed Carys's makeup bag and his and Aidan's toiletries.

"You didn't make a mess," Zach said from the outer room. "You did what you could with what you were handed. Everyone was impressed you could even find the fucker. He was well hidden, but you tracked his ass down. You couldn't know you were going to walk in and find The Jester face down on the floor, man. You did what you had to do."

"Nice of you to…" Tristan stopped, focused on what Zach had just said.

Face down on the floor.

By the time Zach had shown up, Tristan had turned him over. He'd had to see if the man could be saved and along with him, his knowledge. When Zach had walked in, The Jester had been lying face up, his unseeing eyes staring at the ceiling.

"Hey, I cleared out Kala's stuff," Zach announced. "She had everything in a duffel. I think we can manage it on our own."

What else had Zach been sent in to do? Who was Zach really working for? Maybe he was being fucking paranoid as hell. Maybe it was a turn of phrase, something that dropped from his mouth without thinking about it.

Except Zach Reed was always precise.

Tristan cursed inwardly because when he'd gotten dressed he hadn't put his holster on. He'd been in a hurry because they'd lain around naked for a while, and then he'd sat there talking to Aidan while Carys was in the shower. When he'd remembered his phone, he'd gotten dressed in a hurry.

Zach rounded the corner. "You need help in here?"

Tristan forced his expression to go blank. "Nope. Got everything I need."

Zach stared at him for a moment, and then his eyes closed. "Fuck. He was face up. You turned him over. Damn it, Tris."

Tris dropped the bags he'd been holding. Zach was armed, unlike him. Tris held his hands up and assessed his odds of getting out of this situation alive. "So you killed him? And if you did it, then who did I kill? I thought I killed his assassin."

His mind worked overtime, trying to come up with any reason why Zach would have done what he'd obviously done. Zach was his friend. Zach was also military. He could have been following orders. But why would Tris have been left out?

"He was a distraction. I hired the man. Trust me, he deserved what he got. I needed everyone to think we'd closed that circle. You should know Tara had nothing to do with it. She was just doing her job." Zach's hands came up, too, as though trying to let Tris know he wasn't a threat. "There's a reason, Tris. Please believe me. I am not here to hurt you or anyone on this team. I genuinely care about you guys."

There were a few scenarios he could come up with. "Your Army bosses wanted The Jester dead? Had they been working with him? Taken bribes from him?"

"It's not like that," Zach replied. "Let's get out of here and I promise I'll explain everything. Just… There are people who can't know. Who can never know what I did. Big Tag…he won't forgive me. Cooper…"

Tristan was about to make a move when a sound split the charged air around them. A knock. Someone was at the door.

Zach's jaw went tense. "Tash would have called."

"She wouldn't have had to," Tris said. "Aidan has a key. I didn't order anything."

Then they heard the sound of something worse. The door in the outer room opening.

Zach pulled his SIG and held out a hand, telling Tris to stay back. "Hide."

He wasn't about to do that. If this was going south, then Carys and Aidan were in danger. He wasn't about to hide behind the fucking shower curtain. Not that there was one. It was a standing shower with glass sides. Where the hell did Zach think he was going to hide?

"Mr. Dean-Miles," a deep voice said. It was masculine and held a heavy French accent. "We know you're in there along with Captain Reed. We have your ladies in custody. Would you like to see them again or should we put them down? It's entirely your choice."

Carys. Fuck. They had Carys. "I'm coming out."

Zach sent him a fierce look, his voice low. "Like hell you are."

"Are we going to let them kill us in the bathroom?" He didn't see they had a choice unless they wanted a firefight followed by the police showing up and then him likely receiving Carys back in a body bag. He didn't even know where Aidan was. Did they have Aidan, too? Was the "ladies" a bit of homophobia stacked on top of these fuckers' criminal behavior?

"I'm not playing," the voice said. "I have colleagues with me, and you'll find we've taken over the hotel. There's no one who will come to your aid and no way to contact the police. You can come with us or we'll kill the women since they'll be of no use."

"I'm coming out," Tris said forcefully, raising his hands as he walked by Zach. "I can't let them hurt Carys, and we don't know who else they have."

There were three "ladies" in the hotel tonight, and Aidan. His gut churned. Could they have killed Aidan? They would have to have found a way to drug Kala or she would fight until she killed them or they killed her.

How had it gone so wrong?

Because chaos was always the point. They'd played Huisman the way they would have played anyone else. Like he had things that mattered to him. Like he had things he loved and wouldn't want to lose.

But what if chaos was all he cared about? Chaos and some revenge no sane person could understand.

Zach cursed behind him, and when Tris glanced back, he'd put the SIG on the counter and held his hands up. "We're both coming out, and neither of us is armed."

Tris went out the door first, though Zach tried to move in front of him. He couldn't trust anyone. He was immediately faced with five men dressed all in black, each carrying a weapon. Two of them held handcuffs.

"Dr. Huisman requests the pleasure of your company." The man in the middle seemed to be their leader. He was tall and lanky, his eyes predatory.

"Where is my fiancée?" Tris asked. "Let her go and I'll tell you everything."

A chuckle went through the group, and the leader shook his head. "You will tell Dr. Huisman everything anyway." He glanced over to his left. "*Prenez-les.*"

Take them.

Before his fight instincts could take over there was a hissing sound and a sharp pain in his thigh. He heard Zach curse and realized two of the men carried tranquilizer guns. He recognized them because he'd recently been hit with one very similar. These assholes shopped at the same stores as his dad.

Tris felt the world go hazy and prayed he would be able to see them again.

* * * *

"I want someone to kill." Big Tag paced like a tiger.

"I know, babe. Believe me, I know, but all Tasha could find were low-level employees who didn't know anything." Charlotte was trying to calm him down. "They worked fast. I think the manager has likely skipped town, but we'll find him eventually."

Carys and Kala had been gone by the time Aidan and Tasha had finally gotten through the entrance to the speakeasy. It had been completely shut down and locked up when they'd gotten there. The big bouncer who'd dressed like a twenties gangster had been absent from his post, and no one they asked knew anything beyond the bar closed at eleven. An hour or so before they'd entered it the first time.

Had Kala walked in when it was open, and they'd decided to use the opportunity? Then Carys had shown up like a lamb to slaughter.

Aidan felt useless. Lost. How could they be gone?

When they'd realized what had happened, they'd tried to call Tris and Zach, but cell service had been out and by the time they'd climbed the stairs to the suite—the elevator had mysteriously stopped working—all they'd been left with was luggage.

Someone had jammed service at precisely the right time. Tasha had to drive a mile and a half away before she'd managed to get her father on the phone to activate the trackers he had implanted in all of what he called his "puppies." Tris, Kala, and Zach should have been trackable.

They'd gotten nothing.

"They must have pulled their trackers," Lou said.

"Or they're in range of a jammer." Adam Miles had been on his laptop when they'd returned to the safe house. He had barely looked up. "They shut off CCTVs around the hotel, too. They just came back on."

"Likely because Huisman has them wherever he wants them." Kenzie paced, too, mirroring her father in so many ways. She'd been tense and shut down, none of her natural ebullience in evidence since she'd learned someone had kidnapped her twin and cousin.

Her father turned to her, his jaw tight. "You need to get upstairs. Parker could be here any minute. He knows Kara's been taken. Won't he be surprised when he sees you here?"

Kenzie's chin came up in stubborn defiance. "Let him. I don't care. My sister is in trouble. My cousin is in trouble. Hell, I'm worried about Tris and Zach because what's going to happen when they realize Tris knows nothing and Zach is barely involved? They'll kill Zach, but they'll likely torture Tris."

"Or torture Carys so Tris will talk." It was the scenario playing through Aidan's head. Carys being hurt over and over again for a secret Tris didn't possess. "He'll try to make up something, but they'll figure out he's lying."

"It'll take them time to verify whatever he tells them," Big Tag said. "Tris is smart. He'll come up with something. He'll buy us some time."

Aidan had to hope so. "My question is why would they take Kala and Zach? I would think they would be more trouble than they're worth."

The logical side of his brain went where his heart didn't want to go. Kala would be trouble. Zach would be trouble. Should they have searched the hotel more thoroughly? Would they have found bodies?

Cooper strode down the stairs. He'd changed out of PJ pants and into black fatigues and a black T-shirt, a tactical vest covering his chest, and he was loaded up. He carried an AR-15, and Aidan counted at least three handguns and two knives.

"Yo, Rambo. Where the fuck do you think you're going?" Big Tag asked, staring at Cooper like he could force the other man to do his will.

Kenzie got a good look at Coop and nodded. "One of us has it right. I'll go with you. Give me a sec to get changed."

Charlotte sighed. "Yes, because running around Canada dressed for war is going to make everything easier. Kenzie, you're not going anywhere."

"I'm not running around," Cooper promised. "I know exactly where I'm going."

A brow rose over Big Tag's eyes. "Do you? Have you carefully considered all the places Huisman could take them and logically narrowed it to one or two buildings? Did you get a listing of all the properties Huisman owns so you could deduce which one would be the easiest to store four prisoners in?"

"If they're prisoners." Tasha sat beside Lou, her hands in knots on her lap. She said out loud what they were all truly afraid of. "I don't understand why they need Kala and Zach."

"We don't know they have Kala." TJ was ever the optimist. Like Cooper, he'd dressed in tactical wear and looked ready for anything. Though he hadn't strapped on an armory yet. "She could be following them. Same for Zach. You said you left him with Tristan."

"Yes, in the suite where there wasn't any place to go," Tasha argued.

"The CCTVs went out before we could see anything. I have no idea if Zach was still with Tristan or if he maybe hid somewhere and followed them," Lou replied. "Kala could have done the same."

Charlotte shook her head. "Kala would have called in. She would have found a way. Same with Zach. We need to go back to the hotel…"

"She's not dead," Kenzie shouted. Her strawberry hair shook, making her look slightly wild. "She's not fucking dead. I would feel it if my sister was dead."

Charlotte moved in, wrapping her arms around her daughter. "Of course you would."

But her gaze went to Ian, worry plain there.

"You guys can stand around here trying futilely to get the trackers back online," Cooper began. "They're not working and won't. Why the fuck do we even have them? Anyway, feel free to sit on your hands. I'm going to go blow up the Huisman Foundation. Then I'll move on to his house and any other place I think he might be hiding until he gives me back my…our people."

Big Tag's head fell back on a groan. "Fuck me."

TJ stood, moving Cooper's way. "I understand the impulse, man, but the minute you start blowing shit up, we all get taken into custody."

"That's easy for you to say since Lou is sitting right there safe and sound," Coop shot back.

Lou turned his way. "Kala wouldn't want you to get arrested. She would want you to play this smart. They didn't leave bodies for us to find which means that wasn't the message they were sending us."

"We haven't gotten the message yet," Big Tag pointed out.

"Or they're not going to send a message at all," Cooper shot back. "They're going to leave us here because they don't care. Huisman wants to know who the bombmaker is. He's figured out Tristan is The Jester, and he took Carys and Kala so he would have leverage to make him talk."

"Then why take Zach?" Tasha asked. "And how would he know Carys would be in the bar when she was? She wasn't supposed to be, you know. This whole plan doesn't make sense."

"He had control of the CCTVs." Kenzie seemed to have calmed down. She leaned against her mom. "According to the report Phoebe sent, he paid the manager of the hotel, which is why they were short staffed. He sent home anyone who might have interfered. We have to think Huisman intended to take Carys and Aidan at some point. When they separated, he decided it was easier to take them out individually."

"He would have to drug Kala." Coop set the AR-15 on the table.

"I know we think she's invincible, but I assure you she can be overwhelmed," Big Tag said. "What I don't understand is why go when Tasha and Zach got there? You're adding in two variables when you don't need to. I understand waiting until later. If I'd been planning I would have gone in at say three in the morning, overwhelmed the group while they were likely sleeping, and take out the four of them. The way Huisman did this, they had to deal with six instead of four."

"It was only luck they went when Aidan and I were downstairs." Tasha was pale, her hands around the mug of tea her mother had pressed into them ten minutes before.

"I don't think so." Big Tag ran a hand over his head, a gesture that screamed of frustration. "I'm missing something."

Aidan sat there feeling utterly useless. They were out there going through god only knew what and he was sitting here. He couldn't do anything. The loves of his life were going through hell and he was…nothing.

He felt like he couldn't breathe. All around him the team was going over possible scenarios, and he was sitting here.

"Hey, Aidan. Are you… I'm sorry. That's a dumb question. Of course, you're not okay." Adam turned his chair around, leaning toward Aidan. "I need you to know I'm going to find them. Huisman can't take over every CCTV in the country. He'll slip up, and I'll be there. This is far from over. I need you to stay calm and be ready in case we need you."

"Need me? I can't fucking do anything. I'm not trained for any of this. I'm not prepared for this life."

"Of course you are. Aidan, you do something none of us can do. You literally save lives with your hands. When all looks lost, you stay calm and find a way to put a human body back together. We might need those skills because once I figure out where they are, there won't be any holding Cooper back," Adam said.

"I wish I'd gone to the gun range more," Aidan admitted.

Adam's head shook. "I'm glad you didn't. I'm glad you spent all these years learning how to save people's lives. We might need that today because I believe they're alive, and we will have to fight to get them back. I know you think you should be there on the front lines, but we need you. We need you safe because when it all goes bad, you are the most important person here."

Adam's words were doing what he'd likely meant for them to do. Easing Aidan's mind. Getting him in the right frame of mind. "I don't have a kit."

Most doctors didn't carry around the tools of their trade. He'd done some training in fieldwork with EMTs. He'd also spent summers in Africa at a clinic run by Nate Carter's mom. They often went into villages and sometimes had to deal with emergencies where there wasn't an OR for miles. But then he had a kit.

"Cooper has one." Adam turned his chair again, and his eyes went back to his screen. "The team is ready for this. The kit will be basic, but you can do it."

Aidan stood. Something to do. He desperately needed something to do. "Let me look through it and make sure I have what I need."

"I'm still stuck on why they would let Kala live," Lou said, sniffling into a tissue. "Huisman has to know who Ms. Magenta is. He knew Uncle Ian and Tash worked for the Agency."

"She's not fucking dead," Cooper barked.

"Hey." TJ stepped in front of Lou like he needed to protect her.

"Everyone calm the fuck down." Big Tag's voice rang out through the chaos.

Chaos. They were caught in a chaotic situation. The kit was sitting on the table in the dining room, but Aidan stopped. This was chaos. Disruption. According to Ben Parker, it was what Dr. Huisman believed in.

Does chaos ever make sense?

Carys had asked the question.

Maybe it didn't to an outsider, but perhaps they were using a logic that didn't apply. They needed to stop thinking like Agency operatives and start thinking like a narcissistic sociopath who'd watched his father die at a young age.

Sometimes our brains make odd connections. Trauma can do funny things to a person. Especially a child. Sometimes revenge doesn't make sense. Carys had said. *The brain can make connections that wouldn't look rational to the outside person.*

Carys's words were playing around in Aidan's head. "Unless this is all about Ian, and then he would want Kala. He would want to hurt her to get back at her father."

"We don't know Huisman even knows who Kala is," TJ argued.

"He does." Big Tag seemed stuck in place. "He knows exactly who she is. He's been watching me and my family since long before there was an Agency team. Damn it. I've been avoiding the truth because it didn't make sense to me. I didn't fucking kill his father. Neither did anyone on my team."

Carys had been on to something. She'd looked at the situation from the outside and slid pieces into place none of them realized formed a different picture. "But you were the starting point. If you look at it from a distorted position, none of it happens if Big Tag isn't there. Levi Green got involved with Huisman's father because he was looking for men under Big Tag's protection. Without Ian they wouldn't have had the money or the resources to run. They certainly wouldn't have been investigating Dr. Rebecca Walsh."

"So he could want revenge on you, and that would mean hurting Kala." Cooper sounded more hopeful. "She can handle pain. She can handle torture. She can stay alive until we find her."

There was a knock on the door, and Charlotte took her daughter's hand.

Kenzie stood there, her eyes narrowed. "No. I'm going to talk to Ben."

Her father got into her space, taking her shoulders in his big hands. "You chose this. You and your sister chose this fucking life.

295

You could be home right this second getting ready to go to whatever job you chose, but you're here because you decided to be a damn spy. So you will walk up those stairs and keep the illusion because you don't get to fucking burn it all down when the inevitable happens. This is where it was always going, little girl. So you will walk upstairs and keep your shit together while I find your sister."

Tears shone in Kenzie's eyes, but she took a deep breath and nodded. "She would kill me if I blew this for her. But you can't leave me here. You have to let me come."

"If I can manage it safely." Big Tag backed down. "Now go."

Kenzie allowed her mother to lead her upstairs two seconds before Ben Parker walked in with Tara. She looked rumpled and anxious.

Parker looked…ready. Hungry. Like he'd been waiting for this for a very long time.

"I think I've brought Mr. Parker up to speed." Tara left Parker standing at the edge of the room, walking right up to Big Tag. "You should also know I called in and they told me I should do whatever you tell me to do. They'll send whatever support you need. My, Tris, and Zach's bosses are going to be working with Langley to get us whatever we need."

"CSIS is ready to help as well," Parker offered.

"They believe us when we say it's Huisman?" Cooper asked.

Parker looked him over, his face a polite blank. "Of course not. They want proof, but they also don't like the idea of US operatives being taken on Canadian soil. Which is why we should get going before they send a team. They'll want to play this as cautiously as possible. If you want Ms. Magenta back, you'll listen to me. Do you believe me now?"

The last question was pointed directly at Ian, who nodded shortly. "I do."

"This is about me and it's about the bombmaker," Parker affirmed. "He wants both of us, and he'll do whatever it takes to get us. He's taken Ms. Magenta because I'm sure he's aware I have…feelings about her."

"We talked about this on our way from the hotel." Tara wasn't staying at the safe house due to sleeping arrangements. She was in a hotel a few miles away. When the shit had hit the fan, Big Tag had woken her and asked her to bring Parker in. "We believe Huisman has found out Tristan has something to do with The Jester and possibly the same connection with Zach, since they work closely together. I'm not sure about that part. Zach has always been behind the scenes."

"What do you mean?" TJ asked. "I would think if they were going to take someone, it would be me. They can't possibly mistake me for Zach. He's bigger than me, and we don't have the same coloring. If what you're saying is true, we have a leak."

"Or he's been watching you far more carefully than you ever imagined," Parker argued. "If there was a leak, he would know Tristan has no idea who the bombmaker is. Then there would be zero reason to start this war right now. He's certain someone knows. If he didn't come after TJ, then he's eliminated TJ as a possible source of information and decided Tristan knows something."

"He doesn't," Aidan insisted. "He would have told me."

"He certainly would have told me," Tara agreed. "We've been struggling to find anything on the man. At one point we thought we'd found him, but by the time we got where we thought he was staying, he was gone. I've always wondered if someone might have tipped him off. What if we do have a leak? What if the leak told Huisman Tristan knows to throw him off?"

"Or what if Tristan knows something he doesn't think he knows." Lou looked thoughtful for a moment.

"Or Zach." Big Tag was still in a way that let Aidan know something was going through his brain. "Tara, I need all the reports. Every single one you have on every mission Zach worked."

"Zach?" Cooper asked. "Why would this have anything to do with Zach?"

"What do you know?" Aidan couldn't see how the big captain was involved.

"I know Zach was placed on this team to discredit us," Big Tag offered. "But now I'm wondering if he didn't maneuver himself into the position. I need everything, Tara."

Tara nodded. "I'll put it together. I'll get it to you and then I'll help Mr. Miles. I suspect he's going through CCTV cameras across the city. I managed to pull the plates of every vehicle Huisman owns along with all the foundation's vehicles, and I have a list of properties associated with his businesses."

He knew Carys worried Tara had feelings for Tris, but it was obvious the woman knew how to do her job. "Thank you."

Big Tag gestured her way while looking at Cooper. "Yes, thank you for being sensible. Now let's sit down and figure out where we're looking. I know I'll get a call at some point."

"You'll get a video," Parker countered. "One that details what your operative is going through. Or perhaps a finger. He won't call you himself. He doesn't need you to acknowledge it was him. He simply needs to know you're in pain."

"It's almost like you hoped this would happen." Cooper was staring at Parker like he was going to use one of those big knives on him. "Is this another situation like the one in Dallas with Lou?"

Parker's eyes rolled. "No. I did not...what? Tell the man I've been trying to stop for years to kidnap a woman I have complex feelings for? It's obvious your feelings for her aren't."

"She's my teammate." But Cooper wasn't trying hard.

He wasn't about to have them fight over Kala right now. "Mr. Parker, do you have any idea where he might take them?"

Adam snapped his fingers. "Hey, Lou, get on your laptop. Tara, too. I think I have something. Ms. Magenta's tracker came back online briefly. I think whoever said they have a jammer is right, and it briefly went out. I've got a location, and I think it's on a street."

Tara and Lou scrambled to get on their systems.

"I would bet he's on a road that will take them to a private airport." Parker moved behind Adam. "You'll be looking for at least two vehicles. He might split them up. Two and two. He'll have almost certainly drugged them."

"Ka...Kara would have tested any drinks," Big Tag said.

Lou stared at her laptop screen. "There's not a lot of defense against a tranq gun. If they couldn't get her drink, they would have gotten them another way. If they didn't drug her..."

"Something would have blown up by now." Even Cooper looked like he was standing down from his scorched-earth plan. "Can we get to the airport in time?"

"No," Tara said, her eyes on her screen. "But I can see who's filed a flight plan. They have to file something thirty minutes ahead of take off since they're in regulated air space."

Parker leaned against the wall, looking over the whole room. "No need. I know where they're going."

"Enlighten us," Big Tag said in a tone that should have had Parker intimidated.

Instead, the Canadian simply smirked. "Back where it all began. We should go to Toronto."

Aidan grabbed the kit. He prayed he wouldn't need it.

Chapter Seventeen

Carys came awake slowly, the peaceful darkness peeling back in nausea-inducing strips. There was light—too much light—and she could hear the sound of boards creaking. Something was moving.

Her brain was heavy, filled with cobwebs she tried to push aside.

Something had happened. She'd been with Kala in the bar talking about Tris and then... Kala. Something had happened to Kala.

She forced her eyes open. Where was her cousin?

"It would be better if you went back to sleep, Carys," a voice whispered from her left. "Pretend if you have to. I don't want to get to the torture part of our day."

They'd been in the bar at the hotel, and someone had drugged them. Except there was a problem with that scenario. Her head was so foggy she barely registered what that voice had told her.

She forced her eyes open because panic was starting to push all that fog to the side. She tried to move her legs but came up against some kind of resistance.

"Or you could ignore me."

There was no way to mistake the sarcastic tone. Kala.

Carys forced herself to breathe, to take stock of where she was. On her back, staring up at a vaulted ceiling. There was a circle of light above her, bright light. Was that a surgical lamp? "What? Where?"

She heard the sound of someone speaking in French in the distance.

"And now he knows we're both awake," Kala said quietly. "Remember we're on a mission, Ms. Taggart."

Why the hell was her cousin calling her Ms. Taggart?

The night flooded back. The mission. They weren't supposed to be cousins. Kala was supposed to be her bodyguard. She remembered right before the world had gone dark someone else had called her Ms. Taggart. "What happened?"

She heard the sound of a door opening, and terror threatened to overwhelm her. But she couldn't seem to move her limbs with any precision. A light came on, brightening the room to a painful degree. That was when she realized she was on some sort of exam table.

"Well, turns out beyond researching new neurological therapies and drugs, the Huisman Foundation also dabbles in ways to make date rape easier," came Kala's reply.

A deep chuckle slithered through the room. "Ah, not true. We created these particular drugs to make it easier to take out the people I need taken out. Date rape is simply a secondary use, though I suspect I'll make some money off of it. Welcome, Ms. Taggart."

Carys felt her stomach roll but forced herself to focus. She knew that cultured voice. Aidan had listened to some of his lectures in preparation for the symposium that wasn't going to happen now. At least not with them attending. "You're making a mistake, Dr. Huisman."

"Am I? Or am I fulfilling a long-term plan?"

He wasn't looking down at her. She turned her head toward where the voice had come from and realized Huisman was standing over Kala, who was laid out on another exam table.

Carys tried to move her arms, but she felt the restraints around her wrists.

So like the ones Aidan and Tris had used on her, and for such utterly different reasons. It was odd how the same items could cause such various reactions based on who was using them. When Tris and Aidan tied her down, she felt safe, beloved, and worshipped. These scared the hell out of her. "I'm Ms. Taggart, by the way. She's just my bodyguard. And she didn't do a great job. Those test strips didn't work. Someone should talk to your boss."

Another chuckle and Huisman turned, unblocking the view of Kala's body. Unlike Carys, she wasn't tied down. Her arms were at her sides, her legs unrestrained.

Why wasn't she killing this fucker?

Huisman took the three steps separating the tables and looked down at Carys. He was a handsome man in photos, with dark hair and seemingly intelligent eyes. His hair was slightly long, brushing the bottom of his earlobes. He had a full mouth, but his eyes held something Carys couldn't explain. Something that scared the fuck out of her.

This was the real Huisman. The mask was gone, and his insanity was clear in those dark eyes. This was the man Parker had talked about, the one who wanted to burn the world down.

"Yeah, I'm probably going to get fired after this," Kala said, only her mouth moving.

"I seriously doubt she'll get fired. As for you, Ms. Taggart, you're slow. The drugs are definitely harder on your system. We've already gone over this. The drugs I gave you aren't covered by those test strips whores use," Huisman said, the almost kindly smile on his face betrayed by his words. He slid two fingers under the restraint, pressing against her pulse. "I have some very intelligent people working for me. They're also morally ambiguous, which I find helpful. Now that we have the explanations done, I can tell you how surprised I am to see you here, Ms. Taggart. I was expecting the other one."

"Other one? I don't have a sister. I have three brothers, and one of them has a particular set of skills." She was starting to feel stronger.

"You're fine," he said with another chuckle. "And I scarcely think Kyle Hawthorne is the one I should be worried about. Like I said, you are not supposed to be here. I wanted the other Taggart. I wanted her sister."

A chill snaked up Carys's spine. "What are you talking about? She doesn't have a sister."

Kala stayed silent.

"Oh, she has two, and a pretty cousin who unfortunately got caught in my net," Huisman said with a shake of his head.

"You were after Tasha." The words seemed forced out of Kala's throat.

"Yes. It's precisely why I sent my men in when I did. I'll be honest, I didn't know if it would work. I thought I could get the whole team here, but I wasn't sure who they would send in with the idiot residents," Huisman admitted. "Though you should know some of Dr. O'Donnell's ideas are interesting. I'll probably steal them and pass them off as my own."

"I don't understand why you want Tasha." Carys was confused.

"I don't understand how he knows," Kala added quietly. "I don't exist. There's nothing to tie me to Tasha."

"Nothing if one only started looking a few years ago," Huisman conceded. "I will admit the CIA does an excellent job. They scrubbed your existence clean. No social media. No government records. No birth certificate tying you to Ian Taggart. I often wonder how much it hurt your parents. Did they feel the ache when they realized playing spy was more important to you and your twin than being their child?"

"You should ask them," Kala replied. "Bring them in. See what they say."

"I think I'll avoid being in the same room with your parents, though it will be interesting to see what they do." Huisman sounded amused at the idea. "To answer your question about how I knew when all precautions were taken, well, it's because my grandfather kept careful records. After Mr. Taggart set in motion the events that would lead to my father's death, my grandfather made a careful study of everyone involved. I have all the real records, including what I feel is a well done but faked birth certificate for one Natasha Federova. I suppose they did that because if her Russian birth was known, the adoption wouldn't have gone through. And Kenzie and Kala Taggart. You might no longer exist in the official records, but you are in my books."

"You know my father wasn't even there, asshole," Kala managed.

"No, but he's the reason everything happened. He gave those criminals the resources they needed to escape Interpol," he explained, his tone going dark and stubborn. "If your father hadn't helped those men he called The Lost Boys, they would have been in jail or dead, and then the man who shot my father wouldn't have been in Canada. My father would be here today. I wouldn't have been left with…" He seemed to shake something off. "The point is, your father interfered with the natural order of things, and now you will pay the price. The sins of your father will be visited upon you, the daughter he can't claim on paper."

"I assure you a piece of paper won't mean anything to my uncle," Carys promised. "And it won't merely be him after you. My whole family will go to war for this. You have no idea what my father and uncles will do to you."

"Don't be a misogynist," Kala quipped. "You know it'll be my mom and Aunt Erin who take this dude's balls."

Huisman ignored them. "I wonder what your sister will do after you cease to be. Will she take over the role and Ms. Magenta will go on? A sad existence when you think about it. They won't be able to bring you back. You consigned all those years to the void, and for what? So you could try to prop up a dying society."

"Why would you trick us into coming here?" Carys asked. The last thing she wanted to do was lie here and listen to the rantings of a mad man. "I don't understand why you would come after me and Aidan."

She needed to figure out what the man knew, though it seemed like he knew everything.

"Because it's time." Huisman sat down on the tall, wheeled stool in between the exam beds. "Because Benjamin is closing in on me. He'll have what he needs soon enough, so it's time to play offense. I'm not about to allow him to smear my good name. I'd rather do it myself."

"Why Tasha?" Kala said, the words sounding croaky.

"Oh, I like to keep a few things to myself. I wondered if you knew, but it seems there are secrets even in the team. But I can tell you she serves a different purpose than you will," Huisman replied.

Kala still didn't move. Carys's brain was starting to work again. It wasn't natural how still her cousin was. "What did you give her?"

"It's an experimental paralytic. She's got an IV, so don't think it will wear off. I'm not foolish. I know my enemies well, and she would kill me in a heartbeat. It probably won't stop her lungs from functioning. Most of the rats I've tried it on survived," he said as though they were talking about the weather and not her cousin being experimented on. "She came out of the sedative very quickly. Likely she's built up a resistance to all kinds of things. Interesting girl. I can see why she's attractive to Benjamin. I wonder if he knows there are two of her? I think not. Don't worry. I won't tell him. Although after I'm done, there will be only one of you, so I'm saving you a difficult conversation."

Carys felt her stomach turn. How were they here? She'd been happy and safe with her men and she'd left because she hadn't been willing to tell them she was still worried. She hadn't wanted to fight. "You can't kill her."

She hadn't fought at all. She'd gotten her feelings hurt and locked herself in a corner rather than doing what she should have done and going after her man. Tris had been worried she would put herself in danger to try to "save" him. How had he felt when she'd stopped talking to him?

Huisman's face was back to looming over Carys's. "I assure you I can. It's easy. Do you see this room? It's my old room. This is the house I grew up in."

"We're in Toronto?" Kala asked, avoiding the whole I'm-going-to-kill-you portion of Huisman's villain act.

"Yes, this is where it all began, so I think it's a good place to start the next portion of my life. After today I'll have what I need to make my statement." Huisman crossed one leg over the other, looking casual. "I knew this time was coming when I realized who knows where the bombmaker is. Or at least how to find the bombmaker. I need that brilliance if I'm going to start to set the world right."

"Right?" Kala asked, sounding a bit stronger. "Come on, man. If you're going to murder me, you have to monologue better. It's easy to see you're going to have some great 'burn the world down for the sake of humanity' kind of bullshit to share."

A look of disdain crossed Huisman's face. "I don't care about humanity. The world would be better without so much so-called humanity."

"Oooo, cool. We're going the Thanos route." Even without use of her limbs, Kala's whole being managed to convey sarcasm. "You going to snap those fingers and get rid of a percentage of the population?"

"Nothing so simple. I don't merely want people to die. I want them to suffer. I want them to learn. When I've caused a sufficient amount of chaos to force society to fail, I'll come in and offer a different way. My way." Huisman stood. "Society is a bloated whale. You know what happens when a whale dies? They rot and explode and ruin everything around it. However, they also feed the smaller creatures. I'm going to make sure the whale explodes, and I'll be the one to control what happens after. Starting with your family and Benjamin Parker. I've watched him. He's obsessed with the woman he knows as Ms. Magenta. I've only seen him this way about one woman before. I killed her, too."

Carys was starting to get the feeling back in her limbs just in time for a chill to cross her skin. "Won't it be better to keep her alive? To torture her? It would kill her father knowing she's alive and he can't get to her."

"Thanks, cousin," Kala said. "It won't work."

"It won't, because I have so many choices." Huisman clapped his hands with apparent glee. "He has so many children. I'll have fun going through them one by one. And a grandchild already. I'll finish with his wife, and then I'll leave him alive with only hate in his heart. As I've lived for years."

There was a knock on the door, and Carys lifted her head to watch a big man in fatigues walk in.

"*Ils sont éveillés*," he said.

"*Emmenez-les dans la salle à manger*," Huisman replied. "Ladies, I will have to leave you here for now, though someone will come for Ms. Taggart in a moment. Carys, that is. I'll keep Taggart's pit bull where she is for now. I hope he wants you safe. You should hope he has some affection for your family."

"Tristan loves me, but he doesn't know anything," Carys said.

"Tris knows everything," Kala replied. "He'll tell you what you want to know. He'll do whatever you want as long as you don't hurt Carys."

"He's not The Jester," Carys insisted.

"Shut the fuck up, Car." Kala had a single tear sliding from her eye. "You let Tris take whatever he has to. He said they're awake. This is going down soon. Apparently in the dining room, unless this fucker is going to serve them a four-course meal before he kills us all."

Huisman was behind her rather than following his guard out. She heard him moving around and then he was at Kala's side, a needle in his hand. He pushed it into the injector cap. "I won't kill you yet, but as long as you're here you can let me know if this works."

"What are you doing to her?" Carys felt panic well again. "What's in that?"

He pulled the needle away, holding it up. "In this? Another experimental drug. This one should make her feel like her veins are on fire for..." He glanced down at his watch. "Well, I'm hoping for hours, but we'll have to see. Watch the clock for me, Dr. Taggart. Though it pains me to call you a doctor when you're nothing more than a glorified midwife. If you ask me, childbirth should be a test, and if a woman can't fulfill her role, let her die. It's one of the places we went wrong, putting all those resources into saving weak women."

Kala's eyes had closed. A paralytic would hold her in place but without a sedative...

Kala's mouth came open, a scream shaking the room.

"Ah, there it is." Huisman nodded as though satisfied. "Watch her for me. Don't worry. Someone will come in and gag her. I wouldn't leave you having to listen to a hysterical female. That would truly be torture."

Kala was screaming as he walked through the door, and Carys tried not to give in to despair.

* * * *

"Where do you think we are?" Zach stood in the middle of the great room of what appeared to be a mansion of some kind. He whispered the words since they were surrounded by guards. "Whatever they gave us knocked me on my ass."

Which meant they had no sense of time or even how they'd gotten where they were. At least they'd been released from the restraints he'd woken up in. Tristan had come to in the back of a van beside Zach. They'd both been led through a big garage and into this massive house. They'd passed through a living room with furniture still under dust covers and white drapes that let in enough light to let him know it was day. Likely morning.

When they'd made it to the elegant dining room, one of the guards had taken the cuffs off.

307

Unfortunately, they were up against heavily armed guards, and he had no idea where Carys was and who was guarding her. He didn't know what the instructions were concerning her if he misbehaved. "No idea, man. But we have to play this cool."

"We have to figure out what he wants and give it to him." Zach glanced around, keeping his voice low. "I know you don't trust me right now, but I swear I'm going to make you understand. When he asks if you're The Jester, admit to it. I'll back you up. We've been making money behind the Agency's back. He'll trust us more if he thinks we're corrupt."

It was the same plan he'd come up with, but he wasn't sure if he could trust Zach. He was sure he didn't have much of a choice. "I'll do the talking. You back me up." He prayed Zach was right and there was a reasonable explanation for what he'd learned back in the suite. "Do you have a count?"

"Four in here," Zach whispered out of the side of his mouth. "But we had five on us at one point. I think he went to inform our host we're here. No. He's back. At your nine on the balcony."

There was a balcony landing that ran from one side of the house to the other, looking over the great rooms. Sure enough, there was a guard standing there.

So they had five known guns on them.

There were rooms off the balcony, and one of the doors opened.

He heard a long scream before Huisman walked through and shut the door, the sound dulling.

"Was that Carys?" Tristan felt his heart threaten to seize.

"Stay fucking calm," Zach hissed. "You make a move and we'll be back in cuffs. We have to wait until the time is right. At least we know where she is."

They would have to take out all the guards in order to get upstairs, and even then, he couldn't be sure what they were going into.

Chaos. Huisman had plunged them into chaos. He'd known exactly what he was doing. He'd attacked before they'd thought a sane man would and given them absolutely no time to prepare. All their recon had been done on Huisman's Montreal compound and the foundation building. Somehow he didn't think they were close to either.

Huisman was saying something, and then the guard disappeared behind the door, that terrible scream threatening to shake the walls again. The door closed and Huisman started toward the stairs. "Welcome, Mr. Dean-Miles. Or should I call you The Jester?"

Good. They wouldn't have to explain. "Call me pissed off. Is that Carys Taggart screaming?"

He needed control. He made every word cold as ice because showing how panicked he was at the thought of Carys in pain would give Huisman what he wanted.

"Not at all." Huisman jogged down the steps. He was dressed in slacks and a black button-down, expensive loafers on his feet. He looked like an upscale doctor, not the fucking psychopath he obviously was. "I'm actually quite sorry she got caught up in this negotiation of ours. I know you will find this hard to believe, but I don't have anything against her besides her last name. You plan on changing her name? Or did you actually move on? I rather thought I saw you at their wedding, though you weren't dressed as a guest. I can't be sure. The imbeciles I was forced to work with couldn't cut into the security cameras, so I had to rely on the drone." A grin hit his lips. "That was a spectacular crash, by the way. I've watched it at least fifty times."

"So it was you who hired the mercenaries?" Tris tried to keep the question somewhat casual. If Huisman was going to be civil, he would keep it that way as long as possible. "I'm afraid I didn't understand the logic behind that particular move."

Had they found the trackers both he and Zach had in their arms? He hadn't woken up with a gaping hole in his bicep, so he thought not. If he hadn't, then all they needed was time because the team would come for them.

Who the hell was screaming? Had been screaming? It seemed to have stopped. That might scare him even more.

Kala. Had they taken her or Tasha? Had they gotten Aidan? He had no fucking idea, and it threatened to make him scream and try to fight his way up those stairs.

"Logic, like many things we think are a collective experience, is actually subjective." Huisman walked into the dining room, his arms coming out. "Welcome to my childhood home. Sorry it's not ready for company, but I had to move quickly. I thought it might take

309

longer. So because I am a fair man, I'll explain it all to you and then you can make your decision as to how we're going to play out this scene we find ourselves in. I broke up the wedding because from what I could tell, Dr. O'Donnell hadn't bothered to announce he was coming to Canada. I truly expected there to be a great outcry."

Aidan hadn't mentioned it because he'd been angry with Tristan. Liam hadn't mentioned it to Big Tag because the man was preoccupied. The wall between the Agency team and McKay-Taggart had fucked them over this time.

"So you invited Aidan to get the team up here in Canada," Zach posited.

Huisman's hands went to the pockets of his slacks while his lips curled up in a secretive smile. "Yes, Captain Reed. I did. It was a calculated risk. I knew Mr. Taggart would either see the opportunities the chance offered or he would be frightened away and I would have to find another opportunity to get what I want."

He would give it to the asshole. He was cool under pressure. "So we took the bait."

"Don't feel bad," Huisman said with a sigh. "It was excellent bait, and I suppose Benjamin is involved now, too."

Tris shrugged. It was too early to let the man in on everything. Maybe Zach could help him out, remind Huisman he was here, too. "Who's Benjamin?"

Zach leaned in, playing his role to perfection. "I think he's talking about the asshole CSIS sent."

The smile on the doctor's face faded. "You know well who I'm talking about. Benjamin Parker. You've met him many times. I've got the woman he's obsessed with upstairs, and I'll deal with her later. She was a gift since I can use the bitch for several different purposes. I'm going to give you some advice, both of you. Don't lie to me. I know everything, and I won't hesitate to hurt the women I have in custody. Carys Taggart lives and isn't in pain for as long as everyone complies."

"I want to see her," Tristan said. "I'm not talking until I see her and Ms. Magenta. She's the other woman you have, right? She was in the bar with Carys. She's CIA, you know. They will come after her."

Huisman's eyes rolled, his head falling back as he groaned. "That's one lie, Mr. Dean-Miles. I'll give you one because I'm sure you've been trained to hide her identity, but the next lie will cost Dr. Taggart a finger. Personally, I don't think what she does is really surgery, so I don't think she needs all her fingers. She might have a different perspective. Bring her down now, please."

"Wait," Tristan began.

"No. I think it's time she joined us," Huisman insisted. "The other Ms. Taggart was also a bonus, though I figured one of the twins would be there. Tell me—and think before you lie—which one do I have?"

Tris felt his gut take a deep dive. He knew about the twins. He likely knew exactly who was screaming upstairs, and this was a test. It was a betrayal to say their names, but the door had come open and the guard was hauling Carys out.

"Kala. You have Kala," he said, his eyes on Carys.

"Excellent. Now we understand each other." Huisman pulled out a seat from the elegant table. It was long, with seating for at least sixteen people. "Bring her here, please."

"You don't need to do this." Zach stood beside him, a hand on Tristan's arm as he spoke to Huisman. "Tristan is ready to talk, and I'll tell you anything you want to know."

Huisman's head pivoted, his eyes catching on Zach. "Yes, Captain. Yes, you will. One way or another. Jean-Marc, when you have her properly restrained, please join me."

The big guard manhandled Carys in a way that made Tristan vow to kill the fucker. She looked terrified, but her eyes met his.

"I'm so sorry, baby," he said. "I'm going to get you out of this. I promise."

She nodded as the guard forced her into one of the ornate chairs. This particular one had arms they bound her wrists to. "Kala's upstairs. Tris, they're hurting her."

"I know." He would do whatever he had to do. They'd used zip ties on her wrists, and he could see the way they bit into her skin. Bile rose in his throat as the guard placed a straight cutter on the table in front of her. It was the type cigar aficionados used. He was certain her fingers would fit nicely. "You hold on."

He couldn't let them ruin Carys's hands. He would rather die.

"Hold on?" Huisman asked. "For what? Oh, are you under the assumption those trackers of yours are still working? No, no, no. I accounted for them, of course. I used something to jam the signal until I could kill it entirely. They're oddly delicate technology. I used a modified defibrillator to scramble your tracker. Think of it as a mild electromagnetic pulse. They don't work anymore. No one's going to save you. Well, perhaps Captain Reed will. Ah, Jean-Marc."

Tris wasn't sure why Zach would be the one to save him, but he watched as Huisman put a hand on his guard's arm.

"Let me see your gun," Huisman commanded. "I need to make a point to our guests."

The guard handed Huisman his SIG Sauer without question.

Two other guards moved in behind Tris and Zach while the others were at attention.

"Please don't hurt her," Tris said quietly. "I'll give you nothing if you hurt her."

"She wasn't the Taggart I wanted, you know," Huisman admitted. "I honestly thought I would have to take my time. My plan was to monitor the so-called bodyguards coming in with Dr. O'Donnell and his fiancée so I could figure out where the safe house was. From there I was going to take the lovely Natasha and use her to get the intelligence I need."

Zach went still beside him. "Tasha?"

Tris didn't understand. He was missing something. "Why Tash? Don't get me wrong, I would come in for her. I wouldn't let you hurt her, but if you want me to..." Fuck. He'd been such an idiot. All along. Big Tag should fucking draw and quarter him. Not once in all of this discussion had Huisman mentioned Tristan as anything but someone he had to deal with. "You didn't want me."

Huisman ignored him, walking up to one of the other guards. "Gervais, how did this happen? You brought me the wrong Taggart."

Gervais seemed to understand something had gone terribly wrong. "My team was supposed to pick up the women in the bar. Pierre told us..."

Huisman brought up the gun and put a bullet in Gervais's head before he could finish his explanation. The sound shook the big room, and he watched as Carys jumped in her chair, tears in her eyes.

Gervais's body hit the floor, and Huisman stepped over him like he was a bit of trash. "From what I can tell, it was bad timing. When I realized the captain and Natasha were at the hotel, I sent in a team to bring them in. Unfortunately, by the time we arrived, they had already gone upstairs, and then Tasha and Zach seemed to have split up. Like I said, poor timing, but that idiot on the floor thought he'd found Tasha because Pierre referred to Carys as Ms. Taggart. They thought they were bringing me what I wanted. Now they understand what happens when they fail."

"Then you don't need Kala," Carys tried.

"Shut your mouth, woman." Huisman sneered her way. "Your voice is not required here, so don't make me take your tongue. I explained why Kala Taggart is a delightful surprise. It doesn't mean the failure to bring in Tasha should go unpunished."

"Baby, just do what he says," Tristan begged, though he was starting to realize how bad the situation was. Huisman didn't want him. Huisman wanted Zach.

Because Zach knew things Tristan didn't. Because he was involved in a way Tristan hadn't caught.

"Why Tasha?" Zach asked, his voice tense. "Like Tristan said, he would come for her, but he would come for anyone on the team."

"He doesn't want me." He turned to Zach. Zach had become important to him, and now he felt the breadth of his betrayal. "Who are you working for?"

Zach's eyes widened. "The United States Army and the Central Intelligence Agency. Tris, don't let him do this."

"I make a close study of my enemies," Huisman explained. "The tech you work with…Tara something…she gets lonely and goes to bars where she happily talks to women she finds attractive. She hides her proclivities well, but it wasn't hard to get her to talk. Not about classified items. She proved quite tight-lipped about those, but she was willing to gossip about her coworkers. Of course she said you all worked at a bank, but it didn't matter. She gave me what I wanted, which was how to get to Captain Zachary Reed."

Tristan thanked the universe Tara didn't know anything about Devi Taggart.

Zach's face flushed. "I don't… You can't know. You can't fucking know."

"I assure you I can, Captain Reid." He snapped his fingers, and two of the guards stepped forward, taking Zach's arms.

Zach started to pull away.

Tristan felt a gun to the back of his head, heard Carys cry out.

Zach went still.

"Now we find out exactly who you are, Captain," Huisman said quietly, studying Zach. "I know everything now, things you don't even know. Certainly things Taggart doesn't. He had a snake in his midst, and he didn't even realize it. My instinct is to tell him, but that's ego talking. It's more fun to think about Taggart worried about you, not knowing all the ways you betrayed his team."

"I didn't." Zach stood still, his shoulders ramrod straight. "I never betrayed the team, Tristan. I didn't tell you everything, but I had my reasons. Dr. Huisman, I'll go with you if you'll let everyone go."

Huisman's eyes narrowed and his voice went low, so low Tristan could barely hear him. *"Tu m'emmèneras vers elle où tu mourras. Le reste n'a pas d'importance."*

"They're important to me," Zach replied.

Since fucking when did Zach speak French?

Huisman got in close, proving he wasn't afraid of the man who had at least fifty pounds of muscle on him. "Then you'll go quietly. I'm having you escorted to a remote site. My business with you is different than my business with the Taggarts. You might survive if you give me what I want. If you don't want to go quietly, I can kill these two right now. As I said, they're of no true importance. I have my Taggart daughter, and I intend to have such fun with her."

"I'm going to kill you," Zach said quietly.

Huisman patted his cheek, a condescending gesture. "I'm sure you'll try. Are you going quietly or shall I start killing them now?"

Zach's hands came up, and he threaded his fingers together behind his head, the action his reply. He stared stoically ahead as one of the guards brought down first his right and then his left hand behind his back, snapping cuffs on his wrists.

Whatever Zach had done, he wasn't giving them up and he could have. Zach likely could have fought his way out or at least tried, but he hadn't.

Because he wasn't willing to put them in danger.

"We'll come for you, brother," Tristan called out as they led him away.

Zach's head turned. "Tell Devi...fuck...tell her I'm so fucking sorry. And Coop…just tell them all I'm sorry."

They carted Zach off, and he was left with Huisman.

"Now we can have fun," Huisman said, clapping his hands. "I have some excellent wine. Let's sit down, you and I, and discuss your boss. But first, would you like a tour?"

This man was insane. "Sure. Why not?"

"This is the house I lived in when I was young," Huisman announced. "You're standing right about where my father died. Our lovely doctor is sitting where Rebecca Walsh was sitting. My father hated her. Women in the workplace. They fuck everything up. That's where we went wrong, you know. We gave up our biological roles in favor of this equality nonsense."

He was down to two guards. Huisman had split his troops. There had been five, and one was dead on the floor and still had his gun in his holster. Huisman held the one he'd killed the man with, so the guard he'd taken it from was down a firearm. Not that the men left weren't loaded up, but it could be the second or two difference he needed.

If he could figure out how to get Carys out of those fucking restraints.

Would she think to try to break the chair? It's what he would do. Would she react quickly enough?

"Fuck them women," Tristan said drolly. "Get back in the kitchen. That's what I always say."

"Somehow I think you don't," Huisman countered. "But then your mother wasn't a whore. I actually admire her. She managed to make an enormous amount of money and didn't have to leave her children behind."

"Your mother didn't leave you. She divorced your father." He knew a little about Huisman, too. "At least that's what you wrote in your biography."

He would do or say anything to put off the moment when Huisman eventually decided to go for blood.

"I wrote what people want to hear. They like a pathetic man who allows the world to walk all over him. Kindness. It's weakness. My father tried to teach me, and when he was taken too early, my grandfather took over my education. He never allowed me to forget what had been taken from me and what is owed to me by the man who started it all."

"He blames the Taggarts for everything," Carys said. "It's why he's got her upstairs. He gave her a paralytic and some kind of medicine... He's torturing her, Tris."

"Like her father tortured me," Huisman replied.

"No, not like that," Carys argued.

Huisman nodded, and suddenly the guards were on either side of Tristan.

Damn it. He knew what was coming. He knew it before Huisman set his gun down and picked up the straight cutter.

"Don't," Tristan shouted, fighting the hold he was in.

Huisman held it up, showing everyone how it would work. "I think your bitch needs to know to obey when I tell her to keep her mouth shut. Shall we start with your pinkie finger? I can take them off one at a time."

Tristan tried to pull away again. This couldn't fucking happen. It couldn't.

"Carys," he called out.

Huisman simply smiled and put her finger through that fucking thing. "You know I watched it. I watched him kill my father. I was sitting right up there."

"You mean here, Manny?" a deep voice said.

Tristan looked up, and Ben Parker stood on the balcony above, a rifle in his hands and his enemy in his sights.

Tris began his fight.

Chapter Eighteen

Aidan forced himself to stay sitting when all he wanted to do was run into that fucking house and put bullets into people until he found Carys and Tris.

It wasn't an impulse he'd ever thought he would have. He saved lives. He didn't take them, but he knew beyond a shadow of a doubt, he would do it if he had to.

"Adam, what have you got?" Big Tag sat in the driver's seat, Adam beside him. They'd flown down, but it had taken hours to get things into place. Unlike Huisman, who'd been prepared.

Every minute had felt like a damn year. He wasn't sure how the team kept their cool. They'd left Tasha, Charlotte, and Kenzie behind, Big Tag unwilling to allow the latter two in the same room with Ben Parker. Tara had stayed behind, too, helping Tasha clear out her and Parker's rooms and briefing their bosses at Langley about what was happening.

"I don't think they brought the boys in at the same time as the women." Adam was in the back of the Sprinter that Parker had managed to procure despite the fact they'd landed before dawn. "I've tracked the plane I believe they were on, and I found the car I think they were picked up in. It's too small for four bodies. I think he brought the women on the plane and drove Tristan and Zach down."

"Keeping them together would potentially give the men a chance to save the women or vice versa." Parker sat beside Cooper, wearing similar clothes. They looked ready for war. "He'll split them up until he can secure them all in the house. But I assure you, he's in there."

"Someone's in there," Lou confirmed. "I have definite movement in the house. He's got a lot of security, from what I can tell, but I think he's got the system off right now. I think they're waiting for something."

They were parked half a block down from the house in question, nestled in a super-wealthy neighborhood in Toronto. One Parker knew well. He'd explained to the group he'd grown up here, too, his childhood home close to Dr. Huisman's.

There was a knock on the sliding door and Cooper opened it, revealing TJ. He'd changed into sweats and a T-shirt, a bandana around his head and sunglasses on. He looked like a dude out for a jog.

TJ climbed in. "They're subtle, but there's at least two guards on the grounds. The garage door was open, and it's definitely the car Adam caught on the CCTVs coming from the airport. Whoever was on the plane is in the house. I don't see any signs of a vehicle they might have brought Tris and Zach in. It looked like they were getting ready for something. I'm not sure. I can't get close, but I did see a park that might have a view. It didn't look like the place had anything more than those drapey things."

"Window treatments." Lou looked over at her boyfriend, adjusting her glasses—the ones that worked again and would allow Kenzie and Charlotte some form of information about what was going on. From what he'd been told, they would be making their way to Toronto via one of the SUVs they'd rented and would find a hotel to hole up in while they waited. Lou's glasses would be their only connection to the mission.

How hard was it for Charlotte to stay out of it, to stay with Kenzie when Kala was in trouble?

I don't know what your sister is going through, but the last thing she's going to need if she survives it is to come out and realize her career is over. You chose this, Kenz. You had the idea of building Kara. You don't get to burn her down now.

Ian had been in a hell of a mood earlier. While Cooper and TJ kept Parker busy, Ian had gone up to the attic, and Aidan had overheard the conversation while he'd helped pack up. Conversation might not be the right word. It had been a straight up lecture.

He wasn't sure Ian was right. The world might have changed in an irrevocable way.

If she survives.

If Kala survives.

If Carys and Tristan survive.

"We've got a van coming up the street," Lou said, staring at her laptop. "Uncle Adam, I think it's yours."

Aidan sat up straighter, trying to get a view out of the tinted windows. Sure enough, there was a van coming up the street, moving with some speed, as though it was late for an important meeting.

Was Tris in that van?

"I need a plate," Adam said.

Parker put a set of binoculars to his eyes and called out the plate number.

Aidan watched as the van drove by.

"That's it." Adam closed his laptop and pulled the pistol from his holster, checking it. "They have to be in there. Let's go."

Ian held out a hand. "Not yet."

"It'll be easier to take them out as they're transporting Tristan and Zach from the van than when they get them securely in the house," Adam argued.

But Aidan knew what Ian's point was. "We tip them off and they either kill the women or move them."

"The doc's right," Parker agreed even as he was also checking the arsenal he carried. "There are numerous ways in and out of that place. We can't cover all of them. I would wait for my team, but we don't have time. Manny is hurting the women. It's what he does. If we wait too long, he'll kill them, and we'll be getting body parts delivered for the next ten years."

"You're a fucking delight, Parker," Ian said with a huff. "So we wait until they're all inside and then Lou loops the security cams. You have that ready?"

Lou nodded. "Yes. But it means I can't see anything. I don't have time to send the real footage to my system while the server inside has the loop going."

"It's okay," Ian promised. "We'll get it done no matter what. I want you to monitor local authorities and let me know if they get any calls. Do you have anything right now?"

"I have Huisman walking up the stairs. He went to the second floor, but I lost him there. There aren't security cameras outside of the halls and shared spaces." Lou's eyes never left the screen.

TJ was maneuvering in the back, pulling a long-sleeve black shirt over his head. "Are we planning on walking down the street carrying rifles? I mean we kind of look like a military team. It could freak out the neighbors, you know."

Parker had explained they shouldn't call the police. Huisman owned too many people in the government. According to Parker, CSIS was dragging its feet about everything when it came to Huisman.

Aidan had overheard Ian and Adam discussing the fact that they believed CSIS's excuses were just that. The Canadians didn't want to upset Huisman until someone had incontrovertible proof.

They were doing CSIS's dirty work.

Aidan did not care. All he wanted was to have Carys safe and sound and in his arms. He wanted to know Tristan was all right, and they could all be together again.

He wouldn't be able to breathe until they were together again.

"I've got confirmation Zach and Tristan are alive and conscious," Lou said, her voice tight. "They were in the van, and they're being taken into the house through the garage right now."

"All right." Ian started the engine. "We're going in the back to avoid the whole freak-out-the neighbors thing. Follow Parker's lead. Retrieving our people is the mission. Am I understood? If someone has a chance at taking out Huisman, take it, but not at the risk of our people."

Aidan's everything was in that house. He agreed with Ian.

"You have your mission and I have mine," Parker said, a stoic expression on his face.

"You go your own way, Parker, and don't expect us to save you if you get in trouble." Ian eased off the brakes and maneuvered the van down the road. These houses were all massive, with huge yards and walls surrounding the estates.

"I don't expect you to save me at all, sir," Parker admitted. "You deal with your people, and I'll handle Manny." He turned to Cooper, who had been damn-near silent all night long. He'd flown the plane and kept to himself, speaking only when required to. "You'll find her?"

Cooper's hands tightened on his rifle. "I'll find her."

Parker sat back, huffing a breath. "All right. Does anyone have any questions about the layout of the house? After Manny's father was killed, his grandfather closed the place up. I think it's roughly the same as it was when Manny was a child."

"We all studied the blueprints on the flight," Adam replied. "Ian and I will go in via the servants' entrance on the west wall. That should lead us through the kitchen and into the great rooms. Cooper and TJ are going to cut out the window in the study and enter through there. The hallway will also lead them to the great rooms but from the opposite side. We quietly take out anyone in our way. Parker…"

"I'm going in through the roof. There's access to the attic on the eastern side of the house," Parker explained.

"And if it's locked?" Ian asked, turning the corner to round the block so they had access to the back of the estate through the alley that ran behind it.

"I'll get through it." Parker seemed supremely sure of his abilities.

Aidan wished he was. "I think I should go with Ian and Adam. I'll stay behind you."

The van stopped, and Ian turned off the engine. "It's better if you don't. I promise I'll give Lou the go-ahead for you both to come in as soon as possible, but I can't watch over you properly."

Because he had to do anything he could to save Carys. "I'll wait."

Ian opened the door and slid off the seat, reaching for his vest. "We'll get them out. I promise. Or I'll die trying."

Adam did the same on his side. "I will absolutely get them out or let Ian die trying."

Ian huffed out a laugh. "I bet you will, buddy. Adam…"

Adam finished zipping his vest. "Say something sarcastic and get it out of the way."

"I'm glad you're here," Ian said.

"Fuck." Adam closed his eyes, taking a long breath. "Only one man I'd rather have watch my back."

Ian reached up and pulled a black balaclava over his head. "Yeah, well, Jake's gotten lazy in his old age. He's probably sitting somewhere with Li complaining about his gout or something. Old men."

Adam did the same, joining Ian. "Speak for yourself. I'm aging backward, man. I'm way sexier than I was twenty years ago."

"That wouldn't be hard. You were a nerd," Ian shot back.

"Sir, you should go now. I've looped the cams." Lou sent them a pointed look.

"The young are impatient," Ian said, putting a hand on Adam's shoulder. "Let's go get our people."

They disappeared behind a big bush running along the wall demarcating the property.

"Take care, baby," TJ said, leaning over to kiss his girlfriend before he followed Cooper out.

"You, too. I love you." Lou watched as they started to make their way around to the other side of the property.

Parker wasn't wearing a balaclava. He nodded to Lou. "If I don't see you after, it was a pleasure as always, Louisa. And if I don't get the chance to talk to her, tell Maggie I'll see her soon."

He quietly closed the Sprinter's sliding door behind him.

Aidan was left alone with Lou, who climbed into the front and slid into the driver's seat, balancing her laptop on the dashboard. "Can you hear them?"

Lou glanced at him through the rearview mirror. "The comms are working. Aidan, it's going to be okay. We're going to get them back."

He wished he could believe her. "How long do these things usually take?"

"Ten minutes. Ten hours. It doesn't matter. It's always too long," Lou said with a shrug. She touched the side of her glasses. "Yes, they're off. It's me and Aidan. I'm sitting in the driver's seat ready to get us out of here if I need to. Kenz, I know what I'm doing."

Aidan took a deep breath, trying to force down his panic. It was fucking torture to sit here knowing Carys and Tris were so close. They were in the house and the house was right there. Only a wall and some doors and space kept them apart. He put a hand on the kit Cooper had given him. It was basic, but he could work with it.

He prayed he didn't have to work with it.

Lou continued to quietly talk to Kenzie and Aidan sat, the minutes feeling like hours. How long had he been here? They were parked in what appeared to be an alley.

How was everything so fucking normal? When he looked out the window, the sky was blue, and in the distance, he could see people walking around what looked like a park. They had no idea the life and death situation going on so close to them.

What was happening to Carys? To Aidan? Was Kala even alive?

There was a tap on the window, startling Aidan out of his thoughts.

His heart rate shot up as he caught sight of a tall man in all black standing at the passenger-side window.

"Hey, is anyone in there?"

"Stay quiet," Lou said in a whisper. "Don't move. He can't see inside."

The Sprinter had come from someone Parker had called Tim, who'd assured them it was fully kitted out. One of the features was the window tinting. They appeared normal, but when put into secure mode, they darkened and couldn't be seen through from the outside.

The guard tried to stare inside and then attempted to open the passenger-side door.

Aidan reached for the gun Cooper had given him. This must be one of the two guards TJ had seen doing patrols of the grounds. They'd been lucky he hadn't seen the team as they'd gotten out and worked their way inside.

They were inside now, right? They had to be.

The guard stepped back and seemed to think about what to do. His hand went to the radio on his belt.

And then a familiar figure stepped in behind him. Aidan felt his eyes widen and heard Lou gasp.

Zach Reed was covered in blood and had handcuffs dangling from one wrist. He also had a big knife in his hand. A knife he used on the guard's throat, slicing into the man's jugular and spraying blood against the window.

"Zach's out. He got away but he looks hurt," Lou was saying over the comms.

Aidan slid open the door as the guard hit the ground. Zach looked primal standing there, his eyes on the guard and blood dripping from his hands.

"Hey, Zach." Aidan kept the words quiet. He felt like he was in the presence of a dangerous predator.

Zach looked up suddenly and seemed to realize who was talking to him. "Aidan."

"And me." Lou had rolled the window down. "You need to get in the van and let Aidan look you over. The team is inside the house. We need to be ready to go."

Zach seemed to shake something off, stepping back. "Good. Huisman sent half his guards with me. They're dead now, so it'll be a fair fight. Doc, Kala's going to need you. Carys, too, if Huisman decides to fuck around with Tris. I have to go."

"Go?" Lou scrambled out of the van. "Go where? You're hurt."

A ghost of a smile hit the captain's lips. "Back to hell, sweetheart. Should've known I wouldn't belong here. Take care, Lou. Aidan, you can get in through the garage. No one's guarding it anymore."

And with that, the captain jogged off looking like the final survivor of a horror film.

"Yes, that was Zach," Lou was saying. "I don't know, Aunt Charlotte. He ran away."

The fact that she'd called Charlotte *aunt* let him know how shaken Lou was. Aidan couldn't be. He couldn't let panic take over. Zach's words rang in his head. Carys might need him. Kala definitely needed him. He secured the pack over his back and made sure the safety was off the gun. His heart thudded in his chest. "Lou, I have to go in."

She nodded. "I heard him. I'll update the uncles...Ian. I'll update Ian. Be safe, Aidan."

Aidan took off, trying to remember the schematics Parker had attempted to drill in all their heads the night before. He retraced Zach's steps. It wasn't hard. He followed the blood.

Was Zach hurt? Should he have tried to stop him? A head injury could have made him do irrational things.

Aidan stopped as he rounded the corner that brought him to the open garage. It was set back from the road, and that seemed like a good thing now since there were bodies everywhere. Zach had put the knife he'd had in his hand to use. Aidan stepped over them, trying to avoid slipping.

He entered the kitchen and could hear someone talking.

"Don't."

Tristan. Tristan had shouted the word. Aidan inched down the hall and then felt a hard hand on his elbow.

Cold blue eyes stared down at him. Big Tag was not happy.

"Zach got away and told me Kala needs me," Aidan whispered.

A brief nod was all he got, and then Adam moved around him with Ian following.

"Carys!"

Tristan's shout threatened to shake Aidan's world. He didn't think. He ran toward the sound, evading Ian and Adam.

He stopped at the edge of the living area, and the sight threatened to take his breath. Carys was sitting in a chair, her arms held down with zip ties and her finger in a straight cutter, tears rolling down her cheeks. Tristan had two guards on him, both with guns at his back.

Huisman was going to take her finger and likely more. He said something, and his lips curled in an evil smirk.

"You mean here, Manny?" Ben Parker stood on the balcony, his rifle trained on his enemy.

The world seemed to slow down as he realized Cooper and TJ were coming from the opposite direction. Aidan lifted his gun because that fucker wasn't going to hurt Carys. He moved in as he heard the first gunshot.

Huisman put the gun he held to Carys's head. "You might be able to get me, Benjamin, but are you willing to bet her life on it?"

Aidan stopped because Carys wasn't the only one with a gun to her head.

"Stay calm, son," Adam commanded.

"I'm not moving." Tristan's hands came up. "Dr. Huisman, you're surrounded. Just let Carys go and we'll all survive this."

Huisman wrapped a hand in Carys's hair, holding her in place. "What would be the fun in that?"

"Parker, do you have the shot?" Ian asked.

"Ah, we're all here then," Huisman said. "You better have a bead on all of us or you're certain to lose at least one of your teammates. My men will execute that one if I die. Maybe we'll get both. As for Benjamin, I wonder what's more important to him. Taking me out or the fact that he's standing in front of the door where I'm holding the woman known as Ms. Magenta. I don't know how much longer she'll last. I gave her a little something. Maybe she's already dead. What do you want more, Benjamin? My head on a platter or your whore? You know how I took care of the last one."

Parker blinked twice, his body stiff. Cooper was already looking for the stairs.

Parker dropped his gun and went through the door behind him.

"How the hell do I get up there?" Cooper sounded panicked.

"You don't," Ian said. "You do your job. Parker's getting her. Huisman, you're surrounded. There's no way out."

"There's always a way out." Huisman looked more relaxed now. "Ah, there they are. Mr. Taggart, I believe you've won this skirmish of ours, but I'll win the war. Right now, though, I think it's time for some chaos. Let's see who you care about more. Jean-Marc, do it."

Huisman ducked behind Carys as Ian tried to take a shot. Aidan turned to Tristan, terrified he would see one of the guards put a bullet in his head. Instead, the guard held up some kind of device and pressed a button. Tristan kicked out, forcing the other guard to the ground, and the fight began.

"Get down," Ian yelled. "There's a bomb."

Aidan ran for Carys, not caring what could happen. All that mattered was protecting her.

He threw his body on hers as the world exploded.

* * * *

Carys felt the chair fall back when Aidan leapt on her. Out of the corner of her eye she saw Huisman running, heard the sound of bullets, and then the blast of a bomb going off. Her head would have banged against the marbled floors if the back hadn't been so high.

"Stay still," Aidan whispered. "I'm going to get you out of here."

"Tris," she said. They'd had guns on him. The ground was shaking, and she could see the chandelier above her rocking back and forth.

The sound of gunfire was added to the chaos.

It was obvious the guards weren't running like their boss had. They also weren't going down without a fight.

She gasped as she felt a bullet fly by her cheek, heat searing her skin.

"That was close." Aidan moved so he covered her completely. "I have to get you out of here."

"TJ, don't you fucking dare," Ian was shouting. "We don't know where that bomb was or how many more he has. We retreat."

"I have to get Kala," Cooper insisted, his voice tortured.

Where was Tris? Was he dead?

"Use this." Then Tris was there, offering Aidan a knife. "We have to move. That chandelier is going to come down, and Ian's right. We don't know what else he's going to blow up. If he prepped for this, he could blow the rest of it sky high once he's out of range."

Aidan nodded and then her hands were free.

"Cooper, Parker has her. Get your ass out of here," Ian shouted. "TJ, get to Lou. Make sure he doesn't take her on his way out."

She got a glimpse of combat boots running by.

The chandelier shook and dropped a few feet.

Tris hauled her up, taking her into his arms and moving right before the chandelier dropped, shaking the floor. It cracked the table in two, spraying glass and dust everywhere.

"Get her out of here," Adam yelled. "The ceiling is going to come down. Get out of the house."

Tristan started running, Aidan at their side.

Carys held on to him, her wrists aching, but she didn't think about the pain. Tris was alive. That was all that mattered. He ran out into the sunlight, forcing her to blink at the brightness.

Tristan moved out to the middle of the lawn before setting her on her feet. "Aidan, look her over."

"What happened?" Aidan was in her space, staring into her eyes. "What did he do to you?"

"They drugged me, but I'm fine. It's Kala I'm worried about." Everything had happened so fast. "Did they get away?"

"I took out the guards he left behind." Cooper stared at the door. "They didn't run fast enough, but Huisman did."

There was the sound of rattling as the roof began to collapse.

"Aidan, I'm fine." She felt weak, but it wasn't anything she couldn't handle. Where was Kala? "They gave her a paralytic. She won't be able to walk on her own."

Through the smoke she saw Ian walking out and then Parker. The big Canadian carried Kala. She was slack in his arms, unconscious.

Or worse. What had the drugs done to her? Tears blurred her eyes as Parker carried her cousin closer.

Cooper hit his knees, and the sound that came from him threatened to wreck Carys. She looked over and tears streamed down his cheeks. Parker stopped in front of him, looking down at Cooper.

"But she's not your girlfriend," Parker said, no inflection in his tone. "She's alive."

"Give her to me." Cooper lifted his arms, taking Kala into them and cradling her to his chest. He'd lost any sort of situational awareness because every cell of that man's body was focused on the woman in his arms. He smoothed back her hair. "Wake up, baby. You gotta wake up for me."

Carys moved in, taking Kala's wrist in her hand. Her pulse was steady. She worked around Cooper, who wasn't giving her up and checked her vitals. "I think she's passed out, but we need to get her to a hospital."

In the distance she heard the sound of sirens.

"Parker, I think you should sit down," Adam said, a frown on his face.

"I'm fine. I need to call my boss." Parker pulled his cell from his pocket even though his eyes were still on Kala. He stopped, and that was the moment she realized his hand was covered in blood. "Shit."

"Aidan," Carys called out. She managed to get to Parker as he started toward the ground. He'd been hit during the gunfire, and the adrenaline of the situation had gotten him through. But now the injury was taking over. "It's a GSW. Damn it. I've got two entry wounds on his back. It might be in his liver."

Aidan dropped to his knees beside her, a calm presence among the chaos. "All right. Let's get him stable."

She nodded and they got to work.

Twelve hours later Carys sat in Ben Parker's hospital room, watching the man who'd undoubtedly saved her cousin. If he hadn't chosen her over taking out his enemy, there wouldn't have been time to get her out. Cooper and Uncle Ian would almost certainly have tried and likely died when the house came apart, falling in on itself. Parker had saved more than one life.

The rest of the team was meeting with CSIS, but she couldn't sit through another round of what Uncle Ian called debriefs.

She would rather sit here and wait for Parker to wake up. It had been a close thing. He'd been in surgery for hours, the doctors working to save his liver. She'd been told he would come through with minimal damage, but he would have to rest.

Carys rather thought the Canadian operative wouldn't listen to doctors.

She'd been surprised no one had visited him. Only a young man who'd introduced himself as Tim. He'd checked on Ben and then he'd gone off to the debrief, too.

Was Ben Parker a lonely Captain Ahab, constantly chasing after his white whale? How much had he given up to try to take down Huisman?

Of course after spending some time with the doctor she rather thought Parker was right.

"Hey, is he still out?" Aidan walked in carrying two coffees. "I checked his chart. All of his vitals are strong. He's a tough son of a bitch. He carried her down a steep flight of stairs with two bullets in him."

"The man deserves some rest. I want to stay here until he wakes up. I don't want him to wake up alone," she whispered back. "Any word from Tris?"

In the chaos she hadn't had a chance to really talk to him. She'd been working with Aidan to save Parker's life, and then the team had met with CSIS to clear up all the details that came with a house blowing up in the middle of Toronto. And there were all the bodies...

"I think they're finishing up," Aidan replied. "He said he would be here within the hour. Ian wants to leave this evening. Hopefully Parker wakes up soon because I got the feeling they're planning on picking us up and taking us all straight to the airport."

They'd been left out again, though this time they'd chosen to stay in their world—the hospital—rather than going into Tristan's. This time it didn't feel like he was leaving them behind. They'd been given the choice, and it was easy to trust him now. "Any news about Zach?"

The whole team seemed sick at the idea of Zach's betrayal.

Though Tristan hadn't exactly put it like that. He'd said Zach was in trouble.

They just didn't know what the trouble was.

"He didn't say," Aidan replied. "We're going to have to sit down and talk, Carys. I know you've been through a lot, and if you need some time, we'll give it to you."

The door came open and there was Tris. He'd showered and changed clothes and still looked tired and rumpled and so beautiful. "Hey. Is he doing okay?"

She needed to make a few things plain to him. To both of them. She walked straight up to Tristan and wrapped her arms around him. "Parker is okay, but I'm not. Tris, I should have been exactly the woman you said I was. I should have found you and dragged your ass back home. At least then we would have talked. I shut down because somewhere deep inside I always thought we would fail. I always thought something as amazing as what we have couldn't possibly last. You should understand I'm never letting you pull this shit on me again, Master."

A long, shuddering sigh went through Tristan, and he held on to her tightly. "Never. I told you, I'm done playing the spy. I'm a happy tech who will hang with Lou and Tash and make sure Ms. Magenta gets out alive."

"Is she?" a deep voice asked.

Aidan immediately moved toward the bed where Parker was waking up. "Go slow, man. You've had a serious surgery. One of the bullets lodged in your liver. The good news is you didn't lose it, but you've got a long recovery ahead."

"I heal pretty quickly." Parker groaned but shifted so he could see Tristan. "I ask again. Is she alive?"

Carys started to let go, but Tristan's arms held her. "Ms. Magenta is alive, thanks to you. I'm sorry to say Dr. Huisman is gone. We believe he left the country a few hours ago. We were minutes behind him."

Parker nodded, scrubbing a hand over his head as though trying to clear it. "Yeah, he had a way out. I should have… Well, let's say he knew exactly what buttons to push. He knew I wouldn't leave her behind."

"How much did you hear?" Tristan asked.

The amount of information about the team Parker might have learned from the conversation Huisman had been having with Tristan was of some concern.

"Uhm, I managed to get into place when Manny went off on his misogynist bullshit. I couldn't see well. Was he going to take her fingers off?" Parker coughed and put a hand to his chest.

"I don't even want to think about that. Ever again." Aidan shook his head.

"Yes, he was going to do exactly that." Tristan rubbed his cheek against her head as though he needed the closeness to remind him they were alive and whole. "You saved more than Ms. Magenta. You saved my fiancée, and I'll be eternally grateful, Parker. Anything you need, all you have to do is ask. I think you'll find the Agency is now taking the threat seriously. CSIS as well. My boss is meeting with yours right now. I believe he's planning on coming down to Langley in a couple of days to talk further."

"I'll be there if they'll let me," Parker vowed.

So stubborn. "Or you could rest and let your body heal."

"See, that would be reasonable, and I happen to know he's not reasonable." The door had come open again, and her cousin stood there.

Kenzie not Kala, because she happened to know Kala was already on her way back to Dallas. Cooper had bundled her up after she'd woken and Carys had decided she was stable enough to travel. She was on her way home where they would assess her to try to figure out what Huisman had given her and if the experimental drugs had any long-term effects.

So it was Kenzie walking in, looking lovely in slacks and a silk blouse. Her heels clicked across the floor as she entered and moved to Parker's bed.

"You look no worse for the wear." Parker sounded wary.

"Oh, I assure you I'll never forget what he did to me." Kenzie stopped at his bedside. "Or what you did." She leaned over, brushing a kiss over his forehead. "Thank you, Benjamin Parker. I can't imagine what it cost you to let him go."

When she started to move away, he caught her hand, bringing it to his chest. "I would make the same choice again, Maggie. I don't care if you think you belong to Cooper McKay. I would still come for

331

you."

Kenzie's lips curled up, and she nodded. "I'll remember." Then she disentangled her hand from his and moved back to the door. "Try to get some rest, Ben. You'll need it the next time we meet."

Parker's eyes never left her. "How about you try not to kill me next time?"

Kenzie winked his way. "*I* won't. Promise." She looked to Tristan. "We're wheels up in half an hour, so we need to get to the airport."

Aidan took Carys's hand and Tristan the other. They followed her cousin out.

It was time to go home.

Epilogue

One week later
Bliss, Colorado

Serena Dean-Miles stood on the porch of the cabin they'd bought so many years ago and breathed in the scent of clean pine. When she closed her eyes and that scent caught her, she was back to a time when her kids had bounced around the cabin and ran through the woods, when they'd eagerly gone off with their dad to fish or begged their papa to take them to the café in town for pie.

Her baby boy had gotten married today. She felt a smile slide over her face. She'd never thought her son would get married at The Feed Store Church, but here they were.

"Well, I personally feel like we've won a war," Jake said, joining her. He'd lost the tie and jacket he'd worn to the small ceremony. It had been far more intimate than the other tries. "We managed to get through a whole wedding without a single assassination attempt."

"Do not even joke about that." Adam rounded the corner. He'd driven up moments before. Unlike Jake, he was in his full suit. "I'm still having nightmares."

He was, actually. He'd woken up in a sweat this morning, and she knew it had to do with what happened in Toronto. He was playing it down for her sake, but she knew it had been bad. Carys hadn't minded telling them all Dr. Evil had almost started cutting off her fingers and then blown up the house around them.

Adam had been there, watching their son nearly die. He'd also watched him be a hero, getting Carys out.

Tristan had figured out what was important. He was making decisions like the husband he wanted to be. The way his fathers had taught him.

"The kids are happily settled into their honeymoon suite, thanks to Stef Talbot," Adam announced. "And Brianna and Devi are staying with Uncle Van and the group."

Jake's brother lived here along with his partner, Hale, and their wife Elisa. They had two girls who would love spending some time with their cousins. "Devi's okay?"

Devi was the only one outside of immediate family who had come along for this hastily put-together wedding. Even so, they'd still descended on Bliss as a large group. Sean, Grace, and their family were in Ian's big cabin. The O'Donnells were at the new B&B in town.

"Devi says she's great," Adam replied. "She smiles at all the right times, and I can't tell if she didn't care as much as everyone thought she did or if she's planning a murder. Though she'd have to find the fucker first. I will give it to Captain Reed. The man knows how to disappear."

Zach Reed's disappearance and the fact that Emmanuel Huisman was still out there were the reasons for the paired-down guest list. Carys had insisted on getting married as soon as possible. They all had. When they'd returned from Toronto, there had been no hesitation in Tristan at all. He'd barely touched down before he'd started planning a Vegas wedding.

She'd negotiated them down to Bliss, where at least the family could attend and they could keep the whole thing fairly quiet in case the doctor decided to try again.

"Big Tag really doesn't know anything?" Jake didn't sound like he believed it. "He worked with Zach for over two years."

Adam sighed and sank down onto the big porch swing Jake had built years before. "I think Tag has suspicions, but he's not going to voice them without proof. You know Tristan doesn't believe Zach truly betrayed the team."

Tristan wanted to reach out to the man who'd been his friend for years. The rest of the team wasn't as sure.

"I'm sure he has his reasons, but I'm worried about Devi." Serena sat down beside him. "I don't care about her smile. She's devastated. She was in love with him. According to Bri, she'd had a crush on Zach pretty much from the moment she met him. Bri and Daisy will take care of her, but I worry about what happens if Tris is right and Zach comes back."

"Devi seems so reasonable, but she's got a lot of Erin Taggart in her genes." Jake took his seat, the one beside her. He settled in, a hand on her thigh. "I'm more worried about Kala. Do you have any idea what happened to her beyond that fucker fed her some drugs? I asked and those were her exact words. It must be fun trying to get her to write up mission reports."

Adam sighed and his arm went around Serena, connecting them all. Like she always wanted to be. "Tristan heard her. Whatever he did it was enough to make the toughest woman I know scream. Whatever it was, I hope it prods Cooper into making some kind of move. That kid is in love with her."

"They'll find their way." Serena believed. Cooper and Kala had been circling each other since they were children. "Like our boy did."

Jake leaned over, nuzzling her neck. "Our boy finally got his head out of his ass. Thank the universe. They can handle anything as long as they're together. I just hope Kala figures it out. Cooper would do anything for her."

She put a hand on Jake's. "Don't go there. Don't make him out to be a saint. She worshipped the ground he walked on when they were kids. He did something, something she won't talk about, and it cut her heart out."

Kala wouldn't have turned from him over nothing, but she was far more fragile than anyone thought. Something had happened between them, and it cost them years. Or perhaps they were like Lou and TJ had been and their time hadn't come yet.

Serena prayed it would come soon because there was something dark in her niece's eyes.

"You're right," Jake allowed. "I don't know the story. I wish she would tell someone." He breathed in and brought her hand to his lips.

"So did Adam tell you enough for a new story?"

There were always new stories. They were all around her if she opened her heart. Writing a story was like making a wish—that those she loved would find what they need, that the world would be a kinder place. When she sat at her keyboard, she created the world as she wanted it to be. Not free of struggle. That was required for growth and to learn empathy and compassion. But a world where love won. A world where her children found what she had found with these men. "Just being with you is enough for a new story every day."

She never stopped thinking up happily ever afters. Even after she'd found her own.

Perhaps tomorrow she would start a story about a brave young woman who most people misunderstood and the heroic young man she'd loved from childhood. She would write about them going on an adventure together, one that would allow her heroine to put aside the past and find a brilliant future. One that ended in two hearts finally beating as one after all these years.

She would sit and write, her words a wish, a dream, a prayer to the universe.

For love. For peace.

For everyone to find what she'd found.

"We have a completely empty nest." Adam sat back as the sun sank beneath the horizon and the nightly show began.

The stars were a blanket of diamonds here. They shone and sparkled, illuminating the night and giving it a softness she'd never found elsewhere. "Maybe we should spend more time here."

"I'd like that," Jake said quietly. "But I think we'll have to get better Internet."

"Hey, I can do the wilderness thing," Adam argued.

And they were off. Her men could fight like brothers. Like only the best of friends could.

Like family.

Serena turned her head up to the night sky and thanked the universe for the story of her life so far.

And for all the adventures yet to come.

Kala, Cooper, and the rest of the team will return in *No More Spies*, coming March 18, 2025.

No More Spies
Masters and Mercenaries: New Recruits, Book 4
By Lexi Blake
Coming March 18, 2025

Kala Taggart has known she was in love with Cooper McKay since she was a young girl. But her wild-child ways sometimes clashed with Coop's apple pie, all-American persona. After the worst night of Kala's life, she decided to give up on having any kind of normalcy. She focused on her future and let the idea of Cooper go.

Cooper knows he screwed up with Kala when they were young, but the adult Cooper is unwilling to let their past rob them of a future. He joins her CIA team not for the thrill of the job but to be close to the woman he's always loved. He spends night after night with her at the club, trying to fulfill her needs, to prove he doesn't need some perfect partner. All he needs is her.

When Cooper and Kala are assigned to a mission in Sweden, they find themselves locked together and forced to face their problems. As the truth of that long-ago night slowly comes to the surface, Cooper has to admit that Kala might be further from him than ever. And all his plans come crashing down as the elusive terrorist they've been hunting makes a move no one is expecting, but the real threat might come from within.

The Bodyguard and the Bombshell
A Masters and Mercenaries: New Recruits Novella
By Lexi Blake
Now Available

The Bodyguard...

Nate Carter left Australia's elite SASR unit after a tragic accident. Shattered by the experience, he thought taking a job in the States might be a good way to start over. His father's former employer, McKay-Taggart, has a position for him in the bodyguard unit. He never imagined himself risking his life for celebrities and the wealthy, but it will do for now. It will also give him a chance to reconnect with old friends, including the girl who'd been like a little sis to him ten years before.

These days, however, his feelings for Daisy O'Donnell are anything but brotherly.

The Bombshell...

Daisy O'Donnell is a girl on a mission, and it does not include falling for one of her brother's best friends. She has plans, and while chaos always seems to follow her, she's determined to see this through. Daisy finds herself in need of a bodyguard when a job goes terribly wrong. She's sure her dad will find someone suitable, but she didn't expect a big, gloriously masculine Aussie to show up ready to take a bullet for her. Maybe spending some time with Nate Carter won't be so bad after all.

An explosive match...

Thrown together by danger, Nate and Daisy can't resist the insane chemistry between them. But when his past and her present collide, they must decide if they can hold it together or go their separate ways forever.

* * * *

Nate turned, watching as she climbed the stairs in her stilettos. She moved as though she was used to walking in what had to be five-inch heels. He would bet she was quite petite, but those heels brought her close to being as tall as most of the men around her.

She might come to his shoulders. Maybe.

His gaze caught on her as she stepped into the lounge. She smiled at the bartender, who seemed to know her, but she waved him off and started toward the railing.

Then stopped and simply stared his way.

Low and sexy hip-hop played through the whole space, forming a soundtrack that could absolutely be used for sex, but it all faded into the background as he got his first good look at her.

She was every bit as gorgeous as he'd suspected.

She turned suddenly, and he realized he wasn't going to let her go. This was the most he'd felt in forever, and he wasn't willing to end it. He could be intimidating, but he could also charm a lady. He suddenly really wanted to charm this one.

Before he could take a step toward her, she turned again, and there was determination in the way she strode toward him.

"Hello, Sir." She stood in front of him, her shoulders back and chin up. "You must be new around here. I wanted to welcome you to The Hideout. If you have any questions, I'll be hanging around tonight. I know the place very well."

So she was a regular. It made him wonder what kind of drama was going on with her that the other Doms seemed to back away. And then he had to admit he didn't give a shit. She was standing there, and it was obvious it had taken some courage for her to get rejected and try again.

Brave sub. Gorgeous sub.

There it was. His cock tightened for the first time in forever, and for a moment it felt like he could breathe again. He hadn't realized how tight his life had become, how like a vise it felt around his chest until this moment.

She'd asked him to come to her if he had questions. He had one for her.

339

"Do you have a partner for the night?" Nate asked.

Gorgeous green eyes flared behind her elaborate white mask. "Do I... No. I don't."

"Would you like one?" He could feel the fucking heat between them. He had to hope the heat he felt seared them both.

Her head nodded. "Yeah. Yes, I would, Sir. If you're the partner, I would like very much to play."

He held a hand out, and when she placed hers in it, he knew the night would change everything.

Author's Note

I'm often asked by generous readers how they can help get the word out about a book they enjoyed. There are so many ways to help an author you like. Leave a review. If your e-reader allows you to lend a book to a friend, please share it. Go to Goodreads and connect with others. Recommend the books you love because stories are meant to be shared. Thank you so much for reading this book and for supporting all the authors you love!

About Lexi Blake

New York Times bestselling author Lexi Blake lives in North Texas with her husband and three kids. Since starting her publishing journey in 2010, she's sold over three million copies of her books. She began writing at a young age, concentrating on plays and journalism. It wasn't until she started writing romance that she found success. She likes to find humor in the strangest places and believes in happy endings.

Connect with Lexi online:

Facebook: Lexi Blake
Twitter: authorlexiblake
Website: www.LexiBlake.net
Instagram: authorlexiblake

Sign up for Lexi's free newsletter!